Power Exchange

AJ ROSE

Copyright © 2012 AJ Rose

Editor: Theo Fenraven
Cover Artist: Robert Junek
Cover Formatting: Theo Fenraven
http://voodoolilypress.com
voodoolilypress@gmail.com general inquiries

This is a work of fiction. While reference might be made to actual historical events or existing locations, the names, characters, places and incidents are either a product of the author's imagination or are used fictitiously, and any resemblance to actual persons, living or dead, business establishments, events, or locales is entirely coincidental.

The trademarked products mentioned in this book are the property of their respective owners, and are recognized as such.

DISCLAIMER: Please do not try any new sexual practices, especially those that might be found in our BDSM/fetish titles, without the guidance of an experienced practitioner. Neither Voodoo Lily Press nor its authors will be responsible for any loss, harm, injury, or death resulting from use of the information contained in any of its titles.

ISBN: 1492110485
ISBN-13: 978-1492110484

DEDICATION

This book is for Theo.
He recognized my words and gave me a reason to write them.
He recognized my mind and gave me the strength to free it.
He recognized my heart and gave me the opportunity to share it.
He recognized my love and gave me a reason to bestow it.
Fen, this is for you. It started with you, and it'll always be for you.

CHAPTER ONE

TWO YEARS ago, St. Louis was listed by the FBI as the most dangerous city in America. Ahead of Washington D.C. and Detroit. Ahead of that one place in New Jersey that "won" it the year before. Not exactly the distinction a cop is proud of. On the other hand, only seven percent of the police agencies in the country are officially accredited by the society awarding such honors, and St. Louis County Police Department is one of these. Still, sometimes the accomplishment is an empty reward to me when I'm on my way to a murder scene. We do the best we can, but sometimes, that accreditation means shit when you walk into someone's house and their dead eyes are staring at you in silent mockery of your prestigious *status*.

"DeGrassi."

I turned at the sound of my name as I exited my unmarked car on a quiet suburban street lined with trees and filled with the sounds of lawn mowers and kids riding bikes. The late spring sun would make the afternoon hot, but just before noon on a Saturday at the end of May, it was warm and pleasant.

Except for this being a murder scene. I made eye contact with one of the patrolmen guarding the front door, the one who'd called my name. He stood as far from the open door as he could get while still manning it and his face looked pale. I didn't know him well, but I didn't have to in order to recognize the haunted look he wore. "Back room, down the hall and to the left."

"Bedroom?" I asked.

He hesitated. "I'm not sure what kind of room it is."

That gave me pause. Stepping into the protective booties that my brother, Cole, would nail me to the wall for forgetting, I let myself in, following the sounds to the back of a well-appointed ranch-style house in one of the more affluent neighborhoods of Chesterfield. Plush carpeting muffled the sound of feet traipsing about, most of them belonging to the crime scene unit. I could tell by the umpteen-syllable words I heard, the language of the truly geeky. As I passed through the front foyer, I spotted a woman with a cute blond ponytail and red-rimmed eyes talking to a patrol officer in quiet tones. Turning down the hallway toward the hive of activity, I came to the door and paused. Veteran homicide detective or not, I still had to steel myself for it, taking one last deep breath before facing the sight of another body.

Even with that bolstering, I wasn't prepared for the view. The victim, a mid-forties-ish man in fairly good shape, was held in place by rope to a wooden X suspended from the ceiling by chains attached to heavy-duty hooks. His chest was crisscrossed with slashes that slicked his torso with blood. He was naked. It wasn't quite Jesus-like, because the cross wasn't T-shaped, and his feet were tied wide apart, but it was damn close. His hands were fisted and purple against the bindings, and his head was held up by a collar around his neck, affixed to a taut chain anchored to the ceiling, forcing his blank gaze outward. It was like walking by a painting and having the eyes follow you no matter where you went. Making the whole thing more macabre were four squiggly black lines drawn down the man's face, from his eyes to the edge of his jaw, two per cheek spaced closely together. The creep aspect went up by a factor of ten because of those lines alone. I suppressed a shudder, trying to don my professionalism like a cloak. The strobe of the CSI cameras gave the whole thing a *Silence of the Lambs* effect, particularly the scene when Hannibal Lector escaped custody. I shivered despite the warmth of late spring.

"Holy shit," I muttered, stepping all the way into the room but remaining by the wall as the techs gathered evidence.

"Holy shit is right, Gavin," a familiar voice said. I looked toward my brother, Cole, his usually merry blue eyes dampened by solemnity as he carefully goose-stepped across the room to stand beside me, watching his techs do their jobs with a strange sadness mixed with pride. Cole's the lead CSI, and I rarely got the opportunity to work with him because of the potential for nepotistic back-scratching where evidence is concerned, but sometimes, there just aren't enough people to assign us to separate cases. We go out of our way to keep the chain of custody impeccable. Cops are family everywhere, but ours was literally so.

"Where's Sawyer?" he asked, voice muffled by the face mask he wore. He held one out to me, but I waved it off. I planned to do nothing but observe so as not to taint evidence, and the masks never did anything to alleviate the smell.

"He was across town with his daughter at a softball tournament. Had to wait for his ex. He's on his way." Trent Sawyer was my partner, and despite his take-charge attitude, I knew he'd appreciate anything I could find out while he was running behind. "What have you got for me?"

"Body was discovered this morning by the vic's ex-wife, who stopped by when he didn't show to pick up their kids for a weekend visit. M.E. hasn't been here to view the body, so we don't have a time of death yet, but from what I can tell by looking at him, the injuries were all pre-mortem. Have to wait for autopsy to confirm."

I nodded, taking notes. "Victim ID?"

"George Kaiser, forty-five, worked as an engineer for a car diagnostics manufacturer."

I gestured to the cross, the ropes, and over on the futon in the corner, an array of implements more likely found at Home Depot than the—what kind of room was this, actually? Addams' family guest room? Den of iniquity?—spare room of a professional businessman. Well, he was an engineer. Maybe this was a workshop of sorts. "Was all this brought here, gathered from around the house or what?" It was the question of the hour, because it was clear the tools had been used extensively on the victim.

"You'd have to ask the ex-wife what she knows about it, but my guess is it was already here. There's no ceiling plaster on the floor to indicate the hooks were drilled recently, and there's a latch up there," he tilted his head so my gaze would follow, "that looks like it fits the bottom of the cross, so it can be secured to the ceiling, out of the way. And that dresser over there," he pointed to the opposite wall where a long, squat dresser sat beneath a window covered with heavy drapes and thick blinds, "has more... equipment in it. The cross wouldn't be easily transported in the trunk of a car, but our perp could have had a truck or SUV."

I gave him a strange look, about to ask more when a voice interrupted me.

"Whoa," Trent said, standing in the doorway, dark eyes wide and staring, his black hair windblown, which told me he'd driven with the top down on his convertible. "Someone had quite the party." He gingerly stepped beside me, and I told him what Cole had found. "Kinky," was all he said. I rolled my eyes.

"This is out of even your league in the bedroom," I said. Trent loved to brag about his mattress Olympics, so I knew more than I wanted to about his exploits, which were many, considering his calculated charm. Victoria told me it was his confidence that was magnetic. I figured he was conceited and just hid it until after a tumble in the sheets. Turning back to Cole as he watched one of his techs take measurements of what looked like a cat o' nine tails, I asked, "Is there a knife or something that matches the chest wounds?"

"No knife, but those look like whip marks to me, not slashes with a blade," Cole said. I gave him a questioning look. "What? I worked an animal cruelty case two years ago where the breeder whipped the horses to train them." His disgust was clear. "Poor animals had to be put down from infections and inability to be around humans. Completely broken. But their lacerations were similar." He pointed to the whip the tech was tagging and bagging in a paper bag so as not to smear prints. "I'll test it in the lab, but that could be responsible for the chest lacerations. Or there might be another one in the pile."

I was about to ask what he made of the markings on the face when my attention was diverted. The soothing grumble of the county M.E. carried through the doorway, and all activity in the room stopped to make way for him near the body. Dr. Stanley Jencopale was a presence in any room, but at a crime scene, he was often the voice of reason in a chaotic swarm. He could take the worst injuries and make clinical sense of them, scrub them of their heinousness, and break down the information into manageable chunks, all without dehumanizing the victim. Something this… exotic would automatically fall to him.

"Oh, you poor, poor thing," he mumbled to the victim, donning gloves with an authoritative snap. He checked body temperature and for rigor, pulling the dead man's eyelids wide as his thermometer did its thing. Throughout his assessment, he spoke to the silent room while Trent and I took more notes.

"Male Caucasian, middle-aged, dead approximately seven to nine hours, which puts time of death between," he looked at his watch, "four and six a.m. this morning, indicated by body temperature. Cause of death, on initial assessment, appears to be strangulation. Petechial hemorrhage across the cheeks, as well as deep bruising around neck area. Significant blood loss from multiple lacerations to chest and abdomen. Bruising of extremities and rope marks on the skin indicate the victim was alive when affixed to the cross, and suspended for several hours. Victim's genitals show signs of loss of circulation from clamp device." Oh god, I hadn't noticed the cock ring, and I tried not to look too closely. "Help me get this cross down from the ceiling."

Cole hurried forward with a swarm of CSI techs, two of whom spread a plastic sheet to keep fibers from transferring between the body and the deep carpeting, on which there was blood splatter, already photographed. They collectively lifted the apparatus to take the weight off the chains, including the one attached to the collar, before removing the chains from the ceiling hooks and carefully lowering the body to the plastic tarp. They stepped back, waiting for the doctor to indicate if he needed the ropes loosened. At his nod, Cole untied the feet and placed the rope in a large evidence bag. Flashes strobed as photos were taken of the injuries sustained to the victim's ankles. Dr. Jencopale waved them off.

"I will photograph the injuries during autopsy. You've got the placement of the body documented already, so leave the rest to me." The reprimand was gentle but enough of a hint for the crowd to back off as he continued his examination. A few of them returned to the futon to resume cataloguing the equipment on the cushion.

"DeGrassi, you have an ultraviolet light on you?"

He clearly meant Cole, since I hadn't had a black light or anything like it since my college dorm days when my then-best friend Pete and I would smoke pot to celebrate the end of each semester, enhancing the effect with dramatic wall posters and a black light. *Damn, I haven't thought about him in years.* I stopped short of wondering what Pete was up to. Inappropriate right now, not to mention I didn't need the reminder in the first place. I refocused on the body as Cole donned a pair of goofy, 3D-looking glasses and shined a light across the victim's skin.

"A little saliva around the mouth, which looks to be the vic's, in a pattern consistent with a gag, but we'll swab it anyway to confirm. I see no signs of semen or other body fluids. Not on the anterior view." He passed the light and glasses to the doctor, who nodded his affirmation.

Cole and Dr. Jencopale untied the victim's hands and head from the cross and rolled him face down. Another sweep of the light brought a collective shake of their heads. Cole grabbed his kit, extracted several swabs and, with the doctor's permission, spot checked specific areas of the body, including the victim's rectum. "We'll see what Trace has to say, but again, posterior examination shows nothing seminal."

"Victim was anally penetrated, and not gently. Microtears around the anus and blood evidence ringing the orifice. An internal check will say more, but it's pretty clear from initial assessment that he was raped." They gently returned him to his back, the plastic sheeting crinkling beneath the weight. Cole and the doctor spoke softly about which evidence needed to be collected from the body right away and what could be done at the lab during post. Jencopale waved two of his assistants into the room after Cole did a single thorough sweep for trace evidence, then backed off as George Kaiser was bagged and carried to the gurney. The CSI crew continued their check of the room, paying particular attention to the cross, now that its burden had been removed. I closed my notepad and motioned to Cole. He pulled the mask down to his neck and stood in front of Trent and me with his hands on his hips.

"What's this fucking world coming to?" he asked, voice soft, disturbed.

Trent shook his head, uncharacteristically quiet, though his gaze was shrewd, and assessed everything in the room.

"You'll get us your initial report this afternoon?" I asked. Cole rolled his eyes.

"Fast as I can. There's a mountain of evidence here. That's both good and bad, since there's bound to be something you can use to nail—" he stopped himself, clearly uncomfortable with the crucifixion reference. "Find this guy." Cole was a sarcastic shit when he wanted to be, poking fun at my shyness or how my wife, Victoria, wears the pants in our relationship, but disrespectful of the dead, he was not.

"Or we'll be buried by more information than we know what to do with. Just get it to me as soon as you can, and we'll figure out what's useful and what's a dead end. Gotta go talk to the vic's ex now."

Trent cringed. "Mind if I stay here, see what they find?"

I nodded. He'd be more valuable in this room than with the victim's relatives. Trent's sense of humor was off-color, the product of more than ten years seeing some of the worst crimes in the most dangerous city in America. He missed very little, but his coping mechanisms weren't always helpful when dealing with witnesses or next of kin. It's one of the reasons I made a good partner for him; he had a knack for sorting through evidence and knowing what was hot or cold, while I got useful information from witnesses and people of interest. I turned back to Cole.

"Keep him in line, wouldja?"

"Not my turn to watch him," Cole deadpanned, situating his face mask again and turning his back on both of us.

"Go see what the missus has to say. Don't leave me hanging." Trent's eyes twinkled.

I groaned at his bad pun. "You're awful. We don't need a lawsuit when the ex-Mrs. Kaiser decides to beat your ass for your sick and twisted commentary. It's a wonder you haven't been shit-canned yet."

"Nah, the boss loves me. Hell, everyone loves me."

I could think of a string of women who didn't love him, but I kept it to myself, leaving the room to find the woman with the pony tail. Another deep breath and I wiped the expression from my face as I stepped toward the front door. Making sure to be plenty loud so as not to startle her, I neared the grief-stricken woman and cleared my throat.

"Ma'am?" She turned her tearful face to me. "I'm Detective Gavin DeGrassi. I'd like to ask you a few questions." She nodded, fidgeting with her nails, twisting the rings on a couple fingers, and looking anywhere but the hallway that led to the back. I supposed she'd just seen the gurney with the remains of the man she'd married wheeled through the door, and her jumpiness was the result. I couldn't blame her.

"If you'd be more comfortable, we can talk in my car with the air on." She nodded and walked out of the house into the sunshine, waiting for me to indicate which of the many vehicles littering the street was mine. I placed a hand on the small of her back to guide her and then dropped it, keeping professional distance. As we settled into the front seat, I reached into the console between the seats and plucked out a small pack of Kleenex, passing them over. She gave me a grateful, if watery, smile. After turning down the dashboard radio, I took out my notepad and got her contact information.

"Kimberly Kaiser," she said in a small voice, rattling off her address and phone number. She didn't live far from the scene. "You're probably wondering why I'm so upset," she said. "George is my ex, after all."

I waited, letting her talk.

"We were only recently divorced, and we have three kids together, a sixteen-year-old girl and two twelve-year-old boys. Twins. Whatever failings were in our marriage, there's nothing I wanted more than for our kids to have a good relationship with both of us. Just because we couldn't be together didn't mean our kids had to choose, you know? George and I remained friends." A fresh tear track appeared on her cheek, and she wiped it away with a well-manicured hand.

"So George took good care of you and the kids?"

The smile on her lips was both wistful and a bit of a sneer. "He insisted on paying a big settlement when we split. I'd been a stay-at-home mom most of our marriage, and he knew it would be difficult for me to get back on my feet, especially in this economy. He didn't want me or the kids struggling. I didn't demand it, if that's what you're asking. I'm not one of those women that needed to punish him for the end of our relationship. George was generous. It was in his nature to take care of people, even if he had a strange way of doing the caring."

Her unusual wording wasn't lost on me, and I wanted to know more, but starting from the beginning would be important for establishing a timeline. I could fill in the blanks and ask what she meant as we talked. The impression I had of her was not one of a jilted ex-wife bent on revenge or life insurance. She clearly still cared for the man, so it was doubtful she had anything more to do with his death than being the unfortunate one to discover him.

"When was the last time you spoke to George?"

"On the phone, yesterday afternoon. I called to verify he was picking the kids up for the weekend this morning, and he confirmed the plans. He wasn't the type to flake on them, so when he didn't show up, I called both his house and cell phone. No answer. It was unusual, so I left the kids at the house and came over to make sure nothing had happened. Thank god they didn't see this."

"What time was this?"

"He was supposed to get the kids at nine this morning. By ten, I started calling. It was about ten-thirty when I got over here."

"Did he mention any plans for the evening? Or were you aware of something he regularly did on Friday nights?"

"Oh, Friday night was club night, where he and his friends would get together every week."

Club night? I'd come back to that. "How did you find the house when you arrived?"

"The front door was closed but unlocked. I didn't think anything of it. His car was in the driveway, and I figured he'd simply had a late night and overslept. I knocked and then stuck my head in, calling for him when he didn't answer. I went in and was on my way to the bedroom when I saw him in the play room. I ran outside and called the police."

"The play room. Can you elaborate on that?"

She considered me for a beat and then took a deep breath. "It's going to come out anyway, and it's not like you haven't already seen. He's a good man, and that's not going to change because of your opinion of him." She stuck her chin out defiantly.

"Mrs. Kaiser, I ask because I need to understand George's life, where he might have crossed paths with his killer, and how his death came about. If I can answer why, I'd like to do that, too."

"Yes, I know, Detective. I'm just... so used to watching out for him, keeping his secrets. It feels like a betrayal to blab it all. But you're going to find who did this, right? If I tell you everything?" Her eyes flashed fiercely, and her protectiveness of her ex-husband's memory jolted me.

"I'll do my best. And my best improves the more information you can give me."

"George was a Dominant. The club he went to on Fridays is a leather club in midtown, Collared. He went there weekly to catch up on the scene, meet others like him, or submissives. There's a whole culture of people there, and they take care of each other."

Suddenly the room—the whips, the ropes, and the heavily covered windows—made sense. "He was a Dominant? Are you sure?" After all, he'd been found restrained and nude. I didn't know much about leather clubs and BDSM, but I did know Dominants weren't usually the ones tied up.

"Oh, I'm positive. George was never on the stinging side of a whip."

"So he could have met someone at this club, brought them home with him?" My pen scratched against my notepad furiously. She gave me the club's address.

"He could have, but usually he would vet a sub before inviting them to his play room. There are some bad seeds in the BDSM world, just like there are in any group of people, but for the most part, it's a tight-knit group."

"How long has he been involved in this lifestyle?" I took care to keep my language and tone neutral, showing no hint of judgment. Truth be told, though, I was fascinated. The things I learned on this job never ceased to surprise me.

"The whole time we were married. I knew about it when we got engaged."

It took a moment to process that. "Is that why you divorced him?"

She leveled me with a stern look, and then gave a perturbed sigh. "Yes and no. I couldn't be everything he needed in a partner. In a way, a lot of the ideals appealed to me. The power plays in the Dom/sub relationship mirror a lot of the ideals of married life, at least how it used to be, where the husband runs the household and provides while the wife takes care of the family and the living space. Archaic and anti-feminist, I know, but I liked the idea of being looked after, of providing him and our kids a happy home. We gave a normal, vanilla marriage a good shot. I never wanted for anything while we were together, either emotionally or financially. But he did."

She didn't sound bitter, merely sad, picking at her cuticles. "Most people don't understand it. I tried to understand it, even tried to be the sub to his Dom, but I couldn't. It was a short-lived experiment."

"Did he resent that about you?"

"Forgive me, Detective, but is this important, why we split up? It doesn't have anything to do with how he was killed." Her eyes welled up again on the last word.

"It provides me with information about George's life and the kind of person he was, which can help us focus on who he knew that is capable of this."

"You think he knew his killer?" Her eyes widened, and then narrowed. "You're asking to see if it was me." A bitter laugh escaped her. "No, he didn't resent me. I didn't hold his sexual proclivities against him, and he gave me the same respect. Domination and submission isn't for everyone. It wasn't for me. Eventually, it got the better of us. But we never blamed each other for having opposite tastes in the bedroom."

"Did you know anyone he was with after your divorce?"

I noticed a very slight hesitation. "I met a couple of them. They all seemed nice. It's not like you can look at someone on the sidewalk and know they like to be spanked, Detective. They seemed like normal people to me. But George was careful. I needed him to be, as the father of our children. He never played with anyone when the kids were at his house, and he kept that room locked up tight."

"You ever hear anyone threaten him?"

"No," she vigorously shook her head, ponytail swishing. "That group of people is close. They talk. What they do can be dangerous, regardless of consent. Oddballs are quickly singled out and lose any chance of finding someone to play with. Reputation is everything in that world."

"How do you mean, oddballs?"

"I don't know, Detective. You'd get more information from the people in the community than me. George and I talked about it some, but it was a world separate from our life together. Mostly, he told me of abusive people hiding behind the Dominant label, or submissives working through traumas there instead of in therapy where they belonged. They didn't last long."

"Did George have personal experience with these people?"

She shrugged. "Like I said, he was careful. If they didn't please him or he had reason to question their motivation, they didn't last."

It was then I noticed she had been playing the pronoun game. "They" and "them" instead of "she" and "her."

"Was your ex-husband involved with submissives of the same

sex?"

She blushed fiercely, and then nodded. "George was bisexual. As if finding acceptance as a Dom wasn't hard enough for him."

The situation shifted again, making a little more sense. A woman would have a hard time stringing George up to a cross and hanging him from the ceiling. He was a well-built guy, probably around two hundred pounds. I couldn't see the average woman hoisting him onto the cross. At the same time these thoughts were playing in my head, a shot of envy coursed through me that George had someone, anyone, in his life so accepting of his preferences. Pete, the one person I'd ever let in on my dark little secret, had shunned me.

"Is it possible someone outside this culture discovered his lifestyle? Maybe decided to teach him some kind of lesson?"

"I suppose," she said, shoulders slumping, the weight of the morning showing clearly on her face. "But if it was a colleague or someone at work, I can't see them having the grounds to fire him, let alone kill him. He kept this far away from his career. I know some of the people he worked with. They'd ostracize him, find a way to get rid of him so he wouldn't taint their company's reputation." She gave a derisive snort. "He worked for an extremely conservative group of people. But kill him? I can't imagine that."

I got the name of his company and would follow up on that, but with Mrs. Kaiser, I let it drop.

"Can you give me a list of names in the leather circle to speak with, his friends or acquaintances? Maybe some of his past or current subs?"

"Yeah, but I'll have to look in my address book. I don't know his recent ones, since I left that part of his life behind with the divorce."

I frowned. She'd met a few of George's new partners, but didn't discuss it with him after the divorce? The timing didn't add up. "Did you have a long separation, before everything was finalized?"

She bit her lip and shook her head. "No. When I said I couldn't handle it anymore, he made it as quick and painless for me as possible."

"So when were these new relationships of his if you met a few of them but didn't talk about it after your marriage ended?"

Her mouth worked but no sound came out. She fisted her hand and put it to her lips, trying to compose herself. "Our last few years together were in an open marriage, Detective."

Trying to formulate my next question to cover my surprise at her revelation, my thought process was interrupted when she stared at me hard, equally defiant and pleading, willing me to comprehend. "Love was never our issue. I loved him enough to try to allow him what he needed, and he loved me enough to respect my boundaries. But love doesn't always conquer all, does it?"

Her eyes were sad, and it hit me exactly how strong she had to have been to do such a thing for her husband. People would judge from the outside, calling her weak or a doormat, but I saw someone resilient enough to set aside her own insecurities and indoctrinated beliefs to put someone else first. Well and truly first.

"One more question, Mrs. Kaiser. The play room in George's house, that wasn't something that was always there?"

"No, he converted it when we split up. I wouldn't allow it with the kids under the same roof when we were still married, and he locks it when he has visitation now. He used to take his subs to a friend's house, who was also a Dom."

"I'll need that friend's name as well."

She nodded, and then gave me a pained look. "How much of this is going to become public? I mean, is this something I need to warn my kids about before they see it on the news?"

I closed my notebook and gave her a sympathetic look. "Every investigation withholds certain details from the press to keep people from making false confessions or to pinpoint suspects who might slip up about something that's not public knowledge. I'll do my best to keep the nature of George's death under wraps, but I can't guarantee something won't become public."

She bit her lip, squeezing her eyes shut as a fresh set of tears escaped, rolling down her cheeks. "All right," she whispered.

"Are you okay to drive home?" I asked.

"Yeah. I'll be fine. I'm a lot tougher than I look."

I gave her a soft smile. "I can tell, Mrs. Kaiser. Please, have that list of names to me as soon as you can. Here's my card, with phone numbers and my email address. If you think of anything else, please let me know. I may need to contact you again with further questions."

She nodded, taking the card. "I was always afraid something like this would happen."

"We'll do everything we can to find those responsible. Thank you for your cooperation."

She popped the passenger door open before turning back to me. "Thank you, Detective, for your sensitivity. George deserves justice as much as anyone. Thank you for not requiring me to remind you."

I tipped my head to her and watched as she walked woodenly to her car in the driveway. Breathing deeply and taking a moment before reemerging into the mid-afternoon heat, my mind whirled. Something about this victim made me protective. I knew sharing the details I'd learned with Trent would open a Pandora's box of derisive jokes. It was how he dealt with things he didn't understand. I knew this about him, but it didn't mean I liked it. For a long time, George's secret had been safe with his wife and community of friends. For a few more moments, it would be safe with me.

But I couldn't solve this one alone, and I doubted even with Trent's help we'd understand everything we needed to about the dynamics surrounding George's lifestyle. I stood in the front yard, a lump of confusion swelling in my chest.

On the one hand, I was saddened by the sickness in our society, that someone could so brutally murder a man. Trent would assume that sickness included George's sexual preferences. I didn't think so. Though she hadn't wanted to elaborate, Mrs. Kaiser had given me the impression it was simply a different way to express oneself and test one's emotional boundaries. On the other hand, I was fascinated by the dynamic and interested in knowing more. It was disconcerting, and I tried to convince myself it was purely professional curiosity but a small, decisive twinge suggested otherwise.

Before spilling George's secret to my partner, I made the uncharacteristic decision to call our Sergeant and request a very specific kind of backup. One thing was certain: if I wanted to keep Trent's macho posturing to a minimum so he didn't offend future witnesses, increasing our chances of learning useful information that would lead to the killer, we'd need a tutor.

CHAPTER TWO

AS PREDICTED, Trent had a field day.

"You've got to be fucking kidding me." He looked around George's play room with new appreciation. "There is no way a woman, even with the vic's cooperation, could hang him from the ceiling like that."

In as detached a voice as I could manage, I answered. "Kaiser didn't always stick to women."

Trent snorted. "Oh great. A pansy ass on top of it."

I glared at him. "And with that attitude, we're going to get no help from George's friends or acquaintances."

"George?" He looked at me askance. "You're already calling him George? Jesus, Gavin. It usually takes you a few days before you get attached to a victim."

"This is the worst thing I've ever seen, Trent. Pardon me for having more motivation than usual to find the asshole responsible." Keeping my face steely, I stared at him, which he turned into a contest. I blinked first. I always blinked first. Dammit.

"Get a puppy, DeGrassi, if you need to save someone. But keep your head."

"I can say the same to you. Just because Kaiser's personal life disgusts you, or you don't understand it, or it offends your manly sensibilities, you don't have room to be a homophobic, bigoted dickhead. In front of witnesses and the victim's acquaintances, you keep your jokes and your judgment to yourself."

Most people on the force overhearing this conversation would think we hated each other. The truth was, we were a well balanced pair. It was your traditional good cop, bad cop, only we played it with each other, not on suspects. He was right. I was a bleeding heart, trying to save the world, one murder at a time. It made me good at my job in some ways, horrible at it in others. I typically got more information from people than he did, but I had a hard time leaving work at work on my off time. Trent swore it was going to send me to an early grave. On the other hand, his lack of empathy made him almost clinical in his assessment of evidence and in seeing patterns that most people missed. I identified with the victim, and he had the cool detachment of the killer. He said I gave people too much credit. I said he didn't give them enough. Together, we covered the psychology of most cases pretty well. Except we constantly argued. Victoria told me I let him walk all over me. I called it picking my battles. Truth be told, Trent wasn't my favorite person, but I grudgingly respected him. I think he felt the same, but I doubted it would ever be said aloud. That wasn't his style.

"Fine," he snapped.

We spent the rest of the afternoon with the crime scene techs, taking the banking information from Kaiser's office once they'd cleared it and signed it over to us. We each had a car at the crime scene, so we separated to head back to the station, and the few minutes of peace on the ride allowed me to get my center back. I began the breathing exercises learned from yoga, which helped me with chronic headaches. Since we'd skipped lunch—and I didn't think I could have eaten a few hours ago anyway, considering what we'd seen—I stopped at a sub shop and ordered food. I got something for Trent, too, to be nice. Chances were good he'd stop and get a bag full of grease and things covered in special sauce that looked like Thousand Island dressing, but just in case, I got him a turkey on whole wheat with everything on it. We'd be working for several more hours, and if he didn't want it, I could count it as a late dinner. On the way out of the parking lot, I called Victoria to tell her not to wait up.

"But I had plans for us this evening," she said, a chill in her voice.

"I'm sorry, hon. I really am. We can play cards with the Fullertons another night, I promise. I have to work while the trail is fresh. First forty-eight hours and all that." The chances of solving a murder decrease exponentially after the first two days. "Why don't you go without me so you're not sitting home alone and bored? If I can get away at a decent hour, I'll head over there."

She gave an exasperated sigh, but I detected a note of acceptance and understanding for me and my socially inconvenient job. "All right, Gavin. I'll pass on your regrets."

"Do that. Love you," I said.

"You, too." She clicked off.

Trent was already seated at his desk, a small space to the side cleared to hold his dinner. The rest of the surface was spread with papers, likely from George Kaiser's home office. As predicted, he'd gotten a double burger, fries, and a soda the size of my head. "How the hell do you keep from getting fat, eating shit like that?" I asked, setting my sandwiches down on my tidy desk.

"I work it off. Run every morning. Gym three times a week." He took another huge bite and squinted at the papers on his desk. "Banks are closed so I couldn't get Kaiser's account information, but he kept a decent record of expenses in his checkbook. Lab techs have his computer, but so far haven't called with anything. Anyway, no out-of-the-ordinary expenses. Mostly grocery stores, gas, restaurants. But wherever he bought the stuff to furnish his—what'd his ex call it?"

"Play room."

"Yeah, if he used his checking account for that stuff, I don't see it. He might've paid for it in cash, or have another account."

I frowned. "We can check, but why hide the bank records if he's going to keep the purchases in his house? Makes no sense."

Trent nodded, leaning forward abruptly to catch dripping ketchup on his foil wrapper instead of his shirt. "True," he conceded. "He does have a few ATM withdrawals, but the balance register only goes back a few months. Mrs. Kaiser said he converted her sewing room after the divorce, right?"

I nodded, tucking into my own dinner, keeping the extra sandwich for later. "We'll have to wait for Monday morning." I spotted a folder labeled "Receipts" on Trent's desk and snagged it. "Maybe something in here."

Most of the items he kept track of were new appliances with owner's manuals, the extended warranty on his washer and dryer, a laptop with numbers for tech support, tax receipts for clothes dropped off to Goodwill... and one to Pleasure Palace for something called a "St. And X," "vmp glv," and a "lthr pnymsk." I picked up the phone handset and dialed the number at the top of the receipt, speaking with a girl who sounded young and continually popped her gum in my ear. I got directions to the store location and the full description of the receipt's abbreviated items.

Trent was looking across his desk at me with a mix of humor and derision. "You don't even flinch when you ask about this stuff. Something you're not telling me?"

I narrowed my eyes at him. "Ha, funny. This receipt is for one St. Andrew's Cross and hardware to affix it to a ceiling beam, something called a pony mask, and vampire gloves."

"What the fuck are vampire gloves?" Trent asked.

Taking my computer out of sleep mode, I typed the term into Google and hit search with a feeling of trepidation. I clicked the first site I saw, and then scrambled to minimize the picture of a woman wearing vampire gloves while cradling another woman's breast. I couldn't minimize the picture without minimizing the text, too, so I made the screen small, which didn't totally obscure the picture, and read quickly. "'The Vampire Gloves are sporty black leather gloves made of soft, thin leather, with a snap closure at the wrist and one other special feature: the fingers have prickly little tacks sticking out of them (96 to be exact). The tacks are short, about an eighth of an inch long, and will prick and scratch the skin like little thorns, but will not pierce the skin unless you squeeze or slap it very firmly.'"

Trent rifled through the papers on his desk and came up with a preliminary listing of all the items in Kaiser's play room inventory. "I see nothing on here about a mask or a set of creepy-ass gloves." I could tell he was holding back further commentary, but a heavy, warm hand fell on my shoulder and kept me from saying anything about Trent's tone.

"DeGrassi, that better be for a case," Sergeant Talcott grumbled, looking at the photo of the topless woman on my computer screen.

My face quickly flushed red and I stammered a moment before I said, "Yes, sir. Preliminary report's on your desk for the BDSM murder I called you about earlier." I hurriedly clicked off the offending webpage and tried to maintain some dignity as I swiveled in my chair to face my boss. "The website had a description of a purchase he made that's not on his home inventory list, but has receipts for. Potential trophy."

Talcott waved his hand to dismiss it, and I breathed again. "Sawyer, DeGrassi, I'd like you to meet Dr. Benjamin Haverson." He stepped aside, and a man I hadn't noticed standing there moved forward with a warm smile and his hand extended. I stared for a moment before realizing it looked rude that I hadn't shaken his outstretched hand. Hastening to my feet, I slid my palm against his, clearing my throat. "Gavin DeGrassi. Nice to meet you." Okay, at least that came out without too much trouble.

Dr. Haverson was young, early thirties, which made him about my age, with deep brown eyes and a warm smile. His face exuded innocence and an open honesty rarely seen in anyone past puberty. With delicate features, a full mouth, and artfully mussed dark brown hair, he was fit for Hollywood, and it was all I could do to keep my jaw shut. Instead, he was standing in the Second precinct with his hand in mine. Which I was still shaking. Well beyond the acceptable timeframe men adhere to during a handshake. I dropped his hand and shoved mine in my pocket, kicking myself for the slip.

"Nice to meet you," he said, eyes dancing as though my *faux pas* hadn't bothered him in the least. I heard Trent snort behind me. Great. All I needed was to have him say something asinine and embarrass the hell out of me. Haverson rounded the edge of my desk to accept Trent's much more acceptably timed handshake.

"Dr. Haverson is a therapist with ties to the BDSM community," Talcott explained. "He's your requested consult on this case. Get everything you need from him. I'm not only talking about help with questioning witnesses. If there's something you don't understand, ask him, like the whatevers you were just looking up online, DeGrassi. He has clearance to know the details of the case." In other words, use the expert and keep this quiet, even around the station. Something inside me bristled at that. Talcott pointed a finger at Trent. "Sawyer, I'd better not get one phone call complaining about your handling of witnesses. There's only so much sensitivity training I can promise before being required to suspend your ass. You got me?"

"Sure, Boss." Trent knew exactly what tone to take with Talcott. They often had drinks together after hours, and while there was no question who was in charge, I didn't doubt our sergeant had covered for Trent's wisecracking on more than one occasion. "I'm sure Dr. Haverson will have us up to speed in no time, Sergeant." At that, Trent's eyes flickered over to me and his grin spread. It made me squirm. Talcott scowled at Trent one more time before retreating to his office. Trent looked at Dr. Haverson, but he spoke to me. "Gavin, where should we do it?" He gave a weighty pause. "The consult, I mean."

"Briefing room," I mumbled, wanting to shrink into the floor. I stalked toward the hallway, not bothering to see if my asshole partner or the doctor was following. Why was Trent so good at reading me and pushing my buttons when he wasn't the people person? I must've been horribly transparent, the thought of which made the tips of my ears burn red. *Victoria, Victoria, Victoria,* I chanted to myself. The image of my wife, hair swept off her elegant neck in an artful twist, eyes flinty and face perfectly composed, rose in my mind. I used the reminder to quash any thoughts that had nothing to do with the case and everything to do with Haverson. It worked. I'd gotten so good at denial that the thoughts didn't have time to fully form before I blew them away from me like a curl of smoke on the wind. It was how I'd kept my secret for so many years.

I keyed in the lock code on the door and flipped on the light. "So we have a victim, a Dominant according to his ex-wife, killed in his play room and in such a way that leaves little doubt it's connected to his lifestyle." Straight to business would help me look more professional, so I threw myself into it with gusto. "We're waiting for the names of a few of the victim's prior submissives as well as a Dominant friend he knew well enough to share a play room with before he had his own. What can you tell us that will help in questioning potential witnesses and friends of the victim's who were at the club where he was last seen?"

"Let's sit, shall we?" Dr. Haverson swept a hand to the chairs laid out in a semi-circle facing the podium and whiteboard at the front of the room. His voice was rich and sonorous, with a tiny hint of an accent, maybe Tennessee or Mississippi. Hell, maybe southern Missouri. Pete was from southern Missouri and had a lilt to his speech. *Quit thinking about Pete. Jesus, Gavin.* It was like a scab that snagged on a sweater. Easily ignored until awareness of it crept in, and then I worried at it until it was open and bleeding. Again.

My feet automatically obeyed the doctor and I sat, wishing I'd thought to bring my notepad.

"Why, Gavin. How would Victoria feel if she saw you looking at our consult like you just crawled out of the desert and he's a Big Gulp of ice water?" Trent whispered as he took the seat beside me. Dr. Haverson grabbed another chair to pull over so we were sitting in a circle instead of in a lecture-type setting. I didn't think he heard us. God, I hoped not.

"The fuck are you talking about?" I asked out of the corner of my mouth. "I'm married. To a woman." Not a denial, exactly.

"Then act like it."

I glared at him, then turned my attention back to the doctor and pointedly ignored Trent while internally berating myself for letting my poker face drop.

"Healthy BDSM, which stands for bondage and discipline, domination and submission, and sadomasochism, has two significant principles: consent and trust. Not all that different from a vanilla relationship," Dr. Haverson began, and I found myself staring again, but at least I could blame it on fascination with the subject. The image of George Kaiser hanging from the St. Andrew's Cross flashed through my mind, a not-so-subtle reminder as to why I was here, and everything else but understanding the doctor fled my mind. "Consent is given up front, and continually given unless the Dom pushes the sub too hard, at which time, the sub will use safe words, which are *always* acknowledged. When a sub safewords, everything immediately stops. Anyone not doing so quickly gets a reputation and is ostracized by the community. People get hurt that way."

"So Kaiser could have found one of these people," Trent said. "Someone who ignored his safe word."

"George Kaiser was a Dominant," Dr. Haverson said. "Typically, Doms don't have a safe word. They're not usually the ones putting their safety in someone else's hands. But it's possible, if Mr. Kaiser was a sub, that yes, he ran across someone who ignored his need to stop."

Trent snorted. "That's an understatement."

I glared at Trent as much as possible without being obvious to the doctor. He ignored me and kept talking.

"So, if Doms aren't the ones in compromising positions, why would our vic let someone tie him up like that?"

"Trent, we don't know that George consented to being restrained," I reminded him.

"For example's sake, let's say he did consent," Dr. Haverson conceded. "A situation like that could happen between a Dom and sub with a long-term relationship in which the sub wants to experience the other side of the whip. A safe word would be established for the Dom and they would negotiate prior to playing the scene what the Dom's limits are. Such a thing, however, is unheard of for a pair playing together for the first time. In fact, it's unusual for a first-time scene between people to happen at one or the other's home. There are private rooms at clubs like Collared. As the players get a feel for each other, there's the safety net of a nearby crowd should either of them need it. If the players are okay with it, there are even public rooms with someone called a Dungeon Master who is there to step in should something go awry."

"I don't get it," Trent said. "What makes someone submit to that kind of treatment at all?"

"That's the crux of the D/s relationship, Detective," Haverson said. "Submissives enjoy making other people happy, and it doesn't have to be only in the bedroom. It's an exchange of power. Believe it or not, the subs have more power than you realize. They have the power to choose whether or not they give themselves to a Dom. Once the exchange is made, the Dom takes up that power to use as they see fit, but it's a power they earn.

"Submissives like to please people and be acknowledged for giving that pleasure, even if it's at the expense of their own. It's a heady thing, to the extent that a sub finds more satisfaction in giving everything they have to their Dom than if they were to be pleasured themselves. It's more than a desire for recognition as the instrument of the Dom's gratification, though the recognition is a sub's reward.

It's the fact that, to a sub, they can give themselves wholly to a Dom, flaws and all, and still greatly please them, be accepted by them, and most of all, be loved. Isn't that what most people hope for? Love despite their flaws? And before you think the sub is weak for completely putting someone else's wants first, ask yourself if it's something you could do. Could you be at someone else's mercy?" The doctor was speaking to us both, but he was looking at me. "Could you, knowing full well that doing so might bring you discomfort and even pain, bring yourself to kneel in front of another and let them push your boundaries for the sake of their own desires, trusting that the pleasure they will rain on you for your total surrender could literally take you to a higher plane?" He paused. "They say it takes more courage to kneel before another than stand beside them."

A thick silence hung in the air. Trying not to stare at the doctor, or let either of them see how his words had affected me, I cleared my throat. Beating back the need to ask more about that kind of surrender—what did he mean, higher plane?—I changed the subject.

"Okay," I said. "So we have several things we need to find out from friends and witnesses who knew George Kaiser. What's the best way to go about it without our ignorance of the subject shutting them down?"

Haverson leaned forward, putting his elbows on his knees and threading his fingers together, looking up at us from his bent position. My heart stuttered and sped up at the beguiling expression on his face. "People in the BDSM community are just like other people, but we do catch a lot of flak from outsiders about our lifestyle. Maintain respect, and you shouldn't have a problem. Do not try to strong-arm submissives. They submit only to those they've chosen, because their submission is a gift given to those who've earned their trust. It's not like subs walk around bowing to everyone in authority."

"I have a personal question, Doctor," Trent said.

Oh shit. Don't be an ass, Trent.

"Please, call me Ben. And you can ask, but I can't guarantee I'll answer."

"Are you a Dom or sub?"

"Why do you need to know that?" I demanded, trying to mitigate the need for Haverson—Ben—to answer and spare him from potential embarrassment.

"Normally I'd say that's not your business," Ben said good-naturedly. "I'm a licensed therapist with a degree from Wash U and ten years' experience in the field, so I'm more than qualified to help you without you knowing anything beyond that. But there's a trust thing going on here, isn't there?" Trent had taken up his stupid staring contest bullshit again, and as Haverson spoke, it dawned on me that I had no need to mediate to keep from offending the doctor. Both were vying for the upper hand, Trent to establish his alpha dog bravado, and the doctor to establish the respect his credentials should have earned him. The doctor continued. "You don't know if someone within the lifestyle can be trusted to be open about it because it's shameful, right? It's a dirty thing to you, so in your mind, I should be embarrassed to be admitting to any of it. If I'm a Dom, I'm beating up on people who, in your estimation, are broken and need to be controlled just like a victim of domestic violence who keeps going back to their abuser. If I'm a sub, then I'm the broken one without the backbone to take responsibility for my half of a relationship and my own safety. Is that about right?"

Trent didn't blink. Neither did Ben.

"I'm a Dom, Detective Sawyer."

Trent jumped on that. "Isn't it a conflict of interest for a Dom to be a therapist for subs?"

"Trent," I warned.

"No, I wanna know," he said, still staring. "I wanna know how someone inclined to like getting smacked around could get help from a therapist who likes to smack people around. Seems to me that's inherently dangerous."

I shook my head. It was clear that Trent was putting his own spin on everything the doctor had said so far. He didn't get it. Great.

"Is it a conflict of interest for a married man to be a woman's marriage counselor, Detective?" Ben asked. His voice was still smooth and conversational, and his expression as forthcoming as it had been since he'd been introduced to us. But it was clear he wasn't cowed, or even slightly intimidated, by Trent's show of ruffled feathers. "Like any therapist, I keep my personal life separate from my professional life. I don't date my patients, as that would be illegal." He gave Trent a slight smirk. "And my being well-versed in the lifestyle and the relationship dynamics that happen in the BDSM world make it easier for my patients to talk to me, regardless of their preferences. Just as, I'd imagine, Detective Sawyer, it's easier for a therapist who has been a detective to counsel other police personnel, as long as it's kept strictly professional."

Trent blinked, losing the staring contest for the first time since I'd known him. His eyes narrowed and his face pulled into a fierce scowl. "How did you know about that?"

Like watching a tennis match, my gaze bounced between the two men, wondering what was going on.

"I do my homework, Detective. I like to know with whom I'm consulting, so when questions like yours arise, I can understand from where they originate."

"What are you talking about?" I asked, completely lost.

"Nothing," Trent mumbled, looking away from the doctor at last. "After Meg and I split, I saw a counselor on the department's payroll. No big deal."

Except it was a big deal, by the way Trent would no longer meet the doctor's eyes.

I do my homework… When had the doctor had time to check Trent's background? It had only been about six hours since I'd asked Sergeant Talcott to call in an expert. Had he checked on me, too? The thought made me distinctly uncomfortable. I stood, breaking up the little powwow, and thus, the tension that had built up over the last few minutes.

"Well, Doctor, you've been a big help." I stuck out my hand for him to shake, trying to keep my face neutral and ignore the tingle in my palm when he wrapped his warm fingers around mine. "Do you have a card or something? So we can reach you when we have more questions?"

Trent snorted, and I thought I heard him mumble, "Subtle," under his breath. Asshole.

"Please, Detective, call me Ben." He pressed a card in my palm and held one out to Trent, who snatched it as he stood.

"Ben," I tried it out, liking how it felt on my lips. "We'll be in touch." I pinched Trent's sleeve and pulled him behind me, getting out of there before the full head of steam he'd worked up had the chance to blow.

CHAPTER THREE

"TELL ME I don't have to worry about you pulling the same shit you just pulled in there on the witnesses, too," I snapped the second we were out of earshot of the briefing room.

Trent laughed. "Oh come on! You don't buy into that power exchange bullshit, do you?"

"That wasn't about whether or not he's credible. That was about you being top dog in any given situation." I didn't know whether I believed Haverson's explanations or not, but I couldn't deny being thoroughly intrigued. I wasn't about to admit that to Trent, though.

"Gavin, give me some credit. He's not a witness, so I pushed him a little. I don't buy what he said. A good relationship is built on trust, sure, but how can you trust someone when they're tying you up and beating you? It's not healthy."

We'd reached our desks again, and I scowled at my monitor. I had a new email, and I clicked over to see Mrs. Kaiser had sent me the list of George's acquaintances. I printed it and then sighed, speaking quietly. "Whether or not you buy it doesn't matter, Trent. The people we're talking to do. Questioning 101: don't alienate your witnesses. Your suspects, yes, unbalance the hell out of them, but not your witnesses, or you don't get shit from them. You better show some respect, or I'll be doing the questioning on my own."

Trent held up his hands in surrender. "All right, all right." Then he realized how he looked and snickered. "See? I'm capable of submission."

I rolled my eyes. "You're an idiot." But the vehemence was gone from my tone. He was exasperating and embarrassing as hell, but Trent was a good cop, and I knew he'd do his job. His ego may have taken up every breathable space in a room, but it also meant he didn't like it when people thought him incompetent. If he had to feign interest—or at least a lack of judgment—to get good information, he could do it. He didn't like it, but he'd do it. "Got a list of George's friends. Let's go."

"Now?" Trent raised a brow, looking at his watch. "It's nine thirty at night. I'm ready to go home."

"Now, Trent. Maybe the majority on this list will be there, and we can get through it faster."

"Amen to that," he mumbled, grabbing his suit jacket off the back of his chair.

We circled the block near midtown St. Louis where Collared was located and found parking two blocks away. The warm air lent electricity to the vibe on the street: cars with windows rolled down and music curling into the night, people walking arm in arm on their way to an entertaining venue. Flowers in full bloom from Forest Park scented the night. The only tarnish was the occasional siren of an ambulance navigating to or from the nearby hospital cluster, a grouping of two hospitals and the buildings housing outlying specialties. I was surprised by Collared's location, though I supposed it wasn't too far from the Loop and the Central West End, where lifestyles were freer and alternative personalities were the norm. Besides, given the clientele of the club, its patrons would likely have no trouble driving to the location from anywhere in the city.

The building blended in with those surrounding it, its brick exterior nothing special. The front entrance was down a set of steps, the sidewalk providing extra privacy to those entering and exiting through the matte black door. Strobe light from inside flashed past the small window set high in the door, the only indication this wasn't another hotel or part of the nearby university. We trooped into a long corridor lit eerily by red can lights along the ceiling. At the end of the hallway, sitting on a bar stool, was a bouncer in black jeans and T-shirt stretched across his massive chest with the word "Mercy" stenciled in a font more likely found on a first-aid kit than in a nightclub.

"Clever," I said as we approached. He stared at me, saying nothing. I pointed. "Your shirt. It's clever." Well, hey. I got awkward when I was nervous, and this place definitely made me nervous. I schooled my expression as Trent flashed his shield.

"St. Louis County PD, Homicide. Detectives DeGrassi and Sawyer," he announced, clearly expecting automatic entry. The bouncer stood, blocking him.

"You got a warrant, Officer?" he asked, crossing his arms over "Mercy," his biceps flexing to the point where I thought his T-shirt would scream in protest. I cringed, knowing Trent hated being called "officer," especially after flashing his badge.

"You got something to hide?" Trent barked impatiently.

I grabbed him by the sleeve and dragged him back a couple steps. He started to protest, glaring daggers at both me and the beefy obstacle in his way, and I simply held up a finger, telling him to wait. He gritted his teeth and nodded.

I returned to Bouncer Guy and flashed my shield, then pulled a picture from my jacket pocket and handed it to him. "Do you know this man?"

"George?" Bouncer Guy asked, startled.

"Yes. Was he here last night?"

"I wasn't on duty, so I don't know," he said. "Is he in trouble? He's not here tonight."

Don't I know it. I hated this part. "Mr. Kaiser was found dead at his home this morning, and we need to speak to some of his acquaintances, as well as others who might've seen him last night."

Bouncer Guy's face went pale. "No shit?" I nodded gravely. "Follow me," he said, sweeping open the heavy door to let a wave of booming techno music wash over us.

Trent shook his head.

"What?" I asked defensively.

"There goes any element of surprise we had."

"Oh, because your way was working so well. You cannot strong-arm these people. And didn't we say I'd do the talking anyway?"

Trent said nothing, sullenly following Bouncer Guy to the bar where he leaned over to speak to the bartender, a tall, lithe man in black leather pants and a tank top with arm holes so large his ribs were exposed. The shirt did nothing to hide his dual nipple piercings. The bartender bent toward me as I stepped up to the spot Bouncer Guy vacated when he resumed his post.

I let my gaze travel the club, the beat of the music syncing with the pounding of my heart. It was a large, single room with a soaring thirty-foot ceiling and massive support beams throughout. The outer ring of seats held deep leather booths accented with metal grommets, where couples and groups sat in various stages of intimacy, from deep conversation to full on make-outs. There were high cocktail tables in a ring inside the booths, where people stood either watching the stage or the dance floor, which was the center circle of the room, sunk into the floor.

Around the dance floor was the kind of railings one would find at a sports arena that divided the stairs from the seating section. To each of these railings, someone was handcuffed. Some were moving sinuously to the beat of the music or straining to reach those dancing nearby who would tease them with caresses and pinches. Some were engaged with their Masters or Mistresses, getting spankings or attention in other ways. All of them were scantily clad and sweaty.

The stage flanked one side of the dance floor and a DJ booth sat at one end. It was from there the lights and strobes emanated, as well as the occasional blast from a fog machine. On stage, a man wearing nothing but a leather jock was tied to a St. Andrew's Cross, a near replica of the one to which George Kaiser had been strapped. He was blindfolded and glistening in the multicolored lights, and a man in tight leather pants and no shirt wielded some kind of short, multi-tailed whip against his skin. It didn't look like the cat o' nine tails bagged at the victim's house. At the stage end of the dance floor, a crowd of onlookers cheered the whipping. The back wall of the stage was covered in mirrors, so regardless of where the Dom stood, the watchers got a view of nearly everything. Behind the DJ booth was a set of wrought-iron stairs leading to a balcony that ringed three quarters of the room. People danced up there, and a hallway led to another area of the club, lit in red like the front entrance. The entire place was a breathtaking, sweaty, writhing mass of bodies in various states of arousal and display. I did my best to ignore the twitch in my groin as a new, shocking sight registered every few moments. It felt dangerous, exhilarating, and intimidating all at once, and I knew I had to keep tight control of what caught my attention. If I slipped in here, stared too long at the wrong thing, gave too obvious a look at another man, Trent would be too shrewd to miss it.

"What happened to George?" the bartender shouted over the music, bringing my attention back to the task at hand. I had to lean closer to hear him.

"Were you here last night?" I asked.

"Yeah. I'm here every night. Jared Nunn. I own the club." Surprisingly, he stuck out his hand for me to shake. Huh, maybe not all of them are standoffish. I noticed his eyes raking me up and down, stopping at my waist, where my suit jacket had slid open and my holster showed. Oh, so it's like that.

"Detective DeGrassi, and this is my partner, Detective Sawyer." Jared gave Trent a nod, and Trent just stared. God, even here he had to play a badass. "Was George Kaiser here last night?"

"He was here every Friday night," he yelled into my ear. Right then, the DJ took the dance music down a notch to something not so difficult to hear over, with a sultrier sound. I had to remind myself to concentrate.

"Did you see him leave with anyone, talk to anyone new?"

Jared shook his head. "Not that I noticed. George didn't make it a habit to leave with someone the same night he met them. And if he did, he'd have told Matt Kinney, his safety net." Matt Kinney was the name Mrs. Kaiser had provided for George's Dom friend.

"What was George's usual habit when he was here?"

Jared shrugged. "Depends on if he had a sub or not. He hadn't had a steady lately, so mostly he talked to friends, kept up on who's doing what or whom, and stayed visible in the scene. You never know when you'll find the next sub waiting for the perfect Dom."

"So he was looking?"

"Yeah. He was alone for a few months, and I think it was getting to him. He had one or two friends-with-benefits, but nothing serious. It's the longest I've ever seen him go without getting together with anyone. Pickings have been slim lately, which is surprising, since subs outnumber Doms twenty to one. Usually." Jared snickered, moving to the side a little to grab a beer from the cooler for a customer. I moved with him, looking at the people close to the bar. A woman smiled at me and winked, licking her red-stained lips and leering. I turned back to Jared.

"So he might've been lonely enough to go with someone new?"

Again, Jared shrugged. "George was always exceedingly careful. Anyone new usually starts by checking references, so he'd have known if someone was interested. There are private and semi-private rooms upstairs where they can get to know each other. That's as much for the safety of the Doms as the subs. Don't want someone who swears they're into it, and then the light of day brings regret and panic so they run to the police accusing someone of assault. George was up there last night, but Lacey would know more about who he spoke to."

"Lacey?" I asked, writing down her name. "Is she here tonight?"

"Yeah, she's the Dungeon Master, making sure everything's peachy upstairs. Keeps everyone in line."

I didn't realize women could be Dungeon Masters, but I kept my ignorance to myself. Trent's eyes glinted with interest. Before he could say anything, I passed over my email printout. "Are any of these people here tonight? I need to speak with them, find out if they noticed anything or spoke to George."

Jared hesitated. He took the list, but didn't immediately answer my question. "These are good people, everyone on this list. I don't see them having anything to do with what happened to George. You have to understand, Detective, things are negotiated between Doms and subs before any play takes place. Limits are established up front, and if things go too far, Master Lacey or one of the other Dungeon

Masters will put a stop to it. We take care of our own. We can't afford not to."

I didn't say anything, simply let compassion color my expression and waited. After another moment, he released a sigh. "Yeah, these three are around here somewhere," he pointed to the names, "and Matt is on stage demonstrating his flogging technique."

So that's what the short whip was: a flogger. I'd heard the term but had never seen one or looked it up. I glanced at the spectacle across the room with the bound man submitting to the whipping. Before I could stop myself, I said, "Looks painful."

A lazy smile played on Nunn's face. "Yes and no. It's one of the milder pieces of equipment. In the right hands, it can be heaven. You should ask him what it's like, Detective." He winked at me and returned to his bar duties.

Trent clapped a hand on my shoulder. "He's giving a demo. Wanna go volunteer?"

I shrugged him off and glared. "No, thanks." I said it low enough not to be heard by anyone else. When we were done with this, he and I were having words.

We navigated through the bodies on the outer ring to stand beside the stage, waiting for an opportunity to interrupt, but neither of us was in the mood to get in the way of the flying tails on a backswing. The music with the frenetic beat had been taken down some, and I realized the DJ was tailoring the songs to the stage show, slowing it down. The man tied to the cross was breathing easily despite the red welts on his chest and thighs. He seemed to anticipate each blow regardless of the blindfold, arching up to meet the thrashes that rained down. Each blow brought a cry from him, but it was impossible to tell if it was from pain or pleasure. He was hard as a rock. Every couple of minutes, Matt Kinney would lean in and whisper something in the man's ear, to which the man responded with a breathless "Please, Sir," or a whimper. I studied Kinney's face as he moved, graceful as a panther. His face was serene, focused, and it didn't appear he was aware of the crowd, like it was him, his subject, the music, and the flogger, and nothing else in the world mattered. Kinney was sweating, and his gleaming skin shifted over well-defined muscles, his hips swiveling with each lash. His breathing was well-timed with the effort of his arm, and his short hair stood on end from the exertion. I couldn't look away.

After a few more moments, Kinney set the flogger aside and fitted his body flush to the restrained man from thigh to chest, his hands caressing the man's tender sides. It made the guy squirm, and he rutted shamelessly against Kinney's hips, a litany of "Pleases" and

"Yes, Sirs" falling from his lips. Kinney kept his voice low as he spoke to the wrecked man, and the crowd enjoying the show cheered and hooted their appreciation. Someone on the opposite side of the stage stood by with a blanket and a couple bottles of water as Kinney untied the man, who was draped over his shoulders limply, completely spent. Well... I don't know if he was completely spent, but I wasn't about to find out.

When the blanket holder stepped onto the stage, we took that as our cue and approached from the opposite side as the sub was wrapped up and Kinney slipped an arm around his waist to support him off the stage through a door behind the DJ booth, led by the staffer who still held their water.

"Matt Kinney?" I asked. He turned to look at me, his face serene. I held up my shield, introducing myself and Trent. He stared at us blankly, and then shook his head as if to clear it. "We need a moment of your time."

"I have to see to Lance right now," he snapped, clearly annoyed.

"It's only a few minutes."

"I'm not going anywhere, but I really have to take care of Lance. He needs me and that can't wait."

"Do you mind if we come along then?" I asked, not thinking before the words were out of my mouth. What exactly did "see to Lance" entail? Trent elbowed me.

Kinney raised a brow and shrugged. "Suit yourself. Just stay out of the way and don't talk until I'm ready."

Bossy little fucker, I thought, but I nodded and followed the couple through the door and into a comfortable backstage area with a couch, a few armchairs, and a mini-fridge tucked into the corner. The lights were dimmed, but they were the right color, and the music there was muted to the point where it was almost soothing. Kinney guided the man, presumably Lance, to the couch and sat with him, pulling him onto his lap and simply holding him. If they spoke, it was in whispers, small murmurs that sounded like endearments and praise, if the tone was anything to go by. I thought I heard the words "Rest now, baby," but I couldn't swear to it.

More than fifteen minutes passed as the two men on the couch cuddled together. I tried not to watch too closely, taking in the room and its peaceful atmosphere instead, but I kept stealing little glances at the couple. Kinney's hands didn't roam, didn't rub Lance's irritated skin. He just held the man, speaking into his ear while Lance gave an occasional nod. Lance's face was somewhere barely shy of bliss, and his breathing changed several times from relaxed to staccato gasps, then back to relaxed. Curled and wrapped up as he was, I couldn't see much more of Lance than his head, and at one point, he turned his face into the crook of Kinney's neck and sighed contentedly. It was a few minutes after that when Kinney finally acknowledged us.

"Sorry. He was flying and I had to make sure he was okay as he came down. What is it that's so important you couldn't give me a chance to regroup?" His irritation was plain, but his voice was low. I glanced at Lance and realized he was asleep.

"You're a friend of George Kaiser's, correct?" Trent started, not keeping his tone soft at all. It was jarring and Kinney narrowed his eyes.

"Yeah, he's my best friend."

"Did you see him last night? Speak to him about anything?"

I could see Kinney's hackles rise, and instinct told me he was about to ask us to leave. I cleared my throat, shooting Trent a meaningful look and leaned forward, matching my tone to Kinney's.

"Please, Mr. Kinney. This is very important."

"Yeah, I saw him last night. He was still here when Lance and I went home."

"What time was that?"

"Around midnight. George was making the rounds and rubbing elbows. What's going on?"

"I'm sorry to tell you this, but George was killed this morning. From what we know so far, this was the last place he was seen."

Kinney's face paled and his hands tightened around the sleeping man in his lap. "Killed how?" he rasped.

"At his home… in his play room," I said, noting how his face changed. Shock, horror, pain, and he looked a little green around the edges. He was genuinely upset.

"Do you know who did it?"

"That's what we're trying to find out," I said gently, "with your help. Did you see him talk to anyone while you were here? Anyone you didn't know or someone you think he might've gone home with?"

He shook his head, dazed. "Um, he talked to some of the regulars, like always. Me, of course, and Lance. The owner of the club, Jared. It was pretty typical. If he met someone new, it would have been after I left. And he'd never have left with someone new without telling me. I'm his safety net."

"About that. What is that exactly?" Trent asked. He lowered his voice, dialing his hard-ass routine way down, apparently convinced of Kinney's lack of involvement.

"This lifestyle can be dangerous for everyone, in different ways. George and I have an agreement that anyone new doesn't go home with either of us without the other one at least meeting them. Occasionally, I'll get a text message from him that he's meeting a newbie to talk to them, but that was always in public, at a restaurant or coffee shop. He rarely did that, though, and I had no text this morning when I woke up."

Three different people had mentioned how careful George was with new potential subs. So how had he ended up at home with a killer and no sign of forced entry? Things weren't adding up.

"Can you think of any reason he'd allow someone to go home with him? Maybe he wasn't expecting to play with the person. Maybe it was someone he knew from elsewhere and they were friends. A work colleague or former classmate. Someone he didn't realize knew about his preferences."

Kinney shook his head. "I guess it's possible he ran into someone he knew another way and let his guard down." The corners of his lips turned down and his grip tightened further on the sleeping man in his lap. "Jesus, I can't believe he's dead. You talk to Kim? Is she okay?"

"Mrs. Kaiser was the one who found him this morning, so we've spoken with her. She's a tough lady," I said.

Kinney nodded. "Yeah, she is. I'll check on her, see if there's anything I can do for her or the kids." His head snapped up. "The kids didn't... see anything, did they?"

"No, they were at home at the time of the discovery." I let him process the information for a moment, hoping something would occur to him.

"He mentioned going upstairs last night to one of the semi-private rooms. He sometimes went up there to inspect new equipment or talk to Master Lacey. Maybe someone up there talked to him."

A new thought occurred to me and I scooted forward on my chair a little. "Tell me, how does one learn Dominant techniques?"

A rueful smile touched Kinney's lips. "There are a few ways, and it depends on the personality. Some will submit to a trained Dom, learn how it feels to be on the receiving end of whatever instrument they wish to learn. Some develop a mentor-apprentice relationship with an experienced Dom, and they'll share the same sub who will later give feedback. Some do neither, and land with a sub who matches their experience level and they grow together over time. There are munches, workshops, demonstrations all over the country, too. Depends on the personality."

"What's a munch?" Trent asked.

"Casual meet-up. Rarely any special attire or play of any kind. It's like the BDSM version of happy hour. We get together at a restaurant or bar and talk, meet new people, answer questions the newbies might have. Informal and low-pressure."

"Is it possible George was approached by an untrained Dom wishing to learn from him? Would George still take his usual safety precautions?" I questioned.

Kinney considered this for a moment. "I honestly don't know. It's entirely possible, but I've never seen George train a Dom, so I don't know how he would react to such a proposal. He might have refused outright if it wasn't his thing. He liked to help people, though."

I stood, pulling a card from my pocket and setting it on the small table beside the couch. "Thank you, Mr. Kinney. If you think of anything else, please call. We'll be in touch." Trent and I left the backstage area through the door we'd come through, emerging behind the DJ booth. There was a new couple on stage, and I stared for a moment at the woman bent over a bench with her hands clenching and unclenching at every blow of a paddle her Master wielded. The crowd counted out the number of spanks as the woman writhed and moaned. She must have had a microphone near her face because the sounds she made were amplified throughout the club. I turned away and headed for the stairs along the wall to our left, shifting uncomfortably in my pants. It was a bit of work ignoring Trent's smirk.

"Sure you don't want to volunteer? You look interested," he chided from behind me.

"Fuck off," I threw back over my shoulder, dodging a few dancers on the steps and catwalk surrounding the room.

"C'mon, Gavin," Trent teased. "You're getting a lot of attention here with your pretty boy looks. From the guys, too. Seems your stunning blue eyes and that calculated stubble thing you have going on is popular."

The heat rising from my neck to my face had me thankful to reach the beginning of the red hallway so the coloring was well hidden. "Trent," I warned. I knew people considered me attractive, and sometimes I used it to my advantage when questioning witnesses, letting my unusually bright blue eyes that contrasted sharply with my light brown hair capture their attention, or using my sincere smile and dimples to put them at ease. But to hear Trent make a joke of it set a worm of discomfort wiggling in my belly.

"What?" he laughed, backing down. "All right, I'll leave you alone. You've had a hard day. Probably can't wait to get home and spread out, relax, take a long shower. Release some tension."

"You need the smartass beaten out of you," I snapped.

"That can be arranged, boys." The purr of a woman clad in a red bustier and shiny vinyl pants licked up my spine and curled in my gut as I turned, startled by the proximity of an imposing woman of about five feet eight with the three-inch heels she wore. Her platinum blonde hair was cut in a sleek bob, and her shadowed eyes and deep red lips gave her a porcelain appearance, but it wasn't the outfit or makeup that made her intimidating. It was her confidence, showcased by impeccable posture and a knowing expression. She smiled warmly. "Would you care for a private or semi-private space to beat his disrespect out?" It was said as if the phrase was an everyday request—do you want your chicken grilled or crispy? Would you care for some coffee? Have you seen my shoes? In no way should asking me if I wanted to beat my partner privately or in front of an audience sound so mundane. It was all I could do to keep from spluttering in my hurry to assure the woman that no, we were not up there to... partake.

"Detective DeGrassi, St. Louis County homicide." I held up my badge. It had the desired effect, and she straightened her already ramrod posture. "This is my partner, Detective Sawyer. Can you tell us where we might find Master Lacey?"

"My apologies, Detective. I'm Master Lacey. What can I do for you?" While she remained friendly, the playful air had disappeared.

"Last night, George Kaiser was up here for a while," I began. Master Lacey nodded, ignoring the sounds coming from some of the rooms behind her. A loud exclamation of "Please, Sir! Please, may I come?" interrupted my train of thought.

"Lacey, could we possibly go to one of those private rooms you mentioned?" Trent asked.

Master Lacey appeared to consider the request and then shook her head. "Sorry, guys. No can do. I need to be available in case anyone runs into trouble. I assure you whatever we discuss will not leave this hallway, if that's what you're concerned about. The offer of a private room was for the two of you only."

I cleared my throat. "We only need a few minutes of your time."

"My time is yours, gentlemen, but my presence out here is required. Rules of the house."

We were getting nowhere, and the sounds around us were distracting. We'd have to make this fast. "Okay, I can appreciate your point. Perhaps, at the other end of the hallway, though? Where those doors are closed, and less... likely to interrupt the conversation?"

"Certainly, Detective."

We followed Master Lacey toward the opposite end of the

corridor, and I did my best to keep my eyes straight. Trent, however, gawked openly. By the third door—which was less of a door and more of an open archway to an airy alcove, presumably one of the semi-private rooms—he elbowed me to look at a young man tied to a bench on his back with his arms trailing to the floor and his ankles shackled to his wrists. He wore a decorative mask reminiscent of The Phantom of the Opera and his erect penis was angry red from the leather strip wrapped around it. The lighting in each room was stark white, and the reddened skin of the submissive's chest stood out like zebra stripes from an apparent whipping. His Dom knelt beside the bench, hands shiny and slick and he stroked the bound man's erection excruciatingly slow for the titillation of three other people in the room watching, one of whom held a video camera.

"Such a beautiful boy for me," the Dom said affectionately. "Mine to play with, to do with what I want, to watch you writhe and beg to come. How long has it been?"

The man with the video camera answered, "I believe two hours of edging, Sir."

"Close to running out of tape, boy. Lucky for you. It's too bad we're not at home, in our space. Could go for hours yet." The Dom's hands moved slightly faster and his boy flexed his entire body, crying out for release.

Before I could stop myself, I asked, "Edging?" Master Lacey turned, noticing both Trent and I had stopped to watch.

"It's a form of delicate sexual torture. The sub is bound and often blindfolded to provide some sensory deprivation and heighten touch. Then they are stimulated to the point of orgasm but not allowed to succumb until their Dom is satisfied with the play. Edging can go on for hours. I've heard tell of a few sessions among some of our regulars that have lasted a day or more."

"Why would someone want that?" Trent blurted, his expression equal parts fascinated and horrified.

"Because, Detective," Master Lacey purred. "When the bliss is finally granted, it can make them black out, take them into subspace if they're not already there, give them a whole body orgasm. The amount of skill required to keep someone on the edge of coming for a long time brings an intimacy between Master and slave that is rarely seen in the vanilla world. Total trust. Total domination. And total immersion in each other. Young Nick there is no longer aware he's being watched or filmed, though his express consent was given up front. He's in his own world, and the only one who can reach him there is Master Zach, who holds Nick's entire well-being in the palm of his hands. It's stunningly beautiful."

Her words wove a spell around me as we watched, and Nick's acceptance of having his body on display, used to make Zach happy, for the Dom to play as a maestro plays a piano, had me staring in awe, wondering how freeing it would be to let someone else take control for who knew how long, to put aside the mental checklist of how many orgasms had been reached and whose turn it was for the next one. To trust that someone was using my body for their pleasure and I had to do nothing but give up control, let them do as they would, take what they wanted without playing games and expecting me to be a mind reader—I wasn't sure if I could let go that much, but the idea intrigued me.

Zach's hands did not change pace, but he did begin to speak. "Nick, my boy, you have a beautiful body and you so exquisitely give up control of it to please me. You've earned your reward." Still the gentle pressure on the cock in his hand, still the same torturously slow rhythm. "It's time, pet. Come... now."

On command, Nick panted, tensed, and spilled over Zach's slick hand, his dick jumping and pulsing between Zach's loosely curled fingers, a slow, deep eruption that went on forever. Zach's hand was nearly covered in semen. I'd never seen someone come so much from one orgasm, even in the porn hidden in the back of my closet.

"You can close your mouth any time, Gavin," Trent said softly in my ear, and I snapped my jaw shut, flushing fiercely again as I realized how mesmerized I'd been. At least, if Trent had noticed my erection—oh god, please tell me he hadn't—he had the good grace not to say anything in front of other people.

"You are intrigued," Master Lacey said. "Would you prefer to watch more or were you interested in asking me some questions, Detective?"

I called up the image of George Kaiser strapped to his cross, black marks on his face and his dead eyes staring at the room, accusatory and betrayed. I had a purpose, and it was not to get off on other people's sexual proclivities.

"George Kaiser was here last night. Did you see him talk to anyone, watch anyone in particular?" I asked, getting back on track.

"He watched a scene or two in the semi-privates, but he didn't talk to anyone new, no. At least, not that I saw. We had a new initiate sub here last night, and I spent quite a lot of time making sure he was comfortable, and that everything stayed safe, sane, and consensual."

I was getting frustrated with the repetitious answers. "Did you see him leave with anyone?"

Master Lacey frowned. "No. He spent a few minutes talking with

Damon Lane, but I think that was idle conversation while the two of them watched a scene."

"Damon Lane?" I asked, writing the name down.

"Yes, he's a master craftsman. Makes fine implements and has earned quite the reputation in the last few years. In particular, his floggers are spectacular, perfectly balanced, and he can tailor the amount of sting to the Dom's exact desires. He often comes up here to see how his clientele are using his equipment or to get an idea of improvements he can make to new designs based on first-hand opinions."

"You have information on how we can reach Mr. Lane?"

Master Lacey pursed her lips, appraising us. "What's all this got to do with George? Has he done something?"

"We're searching for leads into the murder of Mr. Kaiser, who spent his last hours at Collared."

Master Lacey's hand covered her mouth, horror stricken. "Oh my god. And you think someone here did this?" Her eyes flashed.

"We're trying to learn if someone saw him leave with anyone or knew of him meeting anyone at another club or for a drink. We have some gaps to fill between when he was last seen and when he was found at his home this morning." I kept my voice as neutral as possible, giving no indication that our pool of suspects would have been any different had George spent his evening at a singles bar or a cabaret. This community talked, and it was apparent they watched out for one another, just as Dr. Haverson had said. Alienating one would alienate them all, and so far, they were the best witnesses we had.

"George left around two-fifteen in the morning. He was alone."

I raised a brow, marking the time in my notes. "You saw him leave?"

"Yes, Detective. Club closes at two a.m. and he insisted on walking me to my car. Rather sweet of him, considering I am never without this." She pointed to what I had thought was an elaborate bracelet snaked around her left arm, but was, in fact, a bullwhip. "And yes, I know how to use it. I can tickle someone with it, or wrest a gun from their grip, depending on the situation. Better than a can of mace, and makes an intimidating crack which sends most would-be muggers running to their mommies. George was a gentleman, though, and I like to be reminded now and then that chivalry isn't dead."

"So he didn't actually leave alone," Trent asked, voice challenging. "He left with you."

Master Lacey's face changed little, but her whole demeanor

morphed into calculated calm, one step short of fury. I could see instantly why Jared Nunn would put a woman such as her on bouncer duty in the back rooms.

"I suppose you could look at it that way, though I was only with him long enough to go to my car, Detective," she said coolly.

"Did you go anywhere from here?" I asked, knowing Trent's alpha tendencies would kick in and there'd be a struggle for control of the conversation.

"I went straight home."

"Anyone there who can corroborate that?" A pointed question, but it would zero in on her or totally rule her out, and my tone was nowhere near as confrontational as Trent's would have been.

"Yes. My girlfriend, Ginger. I called her from my cell as I drove and talked to her until I reached home. Ginger was already there, waiting for me."

I took down Ginger's information, doing a double take at the surname. Trent, the bastard, couldn't seem to help himself, not connecting the dots on Ginger's name.

"Is Ginger your sub?"

"She is," Master Lacey answered.

"How do we know she won't simply corroborate your alibi out of fear of you or your punishment?"

That I was uncomfortable was an understatement, especially under Master Lacey's piercing gaze. We took spouses' and significant others' word on alibis all the time, though every now and then, they proved false. That had nothing to do with Trent's question, however. He was merely taking a jab at the lifestyle, and his narrow opinion of it being deviant made clear why these people were wary of authority outside their world. But then Master Lacey smiled a triumphant sneer as she answered Trent's question. "Because you know her, Detective. Ginger Graham, St. Louis County District Attorney's office. She would know better than anyone the consequences of lying me an alibi. I will make sure when you speak to her that she relinquishes her cell phone records as proof of the call and have her give you explicit detail as to what went on after I arrived home last night."

§§§

THE HOUSE was dark and silent when I slipped in the front door, leaving my shoes in the foyer. I let my eyes adjust before walking down the hallway to our bedroom. There was a narrow strip of light from under the closed en suite bathroom door, the only light

Victoria could stand to leave on for me when I worked late. Quietly entering to brush my teeth and remove my contacts, I listened to the rhythm of her breathing, trying to determine how soundly she was asleep.

I stripped out of all but my boxer briefs and climbed between the cool sheets on my side of the bed. Victoria automatically rolled into me and I moved to wrap her in my arms.

"Ugh, you smell like smoke." She rolled away with a wrinkle of her nose, mumbling. "Where've you been?"

"Working. New case and the victim was last seen at a leather bar near midtown. Went to question the regulars."

"I just changed the sheets and you're going to stink them up," she complained, awareness chasing away the hold sleep had over her. "Go shower, please."

Grateful for the dark room so she couldn't see me roll my eyes, I threw back the covers and did as I was asked. The hot spray relaxed a tension in my shoulders I hadn't realized I was carrying, but I made it quick, the brutality of the day catching up to me and sapping my energy. Every time I closed my eyes, George Kaiser's face swam up in my mind. A fierce sense of purpose welled in my chest.

"I'll find who did this to you," I promised him, thinking of the people at Collared who had been shocked to find out about the killing. None of them seemed a likely candidate, not even Master Lacey. There was no crime in being the last person a murder victim spoke with, and I was quite certain her alibi would be airtight. I did want to talk to Matt Kinney again, given that he'd been close to the victim and the timing of our questioning of him had been poor. Maybe different circumstances and setting would turn up more information.

An image of Matt Kinney swam up in my mind, the powerful arc of his arm as he whipped his sub on the cross in front of an audience, how blissed out Lance had looked from receiving the whipping, and how intimate the moments backstage were immediately following the flogging. For what felt like the fifteenth time that night, I got hard. Another image, a whispering Dom leaning over his pliant but restrained sub, giving him a two hour long hand job, solidified my erection. It wasn't only the fact of two men so open about their sexuality that they allowed others to witness it, though that would have been more than enough. It was what Master Lacey had said: exquisite torture, absolute trust, and the knowledge that new heights could be reached by letting oneself go that far, trust in another that deeply.

I turned off the water and toweled dry, foregoing underwear

before sliding back between the sheets and gathering a sleepy Victoria close. She immediately noticed my nudity and my caressing hand on her hip, feeling her smooth skin slide beneath my fingers. Sighing heavily, she mumbled something I didn't catch. I kept stroking her until she slapped my hand away.

"I said I'm too tired," she groused. After a moment, she rolled onto her back and peered at me with one sleepy eye. "That club full of perverts didn't put you in the mood, did it?" Her tone was clear that if that were the case, she was wholly disturbed by it.

"No," I lied. "I just miss my wife."

"S'not my fault you don't have enough ambition to go for a higher rank so you wouldn't have to work so many hours."

My arms went slack, letting her go. She rolled onto her stomach with her face turned away. "I'm happy where I am. I feel like I make a difference, even if it's a small one."

"You could make more of a difference if you were a sergeant, or even a lieutenant. You'd have people in the trenches for you, more power over fighting the criminal element."

"Yeah, and I'd be doing paperwork all day. And press conferences. No thanks." I rolled to my side, away from her, tired of the same discussion that went in circles and was never resolved. She scooted into my back, her breasts pressing into me through the thin fabric of her T-shirt. After the night I'd had and how I'd felt only moments before, I should have regained my interest. Instead, tiredness and her lack of understanding leeched any energy I might have had.

"You know, you swear you won't like being a higher rank, but you've never done it. How do you know?"

Because the paperwork part of my job always sucked my soul from my eyeballs? Because the idea of standing on the sidelines while other people brought down the bad guys made me twitchy and restless? Because I knew it was her ambition and not mine?

"Just like you know you'd be uncomfortable in a biker bar. It's late. We have to be at my parents' tomorrow by ten." Sunday brunch. Never missed a week without a damned good reason. As I closed my eyes, I found myself thinking of acceptable reasons to beg off and wondered if it was possible to will myself a stomach bug or an earthquake only beneath our house. It was the last thing I remembered before dreams of being spanked in front of a crowd swallowed me whole.

CHAPTER FOUR

"HEY, GAV, Victoria." Cole greeted us from the living room floor, where he lay sprawled with Annalise and Marcie, our nieces, playing Candyland. "You gotta get in on this game, bro. Did you know that if you get the Ice Cream Princess, it means you really get ice cream? I think Mom and Dad held out on the proper rules when we were little."

I grinned, passing the pie I was holding to Victoria, who walked stiffly to Ma's kitchen. She'd been pleasant but distant this morning, and I knew she was still thinking about the previous night, about my reticence with climbing the rank ladder. I knew it would blow over if I gave her some space. It always did.

Cole watched her with curious eyes before turning his baby blues back to me. I shrugged at his raised eyebrows. He sat up, announcing he'd pulled the Gum Drop Mountain card and that meant he was stuck there for the rest of the game. New rule. Annalise looked at him with her shrewd four-year-old face. "Uncle Cole, that's not a rule."

He grinned at her. "Did the instructions say it wasn't?"

She grabbed the box and looked for the directions, pretending to read. "Where are the 'structions?" Marcie grabbed them from Annalise, who started to splutter in indignation.

"You can't read yet, Leesey," she said with six-year-old superiority. She looked at the directions with narrowed eyes while Annalise crowded her to grab the box back. Cole reached down to pluck Annalise off the floor before an all-out slap fight could ensue.

"C'mon Leesey. Maybe Nana or Aunt Victoria has a frosting spoon you can lick."

"Frosting!" Annalise crowed, shooting a glare at her sister over

Cole's shoulder as he carried her through the dining room to the kitchen. A few minutes later, he returned, kid-free and grinning.

"Glad she's not my kid. She's gonna leave here so hopped up on sugar she could probably run alongside the car and beat them home."

"I'm sure Mason loves you for that," I laughed. Mason was our oldest brother, and the only one of us with kids. We loved spoiling his girls rotten and then leaving him to deal with the aftermath. It was the only way to get under his skin and rattle his perfect composure. While he definitely had the big brother protective streak, there were times when he got sanctimonious, and Cole and I, being the two youngest, were usually the recipients. It happened in a family with four boys, all of us two years apart in age. There was no doubt Mason had a good head on his shoulders. I just liked my Sunday brunches without the side of pompous ass, and he had less time to do that with hyper children. His wife, Sandra, was a saint, and a very easy-going woman who wasn't afraid to remind Mason he wasn't our keeper.

"So, anything on Kaiser?" Cole asked softly, tilting his head to silently ask if I wanted to go outside and sit on the porch swing. An unwritten rule at my parents' house was no shop talk at the table, and our dad was the only one who could get away with breaking it. Even though we hadn't yet sat down to eat, we didn't want to risk the glare from our mother if she overheard us.

The late May sunshine was brilliant, and it promised to be another gorgeous day. Cole dropped onto the swing and propped his feet on the porch railing, pulling out a cigarette and lighting up.

"When are you going to quit that shit, man?" I asked. "Ma know you do that?"

"She knows," he replied, blowing smoke away from me. "She yells at me for it, but I'm twenty-eight. I can smoke if I want. Don't change the subject."

I leaned against the rail by his feet, crossing my arms over my chest. "Nothing worth mentioning. A couple more people to question. No one saw the vic talk to anyone new, and he left his last known location alone. Whoever did the deed, they didn't ride with him."

"Makes sense," Cole said, watching the neighbor kids riding bikes on the sidewalk across the street. "His car was still in the driveway. Not like the guy would have called a cab from the scene."

"Not if he was smart." I made a mental note to check with cab companies anyway. Sometimes, the stupidest thing led to a collar. Collar… That word made my skin heat up with the memory of the club the previous night.

"What?" Cole asked, noticing.

"Nothing. You have anything from your end?"

Cole shook his head, puffing on his cancer stick. "Not really. Nothing you don't already know. We're still testing the evidence. When's the autopsy scheduled?"

"Got an email from Jencopale first thing this morning. It's set up for tomorrow. Would have been today, but he doesn't work Sundays. Ever."

"Don't blame the guy. I couldn't do what he does for a living without needing a good couple days a week to decompress."

"Yeah, well I couldn't do what you do without decompressing either." Cole flicked his butt into the bushes. "Ma will kill you if you leave that there," I warned.

Cole stuck his tongue out at me. "I'll get it when I go. I couldn't talk to witnesses like you, either. The evidence, that's black and white, yes or no. Once I get it to the lab, it's just another test I need to run or report to write. Kinda sanitizes the whole thing. You, you've got to deal with the aftermath, families and the murky world of emotions. I couldn't do it."

"Good thing you found a loophole in Dad's 'I-will-only-pay-for-a-criminal-justice-degree' rule." Cole was considered the black sheep of the family, still in law enforcement, but technically not a cop. Dad had about blown a gasket when Cole had announced a double major in Criminal Justice and Chemistry so he could become a CSI. There'd been talk about making him pay his own way through college, but Ma had convinced Dad that Cole was the smart one and that would be like punishing him for trying harder. It was still a sore spot but Cole took it in stride. Dad was an old school cop, relying more on good police work than "all that damned science" to solve cases. Of course, Dad had retired from a desk job and hadn't actually closed a case himself for years prior to that. He'd been a lieutenant and was proud of his boys, all four of us cops in one form or another.

Right then, Shawn pulled up in his nondescript Impala. He was two years younger than Mason, two years older than me, and the quietest of us all. All of us had light brown hair and blue eyes, though Cole was vain enough to highlight his blond, and Shawn had the most delicate features, almost elfin. To compensate, he had a short, well-trimmed beard and had let his hair grow a little shaggy. His girlfriend of three years, Chrissy, got out of the passenger side, her long chestnut hair pulled back in a French braid. I kissed her cheek as they passed, and she gave me a bright-eyed wink and a smile that showed a dimple in her cheek. Chrissy could only be described as adorable, very girl-next-door.

"You look tired, Gav. You taking care of yourself?" she asked.

I waved her off, smiling reassuringly. "Late night working a case. I'm fine."

"Oh damn," she said, mock disappointed. "I was hoping you were up late with the little missus working on becoming a daddy."

I groaned at her teasing, inwardly cringing at the very idea, but not letting it show. "We have to plan for that kind of thing. Victoria's scheduled it for next year."

She laughed and made for the door Shawn held open for her. "Oh, well then, who am I to rearrange the schedule?"

"Be nice," Shawn said quietly, giving me a wink over the top of her head.

"Speaking of schedules, when are we getting that wedding invitation in the mail?" I teased her in return. She turned back to me, shaking her head and laughing.

"You'd have to ask your brother." She playfully punched Shawn in the ribs. "But I'm not in any hurry. I already know I've got him hooked."

Shawn's lips twitched like he was fighting a smile. "When I know, you'll know, pretty girl."

Chrissy sauntered into the house singing, "If you like it then you shoulda put a ring on it."

"I like her," I said to Cole when they were out of earshot. "She's not hung up on appearances or expectations."

"You mean like everyone else in this family?"

"Yeah, well..." I trailed off, looking out over the street.

"Dad say something about you being stuck at detective again?" he asked, knowing damn well that if it hadn't come up, it was only a matter of time.

"Not today. Yet." I shifted uncomfortably. There were a lot of things I kept close to the vest where my family was concerned. Of all of them, Cole was the one I was closest to, the one—were I so inclined to tell someone the one deep secret I'd had locked in my chest since I was a teenager—to whom I would unburden. He'd be shocked, I was sure, but I didn't see how that would happen. I had Victoria. She was what I needed, for now.

Suddenly uncomfortable, I knocked Cole's shoes off the railing. "Let's go see if we can cause some trouble in the kitchen under the pretense of helping." Cole stared at me silently for a moment, and I headed to the door, but his hand on my elbow stopped me.

"You know you can tell me anything, Gavin. If things aren't great and you need to vent. I won't judge."

I smiled at him, touched. "You're the brave one in the family, not me. I don't have anything to tell." I'm not willing to, anyway.

He gave my elbow a squeeze. "Okay. Offer's open."

We couldn't have timed our return to the house any better. Victoria and Ma were setting the last of the food on the table, and Annalise and Marcie were being herded to their places between Mason and Sandra, the picture of well-behaved girls until Marcie bit back a wicked grin and kicked her sister's foot under the table. Annalise yelled, "Hey!" and kicked back, which necessitated a rearranging of seats, with Mason between the girls as buffer. He scowled at them and their postures immediately snapped straight, eyes down on their plates. "Sorry, Daddy," they chorused.

God, was I ever grateful I didn't have the stress of parenthood at home. I wasn't there a lot, and I knew having grown up in a cop's house what it was like. I wasn't sure I'd wish that on a child, let alone my own. I couldn't even picture being a father. I got all the kid-fix I needed from my nieces. As I held Victoria's chair out for her and took my own seat, she leaned close, speaking softly.

"You okay? You look like you have heartburn or something."

"I'm fine," I answered. "Just hungry and have a lot on my mind."

"Care to share?" she asked, passing the plate of rolls my way.

"Not here," I took one and passed it on.

There was mostly silence for several minutes as we filled our plates and settled into the food. Dad was the first to speak up.

"You know Megan Carroll recently got out of the Academy? Got her degree in computers and wants into the white collar stuff."

Ma gave Dad a look, but said nothing about him talking shop at the table. It wasn't really shop talk exactly, since the Carrolls had been our neighbors long before I was born and we had spent years running the neighborhood, playing hide and seek until the streetlights came on. Megan Carroll was Cole's age, twenty-eight, with two kids and a fresh divorce. She'd often been the subject of brunch conversation as my parents watched her marriage implode from their concerned, neighborly vantage point. Megan had moved off the street, but her parents had not, and they gathered at dusk for iced tea on my parents' porch or the Carroll's backyard patio often, especially during warmer months.

"What station is she assigned to?" Mason asked, chewing thoughtfully.

"Seventh," Dad answered, giving Mason a pointed look. "Thought you'd know that already."

Mason was sergeant at STLCPD Seventh precinct, a great source of pride for our father, given he was one of the youngest to earn the rank at only thirty-four. But Mason always did like playing politics, and he was good at it.

"New hires listings don't come out for three more days, Pop," Mason said. "But I'll look out for her. Surprised she went the cop route, with her kids and all."

Megan's decision to go to the academy had not been popular with her parents, but she'd held her ground. I was proud of her. She'd taken enough crap from her deadbeat ex to let anyone else give it to her.

"White collar, though. That's safe, soon as she can get off patrol. She always was a computer nerd," I said, jumping to Megan's defense. Victoria eyed me sideways. I ignored her. She already knew I'd dated Megan my last year and a half of high school, taking her to prom and homecoming. Megan was the first relationship I'd had, first girl I'd slept with, and my family had a soft spot for her. There had been talk amongst our families that we would get married, but when I went to college, Megan and I had backed off. My family had been upset, and I couldn't tell them the real reason Megan wasn't right for me. Then I'd met Victoria my senior year, after deciding to remain firmly closeted. Choosing Victoria had cemented that decision, though I often wondered if Megan would have been an easier choice. Regardless, Megan and I were simply friends now. I didn't see her all that often, but that might change if she was on the force.

Conversation flowed around us, and slowly, the clanking of silverware against china tapered off. Ma and Victoria brought in dessert and I was beginning to hope this week would be calmer, less filled with the whole Gavin's Ambition campaign, when Dad leaned forward.

"There's talk of Mitchell retiring soon. Isn't he your lieutenant, Gavin?" Jake Mitchell was my sergeant's boss.

I gulped the rest of my tea before answering. "Yes, he is. Wants to move to Florida to be closer to his kids, so the rumors say."

"You know us old timers, we talk, right?" he started. "Jake and me met for drinks last week at Blues, and he says your sergeant, Talcott, is on the short list."

Victoria set a warm apple pie on the table with small plates, ready to dish up for anyone who wanted it, but she stopped short, listening intently.

"I hadn't heard anything," I said noncommittally.

"Didn't hear or didn't want to hear?" she asked, handing me a plate with pie and a scoop of ice cream.

"Now, son, why would you ignore an opportunity like that?" Dad asked, taking his dessert from Ma.

"I'm not ignoring anything," I protested, shooting Victoria a look. She knew how much I hated this part of brunch, knew I got angry when my dad pushed me. Most times, he didn't have anywhere to push me to. It's not like I could make a promotion appear out of thin air, though that's exactly what Mason had done when he'd made Sergeant.

"So you'll be putting in for Talcott's job if he gets promoted?" she asked, zeroing in.

"I didn't say that either."

"Why not, son? Can't stay in Homicide forever. It's hell on families, and your ma mentioned to me the other day how it would be nice to have another baby around here. Can't start a family if you're not around much."

"Victoria and I haven't even talked about kids. Sorry, Ma," I turned to her, trying to lighten the tension growing over the table. "You'll just have to be a little more patient."

"We haven't discussed it yet, Dad," Victoria said politely, but I could hear the ice in her tone, directed not at him, but at me. It sounded like she'd been meaning to bring it up with me, and maybe that's what her increased efforts to steer my career had been about. She might have even discussed it with Ma, gotten my parents' hopes up. I couldn't be sure, but the look that passed between her and my mother didn't reassure me. In fact, it made me angry.

"Sit, Victoria. Have some dessert," I ordered, diving into my pie for the distraction.

"I'm watching my weight," she said airily, but she did resume her seat.

"Well, son," Dad said, pointing his fork at me. "You're the next to move up the line. Make me proud." He beamed as if the discussion was closed and there was no other conclusion than the one he wanted.

"Technically, isn't that me?" Shawn cut in. Ever the peacekeeper, Shawn was. He could read a room like no one else and defuse almost any situation. Shawn had saved me from several knock-down drag-outs when we were kids, both within the family walls and without. When you're an easy target, like I was, Shawn was good to have around. He always had my back, though I had learned he didn't do it to help me so much as keep things even.

Dad waved him off. "You're in IA. You don't count."

Shawn rolled his eyes but said nothing. He put up with a fair amount of shit for "going to the dark side" as Cole put it. But Shawn still had aspirations, and even Dad wasn't going to admit there weren't sleazy cops out there my brother could bust. Internal Affairs had its own hierarchy, and though Shawn was roughly the same level as me, he was going places.

"Yeah, well, if Gavin's happy where he is, what's the big deal?" Cole asked, throwing his gloves into the fray.

"The big deal, Cole, is that Homicide is where every academy cadet wants to be. People are always gunnin' for your job and the glamor of the Homicide dick." Dad put sarcastic emphasis on the words, really winding himself up. "And if you don't work eighty or ninety hour weeks, you get replaced. You get higher up than detective, you don't gotta worry so much, don't gotta work so hard. Can have yourself a coupla rugrats and keep your wife happy. Right, sweetie?" he asked, leaning over to peck Ma's cheek.

"Not to mention the safety thing, dear," Ma said to me. "You know I worry."

"And who wants to be at someone else's beck and call all the time?" Victoria asked. I looked at her in disbelief, knowing she wanted me at her beck and call. I was astounded at her hypocrisy, and I finally let my anger boil over.

"It's not like I'm on SWAT or pulling traffic detail with people who'll run because of unpaid parking tickets. I mostly talk to people. Sometimes I go to court. I'm not gonna get hurt, Ma." I turned to Dad. "I like where I am. I get to bring the bad guys in and go looking for more. It makes me feel like I do some good. Isn't that what being a cop is about? How many times have we heard your 'protect and serve' speech? How many times did you tell us before college how important the job is to the very fabric of our society? I'm good at what I do, and I don't think I'd be good at kissing asses and schmoozing reporters. Sorry, Mason, but I'm not good with politics. I don't have superiors eating out of my hand like you." I turned to Victoria, who glared back at me. "And I didn't even know you wanted to talk about kids right now. Way to spring this on me in front of everyone." Throwing my napkin down on my plate, I scraped my chair back and stalked from the dining room, silence following me all the way out the front door to the porch.

I fumed for a few minutes and flinched when the front screen door squeaked open. I heard the flick of a lighter as Cole came up beside me. "Well, that was fun," he said. I glared at him, then swiped his cigarette and puffed once before returning it to him. His face registered surprise, but he said nothing, only shaking his head, turning around, and leaning on the railing to face me. "Wanna get a drink later?"

I shook my head. "Nah, I'm going in to work. Need to think about something else for a while."

Cole hummed and then finished his smoke. He punched me on the shoulder. "You finally stood up for yourself. That was kinda fun to watch."

Suddenly, the fight went out of me. "Whatever floats your boat. The real fireworks start when Victoria and I leave."

Cole winced. "Yeah, wouldn't wanna be you. But you'll be all right, yeah? Call me if you need to?"

Nodding slightly, I turned to follow him back inside to get my wife so we could leave. "I may need to."

§§§

THE STILTED silence in the car was deafening, both of us concentrating on the scenery that passed the windows. I drove carefully, keeping the flash of anger in check.

"You humiliated me," Victoria finally said. "Not only did you make it look like I went behind your back about having kids, you made me feel like I'm in second place to your job. Your dad said this life is hard on marriages and families, and you just barreled on through with 'I'm happy where I am, so screw the rest.'"

"You did go behind my back about having kids. You haven't mentioned it to me once, and yet Ma knows? It's like you planned for them all to gang up on me, to railroad me into doing exactly what you want. I'm not your game piece, Victoria. You can't just move me where you'd like me to be."

She whipped her head around, glaring at me. "If this were a game, which it's not, you'd still be on the starting line, Gavin. Why not consider putting in for Talcott's job? It's stupid not to, especially with the pay bump."

"Money isn't the issue, here. Mitchell's retirement hasn't even been announced. Don't you think it's premature for me to go after my boss's job when he hasn't even made a move for his boss's? Talk about pissing off The Powers That Be. You don't know how the station runs or how these people operate, so quit pretending you do." I took the Olive Boulevard exit off of I-270, headed toward home, but I didn't feel like going there.

"But you're not even entertaining the idea if the opportunity does come up. You may be happy with settling, but I'm not."

"So don't settle!" I yelled. "Climb the corporate ladder at your own job, but stay the fuck outta mine!" Victoria worked for one of the local colleges in the recruitment office. Most of the upward mobility there was reserved for professors and those with higher degrees than hers, but she'd been taking business courses to change that situation. Apparently it wasn't happening fast enough for her tastes.

"Is this a partnership, or not? Are we not in this together?" she asked coldly. "I thought we wanted the same things. Good, stable home life, a couple of kids, some disposable income and time to travel. We won't get that kind of life if you're chained to your Detective shield. Jesus, Gavin. It's like you don't even give a shit what I want anymore! This is everything we've talked about for years."

She was right. We'd discussed the big picture many times, but now that taking steps to achieve that picture loomed closer, I wasn't convinced I could keep it up, keep the lie going. How far was I willing to go to hide? I'd already had a series of girlfriends starting with Megan Carroll, and now a wife. "I don't know what I want anymore." Guilt at how unfair to her I was being stabbed at me, but not enough to dampen my anger at her underhanded methods with my family.

She snorted. "Oh that's great, Gavin. Fantastic. You don't think you could have told me this before, I don't know, we got married?"

That stopped me. "Are you saying you wouldn't have married me if you'd known I didn't want to be more than a detective?"

Her shoulders sagged. "I don't know, Gavin. This is a lot to throw at me all at once. This changes a lot of things."

Whipping the wheel to the right, I parked along the curb in front of a liquor store that had seen better days. Slamming the gear shift into park, I turned to her. "Why does the job I do have any bearing on whether or not we have a family or time to travel? I have four weeks of vacation time built up, but you've not once mentioned wanting me to use any of it so we could go somewhere. It's not like I can't get away if we need to."

Looking anywhere but at me, she spoke softly. "It's not the traveling, Gavin. Tell me, if I were to say, 'Let's take a trip, right now, start planning it as soon as we get home and leave next weekend,' what would you say?"

Picking at my cuticles, I was slow to reply. "I'd say I can't right now. I have an active case and it's not good timing." She huffed in righteous indignation, and I held my hands out, palms up. "That's hardly any notice for something like that, and you know it."

"And after this case, there'll be another one, and another one. There always is. And when we have kids? How many times are you going to have to beg off Little League games or dance recitals because of a case that's ongoing and not convenient to set aside for a few hours? I don't want to bring kids up that way, Gavin. And I don't think you do, either. You being promoted is a chance for us to have a life that doesn't revolve around your job." She turned to me, eyes pleading. "It's a job, Gavin. Not who you are. How you treat the people in your life, that's what makes you who you are. You don't have to be everyone's hero. Just mine."

My spine went twitchy at her words. She had a point, and it was obvious why this job had such a high divorce rate. How do people choose between putting aside the needs of the many in favor of the needs of one or two?

"Victoria, I'm hearing you. I am. But I am not cut out for more than what I already am. You're asking an awful lot from me, and not giving me room to have some doubts, to think it over. It's like you have decreed it, and therefore, it shall be. I should simply fall in line. Put yourself in my shoes."

Her eyes went steely. "Oh, like you're putting yourself in mine? Alone all the time because of a workaholic husband? Left to make your excuses time and again when you have to bail on our plans? Wondering half the time if your phone calls telling me you're going to be home late again are legitimate or if there's something else going on?"

I recoiled as if slapped. "You think I'm fucking around on you?"

"It has crossed my mind. Like last night. You get home smelling like Satan's whorehouse and poking me in the leg with your hard-on, and I have to wonder what you've been doing."

Fuck this bullshit. I pulled back out into the street, not looking over my shoulder as I shoved my way into traffic again, earning a blaring horn and a finger out the window of the car behind me.

"If I were fucking around on you, I wouldn't have been interested last night. You know, if you want kids, you are going to have to fuck me sometimes. That's how it works."

"Yeah, well, after today, you'll be lucky if you ever get laid again," she snapped, returning her attention to the window.

Ten minutes later, I pulled into our driveway, and put it in park, but didn't turn the car off.

"What are you doing?" she asked.

"Going to work."

"It's Sunday."

"Gotta make a good impression if I want that promotion, don't I?" I sneered.

"Fine, Gavin," she said, yanking open the passenger door and getting out with jerky movements. She bent down to look at me, holding the door open. "I won't wait for you for dinner." The reverberation of the door as she slammed it set my teeth on edge. I watched her tense posture as she approached the front of the house, pulling out both her cell phone and her keys to let herself in. I heard her ask whoever she was calling if they were free for the afternoon, and then she disappeared inside.

A few minutes went by while I got myself under control. Backing out of the drive, I called Trent on his cell. I heard the telltale click of call waiting before his gruff voice came over the line.

"Sawyer."

"It's me. I'm going in today. What are you doing?"

"It's Sunday. I'm not working, man, and neither should you."

"Fuck you, Trent. I'll work when I want and how I want, and no one can say a goddamned thing about it," I barked, knowing full well he didn't deserve the tirade.

"Whoa, okay. All I meant was that everyone needs a day off, partner, and I wasn't planning on working today, so we should enjoy the time off."

"Tell that to the Widow Kaiser."

He was silent for a long moment. "You keep going like this, you're gonna burn out, buddy. Everything okay?"

"Well, if I don't work my ass off, somehow I'm not ambitious enough. I have people to impress, right? But if I work too much, I'm not a good family man and I'm neglecting my wife." I hadn't meant to come out with all that, but if anyone understood, it was Trent. He had one ex-Mrs. Sawyer, and always joked that he was on the lookout for numbers two and three.

"Ah, the cop's ex-wife mantra. Didn't expect that to happen to you for another year or two." The minute click of his call waiting said whoever he'd been on the phone with had hung up. I got to the point.

"I'm going to talk to Damon Lane, and maybe Matt Kinney again. He might remember more today after having thought about it." I headed up Ashby Road toward the station, wanting to hit my desk and see if anything new had come from the lab, and knowing I needed to breathe before tackling any witness questioning.

"That can't wait until tomorrow?" Trent asked, his chiding bordering on whining. I rolled my eyes.

"Relax, pretty boy," I said. "I'll cover this solo. I have a feeling talking to these guys at their day jobs would get us even less information than usual, so I don't want to wait until tomorrow. Who knows what their employers know of their personal lives? Kinney might be more receptive to talking to me alone anyway, since you were a jackass last night."

"Who you callin' pretty? You're the one with the face the girls get all swoony over. All you DeGrassi boys are. But you're probably right about their openness in front of coworkers. I hadn't thought of that. And I wasn't a jackass. You seemed hell bent on believing every word out of everyone's mouth, so caught up in the spectacle of the place. One of us had to stay objective. Autopsy tomorrow, right? Rock, Paper, Scissors you for it."

Trent hated viewing autopsies, and I couldn't say I blamed him. I didn't like them myself, but I felt more comfortable with the facts of a case if I was there when the M.E. did his exam. I got more understanding by seeing than by reading the report or hearing it from Jencopale. Plus, he didn't mind if I asked questions.

"No need. I'll take it. See how Victoria likes me coming home smelling like a morgue instead of Satan's Whorehouse, as she so delicately put it."

"Oh, ouch. First rule, man, never crawl in bed with a woman who wasn't at the same bar as you without showering."

"Noted. Enjoy your day off."

"I plan to. Later, man."

He hung up and I pulled into the station, a squat brick building that was nothing to look at, its mirrored front windows glinting in the sun. The cool rush of air conditioning hit me just as much as the hush of the main room of cubes. Sundays, not many people in who didn't have to be. The somewhat hushed conversation and the familiar smell of industrial cleaner and burned coffee soothed my raw nerves. I didn't care what Victoria thought. This job was not a crappy stop along some grand career map I should be adhering to. I felt at home here, and the decisions I made mattered. I grabbed a cup of coffee before sitting down and signing in on my computer. I had an email from one of Cole's lab rats that none of the implements gathered from George Kaiser's play room had any DNA on them other than the victim's, so his guess was the perp wore gloves, no skin abrasions to leave tissue or blood on the ropes or whips. The cat o' nine tails was confirmed as the weapon that had made the lacerations on the victim's chest. Pictures of the whip and the dummy on which they'd tested it were attached to the email, both before and after. I winced, noting the marks, etched with blue paint so the depth and breadth of the injuries was more visible in the forensics gel. At least they hadn't used red paint. The picture also included a tape measure to provide scale and to measure the slashes, and a side-by-side comparison of photos of the victim's wounds taken at the crime scene. Measurements matched, as well as the patterns.

"Jesus, people volunteer to be whipped with these?" I asked aloud, shaking my head. I supposed the force of the swing made a difference, but damn. Then I remembered the flogging I'd witnessed the previous evening, and wondered if that instrument was capable of the kind of damage shown in the photos. If so, it really did depend on the wielder. What I'd seen of Lance's skin after his whipping showed only a few raised welts and an abrasion or two. Hardly life threatening. I'd have to wait for the autopsy in the morning to see how much the lacerations had contributed to George's death.

Even reading the preliminary report from the lab told me I was veering out of my depth again, that they could describe and test all the equipment in George's play room and I still wouldn't grasp the meaning of everything or recognize a breakthrough when I saw it. That brought to mind the business card I'd left in my drawer, which I extracted and stared at for a few moments, elbows resting on my desk. I wondered if it would be inconvenient for Dr. Haverson to speak with me again, with it being Sunday. After a few moments of indecision, I realized the worst he could say was no, and if he was busy, I could arrange a time to go over my questions at his earliest convenience.

Sure. Keep telling yourself that, my inner monologue chimed in. Just ignore the increase in your pulse and the thrill ping-ponging up and down your spine. To shut the voice up, I punched numbers into my desk phone and listened to the ring at the other end.

"This is Dr. Haverson," came the answer in that rich, velvety voice with the hint of southern politeness. I cleared my throat.

"Doctor, this is Detective DeGrassi. Would you have time today to answer a few questions?" Nothing like getting right to the point. And keeping it professional.

"Absolutely, Detective. I'm free until around four." We arranged to meet at a nearby barbeque chain restaurant, though food was the last thing on my mind. I checked my watch.

"Is one o'clock too soon?" It was a little past noon.

"No, that's perfect," he said accommodatingly.

"See you there." I hung up, my finger lingering on the receiver for a moment as I stared into space. Then I shook myself and spent the next twenty minutes listing my questions so I'd stay focused. At least without Trent around, I didn't have to pretend I wasn't distracted by the doctor.

The restaurant was three-quarters filled with people finishing their lunch when I arrived just before one o'clock. Rough-hewn wood interior was the restaurant's trademark as well as red-and-white checked patterns on the tabletops and napkins. Squeeze bottles carrying different types of barbecue sauce made up each table's centerpiece, and the waitresses were dressed in jean shorts and red shirts sporting the establishment's name, as well as slogans like, "Napkins optional," with a picture of a man licking barbecue sauce from his fingers.

Well, it wasn't The Hill, with its fine Italian restaurants, or downtown, with views of the Arch and the Mississippi River, but it suited my purposes. I was seated quickly by a perky girl with twin braids down each side of her head and a chipper smile, and I ordered a Coke with instructions to keep them coming. It was getting too hot for coffee in the afternoon, and I needed the caffeine after sleeping so poorly the night before.

Haverson arrived a short while later, and I smiled and waved as he scanned the dining room before finding me and sliding into the booth across from me. He ordered a tall iced tea and perused the menu for a moment. He'd apparently just showered, as his hair was wet and sticking up in tufts. "I hope you don't mind if I eat," he said, grinning and showing a slight gap between his front teeth. "Mornings at the gym have me starving in the afternoons."

I let my eyes fall to his broad shoulders and the patch of throat that peeked above the open collar of his polo shirt, where a defined clavicle disappeared beneath the fabric. Yes, he definitely worked out regularly. "Not at all. I hope you don't mind if I don't order anything. Large family brunch, and I'm still full."

"Ah, the Sunday gathering tradition. I know it well." He smiled. The waitress appeared, and he ordered a pulled pork sandwich with fries. The girl flashed a big grin at him and sashayed away with his order. I suspected her hips gave a more pronounced sway with the doctor's arrival, but if he noticed, he didn't show it.

"We took a trip to Collared last night to find out what we could about our victim's last hours and speak to those who knew him." I fiddled with my straw, trying to remind myself that this was work, and there was no reason to be embarrassed, so the flush that crept up my cheeks was quite unnecessary.

"Oh? How'd that go?" he asked, genuinely interested. He leaned forward and gave me his full attention, and I wondered if he was pulling the therapist bit on me. Funnily enough, I didn't mind.

"It was... interesting. Eye opening. Enlightening. And we got very little from the witnesses." He laughed heartily, his eyes dancing with mirth. I failed at suppressing a smile. "To tell you the truth, Doctor, I was fascinated. It's a world I never suspected existed, and there are codes of honor and rules and depths to the relationships that go beyond anything I've ever seen before. It's like waking up one morning to find a veil over my eyes was removed, and I can see a whole element of life I've never noticed."

Haverson nodded, lacing his fingers together. "Please, for the last time, call me Ben. And that's how it was for me when I was first introduced to the scene. It was overwhelming, and I didn't know where to look first, let alone where to begin to get further involved. Best advice I can give you is to find someone who's open to explaining things—and you'll find that most people are—and ask questions. But I guess you're doing that, aren't you?"

He had a boyish innocence about him, one that I knew was simply a by-product of his looks, because to be who and what he was, he had to have seen and done some incredible things. Perhaps it was a combination of his open face and his lack of judgment in my not-completely-professional interest in the lifestyle that made me comfortable talking to him in a way that I couldn't talk to anyone, not even Cole.

"Yeah, Ben, I guess I am," I smiled. "Tell me, how much damage can a flogger do? Is it comparable to a cat o' nine tails?"

"Well, that depends. There are different details in the construction of a flogger that can change how it impacts. The cut of the ends for one, the weight and width of the tails, the material it's made of. For example, a narrower lash will sting more, and a wider lash will have a more thudding impact because the force of the blow is spread over a wider area. But the heavier the flogger, the harder it is to wield, and wider lashes weigh a flogger down. Depending on the person being whipped, standard usage is between twenty-five and thirty strokes. Beveled or rounded ends hurt less. Slanted ends, if the wielder is good at it, can make the tiny points sting so nicely. Depends on what you're looking for in the flogging. A cat is much narrower in construction and often knotted at the ends of each lash, designed for maximum impact. It's like the difference between a knife and a spoon. Both are made from the same material, but the thinner the edges, the more dangerous. Cats are tricky to wield, and for the most part, yes, can do more damage."

I stared at him. He was talking about whipping someone as if he were describing different types of golf clubs and whether someone preferred a gloved hand to a bare one.

He laughed at my expression. "What?"

"Nothing," I shook my head, dropping my eyes to my hands. "You obviously know what you're talking about, but you're so comfortable with it despite what people might think of you."

"Well, Detective, you asked me to help with your investigation, so I see no reason to hide behind society's rules about what is and is not acceptable conversation in public, and yeah, I'm comfortable with it. I've gotten my share of judgment from people, but I've learned that this is who I am, and if they judge me, it's either out of fear of the unknown or an unwillingness to learn, and in both cases, why should I care what someone like that thinks?"

"That whole 'if they're ignorant, what does their opinion matter anyway' bit? And please, call me Gavin." I hadn't given him permission before, with Trent present, because it would have landed me a heap of teasing, but it felt all right. "I guess it's not something I'm used to hearing. In my line of work, people are rarely this frank with me, and at home—" The image of Victoria's cold expression arose and I frowned. "Well, there's a lot of reading between the lines there, too." And walking on eggshells.

Ben leaned forward again, and this time I caught the whiff of his cologne, a spicy, woody scent I couldn't place but liked very much. "The fundamental difference, and probably the reason I do this at all, is the level of communication in a Dom/sub relationship is so much deeper than anything I've ever seen in the vanilla world. There's no room for playing with words, reading between the lines or being coy because mind reading can get you hurt. You have to be a hundred percent honest about what you like and don't like and your limits because if you don't? Someone can take you to a place you never wanted to go."

"I noticed that last night, between this couple we passed in the upper rooms of Collared." My skin colored thinking of the boy and his Dom, who had been masturbating him for hours. I explained enough to set the scene for Ben, though it was difficult to describe in non-embarrassing terms, and to keep him from catching me shifting in my seat. "But what I noticed most was how well the Dom seemed to read his sub, seemed to know where his boy's body was at all times, and what he had to do to keep him where he wanted him. He trusted his sub to turn himself over, and the sub trusted him to take over. It was an intimate thing to watch, even aside from the sexuality of it."

"Ah, the power exchange. A submissive's greatest gift is giving someone else control. As I said last night to you and your partner, it takes more courage to kneel before another than to stand beside them. Subs are not weak. They simply choose to let someone else fulfill their desires, and trust that person to do so. They put their Dom's wishes ahead of their own, and their payoff is a happy Dom, who also rewards them with praise and love and the safety net of guiding them around life's obstacles.

"Unfortunately, a lot of the patients I see are people who had something bad happen to them at the hands of someone dangerous, who either failed to see or didn't acknowledge their limits and went beyond them. Or people who have traumas in their past for which they think they deserve punishment and are seeking that through submitting to others. The good Doms see this for what it is and won't oblige until the sub gets help, but like any subset of people, there are bad eggs."

"Like my killer," I supplied.

"Like your killer, though he went after a Dom, not a sub. I've read the file you gave me and the amount of trauma Mr. Kaiser suffered speaks of someone with a point to prove. Either someone in his past disparaged his ego and he's showing off, or he's got a vendetta. George wasn't merely killed by his own toys. He was humiliated by them. Hung on his own cross. Whipped with his own cat. I'm quite certain at some point, even had Mr. Kaiser consented to being tied up and switching roles for the night, he would have used his safe word, and been duly ignored, which is the most grievous sin a Dom can commit."

"So my killer, is he really a Dom then?"

Ben shook his head. "Hard to say. He certainly knew his way around Mr. Kaiser's equipment. But the foundation of a D/s relationship is safe, sane, and consensual. Mr. Kaiser didn't consent to this. No one in their right mind would. He fell prey to a predator, plain and simple. You're looking for someone in the community, but likely not wholly immersed. Someone who knows enough about the play to recreate it, but has probably never done it or never submitted before. Someone who doesn't hold to the truth of a power exchange, and simply takes the power he wants for his own use. He's inexperienced and doesn't care to become experienced, since he's unconcerned about hurting his subjects too much. The purpose is the pain and taking his pound of flesh, not the submission. I'm no profiler, but my guess is someone in the community hurt him in some way. Maybe not him directly, but someone he cared about. If it wasn't specifically Mr. Kaiser, it was someone whom Mr. Kaiser represented."

A shiver raced up my spine and bloomed across my scalp. "If it wasn't George Kaiser, then he could kill again, another Dom who represents his revenge."

"Let's hope not," Ben said seriously.

We both fell silent for a moment, and during that time, Ben's food arrived. Despite the weight of the conversation, he dug in with gusto. I watched, bemused, as he got messier and messier. Tearing a paper towel from the holder on the table, I passed it to him. Not that I didn't enjoy watching him lick his fingers, but really, I wasn't there to ogle.

"All right," I said, switching tracks. "I spoke with Matt Kinney last night, who was Kaiser's closest friend. Do you know him?"

"Yeah, I know Matt. Good man. Good Dom. He takes it seriously, and he's had the same sub for the last three years, Lance Marsh. They seem happy together."

"We caught him right after an on-stage flogging, so I'm guessing our timing could have been better."

Ben grinned, licking his fingers again, seemingly oblivious to the effect it was having on me, not that I was trying to be obvious about it. I shifted in my seat, willing my pants to cough up more room.

"Your timing, pardon me for saying, likely sucked. He was in top space, which is similar to a runner's high, but significantly more intense. The chemical makeup of the body is the same: the rush of endorphins, the singular focus, the feeling of invincibility. For him to even have answered your questions is a miracle in itself. It can take hours to come down from that high."

"Will I have to ask him the same questions again? I'm going to try to catch up with him when we're finished here."

"Nah, he was probably more truthful last night than you'd think, with his mind flying. He wouldn't have had the wherewithal to carefully word his answers. But it couldn't hurt to talk to him again. He'll remember your conversation and probably have a better idea of how to help. You don't finger him for this, do you?"

"Oh, no. His reaction didn't give that impression, and he has an alibi, even if Lance wasn't in a position to corroborate it last night. It's one other thing I want to confirm, and he indicated they live together, so I can ask Lance some questions while I'm there. Any helpful suggestions?"

"Well, they're an intense couple, but they're not twenty-four seven."

"Twenty-four seven?"

"Yeah, that's shorthand for submissive all day, every day. Lance isn't Matt's slave. They live together, and there are probably bleed-overs from the bedroom, but from what I know of them, they're mostly equals when they're not playing. Lance will be free to answer your questions and probably wants to, since he'd consider Mr. Kaiser a friend, too."

The waitress came by then to refill our drinks, and I found myself wanting something to do with my hands, which kept fluttering in my lap, so I ordered some fried pickles. Ben finished his sandwich and continued to munch on french fries.

"So tell me, Detective. Sorry, Gavin. The lifestyle intrigues you. Is it something you could see yourself trying?"

I spluttered and coughed, having just taken a drink of my soda and swallowed it wrong. "Well, I don't know, Ben. I can't see my wife giving me much room to play like that." His eyes softened from the piercing gaze he'd leveled at me, and he nodded. Dammit, I thought, and then chastised myself. I wasn't flirting with him, and I doubted very much he was flirting with me, though I couldn't be sure, with the vibe I was getting. I couldn't tell if his open honesty was typical, a product of his therapist persona, genuine interest in what I had to say, or something more. It seemed, however, that with the mention of my wife, some of his openness drained away.

"You're married."

"Yes, going on five years now."

"Kids?"

A cloud broke over my face, much of the sting of the morning returning. "No."

He chuckled. "What's that look for? Do you want kids?"

I sighed. "It's hard to say. Doesn't almost everyone grow up thinking they're going to get married and have kids? But with my job, it's a hard thing to commit to. My hours suck, and my attention is not always focused where it should be. At work, I have purpose, but at home, I kinda… drift. Do what I'm told, which I don't mind, and it makes Victoria happy, except, well… It used to be a lot of give and take between us, and lately, it seems I give, she takes, and then doesn't even acknowledge what I've given."

As soon as I stopped speaking, my eyes widened at how much I'd revealed to a virtual stranger. There was just something about him that made it easy to open up. Because of that, I started babbling.

"Wow, okay, I didn't mean to get into all that. I bet you're one hell of a therapist, having the effect on people that makes them want to spill their guts."

Thankfully, my pickles arrived and despite the steam rising from them, I dunked a couple chips in the ranch dip and stuffed them in my mouth, scalding my tongue. It was worth it to shut myself the fuck up.

"You wanna know what I think, Gavin?" he asked, a smile playing at the corners of his lips as he sat back and wiped his hands on a napkin, pushing his plate to the side and out of the way. He'd gotten messy with the food, but had managed to eat it without getting a speck of barbecue sauce on his shirt. I was impressed.

"What do you think, Ben?"

"I think you'd make a fantastic submissive." He hurried on when I opened my mouth to protest. "Think about it. You like to make your wife happy by doing what she asks of you when you're home, but you have little direction when you're there. You thrive in the more structured environment of your job, where there are rules to follow and procedures in place for how to behave. You emotionally submit to your wife, but she acknowledges little of that gift, and so you think she doesn't appreciate you or what you do for her when a simple thank you would go a long way. How far off base am I?"

"Not far, I guess, but don't most people want a little acknowledgment when they do something for someone? It doesn't make them submissives."

"Sure, but it depends on how often they do things for others and what they expect to get out of it."

I let out a breath before peering at him from the corner of my eye, trying to figure how much to say. "I'm not normally this down on my home life. You happen to be seeing me at work on a Sunday trying to get some peace after a big fight in front of my whole family. She's normally a great person, driven and ambitious, and incredibly smart."

"But…" he prodded, waiting for me to continue.

"She wants more for me than I want to give. She wants me to become a sergeant or lieutenant, and I'm happy being a detective. I get to help people more in this role, and I don't have to play the politics. I come from a family of cops, and except for my brother Cole, who's a CSI, they're all clamoring to get that stripe on their shoulders. My brother, Mason, already has it, and he's only thirty-four. I don't want it. I don't need it. There're people better suited than I am for that job. Take Trent."

"Your partner."

"Yeah. He's a much better politician than I am."

"Well, he certainly has his superiority down pat, if last night is any indication."

I winced at the memory. "Sorry about that."

"What are you sorry for? He was the jerk, not you."

"Yeah, well, what he does reflects on me, and vice versa. You handled him well, though. Not many people can, and he'll afford you a lot more respect the next time he sees you, I'd almost guarantee it."

"And you think his attitude makes him suited for a higher rank?"

I shredded a napkin, not looking at Ben. "I think so. He's always having drinks with our sergeant, and getting himself invited to golf with the Chief or to some barbecue at a lieutenant's house. He likes that life. I don't want it. A fact that makes my wife mad, because by choosing this life, I'm choosing longer hours and more danger and time away from her. She feels like I put her second, and I feel like she's using my family to manipulate me into having a kid and force me to choose a different career. It was ugly."

"Sounds like it. Did anything get resolved?"

I shook my head, biting into another pickle. "I dropped her off at home and went in to work. We both needed to cool off. I don't know how to fix this one, and this time, I'm not going to just give her what she wants. Not without some recognition that there are things I need and unless there's a way around this so that we both have our needs met, I'm afraid we're at a stalemate."

"Negotiation. The tools of a solid relationship. Both people meeting their needs and talking it out. Another mark of a good sub."

I threw a pickle at him, which he dodged , laughing. Okay, definitely flirting now. Knock it off. "All right. For a second, just for a second, say I'd be a good sub. That doesn't mean I'll ever be one. First, Victoria would have to be a… What would you call a woman who dominates?"

He smiled deprecatingly. "Don't ever call a Dominant woman a Dominatrix. You'll get yourself hurt, and not in the fun way. Mistress, Master, Dominant or Domme with feminized spelling works." He spelled the word out. "You don't think she would?"

I snorted. "Oh, hell no. Anything that's out of the ordinary, she won't even discuss. One of her college friends asked Victoria to be in a threesome with her and her boyfriend. She refused and never spoke to the friend again. They'd been close since high school. She was able to turn her back on every aspect of that relationship because someone who could be adventurous in bed must be dangerously adventurous in other ways. Victoria didn't want to associate with someone like that."

"She's very adherent to societal image and position. I can understand that, even if it's not something I'd personally practice."

"Are you always so diplomatic?" I asked. "I haven't exactly painted my wife in the best light in the last few minutes and yet, you haven't said one word that could be insulting, despite making it clear you see where I'm coming from. How do you do that? Not to mention getting me to talk to you about things I haven't even told my brothers."

He grinned. "Years of therapy."

I laughed out loud, and the waitress came by to clear our dishes and ask if we needed anything else. I shook my head and asked for the check, reaching for my wallet.

"Oh, let me get this," Ben offered.

I waved him off. "I can expense it. Let me pretend for a moment that this was the best date I've had in years, okay?" What. The. Fuck, Gavin? I froze, barely courageous enough to look for Ben's reaction. But I did. I had to. He could get me fired for saying such a thing. We were, after all, working together.

"All right," he said, calmly. "I could have expensed it, too. Either way, the department pays, right? So nice of them to chaperone." He wasn't careful in how he spoke or looked at me. He smiled the same as before. If he'd taken offense, I couldn't tell. Then, I felt his shoe against mine beneath the table. It was subtle, could have been an accident, but when I shifted my foot to give him room, a moment later, the pressure of his shoe returned and stayed there until the waitress dropped off the bill.

"You know," he said. "Other than the bit about safe word-ignoring Dom killers and revenge motives, this was a pleasant conversation. And good food. Thank you. I hope things work out for you at home. Think about what I said, though. Even if it's only in light of negotiating better with your wife to keep from being pushed beyond your limits."

Not meeting his eyes while I looked over the bill, I swallowed, signing on the dotted line after figuring the tip. When I finally did look up, he was wearing a soft, almost sympathetic expression. "Thanks. I'll remember that."

He finished his tea and set the glass on the table, hesitating. It was the first time I'd seen him anything but completely comfortable in his own skin. "And if, for any reason, you need a shoulder, you've got my number." He stood and left without waiting for my reply.

§§§

I DIDN'T get any more from Matt Kinney or Lance March, other than corroboration for Kinney's alibi, and the names of George's two most recent subs that Mrs. Kaiser hadn't known. Kinney hadn't had their contact information, though, suggesting I get that from Jared Nunn, who kept as much info on his patrons as they would agree to.

The pair was obviously grieving over the loss of their friend and wanted to help in any way they could. Kinney was more forthcoming without my glowering partner at my side, but he only reiterated what he'd said the previous night. George Kaiser was careful. Good Doms never drank if they expected to play, and as far as Matt knew, George hadn't been partaking that night, so he could have met someone. I thanked them for their time and left.

While I considered tracking down Damon Lane, my stomach rumbled and I realized that it was nearing dinner time. Victoria's parting shot had been that she wasn't intending to wait for me, but it was early enough I decided to grab something from the Chinese place near our house. She didn't usually start dinner until around six, and it was only four-thirty. Maybe she was calm enough to talk about things. I thought about what Ben had said about negotiating, and I wanted to see if there was a way Victoria and I could think of a solution to the mess that had sat like a gluey ball of distaste in my gut since brunch.

As I pulled into the driveway, I noticed through the big front window that the lamp in the living room was on. Victoria often read or worked on her needlepoint in the chair by the lamp, especially when she needed distraction, so that told me she was home. Letting myself in quietly, I deposited the food on the kitchen counter.

Sounds emanated from the back of the house and I cocked my head to hear if she was watching TV in our bedroom or on the phone. If she was talking to a friend, I might get a read on her mood if I could hear her half of the conversation.

Walking softly down the hall, I approached the bedroom, listening intently. A soft moan sounded, and my shoulders relaxed. That had to be the TV. At least I wouldn't overhear her bad mouthing me to anyone, even if it would help me figure out how to approach her. I didn't begrudge her the chance to vent about me to her friends when she needed to. Today had been a rough day, and hadn't I just vented to Ben?

I got closer to the bedroom, wanting nothing more than comfortable clothes and my dinner. Another sound stopped me short. A laugh, more immediate than the TV. I hugged the wall so the creak I'd been meaning to fix in the middle of the hallway floor didn't give away my presence. I tuned my ears to the bedroom, straining to hear.

"Oh yeah," came muffled through the closed door. "That's it. Right there." A man's voice. There was another noise, the rustling of fabric, and a softer, feminine moan.

Son of a bitch. My face flooded with heat as fury roared in my belly and my pulse pounded in my temples. I no longer cared if my approach was heard, and when I reached the door, I opened it to see my wife, naked as the day she was born, sitting astride my partner, riding Trent's cock like she was in a race to the finish line. She threw her head back and cried out, "Oh! Oh! Oh, Trent!" and flung herself forward. Trent gurgled out an incomprehensible sound, his hands circling Victoria's back to stroke her skin. They hadn't heard me. I leaned casually against the door jamb, wondering how long it would take them to notice me there. I sincerely hoped they were finished, though. I wasn't that interested in watching.

"You sure Gavin's not coming back for a while?" Trent asked, mouthing down her throat. "A couple witnesses won't keep him all day."

"I told him not to come back for dinner. We've got hours yet," she purred.

"I believe your exact words were, 'I won't wait for you for dinner.' That didn't mean I wouldn't come back to eat," I said coldly, arms folded over my chest. "But don't let me interrupt your plans for another round."

They both gasped and Victoria whipped around, yanking the sheet over her chest, her hair a mess. Trent sat up and reached for his boxers, which had landed on the lamp shade on my side of the bed. I laughed, startling both them and myself.

"I'm just going to pack some things and I'll be out of your hair. Promise."

"Gavin, I—" Victoria started. I ignored her.

"Hey, man, it's not what it looks like," Trent said, his cop voice taking over, the one that made people stop and listen to him.

"Oh, it's exactly what it looks like. My wife used my afternoon of trying to get a clear head after our fight over kids to find herself another sperm donor. My partner, ever the sleaze, couldn't resist a chance to notch his belt again. Unless Victoria's a previous notch, and I didn't know it."

"Gavin, please," Victoria said, her chin and lower lip trembling.

"Save it. You've just made my life a lot easier, Victoria. I should be thanking you."

"Thanking me?" Her voice sounded so small, not at all the overbearing, demanding shrill I'd become used to.

"I was afraid I'd have to give up the job I love so you could be the social climbing wife of the brass, doing the whole PTA bit and lording your matriarchy over the whole manor. Now all I need is a good lawyer."

"Let's talk about this, Gavin, please."

Calmly, I took out my cell phone and snapped a picture of the two of them in my bed, Trent in his boxers and trying to surreptitiously toss the condom, and Victoria still demurely covering her chest, lipstick smeared and tears starting to roll down her face.

"There, that should be sufficient." I moved to the closet and dragged the suitcase from the top shelf, propping it open on top of the laundry hamper. A few trips back and forth to throw shirts and slacks into it, a quick swipe to empty my underwear drawer, some khaki shorts and T-shirts for off-duty hours, and I was just about finished. I grabbed my shave kit from the bathroom, my phone charger, and the laptop on the corner desk. Packing to leave my wife took all of five minutes while they spluttered and made excuses and tried to justify what they'd done.

"Gavin, please!" Victoria shrieked as I moved to the door. She dropped the sheet and shrugged on her bathrobe, intent on following me out. "You can't leave! I'm sorry, okay? I'm sorry. You don't have to try for a promotion. Just promise me you'll be home more, and I'll be happy! All I ever wanted was more time with you."

"That's not true, and you know it. And if I stay, in a year or three years, you'll be hounding me again that what I do isn't good enough, only by then, we'll have a kid whose life will be torn apart when the walls come crashing down. I will never be able to make you happy because I don't want the same things you do. You want prestige and social standing and the kind of power being married to a high ranking police officer brings, even if the money's not enough to get you into the country club. And I want..." I stopped short of saying it, but for the first time ever, I didn't shove the thought away, didn't slink from it or hide it from myself. I want to be with a man. "Well, I think this might just be the best thing that could have happened to me. Thank you." I leaned over and kissed her tear-streaked cheek. Yes, it was a sarcastic move, but dammit, she'd sucker-punched me again. Twice in the same day. "Enjoy your life, Vic," I said, using the nickname she hated.

"Gavin," Trent called. "You ass, at least talk to her about this. She wouldn't have been looking for something else if you'd made her happy."

I'd almost forgotten the self-righteous prick was still there, in his underwear in the bed I'd slept in for the last five years.

"I'll talk to Talcott tomorrow and see if there's another precinct with an opening in Homicide. I wouldn't want you to get stuck in Vice or Narcotics because there are no more Homicide openings. Or worse, get you busted back to patrol." I briefly wondered if he had been maneuvering for the same promotion Victoria had wanted me to put in for, and playing musical precincts would take that away from him. Served him right.

Trent's eyes narrowed. "You wouldn't," he snarled.

"Oh, I think I would," I said, a near impossible-to-control burst of giddiness growing in my chest. I suppressed the laugh but not the smile. "And if you fight me on it, I'll make sure your reputation precedes you." I waved my phone at them both. "Stabbing a brother in blue in the back like this. What kind of cop are you, Trent? No one will want a partner like you when word gets out what you did to me. And they certainly won't give you Talcott's job now."

"You asshole!" he yelled at my back as I retreated down the hall to the front door. I paused long enough to grab the food off the kitchen counter, and carried the start of my new life to the car.

CHAPTER FIVE

THE RAUCOUS beat vibrated through my chest as music and lights assaulted me, and the heavy steel door clanged shut at my back. It was a Sunday night at Collared, not very busy, and I didn't have a plan for where else to go. I figured I'd get a drink, people watch, and then grab a hotel room close to the station. Why I ended up at that bar, I couldn't say.

Well, actually, I could say. I was free. I had a legit reason to be there aside from curiosity, and if anyone asked, my explanation was rock solid. It was the perfect cover, not that I expected to run into anyone I knew. The truth was, curiosity and an overwhelming sense of rebellion got me through the door. Fascination and a shaky anticipation kept me there. I had no constraints and no one to whom I owed a damn thing. Perhaps alcohol wasn't a wise decision. The demise of my marriage was hours old, and no one knew where I was. Not to mention, someone among the sparse crowd could have been my killer. Not the right time or circumstances in which to lower my inhibitions. But Victoria and Trent going at it in my bed had completely broken my give-a-fuck.

"Can I get a Bud Select, draft?" I signaled the bartender, shirtless and clad in black jeans with strategically placed rips beneath each ass cheek. He turned and smiled when he caught me ogling, grabbing a fresh glass and pouring.

"Detective! DeGrassi was it?" Jared, the owner, asked. "I wouldn't expect you to order a drink when you're here."

"Off duty."

His eyebrows shot up. "Really?" He seemed pleased with my answer. "Have we got a new convert?" After placing my glass on a coaster in front of me, he leaned forward, resting his forearms on the bar.

I took a large gulp of the cold beer before answering. "Depends on what you think I'm converting to."

He threw his head back and laughed long and hard, then waggled a finger at me. "I could tell last night that you weren't like other cops."

It was my turn to raise my eyebrows. "Oh? And what's different about me?"

"Attitude, for one," he said, grabbing a cloth and polishing the already gleaming bar. "You only give it when you need to. Judgment, for another. You didn't look uncomfortable while you were here last night. Master Lacey said you were particularly intrigued by the semi-private rooms. Asked all kinds of questions."

"Questions are my job," I said, drinking deeply again. "And so are statistics. Probabilities of who might've committed a murder. I bring 'em in. It's the jury's job to judge 'em."

"You know that's not what I meant."

I said nothing

"So what brings you here as a patron and not a detective, Detective?"

I watched for a moment while he poured one of the waitresses a flurry of cocktails, his attention still half on me.

"I'm having a problem with my wife."

"Tell her you're at the office and come here to get away for a few hours?" He gave me a knowing wink. "Honestly, I didn't peg you for married."

"Something like that. And I won't be married much longer." His busy hands paused as he looked at me. I could tell he wanted to ask, but knew better as both a good bartender and a discreet member of an exclusive society. I let him wonder. No one's business, really, and I didn't want to talk about it. Not with him.

Jared seemed to realize I wouldn't elaborate, resuming his attention to cleaning glasses. He did throw me a bone, though. "That sucks, man. Next round's on me."

"Thanks." I drained my glass and pushed it towards him, watching as he silently refilled it.

"So now what?" he asked. "Looking to try the dark side? I can arrange something, if you're interested."

"I doubt that's a great idea in my current state of mind. As for what's next, all I know is I have my whole life in my car, and I should probably find a hotel room."

He shrugged. "Well, holler if you change your mind or need another brew." He sauntered off to help a couple of college girls fresh from the dance floor. I sat, idly watching the club in the mirrors behind the bar. There was very little in the way of public entertainment, mostly just couples talking and drinking and some dancing. The stage was empty, and most of the people at the bar were engaged in conversation or doing what I was doing—people watching. I noticed a guy at the other end eyeing me, curiosity on his face. I tipped a nod in his direction to acknowledge him, but honestly, he wasn't who I wanted to talk to. He seemed to take the hint, though, because after a salute with his beer bottle, his focus shifted to the dance floor. I wondered who he might be, and why I'd caught his eye, and I thought about flagging Jared to find out who he was and if he'd known George Kaiser, but I let it go. I was off duty and drinking.

I didn't know how many beers I'd had before I felt a warm hand on my shoulder. Maybe three or four which wasn't enough to explain the tailspin I went into at the sound of a certain velvety voice in my ear.

"Mind if I join you?" I looked into Ben Haverson's face and felt my breath stutter, so I simply nodded, gesturing to the barstool beside me. "I take it since you're here and not at home, things didn't go well with your wife."

I shook my head. "She was too busy fucking my partner to talk."

I guessed Ben didn't often register shock at the things he heard, but his mouth fell open and his eyes widened. "Seriously?"

I gave a derisive snort. "Who knows how long it's been going on. So I stopped in for a beer or three, and I'm trying to decide if I want a hotel near here or closer to work."

He placed a hand on my forearm, his palm warm and dry against my skin. "Wanna get a cup of coffee? Talk about it?"

"Nah, beer's good. Probably better for calming me down than a bunch of caffeine. I feel like I'm bouncing around in my skin as it is."

Ben raised his hand and signaled Jared, ordering me another beer and a glass of merlot for himself.

"You know," I peered at him sideways, a good buzz ricocheting through my veins, "you're a really classy guy. None of that bullshit bravado that so many men have. You eat barbecue without turning your shirt into a Rorschach inkblot, and you come to a BDSM club and order wine. But you don't have an ounce of snobbery to you."

He laughed, his deep brown eyes crinkling at the corners, the tiny gap in his top two front teeth catching my eye. "Thanks, I think."

"I mean it. Maybe I'm not getting my point across well, but I don't know... There's something about you. You're so comfortable with who you are and your surroundings. I wish I felt that way." I knew I was getting philosophical, though I doubted there was any stopping it. It did make me decide that my current beer would be my last.

"Why are you not comfortable, Gavin?" he asked, swirling his wine around the bowl of the glass, watching the legs meander before sipping.

"Because my wife is fucking someone else, and instead of being devastated, I'm elated. The most appropriate feelings I have are anger that it was Trent, and embarrassment that I was stupid enough not to know. But I shouldn't be sitting here thinking how glad I am not to have to follow her rules anymore, or how I don't have to feel guilty for working overtime, and my off time will be my own again. This should hurt, right?" I looked up from my hands to find him studying me. "It doesn't hurt, and I wonder if that makes me defective."

Ben narrowed his eyes, calculating his next words. He seemed to come to a decision, leaning forward into my personal space. I didn't back away, and I probably wasn't all that subtle in sniffing his cologne.

"Mind if I guess at why you're not reacting the way you think is socially acceptable?"

Dangerous territory, but I felt reckless. "Knock yourself out," I said, resting my chin coyly on my shoulder. Our eyes locked as he spoke, and I felt that strange twinge in my gut again, like someone had taken a live wire to my internal organs and given me a jolt. His voice wove around me even over the jarring music, blotting everything else out.

"You've been painted into a corner for a long time and you now have a get-out-of-marriage-blame-free card. No one will judge you for leaving her. No one will think there's another, deeper reason for things not working out. It's cut and dried, and her bad judgment takes away the burden of a very difficult decision, which is whether to stay with her and be miserable, or leave and be the man you want to be, regardless of others' opinions. You are not defective. You're unchained from the consequences of marrying the wrong person. It's no wonder you're crawling out of your skin. You're free to be who you want to be, now."

I nodded sagely, the alcohol letting me think it was a good idea to keep staring, to study him with bright interest. "And who do I want to be, Ben?"

He considered me, tilting his head to the side, his dark, artfully mussed hair glinting in the neon light from behind the bar.

"Honestly?"

I kept staring. I liked looking at him. "Honestly," I confirmed.

"You want to be Detective Gavin DeGrassi, ridding St. Louis County of the criminal element. Outside of work, you want to lay that responsibility down and let someone else take over the heavy lifting. Trust someone else to handle the details, and you can simply make that someone feel good and happy and loved. You didn't have a name for it until yesterday, and you still need me to say it for you, but you want to be Gavin DeGrassi, submissive." He paused and lowered his voice, either for dramatic effect or propriety. I couldn't decide which. "And you want that someone to whom you give your burdens to be male."

I blinked, breaking his spell over me, but I was too stunned to speak for long moments. When I did find my voice, it came out in a half-croak. "How did you know that?"

"Today at lunch. When I asked for your impressions of your trip here, you told me about a guy edging his male sub and how fascinated you were. You spoke of Matt Kinney's stage show with Lance. Not a single flinch at the mention of Matt and Lance living together and no hesitation whatsoever to go to their home, regardless of what you might interrupt. I know what Collared looks like on a Saturday night, Gavin," Ben said softly, hypnotizing me with the cadence of his voice. He still leaned close, still held my gaze, and the hand not holding his wine glass slipped along the backrest of my barstool, closing out the rest of the club by completing a circuit between our bodies without even touching me. "There are girls dancing half naked, equal amounts of women being spanked by men, but it was the men you noticed. Then you tell me how your wife is trying to steer your career, and if she's concerned about her image, which you said she was, she'd try to steer your personal life, too. The final clue was you talking about her dumping her good friend for a slightly adventurous sexual appetite.

"You're so far in the closet you may never come out. And why should you? The people you're closest to are cops, inherently judgmental and bound by a code of honor that's archaic about homosexuality at best and bigoted at worst. Your wife would've had an aneurysm if you'd even hinted at being attracted to men. All of that is fairly potent pressure to stay in the closet. And when you finally do break free of the mold you've adhered to for so long, you come to a sexually liberated, mostly judgment-free kink club for 'a beer or three.'"

Jesus, put that way, I couldn't believe how obvious I was. My face flooded with heat and embarrassment, and I dropped my eyes to my empty glass.

"Like another beer?" Ben asked, letting me out from under his gaze. I shook my head, both in answer and to clear my mind.

"Probably had enough to drink tonight if I don't want to be hung over for George Kaiser's autopsy in the morning."

"Wise," he said, turning his profile to me once again and sipping his wine.

Companionable silence descended and the beat of the music, mostly beneath my radar since Ben had sat down, insinuated itself again. I twiddled a napkin, debating whether or not I needed to stand up and leave, or if I was here for a reason and chickening out wasn't getting me anywhere and never had. Fuck it. It's now or never.

"So do you have any suggestions on how I handle this restlessness?" I kept my tone low, going for seductive and feeling like a fool. "I can't sit still. And I know I don't want to bounce around an empty hotel room yet." The flirting was foreign, and I had no idea if I pulled it off. I was completely out of my depth, not even knowing how to articulate what I really wanted or having a clue how to bring it up. Hell, even contemplating acting on the desire was new territory, including whether or not I was right about Ben being receptive to a man's advances. I didn't just have a rusty gaydar, I had no gaydar. But I had to know.

"You don't need any more to drink, and you shouldn't be alone." Ben looked up from his wine thoughtfully, again tilting his head to the side. It was endearing, that look. No other word for it. He called Jared over and paid both our tabs, then leveled his gaze at me. "Let's get out of here."

Warmth spread through my gut and my nerves fired all at once as I nodded and stood. "Lead the way, Doctor."

"Give me your keys." He held out his hand.

I stared at him. "What?"

"You've had, what, six or seven beers? Give me your keys. We'll take your car and my partner can bring me back for mine tomorrow."

That brought me up short. "Partner?"

He dropped his hand to his side, his face going serious. "Yeah, my partner. Doctor Laura Ribaldi, the other half of my practice."

"She knows you come here?" I asked, feeling stupid and handing over the keys to my Camry.

"She comes here, too, with her Master."

The relative quiet of the street was deafening in contrast to the club, and Ben waited for me to walk in the direction my car before falling into step beside me. "Your business partner is a sub." Way to state the obvious.

Ben nodded, bumping my shoulder companionably. "Yeah, some of our patients are more comfortable talking to a Dom. Some would rather see a sub. Not everyone we counsel is in the lifestyle, but most of them are. We don't try to shrink the kink out of them like so many other psychiatrists in the vanilla world. So we balance the practice to cater to the needs of everyone who comes in."

"That makes sense. Hell, everything you say makes sense. I've never met anyone like you, Ben. Talking to you is... Well, it's just different."

He grinned and unlocked my car with the remote as we neared it. "I have that effect on people."

Over the roof of my car, I gave him an appraising look. "Is this kind of thing common for you?" I flapped a hand to indicate him and me, us, leaving a bar together, to go... well, I didn't want to assume, but I thought I knew where we were headed. My stomach was still undulating at the very idea.

"What, leaving with a friend whose marriage just imploded? Not usually. Most of my friends aren't married. Collared, yes. Married, no."

I blinked. There was so much in that statement I wanted to clarify that I didn't know where to begin, not to mention he hadn't really answered my question. Is that what this is? A pity fuck? Am I a charity case? Am I misinterpreting this? Is he going to drive me to the Hilton, tuck me in and leave? "Collared?" I asked, shoving down the rest.

"Yeah, it's a semi-public ceremony where a Dom collars their sub, announcing to everyone else in the community that the sub is owned."

"Owned? Like property?"

"Some of them are like that. But most of them, no, it's a commitment ceremony, and instead of a wedding ring, the sub wears the Dom's collar to announce not only that he or she is off the market, but often times, to whom they specifically belong. The collars can be simple or elaborate, are sometimes engraved, and usually lock or screw together. The only person with the key is the Dom. Anyone seeing the collar knows that sub is permanently spoken for. There are occasions when a collared sub is dismissed, but they're rare."

We climbed into the car and I cranked the air conditioner to cool my alcohol-heated face while he pulled out of the lot, picking up the side streets surrounding Forest Park. I loved this part of the city: grand old homes, towering trees, historic buildings. Keeping my attention on the scenery, I asked, "Dismissed?"

"It's like a divorce, but it does carry negative connotations for the sub. More often, when a collaring doesn't work out, the couple quietly breaks their contract, just like in the vanilla world."

"Wait, contract?"

I studied his profile for a moment in the fading twilight and he smiled. "I keep forgetting how much you don't know about this. When a Dom and sub enjoy playing together regularly, they'll consider drawing up a contract, tying that sub to that Dom for a specified period of time. Could be a month, six months, a year. The contract will specify when negotiations are revisited. It's during negotiations that the sub sets their hard and soft limits, requests things they want to try. The Dom does the same, stating their requirements of the sub. When the terms are right for them both, they sign and are bound to each other for the contract period. When that period is up, they decide if they continue for another term, a longer term, or part ways."

"Sounds so clinical," I said drily.

"Let me ask you something. You've just been seated at a nice restaurant with, well, let's say your wife, since that's a concrete example and you know how she reacts to things. You know this date is important to her and the night's going well, but shortly after you order the wine, your cell phone goes off, and you're called to a crime scene. What happens?"

"I pay the bill, apologize profusely and start thinking of ways I can kiss her ass while I call her a cab and head to the scene."

"That's a term you have. No matter where you are or what you're doing, if you get that call, you have to go. Now, if you'd talked about it up front, and she'd said, 'You know, I understand why you have to leave, but when that happens, it frustrates me. So you have to agree that every time it happens, you will take a day off work and spend it with me, no interruptions.' Think she'd be less irritated at you being called away?"

I considered it. "You know, she probably would be."

"That's what I mean by negotiations. It happens in every relationship. We just write the terms down, mostly for the safety of everyone, since we play with dangerous toys. Boundaries are good to push, but not cross. It's also one reason D/s relationships get deep fast. There are few things hidden, less room for resentment to grow. If something bothers one person, they have a way to bring it up, in the context of their negotiations. Some couples even contract to having set times every week to discuss their needs in a safe way. I'm a big proponent of that."

I'd been lulled by his voice again, but was pulled out of it when he turned into one of the most historic neighborhoods of the city, just north of Forest Park. Beautiful, stately homes graced massive lots on each side of the street and even in the dim light, I could make out well-manicured lawns just brightening with artful landscape lighting. Ritzy. I had slipped even more out of my element. "Know someone in this neighborhood?"

"Yeah, several people. My neighbors."

I swallowed nervously, watching the enormous houses slip by before he pulled into the long driveway that wrapped around a Tudor with sharply peaked gables and ivy hugging the walls. "You live here?"

"Yep," he said, stopping in a cobbled courtyard between the house and detached garage, turning off the car and looking at me. He leaned toward me, elbow on the console, speaking low and serious. "If you're not comfortable, I can take you to a hotel and get a cab. It's no big deal."

Somewhat sheltered in the courtyard surrounded on three sides by his house, trees, and looming darkening skies, away from the street and prying eyes, I gathered my liquid courage, closed the distance between us and kissed him lightly. My heart hammered in my chest, blood roared in my ears, and my fingertips tingled with the kind of anticipation I hadn't felt since I was a kid on my first roller coaster. The touch of our lips was electric, soft but not tentative, and he didn't push me away. It was nothing like kissing a woman and it thrilled me. After a few seconds, I pulled back to see his face, his reaction. That warm openness was there in the slight upturn of his lips, and though I couldn't see his eyes well in the dark, they seemed to shine in the reflection of the lights still glowing on the dashboard.

"I don't have a clue what I'm doing, but I don't want to stop," I murmured.

He smiled, his hand covering mine with a quick squeeze. "Then let's go inside."

We entered through a back door beneath a covered patio that held a fireplace surrounded by comfortable outdoor furniture, and the interior view of the house took my breath away. Soaring, exposed-beam ceilings drew the eye to a loft overlooking the massive living room dominated by a fireplace between enormous bookcases that held knick knacks and photos as well as enough reading material for a small library. A wrap-around breakfast bar separated the kitchen from the living room and stainless steel appliances gleamed in the soft glow of tasteful under-cabinet lighting. Another door opposite the kitchen led to more rooms, but the place was so big, I was afraid any exploration would get me lost. I gave a low whistle.

"I'm in the wrong business," I said, eyes still sweeping the luxurious surroundings. Ben set my car keys on the kitchen counter. He flipped a light switch and wall sconces around the room threw off a cozy glow set on a dimmer, which he adjusted to his liking.

"Can I get you anything?" He stepped behind me, stopping a couple feet away, and his silky smooth voice coiled around my spine. I turned, hands in my pockets, suddenly shy and unsure of myself. I shook my head, trying not to appear as though I was avoiding his gaze but having a hard time looking him in the eye just the same. "Nervous?" he asked.

I did look at him then and blew out a breath. "Little bit, yeah."

"C'mere," he soothed, holding out a hand. I took it, and he pulled me close, our chests brushing. He was about my height, and his warm brown eyes appraised me, glinting in the dimness of the room. His heat seeped through my shirt, and he rested his hands on my hips. "You call the shots, okay? If you want to stop, we stop." I nodded.

Slowly, he leaned into me, tilting his face and once again, our lips met. I felt hands at the small of my back, pulling me closer. My arms wound around his shoulders, I brushed my fingers up into the hair above the nape of his neck. Like a fourteen-year old kid with no control whatsoever, my dick swelled, the very thought of kissing a man fueling me in a way nothing ever had before.

Emboldened, I flicked my tongue against Ben's bottom lip, inviting a deeper, more insistent kiss. He responded with a sigh, parting his lips to allow me entrance. Despite his baby-faced jaw, his skin was rougher than I was used to, the hint of whiskers setting a flurry of firing nerves through my face and down to my gut. I lost myself in it—the feel of strong arms, a definable ridge of flesh pressing into my hip. I groaned, my hips involuntarily rubbing against him. My face flooded with heat, embarrassed by how shameless I was, but the reaction it elicited from him was not admonishment or even amusement. He simply pushed back, his hands gliding down to grip my ass as he held me firmly against him. I gasped, and he took the moment to slide his lips along my jaw and suck in air from a break in the kiss that left us both breathless.

I tilted my head back, shivering slightly. My neck had always been a sensitive spot, and this was no different. His hands released my ass and slid up between us, rubbing my chest as his lips meandered toward my ear.

"Good?" he asked, his hot breath caressing my skin and sending delightful shock waves through me.

"Mm-hmm," I mumbled, loosening my arms slightly to make more room for his hands. He began to work open my shirt buttons as he captured my mouth again. Oh god, this is what I've been missing. I dropped my hands to his waistband and untucked his shirt, fingers finding the warmth beneath. It was his turn to shiver, and he pulled away from the kiss to look down, watching as he exposed my torso inch by inch.

"God," he breathed. "I couldn't take my eyes off you during that first meeting. I was so afraid you'd complain about harassment or something."

I chuckled. "I spent that whole time wondering if I was staring too much and if my dickhead partner would notice. Which, of course, he did."

My shirt hung open as Ben moved his hands along my waist, the slide of his palms dry and reassuring. I lifted his shirt, forcing his arms up to bare his chest, and when I had it off, I tossed it toward the couch. The need to touch every inch of him overwhelmed me, and I did as much as I could while he licked and sucked his way along my neck again, eliciting a low moan from me. His chest was devoid of hair except for a few strays circling his nipples, which responded deliciously to my touch. I rolled them between the thumb and forefinger of each hand, loving how they pebbled between my fingertips.

His hands returned to my hips, caressing my sides before pushing my shirt off my shoulders. I wanted to savor every moment of this, every caress and kiss, and I had no idea if he was enjoying himself as much as I was. The ridge of his cock against my hip suggested he was, but I wanted more feedback. I snaked my tongue out to taste his neck and licked lower, along his collarbone and down his smooth chest, reveling in his hands tangled in my hair, holding me captive against him. The scent of him, clean and male and intoxicating, filled my nose, adding another layer to the taste of him.

I gave a small groan when he pulled completely away from me, confusion on my face, disappointment welling up in my chest. It lasted just a moment, though, as he caressed my arm from elbow to wrist, took hold of my hand, and pulled me toward the door next to the bookcase and into the bedroom beyond. It was enormous, with a fireplace along the same wall as the one in the living room and sharing the same flue. The carpet was deep, and there was a sitting area on the far wall in front of a door that led out to the same patio through which we'd entered. The other end held the en suite bathroom, dark but for the light seeping in from the living room. Ben led me to the middle of the room and turned on a table lamp.

By far the most dominant feature was the bed, a California king covered by a down comforter in a chocolate colored duvet cover. The pillows stacked at the head of the bed were deep red and inviting. He pulled me to the edge of the mattress, which came to just below my hip.

The strength of his tug sent me into him, and I clung like a barnacle, kissing him with a passion I hadn't known existed before this moment. He moaned into my mouth, and the feel of his tongue sliding against mine was heaven. With more deliberation, my hands found the globes of his ass and pulled his pelvis closer, and I smeared my hard-on against him with complete abandon. He ground his hips into me in return and a low growl escaped him. I pulled back with a startled look, studying his face. The desire there set off a shiver beneath my skin again, and his hands found my belt buckle, undoing it and pulling it slowly from the belt loops of my pants.

I wondered if he would use the belt on me, and it pulled me up short. This wasn't just any man. This was a Dom, and I wondered if he would enjoy this without the element of submission on my part. I was as much an active participant as he was, and I didn't know if that's how he liked it or if he wanted me to let him do whatever he pleased.

"Stop," he murmured, dropping my belt on the floor and flipping the button of my pants open with an easy flick of his fingers. "I can get into regular sex as much as the next guy, so quit overthinking."

"Are you a mind reader?" I asked, shuddering as he lowered my zipper, my pants sagging around my hips.

"Your face is so open, it's hard not to see what's written there."

"My poker face only fails around you." I captured his mouth again, nibbling on his lips. His hand insinuated itself inside my underwear and gripped my shaft, already hard from the mere idea of what we were doing. The added stimulation nearly had me coming in prepubescent record time. Suddenly desperate to do everything possible before I embarrassed myself, I opened his pants and pushed them and his boxers down. He kicked off his shoes and stepped out of his clothes, standing before me naked but for his socks. I made no secret of my appraisal, devouring him with my eyes. He was gorgeous, lean and lithe, with the most beautiful dick I'd ever seen, the shaft curving gracefully from a trimmed thatch of dark hair. He was long, not incredibly thick, but had a pronounced flare to the glans. He leaned back, letting me get my fill.

After shucking the rest of my clothes, my desire was obvious, and when he sat on the bed and held out a hand, I went to him and stood between his spread knees, leaning down to kiss him again. The soft sounds he made, little purrs and gasps, spurred me on. For the first time in my life, I gave in to the need to touch another man in that way, wrapping my fingers around his silky hard skin, caressing his prick. A shuddering breath escaped me. This was real, honest, and right. Not a sham, or a quick let's-do-this-before-you-figure-me-out rush to the finish line.

"Oh god," I whispered, sinking to my side on the bed beside him as he went down on his back, his arm beneath my shoulders and holding me close while I jacked him, watching every muscle twitch. I was torn between the sight of his shaft passing through my hand and the parade of expressions on his face. Pleasure, relaxed enjoyment, consideration of how I was feeling at the revelation of being with a man for the first time. I chuckled at that last one, gave him a kiss and sped up my hand.

I threw a leg over the one nearest me, pressing the head of my cock into the smooth skin of his flank, and gave a few short, involuntary hip thrusts. He turned into me then, pushing me to my back and straddling my thighs. He gently grabbed my wrists and pinned them above my head as he plundered my mouth with his tongue.

"Want you," he murmured against my lips. To punctuate the point, he ground our cocks together, the sensation ripping a gasp from me. I tried to lift my hands to get at him, to caress his lean muscles or wrap my fingers around both our erections, but he wouldn't let me, a serious look crossing his features. He pulled back enough to gaze down at me. "What do you want?" he asked softly.

Saying "everything" to the Dom straddling me could mean more trouble than I could handle at the moment. My go-to fantasy, however, tumbled off my tongue before I could stop to consider if I was ready. "I want you to fuck me."

"You're sure?" he whispered, not moving a muscle or distracting me in any way.

"Yes. No. Oh god, yes, yes I'm sure," I babbled. He raised a sardonic brow at me, the corner of his lips tilting up.

"This isn't something you can take back. Once it's done, it's done."

"I want it. With you. I want you," I said, shaking with nervousness and anticipation. Thankfully, before I could sink too far into my thoughts, he kissed me breathless, releasing my hands and curling over my body protectively.

"I'll make it good for you," he said, lips teasing my throat again. I groaned and thrust up into him, hopefully conveying that I wanted it sooner rather than later. He got the point, stretching away from me to get into his nightstand. The supplies thumped to the bed beside my head and a body tremor coasted through me. I'm doing this. I'm actually doing this.

His marvelous tongue curled against my skin, traveling down my chest, flicking wetly at my nipples and lower, into my belly button. I shivered and laughed nervously. His fingers wrapped around my shaft and pulled it from my abdomen, his tongue licking around the head and pushing into my slit.

"Holy fuck," I gasped, eyes glued to the spectacle. When he engulfed me in the heat of his mouth, I was afraid I'd come right then. It was like no other blow job I'd ever received, eager and everywhere at once. His hand curled around the base of my shaft and pumped where his lips didn't reach. When he shifted position to his knees, swallowing me down seemed easy for him, and when my dick bumped the back of his throat, my eyes widened and my breathing ripped from me in staccato bursts. He popped off with an audible sound, moving lower to mouth my balls and bathe my skin with his tongue. I spread my legs shamelessly and fire curled in my gut when he licked up the crease between leg and pelvis. Flushed and wanting, breathing raggedly, I groaned when he sucked me down again. It was the most enthusiastic head I'd ever received, and I was way too close, way too fast.

"Ben," I said, hands tangled in his hair to try to dislodge him. "Ben," I said again when he ignored me the first time. He looked up, dark pupils blown with desire, my cock stretching his lips wide. He hummed at me questioningly, the vibration piercing my dick like an arrow to my gut. "Oh god, I'm… come on, you gotta—" I groaned uncontrollably. "Close," I managed to stutter.

He gave my cock one last suck that had my eyes rolling back into my head, before kneeling up and releasing me completely.

"Move up the bed," he commanded and I did, scooting backwards and turning so my head rested on the mountain of pillows. I watched in the dim lamplight as he grabbed a bottle and flipped open the top, pouring a generous amount of liquid into his hand. Lube, I realized, and grinned both at the fact that I'd never thought of it, and the realization that we needed it. Somehow, even with my fingers around his cock, his tongue in my mouth, or my dick down his throat, this had been a little surreal, like a fantasy I was afraid I'd wake from. His slick fingers dancing downward between my ass cheeks made it real.

"Hold your legs back, behind your knees." He pushed my thighs apart and I did the rest, spreading myself for him. Vulnerability crashed into me and my eyes roamed him in need of reassurance, drinking in his open face, his obvious desire, his erection and his hand disappearing between my cheeks just before I felt the caress of his fingertips at a place I'd only ever touched myself. I groaned as one of his fingers dipped inside, gently. The intrusion wasn't uncomfortable, but it was strange, and it took me a moment to acclimate.

"Don't fight me," he murmured. "Push out. Counter-intuitive, I know, but it helps."

I nodded and did as he said, and the pressure eased even as he inserted the whole finger. I breathed steadily, relaxing as his other hand gently caressed the inside of my thigh, soothing my jangling nerves. He wouldn't hurt me. A few thrusts and I felt the blunt press of a second finger alongside the first. This time, he went faster, and the stretch made me groan, the invasion becoming pleasurable instead of merely strange. His eyes darted up to my face, and I smiled as reassuringly as I could. I was just beginning to wonder if this was all there was to it, and that it wasn't as scary or painful as I'd feared, when a jolt shot through my pelvis and made my dick stand straight up before slapping back against my abdomen. I looked at him, shocked.

"Meet your prostate," he chuckled, rubbing the same spot again. Lightning crackled along my spine and I writhed, seeking more. He rubbed mercilessly, and I gave a panting cry, fisting my hands in the duvet to keep from jumping out of my skin. After a few moments, he pulled his hand back and gripped my knees, shifting to kneel between my legs. "Last chance to change your mind," he said softly.

"Not on your life," I growled, spreading myself open further in wanton invitation. The rounded head of his cock, sheathed in a condom that he'd rolled on while I was busy trying not to scream in joy at the prostate massage, pressed against my opening and stretched me beyond what his fingers had. I hissed as the pressure increased, trying to remember to push out. When the ring of muscle gave and he slipped inside, I gave a low whimper, gripping his forearms and shaking my head at him, eyes wide and breathing uneven. The burn overtook the pleasure he'd built up, and I was a mess of nerves all over again. Now that I was actually in the moment, that he was inside me and it hurt as much as it did, I began to quietly freak out. If it was that painful, why would anyone do it more than once? Hell, why would anyone let it happen at all, after that first searing breach?

He made calming noises, his hands rubbing up and down the backs of my thighs while still holding me spread for him. He punctuated the light massage with encouragement, words I'd never expected to hear from another man.

"Damn, you're so beautiful," he smiled at me, eyes alight. "You feel so good around my cock." Heat sizzled through the small of my back and into my pelvis, and clearly, my dick approved of the dirty talk. To my surprise, the burn abated and the fullness of him—even only partially seated and wholly unfamiliar—became pleasant. Remembering the exquisite pleasure his fingers gave me, I wondered if his cock would do the same, and I realized I had to know. I nodded, signaling that I was ready for more.

He slowly thrust inside me, not stopping until he was fully buried, but not rushing either. He breathed through clenched teeth before releasing my legs and lowering himself to his elbows on either side of my shoulders. With a long, languid kiss, I was penetrated by his tongue and his dick. I flew with the rush of sensations. Gently, he began to rock, gradually increasing the thrusts until the pace was measured, strong, and sure.

"You feel incredible," he whispered, tongue flicking my earlobe and downward. I bared my neck and reached down as far as I could, resting my hands on his hips, feeling the sides of his ass flex beneath my fingers. I caressed the skin I could reach, moaning low with each push in, speared and filled and complete in a way that was new and profound.

"You, too," I answered, getting my own hip gyrations involved. He braced himself above me on his hands and knees, and experimentally slammed home once, hard. My gut burned and my toes curled, hands scrabbling at him to hold on.

"Oh!" I cried out, eyes wide and pierced by his intense gaze. "Do that again, yeeeeeeesssss." He complied, his thrusts slapping his balls against my ass—yet another feeling to memorize and revel in. I wanted it, him, so badly. I hooked my hands behind my knees and hiked them back, my hamstrings screaming in pleasurable agony. "Fuck me," I demanded, growling at him.

He changed his grip to my shoulders and pounded me into the mattress, low grunts escaping his lips as sweat beaded on his forehead. Every thrust was accompanied by a yank of his hands on my shoulders, and I submitted to his need filling me, stabbing me, reaching inside me to places I'd only dreamed of. My thoughts jumbled, and I hung on for the ride.

He reared up and gripped the headboard of his bed, changing the angle at which he fucked me, and I howled as his dick rammed my prostate on every thrust. White fire zinged through my gut and lower, and without even a hand on my cock, I came, long ropes of semen splattering my stomach and chest. Stars danced behind my eyes and I did my best to keep looking at him, watching his beautiful body dance against mine, sweat glistening on his skin and making him glow.

Ben's eyes widened at the sight of my orgasm and his hips stuttered and froze. He threw his head back and cried out. From within, I felt the pulse of his cock as he emptied into the condom, erratically thrusting with convulsions that wracked his body. Cords stood out on his neck, and his biceps and pecs flexed and relaxed, his tight abs quivering until he released a gulp of breath and collapsed on top of me. I was mesmerized.

Unable to resist, I licked his skin and tasted sweat as my legs fell apart and my arms wound around his back. He was heavy, but I could still breathe, albeit shallowly. When he began to come back to himself, he knelt up again, carefully pulling out and sitting back on his heels, his chest heaving.

I didn't know what to say. Completely unselfconscious, I stared at him with wonder, licking my dry lips and willing my breathing to calm down. Silence reigned as he stripped off the condom and dropped it in a small trash can beside the bed. I lay there, with no motivation or ability to move, other than to flop a hand out to touch him, running my fingers down his ribs to rest on his hip as he sat at the edge of the bed. He was shaking. That snapped me out of my pleasure coma and to my knees, hastily mopping up the semen from my torso with a tissue before wrapping my arms around him from behind.

I said nothing, just kissed his damp shoulder and nuzzled the back of his neck, still a little shocked at the ease I felt at holding another man with such intimacy. He turned his cheek to rest it against my forehead and, almost as though he were afraid of the answer, he spoke quietly.

"Are you okay?"

I murmured assent, pressing my nose into his neck and inhaling. As soon as I rediscovered speech, I said, "I'm good. Beyond good. Phenomenal. You?"

"I, uh..." he hesitated, running a hand through his hair. I pulled back, afraid he was going to tell me to get out or, worse, run from me, push me away, say that I'd disappointed him somehow or done it wrong. He turned, bending a knee to raise his leg up onto the bed, foot hanging over the side. "That was intense," he said, searching my face, for what I didn't know. "You sure you're okay? I didn't hurt you?"

"That," I said, pressing a soft kiss to his lips, "was perfect." A tension I hadn't realized I'd held bled from my shoulders at his words. I hadn't made a fool of myself, or done something stupid. I'd fucked a man. Correction, I'd just been fucked by a man, and to my surprise, I wasn't the least bit uncomfortable, aside from a resonating ache in my asshole that felt more good than painful at that moment. "That was everything I've always thought it might be, so no, you didn't hurt me."

He shifted on the bed, yanking the covers down. I scrambled out of the way and slid my legs between the sheets, not bothering to grab my underwear before beckoning him to join me. The high thread count made me purr, my mood soaring.

"You sure?" he asked, lying on his back and curling his arm around my shoulders to pull me to him, urging me to rest my head on his chest. His fingers threaded through my hair, and that jumpy feeling I'd had since leaving my house finally dissipated like smoke on a strong wind, replaced by a deep calm.

"I'm sure, and as soon as possible, I want to do it again."

He chuckled, and then yawned, and I tightened my arm across his torso, throwing my leg over his beneath the covers. Post-coital cuddling was something I wasn't used to. Victoria always shoved me off, grumbling that I squashed her. Ben turned off the lamp and settled around and beneath me again. I fell asleep to the rhythmic run of his fingers through my hair.

CHAPTER SIX

THE DISTANT bleep of my cell phone alarm woke me, and I rolled to my side to reach for it on the nightstand only to find that my nightstand was different. Nor was my cell where it usually sat. I looked around, bleary eyed, at the unfamiliar surroundings. I could make little out with no light filtering in from any windows. I realized my phone was in my pants. On the floor, several feet from the bed. Beside Ben's pants. Ben's bedroom. Oh yeah.

Recollection of the previous night bloomed and I tried to get out of bed smoothly so as not to wake Ben, who had an arm flung across my chest. I slid free of the sheets and reached for my clothes just as the alarm went silent. Five-thirty was way too early. The sour taste in my mouth reminded me of the beer from the night before, and I would have given my left arm to brush my teeth. My bags were still in my car, and I'd be damned if I was going outside naked for them. Getting dressed in yesterday's clothes was far too much trouble.

Ben stirred, feeling the empty space beside him. He lifted his head and squinted at me, his hair a flurry of wild directions. "Wh'time is it?"

"Before dawn. Go back to sleep," I said, voice low.

"I brought your bags in," he mumbled, burying his face back into the pillows. "Living room."

I stared at him for a moment, surprised, then padded to the living room for my shave kit, feeling self-conscious about walking naked in another man's house. After taking care of my bladder and teeth and resetting my alarm for another hour, I crawled back in bed with Ben, seeking his warmth. He purred, pulling my arms tighter around him so I was the big spoon. I couldn't help but think how well we fit together, and the miles of smooth skin against me begged to be caressed.

I tried to go back to sleep, just for a little bit, but thoughts of the previous night kept my mind active, and the solid body next to me was too tantalizing to ignore. I thought about what I hadn't had the opportunity to do, things I'd fantasized about for years. Before I could overthink it, I untangled my arms from Ben's and pulled the covers up, slinking down the bed and along his body until my head was aligned with his hips. Gingerly, I licked along his ass cheek up to his hip, the sleepy heat of him magnified beneath the heavy covers. He stretched, straightening his right leg out and rolling onto his back. I repositioned myself over his legs and trailed my tongue up his left inner thigh. I could see nothing, going simply by feel, and the smell of his maleness filled my senses the closer I got to his cock. Lapping at the skin next to his balls, I heard him huff out a breath before his knees bent and his thighs parted. Hooking my forearms beneath his legs to rest on my elbows, I ran my tongue across his lightly fuzzed nut sack and up along the length of his dick. He'd had half-hearted morning wood when I'd started, but the shaft rose to full attention beneath my lips. Tracing the veins along the underside, I savored the taste of warm saltiness on the flat of my tongue. I heard a muffled groan through the covers just as I wrapped my lips around the head and sank lower, engulfing him with my mouth.

I didn't have much idea of what to do, only having experience with what I liked done to me. Recalling the previous evening, I gave extra effort to be as eager for Ben's cock in my mouth as he'd been for mine. Keeping to one elbow to prop myself up, I raised my arm to rub a hand along his flat stomach, up his smooth skin and down his side, the ridges of his ribs giving me a map to his body. I reached to flick his nipple with my fingernail, earning a hiss and a small thrust of his hips. It pushed his cock too far into my mouth and I had to pull off, suppressing a gag. How the hell had he deep throated me the night before? Rising up on my hands and knees, I flung the covers off, taking in a gulp of cooler air and diving back down, determined to blow Ben's mind.

One hand on his hip, the other wrapped around his shaft at the point where I could reasonably swallow him down, I sucked, hollowing out my cheeks and looking up at his face to see his reaction. He looked down at me, biting his plump lower lip, his hands fisted at either side of his head in his pillow. I hummed approval and his eyes rolled back in his head. Trying to get him to do that again, I sped up, getting my hand pumping along the base of his cock, and using the other to fondle his balls. I liked my balls played with during oral sex, so I gave it a try. He groaned, throwing his head back, his buttocks flexing and releasing which pumped his hips a little bit, but not any more than I could handle. A few drawn out minutes, and his voice, rich and buttery, broke the near silence.

"Gavin," he warned. I raised my eyes to his face, still sucking. His brows were furrowed and his mouth was open, his breathing rapid and sharp. "Gavin," he said again. I knew what he meant, and I ignored him, wanting this after years of picturing it, imagining what it would feel like, taste like. After one more deep suck, he groaned, arched his back, and flooded my mouth with hot, bitter spunk. I swallowed what I could, the convulsions making his cock dance on my tongue. If it weren't for the speed he filled my mouth, I would have been better at swallowing it. I also realized there was something to be said for watching him splatter his stomach, though. Next time, I thought, registering that I wanted there to be a next time.

Ben pulled me up beside him and wrapped his arms around me, nuzzling my neck and hooking the covers back up over us. I realized I'd probably have to get up and shower soon if I wanted to grab Talcott first thing before George Kaiser's autopsy. The thought of leaving the bed's warm cocoon with its irresistible occupant left me grumpy.

"That was quite the surprise," Ben said. I noticed his slight Southern lilt was more pronounced when he was sated or sleepy. It made me smile as he pressed a kiss to my temple, his hand reaching down to fondle my hard-on.

"I've always wanted to do that," I breathed, as his fingers tightened on me. "But I didn't do it so you'd get me off, too." I pushed his hand away, not wanting to get carried away with the time. If he touched me even half as intently as last night, I'd never make it to work on time, if at all. "I have to shower in a minute."

"Mmm, want company?" he asked, mouthing my neck and making my limbs weak. He worked his way down my chest.

"Normally, I'd say yes, but I have to be in early this morning," I said regretfully, threading my fingers through his hair, surprised that this morning-after stuff with Ben wasn't stranger, more awkward. But it felt easy. Of course, that could have been because he was relaxed and post-orgasmic, and I was just thrilled to have popped my homosexual cherry. It didn't feel that trivial, though. I pushed the thoughts away, not wanting to lay too much importance on the matter. Ben was a good man, and I respected him a great deal, but one night in bed didn't mean he'd necessarily want a repeat, especially with a horribly closeted, still married man with zero experience not only with D/s dynamics, but other men in general.

"Why so early?" he asked, tonguing my nipple. I closed my eyes and tried to keep thinking with my brain.

"Autopsy," I answered. "Plus, I need to get my partner reassigned."

Ben raised his head, his eyes serious. "You think your boss will give you any trouble for that?"

"Sergeant Talcott is Trent's friend, which normally would make it harder for him to believe me, not that he'd outright accuse me of lying. But I covered my ass yesterday." I swiped my phone off the nightstand and tapped the screen, turning it to show him the picture I'd snapped before leaving home for good. "Proof."

Ben gave a low whistle. "I'd say you're good, then." He resumed kissing across my chest. "Very good." His voice was muffled against my skin. It felt heavenly.

"Ben," I said, trying to stop him and failing. "I have to shower. Come on, I can't." I sat up, and if my dick could talk, it would have grumbled wholeheartedly at my thwarting its pleasure.

"Okay," Ben acquiesced, letting me out of bed. I rifled through my bag for a fresh pair of boxer briefs and disappeared into his ginormous bathroom.

Black marble stood in stark relief against the white walls. The sinks were the kind that stood as giant bowls above the counter surface. I brushed my teeth again and stepped into the large tub that split the vanity in two with a sink on each side. As I fired up the dual shower heads and drew the curtain, I let the hot water wash away the last of my tension from the previous day. I wasn't in there more than a few minutes with my eyes closed and shampoo sluicing from my hair when I heard the curtain rattle as Ben joined me. He said nothing, and before I could get all the suds out of my hair, I felt my cock engulfed in his wet, hot mouth.

"Jesus Christ!" I moaned, giving in. Ah, fuck it. What will it hurt? The way Ben's mouth moved on me, he'd have me finished in no time anyway.

§§§

"SARGE, HAVE you got a moment?" I asked, stalking past my empty desk, thankful Trent hadn't shown up for work yet. It was nearly seven-thirty, way too early for the scumbag to be in unless he had a specific reason, though I half expected him to try to head me off. Unless he'd called Talcott last night, beating me to the punch. I shook my head. No matter. I had what I needed to get my point across.

"Sure, DeGrassi. What's up?" He leaned a hip against my desk and crossed his arms over his chest, looking at me expectantly.

"Uh, can we go in your office?" Few people were there to overhear me, but I wanted no one eavesdropping. Much as I was disgusted with Trent, I didn't have any desire to smear him to everyone we worked with, though that would happen as soon as word got out. Not my problem, though.

Talcott nodded, brows drawing together as he led me to the hallway lined with gunmetal gray closed doors. He opened his and stepped into his office before grabbing his seat and gesturing me into one of the two in front of his desk. "Everything all right?" he asked, not quite exhibiting fatherly concern, but close.

"Well, yes and no. I'd like to request a new partner."

Talcott went still, appraising me. "Well, now, that's a pretty big request, DeGrassi. You two are in the middle of a rather sensational case. If the media gets wind of the extenuating circumstances of the Kaiser murder, it'll be very public quickly. I need my best guys on this. Bringing someone else on board would slow the investigation as they got up to speed. You and I both know this isn't a bar brawl that got out of hand and the perp is hiding out at his girlfriend's house and not answering the door. This one was premeditated. That alone is disturbing. A new partner is going to have no impressions of your first witnesses, no idea what reports have been requested or are still pending. You'd better have a damn good reason for this request, Detective." The more Talcott spoke, the sterner he became.

Silently, I thumbed at the screen on my phone, finding the appropriate picture. I figured the photo would do my talking for me. "You've met my wife, Victoria?" Talcott nodded. "Then you'll recognize her," I said as I handed over the incriminating image.

"Aw shit, Trent," Talcott growled, furrowing his brows and frowning at the phone as if it had personally insulted him. With pursed lips, he set the cell on his blotter and folded his hands behind it. "All right," he nodded, turning to log into his computer. "I'll make some inquiries. When he comes in today, I'll recommend he take a mental health day. How many other people have seen that photo, son?" he asked.

"One friend outside of work whom I trust implicitly, and I intend to show it to my attorney for the divorce I'll be seeking. Beyond that, I'll keep it quiet. I don't need to embarrass them publicly, sir. I just need to end both relationships as soon as possible. No one else's business why."

In a perfect world, that would fly. But I knew the minute I told my family, they'd have to know why, and four cops, one of them a gossipy retiree, keeping their mouths shut about Trent's behavior?

Especially my protective brothers? Not fucking likely. Trent would be lucky if he got his new partner assignment before word got around.

"Go through his desk and grab the files he has on Kaiser and any other open cases you two are working. I'll make some calls and have a chat with our boy when he comes in. You might want to make yourself scarce for the morning. He's been angling for a promotion and won't be happy being taken off that list. It could get ugly."

I was surprised Talcott was that free with the promotion information, but I shrugged. Far as I was concerned, as long as Trent wasn't at Second anymore, I didn't give a shit what title he had. "He should have thought about that before fucking my wife," I grumbled. "I'm leaving in a few to go observe Kaiser's autopsy. I'll be gone until well after lunch. That enough time?"

Talcott nodded. "Now get outta here. Disruptin' my precinct, is what you're doing," he grumbled. I smiled slightly, knowing he was just busting my balls. I did as I was told, grabbing all Trent's pertinent files and locking them in my desk before heading out to get more answers on the real matter at hand.

The drive to the M.E.'s office took longer than necessary, with rush hour. Mondays were always the worst for traffic, the drivers grumpier and shorter tempered than any other day of the week. That I had to pass by the airport with people obliviously ogling signs and trying to figure out where they were going was just the icing on the cake.

I parked and hurried inside, the cool blast of air conditioning hitting me just right. The receptionist saw me and buzzed Jencopale right away, already aware of why I was there. The doctor emerged and waved at me to follow him, his smooth baritone calming despite the purpose of my visit.

"Morning, Detective." He showed me into his office, where I left my jacket after grabbing my notepad from the pocket and followed him through the double doors into the heart of the building. People tend to think of morgues as creepy, but I never have. There are disturbing things to see, but it's just as clinical and sterile as a doctor's office or hospital. After giving me a disposable gown to protect my clothes, Dr. Jencopale washed his hands and gloved up. I stayed out of his way. I would be touching nothing, so I had no need for gloves.

"Have a good weekend, DeGrassi?" Jencopale asked me. He was the type to make whomever he was speaking to feel like the most important person in the world. I genuinely liked the man. However, the last thing I wanted to discuss with anyone, including him, was my weekend. As much as I respected Jencopale, there were things I'd never talk about with the man. Mundane weekend events? Sure. This particular weekend's? Not on your life.

"Well, it's been an interesting one. Most of it taken up by this case. How was yours?" I asked, deflecting.

"Truthfully, this one's weighed on me," he sighed, gesturing to the body as we entered the autopsy suite. George Kaiser had been kept in his body bag to preserve evidence, and as we approached the table, one of Jencopale's assistants came over to help him remove the bag. He began to speak slowly into a retractable microphone that hung from the ceiling and recorded his notes as he worked so he could remain hands-free during the autopsy. This was the reason some of the M.E.'s assistants didn't allow questions during their autopsies, but Jencopale welcomed mine, not minding the extra dictation. He told me it helped him answer every possible question before releasing the body for burial.

Once George Kaiser was laid out on the table, Jencopale began.

Reading out the case number and date, his voice was the lone sound in the room, the other assistants either stopping to watch or leaving the lab altogether. "Autopsy of George Kaiser, forty-five year-old male Caucasian. Present with me is Detective Gavin DeGrassi to observe. Victim has several chest and stomach lacerations, measurements of which were taken at the scene by the crime scene investigators." Despite that, Jencopale retrieved a protractor and took his own pictures. "Depth of the wounds, half an inch. Length varies between seven and nine inches. Blood loss and bruising evident. Wounds inflicted antemortem." He continued to move around the body. "Petechiae on the cheeks and the sclera of the eyes indicate the victim's air supply was restricted." He prodded his fingers around the outside of George's throat. "Fracture of the hyoid bone and bruising around the neck along with small abrasions. Probable cause of death, strangulation."

At that moment, Jencopale waved me over and pointed to Kaiser's neck, specifically the abrasions. "Look at these. You ever seen anything like this?" he asked. Small red dots covered the bruising all along Kaiser's neck, as if someone had taken a small needle and punctured the skin at patterned intervals all along the bruises. I shook my head.

"They're not deep, are they?"

"Hard to say." Jencopale grasped a pick tool, typically used to collect fingernail scrapings, and probed one of the punctures. "Tiny. About an eighth of an inch deep."

I frowned, shaking my head.

Dr. Jencopale grabbed a UV light and glasses that would allow him to see foreign substances on the skin of the victim. Running the light over the entirety of Kaiser's body, he remained silent, collecting nothing in the way of hair or fibers. I blew out a frustrated breath, but kept quiet.

"The only notable trace on the victim is artificial black marks drawn on his face," Jencopale said into the microphone. "UV illumination shows they outline saline tracks. Spectral imaging data to be sent to the crime lab for ink analysis." Jencopale took several pictures under different UV light sources with a UV camera and passed me the memory card after marking the case number and noting it in the evidence transfer log. I frowned down at the card in my hand, then at Jencopale.

"Wait, the killer drew around the man's tears?"

"It looks that way."

"Why?" I asked before I could stop myself.

"That's your job, Detective. My guess, considering the position and location of the body, the victim's lifestyle, and the killer's display of the scene, is that he wanted to humiliate the victim. He got a Dom to cry, and wanted to let everyone who saw the man know it."

"Reasonable," I nodded, making notes. "No hair or fibers?"

Jencopale shook his head. "None. Either the killer wore a hood and gloves, or he scrubbed him down after. Considering the blood left behind, my money's on the former."

Gloves.

"How deep did you say those tiny prick marks were?" I moved to the head of the table, pointing to Kaiser's throat.

"Eighth of an inch," Jencopale answered.

"Vampire gloves."

"What?"

"Vampire gloves. The victim had a receipt for the cross and had purchased a mask and gloves on the same trip. They're gloves that have little tacks in them, used for scratching and spanking, but designed not to break skin unless used roughly. Strangulation's rough, in my opinion."

Jencopale nodded. "It would also explain the lack of transfer. As much interaction as the killer had with the victim prior to death, I would have expected something to transfer between them. There's nothing."

"No, there's something," I murmured grimly. "We just don't know what it is yet."

Jencopale called an assistant to help roll George onto his stomach for posterior examination. An array of pinpricks like those around his throat peppered George's back in large swaths, particularly lower, around his butt and thighs. Abrasions and welts similar to what I'd seen on Lance March's back were also present. At the very least, he'd been flogged, possibly whipped with more of his implements, and smacked around with the vampire gloves.

I made notes while Jencopale continued. "Contusions along the flanks and buttocks are consistent with whip marks, though which of the whips present at the scene was responsible, I couldn't tell you."

"Got it covered." I recalled the photos of blue slashes in the forensics gel Cole had sent.

"External examination indicates small tears around the victim's anus, as well as bruising and bleeding consistent with rough penetration." I looked up at the M.E.'s words to find him studying the area between the victim's buttocks. A flush crept up my face, and a flash of the previous night's events played in my mind: Ben spreading my ass and delving gently with his fingers. The memory of some discomfort even at Ben's gentle touch made me wince that George had had it rough. Something else gnawed at me.

"Traces of lubricant or semen around the area, Doctor?" I focused on the body, hoping he wouldn't see something on my face, which I kept as blank as possible. Jencopale retrieved his light while instructing his assistant to hold Kaiser's buttocks apart so he could aim the beam. A few minutes' exam and he turned it off and removed the glasses.

"None on external examination. I'd say he was penetrated dry and that contributed to the bruises and tears. But he was definitely raped."

I frowned. "How does a man hanging spread eagled on a cross that leaves him several inches off the ground get anally raped? Is the man we're looking for supremely tall, or did the rape occur before he was put on that cross?"

"I can't answer that question," Jencopale said, focused on taking swab samples from Kaiser's rectum. "Maybe he wasn't penetrated by the killer himself, but an object."

"Is there evidence of that?"

Jencopale leveled a gaze at me, his tone droll. "Detective, with the creativity of the sex toy market these days and the anatomical correctness they achieve, I would never be able to confirm whether the killer used a toy or his own penis."

I cleared my throat, somewhat embarrassed. "Of course, Doctor. I'll have them run trace on any toys recovered at the victim's home to see if any match."

The doctor nodded. "I'll make sure any photos are useful if you do find an object with evidence."

The autopsy continued, and Jencopale took several syringe samples from various points on the body, including the bladder, liver, stomach, spine, and the one that always made me turn my head and fight nausea, the fluid from the eye.

"I'll send these for tox and let you know if there are any revelations," he spoke to my back, tone light and understanding. "You can turn around now," he said gently.

Resuming my vigil, I watched as he completed his external exam and with the help of his assistant, cleaned the body and got ready to explore the inner workings of George Kaiser and his murder. I settled in for the long haul, observing intently, asking any questions that came to mind, and in general, learning the victim's body and manner of death inside and out.

By the time they stitched Kaiser's body up, it was nearing noon, and I felt the need to decompress. I went back to the station and checked my messages, ignoring the stares from other people. Lawanda, the receptionist, murmured a hello to me as she passed over the small slips with calls I needed to return. She leaned close, speaking low.

"You okay, DeGrassi?"

I spared her a glance. "Yeah, why?"

Her eyes darted around the room to make sure she was being quiet enough, but she wasn't the only one attuned to my presence. "Well, Sawyer came in here after you left for the M.E.'s, and he went straight to the Sarge's office. There was yelling, but no one knows what about, and then Sawyer packed up his desk and Talcott walked him out. You two not partners no more?" She looked at me with wide-eyed curiosity, and I felt my poker face slip into place.

"No, Lawanda, we're not."

"What happened?" she asked. I sighed, knowing it wasn't the first time I'd be asked.

"He's being assigned to another precinct, where I'm sure he'll do his job and do it well. Don't concern yourself over Sawyer. He'll be fine."

She huffed, crossing her arms over her chest. "Honey, I ain't worried about him. I'm worried about you. He was a womanizing dirtbag, you want my opinion. Good cop, lousy human being." She lowered her tone conspiratorially. "I wouldn't be surprised if he got caught screwing some higher up's wife or something and got the boot."

"If that's the case, Lawanda, then he'd be incredibly stupid. Don't worry about me, though. I'm sure I'll be happy with whoever they assign in Sawyer's place." I tapped the edge of the messages on the counter, smiling down at her. "You hear anything about that through the grapevine, you let me know, huh?"

She nodded and winked at me. "You got it. Oh, and a Doctor Haverson called while you were out. Didn't want to leave a message, but asked if I'd let you know he called."

Her tone was all business and I kept from showing any kind of expression, though my insides jumped. Whether that was from the skittishness after witnessing the autopsy or because Ben had that effect on me, I couldn't tell. Probably both.

I pulled out my desk chair, logged onto my computer and checked email to find more reports from the CSIs had landed. I printed them out while I looked up contact information for Damon Lane, the man who'd also talked to Kaiser on his last night whom I hadn't had the chance to question. I made a quick call to arrange a time and place to meet with him, away from his acquaintances or coworkers if he had a day job aside from his tool making business. He agreed to meet me at the Coffee Cartel, a shop in the Central West End somewhat near Collared. I grabbed my jacket from the back of my chair, shut down my computer, and headed out, palming Ben's business card in my pocket.

Driving to Ben's offices, located in the Clayton business district, I chewed over the details of Kaiser's postmortem. The marks on his face stuck out particularly, and it pointed to the fact that the method of torture had meant more to the killer than just a means to bring about death. The role reversal, humiliating a Dom, was not lost on me. Had George hurt one of his subs in the past, someone the killer knew and cared for enough to seek retribution? None of those who knew him seemed to think so. I remembered the list of George's previous subs from Kimberly Kaiser and the two names provided by Matt Kinney. They could paint a more accurate picture of the man's Dominant side. We hadn't had a chance to track everyone down that night at Collared.

Turning into one of the many parking garages in Clayton's downtown, I parked and locked my car, making my way into the office tower where Ben's practice was located. The silent elevator ride contrasted with the nerves in my stomach. Was I overstepping my bounds, coming to his office? I figured I'd offer him a ride to his car at the club since I was the reason he'd left it there. But for all I knew, he wasn't interested in seeing me outside the case. I shoved my doubts aside. He'd called me, and whether that was for business or otherwise, I wanted to find out.

The plush offices were as tastefully decorated as Ben's house, with art on the walls that spoke of attention to detail rather than cheap space fillers. Fresh flowers stood on two corner tables and the magazines appeared current. I stepped up to the receptionist's desk and spoke low.

"Detective DeGrassi to see Doctor Haverson."

The homely woman at the counter looked at her computer screen and frowned. "Do you have an appointment, Detective?"

"No, but Doctor Haverson called me this morning, and I thought I would swing by to see what he needed."

"Just a moment," she pressed a button on her phone and spoke into the headset she wore, announcing me. After a beat, she waved me through the door leading back to the offices. Not knowing my way, I picked a direction, poking around and listening for Ben's voice.

"Ben, this isn't necessarily a bad thing," I heard a woman's confident tones ring out, a hint of exasperation underlying the words. I didn't catch what Ben murmured, but it gave me a direction to follow.

"We'll talk about this later, Laura. Okay?" Ben said with finality as I neared the door where an extremely short woman with chestnut brown hair pulled up into an elegant twist stood, her smart suit marking her professionalism. Ben's business partner. She turned as I approached and smiled, eyes flicking to my belt where my shield glinted in the muted light.

"You must be one of the detectives Ben's been consulting with. Dr. Laura Ribaldi, Ben's partner," she introduced herself, holding out her hand, which I shook. For such a small woman, she had a hell of a handshake. I found myself smiling at her in return, though it faltered slightly when I remembered she was a sub. Not exactly information I got about people before ever making their acquaintance. If she noticed my reaction, she didn't let on.

"Gavin DeGrassi," I answered, letting her hand go. He must not have told her any more than that I was working with him, so I kept it reserved. "Yes, Ben's been helping me on a case and he's already made himself indispensable."

She smiled warmly. "Ben does that with everyone." She stepped aside so I could enter the room. "Still need that ride, Ben?"

The office was large with a sitting area containing comfortable furniture and a book shelf in the corner filled with volumes. Between this one and the two massive bookshelves at his house, Ben sure read a lot. He didn't strike me as the type to have that many books just for show. One wall was a bank of windows overlooking the city, and the lighting was open and airy, with lamps dotted around the room offering a soft glow as opposed to the usual harsh fluorescents in most doctors' offices. Ben sat at a large cherry wood desk with a widescreen flat panel monitor at one corner. The rest of the desk was neat and uncluttered. A few knickknacks, a desk blotter, a phone, and one or two files were all that sat in view. The man himself looked professional in an obviously expensive dress shirt and slacks, the silk tie adding color to otherwise conservative clothing I'd not seen before leaving his house that morning. I wanted to lick him from head to toe. With Dr. Ribaldi behind me and unable to see my expression, I looked him up and down with blatant interest.

He cleared his throat as he met my eyes and answered his partner. "No, Laura, thank you. I'll see if the detective will drive me to my car."

"Okay, then. I'll see you after lunch unless you're later than usual. My afternoon's booked," she said with a significant look before disappearing down the hall.

I raised a brow at him. "She's nice," I said, making myself comfortable in one of the chairs in front of his desk. Ben pinched the bridge of his nose like he had a headache.

"Yes, she's very nice," he agreed, his voice tired, with less warmth than I was used to from him. I shifted uncomfortably, peering at him sideways. Was he uneasy with me there? I sincerely hoped he wasn't regretting the night before, but he had called me.

"So, you left me a message?" I asked, brushing lint off my knee to avoid looking at him in my discomfort.

"Yeah," he said in a clipped voice. "I wanted to see if you would mind taking me to my car. Laura's busy today." I did look up at him then, hopeful that he wanted more than a taxi, but his expression was carefully blank. "I also thought I'd ask how it went this morning requesting Trent's transfer."

My spine went stiff. The man in front of me was completely different than the one I'd slept with, woken up with. That early morning shower seemed light years away.

"About as well as expected," I answered. "The photo convinced my sergeant with minimal trouble, but I heard later that when Trent got the boot, he made his displeasure known to the entire station. Not my problem," I waved my hand dismissively, my own irritation growing.

Ben sat back, eyeing me calmly. I couldn't read him as well as he could me. A product of his occupation? Or his domination? I didn't know, and the scrutiny unnerved me, made me wonder what he noticed, what he saw. I could discern nothing, so I averted my eyes again.

"Find anything useful at the M.E.'s office?"

Strictly business. All right then. Even though I deflated inside, I didn't let it show in more than a momentarily clenched jaw to keep from saying whatever flew out of my mouth without thought. Adopting my cop voice, I spoke. "Several things. The victim was raped without lubricant and humiliated before being strangled. The black markings on his face were marker, used to outline tear tracks. Way I see it, the killer was permanently showing a Dominant his own weaknesses in the last moments of his life. Humiliating him with his own equipment and punishing him for some wrong the killer put on Kaiser's shoulders. Strangulation is a very personal way to kill someone. Hands feeling their pulse, right up in their face. It fits with your theory that the killer's motivation is vengeance. I should have the tox results back in a few days. I still don't know how the killer subdued the victim, and it's obvious he did because there were no skin scrapings beneath Kaiser's fingernails, or defensive wounds. What happened to him took hours. The killer stayed out all night, and that would be noticed if he's married or living with someone, so my guess is he's single and lives alone. If he is in a relationship, it's not serious."

Ben nodded thoughtfully. "There's a role reversal here, the Dom becoming the sub."

"I thought of that," I mused, looking out the windows and thinking. "If the killer had a previous relationship and was somehow wronged by George, wouldn't that get around the community? I've heard time and again how you look out for your own." I used the specific pronoun of "you" and "your," distancing myself from it, holding him at arm's length, unsure what his careful demeanor meant. I moved to stand at the window, looking out over the city, trying not to read into Ben's standoffishness, and failing.

"If George had hurt someone badly, yes, it would be well known. I personally would have heard not only because I'm a Dom, but also a therapist. Dr. Ribaldi and I are the local subject matter experts. Anyone seeking therapy after a trauma visited on them by a Dom typically does hit our radar through consults with other therapists if they're not our patients. I can't remember anything like that associated with Kaiser. He was a good Dom, by reputation and from what I knew personally of him."

"Wait, you knew him?" I turned, eyes narrowed.

"Not really. He was more a friend of friends. I knew who he was; he knew who I was." It hadn't occurred to me that Ben might have a connection to the victim.

"That might have been pertinent information to know, Doctor,"

I said coldly. Ben looked surprised before the blankness returned.

"Like I said, he was a friend of friends. I may have said five words to him in all the time I knew of him."

I sighed, lowering my gaze. Mrs. Kaiser hadn't mentioned Ben and neither had Matt Kinney. I had no reason to believe Ben wasn't telling the truth. But something was definitely going on here. Even the night I'd met him, at the station, he'd been more open and warm than this clinical man in front of me.

"Didn't you mention getting your car?" I asked, mentally letting go of the idea of having lunch with him. He'd thrown me off balance, and I wanted it back. It bothered me just how vulnerable I'd let myself be with him. He knew the one thing about me no one knew. I still trusted him to keep it confidential, but it had become a grudging trust.

"Yes, that's a good idea," he said, grabbing his keys from his desk drawer and leading me out of his office. He told the receptionist he'd be gone for a couple hours and to call his next patient to ask for a reschedule. Driving him to his car wouldn't take more than twenty minutes, but I wouldn't let myself wonder why he was planning such a long lunch. It wasn't my business. Walking stiffly down the hall to the elevators, I remained quiet while my mind whirred and clicked over questions and potential explanations. None of them satisfied.

"Are you all right, Gavin?" Ben asked while we waited for the elevator to arrive. I kept my focus on the numbers above the doors.

"Yeah, I'm great. I'll be even better when I catch this bastard." The answer was safe, and had the benefit of being the truth, except for the last half hour or so when I'd become more confused than great.

"You will," Ben said softly, stepping aside to follow me into the elevator when the gentle ping sounded. The car started its descent and a second later, Ben had me pinned to the wall, his mouth pressed hungrily to mine, sending me spinning off kilter again. Despite my confusion, I kissed him back with fervor, a small growl escaping my throat. His hands gripped my waist, fingers massaging through the fabric of my shirt, and everywhere I could feel him flared with heat. When our mouths separated, he rested his forehead against mine.

"I'm confused," I murmured. "A minute ago, you acted pissed that I came by, like last night hadn't happened."

"I didn't think you'd appreciate me outing you to my partner, and when she left, you clammed up, turning the cop on and Gavin off. I assumed you were uncomfortable with things. But I can't seem to help myself." He shoved his nose in my neck and breathed, humming quietly.

Nothing about that added up, but what could I ask that didn't make me sound like a needy teenage girl? You weren't looking at me right. I thought you were the one clamming up. I shook my head, threading my fingers together at the small of his back. "I appreciate the courtesy in front of your partner. But I took my cues from you, and you seemed, I don't know, put out."

He shook his head, moving up my cheek, nipping at my jaw. I shivered. "No. Irritated with Laura, yes. She brings out the big brother in me. Most of the time, I'm just protective of her. Sometimes, I want to throttle her." He smiled and kissed me again. "Thought about you all morning," he murmured against my lips.

I sighed and gave him a gentle push as the elevator pinged and stopped. He backed off and allowed me to lead the way to my car. We rode with the windows down, the day shaping into one of St. Louis's rarities—low humidity, gentle breeze, and warm sunshine without tipping into hot. I savored it and let my mind wander.

"What's that look on your face mean?" Ben asked, noticing the slight smile on my lips.

"Just how a couple days ago, I was nervous about coming to this club and it's fine now. Almost normal, like a run to the gas station. Just another place, really."

"It can be more than just another place," he said, then fell silent to let me ponder his words as I turned into Collared's parking lot.

I was all set to let him go and head back to the station when he asked where I wanted to eat. We agreed on a nearby café, driving separately and opting to dine outside as the hostess seated us and gave us our menus. After we ordered, I cleared my throat and took a long drink of tea.

"So, what do you mean, Collared can be more than just another place?" I asked.

Ben leaned forward and spoke quietly to prevent eavesdropping. "For some people, it's a reprieve from the rest of their lives where they can openly express themselves without fear of censure. For others, it's a haven to safely meet people with specific proclivities." I didn't interrupt him, though I wondered how safe it was, after George Kaiser's murder. "Still others find it a comfort to go somewhere they'll always be accepted, like a leather version of Cheers, whether or not they will ever venture into the lifestyle or merely watch from the sidelines." He dropped his eyes, smiling at his hands folded serenely on the table, then gracing me with a piercing gaze. "Where do you fall, Detective? You weren't there last night for work."

I didn't answer right away. I wasn't sure I knew what the answer was, but I felt compelled to give him something. Jesus, he smiles at you and you're putty. Just twenty minutes ago, you thought he didn't want to see you again. I took another drink of tea, pondering the question. "Well, I don't know exactly. I've been there twice. It's fascinating. It's filled with people and situations I'm interested in knowing more about. And frankly, it's hot as hell."

Ben laughed heartily from deep in his chest and his dimples stood out. The longer we were away from his office, the more relaxed he became. Maybe discomfort of having me at his office was all it was. I smiled at his reaction.

"So I think we can cross you off the list of those disgusted by Collared's patrons," he smiled.

"Yes, cross me off that despicable list. What people do in the privacy of their own homes is their business as long as everyone consents. Who am I to look down on anyone?"

Ben sat back, a teasing expression on his face. "So I take it the crisis you were having last night has passed."

I felt my face heat, clearing my throat as the waitress set our plates in front of us. When she left, I spoke low and carefully, trying the words on as I voiced them. "Today was the first day in a long time I woke up feeling comfortable in my own skin."

His eyes danced a little, his lips turning up in a wry smile. "First day I woke up comfortable in your skin, too," he chuckled. The heat in my face skyrocketed and I ducked my gaze. "How do you feel about things?" he asked, quietly, tone warm.

Digging into my sandwich, I stalled by taking a bite, chewing deliberately before swallowing. "Better than I expected." Except for the few minutes in your office. I still wondered if he'd been honest with me in the elevator, but it wasn't worth dwelling on. "It's almost a relief. The big question has been answered and I don't have to deny it anymore. I'm gay."

"Big revelation," he said. "Scary?"

"Not really. The scary part will be telling people I care about. But I'm not ready for that. First things first. I need a place to stay until I can get an apartment. I need to meet with a lawyer as soon as possible, and I need a new partner. One thing at a time."

"So tell me, Gavin. What will you do when you're not covering the logistics of divorce or working?"

Meeting his stare, eyes roaming his face to take in his features and that indescribable openness he once again wore with such confidence, I nearly couldn't speak. With a small, hopeful smile, I said, "Well, I'd like to see you again."

"I'd like that, too," he replied.

The bright May sunshine punctuated the importance of the moment, searing it into my memory. Such a significant thing, I knew I'd carry it with me forever, whatever my future held. Not knowing what to say that wouldn't ruin the mood, I silently resumed eating. When Ben's shoe brushed mine beneath the table, I turned my foot into the contact and kept it there for the rest of our meal.

Leaving Ben to return to his office after lunch, I called one of the lawyers with whom I dealt on a regular basis, asking for a recommendation for a good divorce advocate. All the lawyers I knew were on the criminal side of the law and didn't handle civil matters. Name in hand, I set up an appointment with an attorney named Marcia Whitlock, cursing when the only time available was the very day and time I'd scheduled to talk to Damon Lane. I booked it, since the rest of her week was full and I wanted to get this done as quickly and quietly as possible. Lane would have to wait, a prospect he seemed fine with when I called to cancel.

The crime lab, Cole's fiefdom, wasn't far from Ben's office, and I had time before my appointment, so I swung my unmarked car into the parking lot and went on a search. I found him at his lab table, face buried in a microscope.

"Hey, Cole." He held up a finger, silently asking me to wait a moment while he made a note about his slide before turning his stool around to face me.

"Still alive, I see," he said, somehow giving me a smile that was both wry and sympathetic. "If Victoria bit your head off, you must have a hell of a plastic surgeon."

"About that," I said, looking around at how crowded the lab was. "Is there somewhere more private we can talk?"

"Sure," he answered, leading me to his office and shutting the door. "Everything all right?"

"I left her," I said without preamble, walking around the room, eyeing the jars on his shelves with preserved specimens of animal parts. I knew the eyeball was a cow's. There was a pig heart and a whole fetal pig. Some other things I tried not to look at too closely. Cole's office was grotesque in a nerdy science way, and it suited him but gave me the willies. Cole pursed his lips, then nodded sagely.

"I didn't want to say anything, man, but it always bugged me the way she harped on you. Hell, it never seemed like she was satisfied. But I'm sorry. Had to have been bad for you to decide to quit her. You never quit anything."

"She was plenty satisfied while fucking Trent." No sense beating around the bush.

"No shit?" Cole gave a low whistle. "Wow. How'd you find out? Sorry, if you don't want to talk about it—" he said quickly.

I waved him off. "I walked in on them yesterday afternoon." Had it really only been yesterday afternoon? So much had changed since then.

For a moment, Cole simply watched me, reading my stiff posture and my closed expression. I wasn't intentionally being standoffish. I just knew too many questions would put me into territory I wasn't ready to discuss. I also knew he'd be misreading my discomfort as having to do with Victoria. It was an assumption I let him make.

"So you left. What about Trent?"

I shook my head, sitting in the chair in front of Cole's desk and meeting his eyes wearily. Suddenly, I was tired of the whole thing. Better to just spell out exactly why I was here.

"I asked my sergeant to transfer him. Trent's already been moved out of Second precinct. I get a new partner. I have an appointment this afternoon with a lawyer to draw up divorce papers, and I already know I'm not fighting for the house or anything in it. I packed up everything I need and the few keepsakes I want."

Cole's face scrunched up. "Where'd you go last night?"

I'd known the question was coming, but I still opened and shut my mouth a few times like a gaping fish. I can spot a lie pretty well, but I suck at telling them unless the lies were part of an elaborate ruse where I could shroud them in a series of truths, like my marriage. My speech becomes fractured and halting.

"I ended up staying with a friend from work." Not a lie and not any more information than Cole needed. I was relieved when he moved on.

"So where are you going tonight?"

I shrugged. "I could get a hotel room until I find an apartment, but I was hoping I could crash with you for a while. I have the money to get my own place, just not the time to search. The longer I stay at a hotel, the quicker my savings diminishes. I can't stomach the idea of going to Mom and Dad's or Mason's, and Shawn and Chrissy would be great, except that Shawn would try to dig into what Trent did."

Cole's eyebrows went up again. "Should he be digging into what Trent did?"

I shook my head. "Worst they can get him for is misconduct, and even that's shaky because the misconduct wasn't on a case. Poor judgment isn't against the law. I don't want to be his partner anymore, but I don't want to ruin his career."

"Trent ruined his career when he pulled such a bonehead move,"

Cole corrected me. "Of course you can stay with me, as long as you need to. I'll have a key made this afternoon. You going to be okay?"

I gave him my most convincing smile. "Believe it or not, I'm relieved. I don't have to live under Victoria's thumb anymore."

"I hear that. Why do you think I never have a girlfriend for more than a few months? When they start getting bossy, I run away."

I laughed at that. Cole wasn't a womanizer, just a serial monogamist. Dating was something of a sport for him, and he was first string. Given his friendly manner, handsome features and big smile, and what Victoria had always called his schoolboy charm, Cole didn't have any trouble attracting women. It was finding one who could put up with his crazy hours and his independent streak that was the trick. The minute they tried to box Cole in, they'd find themselves unceremoniously dumped. In a way, I admired his backbone. He always stayed true to himself. Victoria had complained it was a selfish way to live, that relationships inherently worked with some compromise and he was deluding himself if he thought he'd find someone who would take him as he was. It made my skin crawl now to remember the times when she said she was glad I wasn't like Cole, that I understood the value of putting someone else first. Ironic, considering she put herself first, too.

"What about Mom and Dad? What do you plan to tell them?"

I shrugged. "The truth. She cheated. They can't blame me for leaving. Though I think I'll leave Trent out of it. Dad's probably going to find out anyway, since he keeps tabs on all of us and the rumors will eventually reach him."

"Yeah," Cole replied, rubbing his face with his hands. "Worse than an old woman when it comes to gossip." He chuckled. "Do you need anything else?"

"No. A new partner, but that's Talcott's doing."

"Wanna get a drink tonight?"

"Not really. I have a few more reports to go over for the Kaiser case and after the lawyer's this afternoon, I'll be at my desk. When you get home, call me. I really just want to crash."

"Okay, bro," Cole said, standing to see me out. Before he opened the door, he pulled me into a brotherly hug. "I'm sorry about Victoria."

"I am, too," I said, hugging him back. But I wasn't sorry it was over. I was sorry it had ever been. Cole gave me a look that said he might have picked up on the distinction, but if he did, he kept it to himself.

I was halfway down the hall when I remembered the SD card in my pocket from George Kaiser's autopsy. I returned to find Cole resuming his post at his microscope, and with a quick notation in the evidence transfer log, I was on my way out the door.

The rest of the afternoon went smoothly. Marcia Whitlock was a gruff, efficient woman with a no-nonsense attitude. She didn't give me any false sympathy, nor did she question my reasoning. She did, however, dig into my relationship with my wife, trying to determine if there was anything Victoria could use to weaken my position in the proceedings. Given the picture on my phone, there was little Victoria could do to draw out the process. Marcia suggested I fight for more of the marital assets, advising me to insist on selling the house and splitting the proceeds instead of simply walking away from everything. I didn't have the energy and while a part of me wanted to put Victoria out in the way I was, I knew a bitter battle for assets would only prolong the transition. Other than half my pension, Victoria could have the rest. Against her better judgment, Marcia agreed to draw up papers simply requesting my name be removed from all financial obligations to the house and other loans. She suggested I take care of my banking immediately, switching my direct deposited paychecks to an account only in my name and freezing the content of our joint savings account so the courts could divide it fairly. She also made me aware that mediation, should Victoria agree, could be complete in weeks instead of months. I quickly agreed.

On the way back to the station, I took the first part of her advice and opened a new account. Ignoring the second part, I withdrew less than half from the joint savings, what I required to get and furnish a new apartment, and left the rest for Victoria, removing my name from the account. From that point on, there was no reason for me to be in contact with my wife until mediation could be scheduled. The remainder of my day was spent poring over forensics reports and ignoring the stares from other detectives and officers. By the time Cole called to tell me he had my key, I was itching to leave. I didn't particularly care for that bug under a magnifying glass feeling. After a quick dinner of pizza and beer, I went to bed. My last thought before oblivion was of Ben, and of what, if anything, I should tell my brother.

CHAPTER SEVEN

THE NEXT two days, I buried myself in paperwork, both personal and work related. I had to fill out a formal request for Trent's transfer and detail why I was asking for it. The forensics reports told me plenty of the how of George Kaiser's death, but didn't point much to the who. Toxicology came back that he'd been roofied, and an inventory listing of the contents of his house showed two of his drinking glasses were missing. Whoever the killer was, he'd left a trace of himself on that glass and in taking both of them, he'd moved to prevent us from finding his method of subduing Kaiser or his identity.

My parents called me shortly after I arrived at Cole's on my second night at his place, asking if they could do anything and offering me my old room. I shuddered at the thought of my mother babying me and my dad asking me constantly about work. I assured them I was comfortable at Cole's and that I'd just as soon get my own place quickly and without putting anyone else out.

"You're still coming for Sunday brunch, right?" my mother asked, a hint of warning in her voice.

Because the last one went so swimmingly, I thought, biting my tongue. "Actually, I'm not up for it, if you don't mind." I surprised myself with the firmness of my voice, and Ma heard it, releasing a sigh but not arguing.

"We love you, Gavin. I'm sorry you're going through this, but you've got family and no matter what, we're here for you." There was comfort in her words, but I couldn't help wondering how deeply it would go if they knew about Ben.

Speaking of Ben, I felt like I was sneaking around to see him so Cole wouldn't find out. We'd had one more lunch date that ended up back at his place and I'd stopped by his office the previous evening just to say hi when he was working late. Unlike the cool treatment he'd dished out the first time I was at his office, he'd been a completely different person. He'd ended up bending me over his desk and I'd watched our reflection in the darkened windows as he fucked me. I was flying high, but I couldn't show anything in front of my brother when I came in late. I'd played it off like I'd stopped for a drink after work, and Cole had given me a sympathetic look, telling me he'd keep me company next time. I'd grunted noncommittally and hurried into the shower to cut off any further discussion. Part of me felt like an asshole for lying, but I had been through enough in the last few days and wasn't ready to face that demon, no matter how supportive Cole was.

I had my finger on the handset of my desk phone, and I was considering seeing if Ben was free for lunch again when it rang. Talcott's extension flashed on the caller ID and I immediately answered, hoping for some kind of distraction from the monotony of more forensics with dead ends and my brain playing an endless loop of should I's about calling Ben.

"DeGrassi,"

"Come to my office," Talcott said. "Bring the Kaiser file."

Immediately, I wondered if he was taking me off the case as some sort of backhanded punishment for getting his buddy Trent banished. Even as I gathered the papers and shuffled them into the accordion file they'd grown into, I knew that was ridiculous. I'd been to the scene, seen the body in its original position, had talked to a multitude of witnesses already, and taking his lead investigator off a case to give it to someone else who only had photos to go on wasn't an intelligent move. Talcott was smarter than that.

I rapped on his door and stuck my head in. He waved me to a chair, and it was only when I entered his office that I saw the other chair was occupied. A beautiful woman perched on the edge of the seat and turned to look at me, her gray-blue eyes bright and her blond hair pulled back from her face. She was striking, with high cheekbones and a wide mouth. If I were the least bit interested in women, I'd have been panting for her.

"Gavin, this is your new partner, Myah Hayes. Hayes, Gavin DeGrassi."

She reached out a hand, her long, slender fingers cool and strong as she gave me a firm handshake. With a professional nod, she returned her attention to Sergeant Talcott.

"DeGrassi's been assigned a particularly brutal homicide, something we're keeping as far away from the media as possible. The sensational nature of the crime would make it an instant buffet of horror for the vultures, er, reporters who dog our steps. DeGrassi has the file," Talcott pointed to the papers in my hand, which I obediently passed to Detective Hayes. "I'd suggest, DeGrassi, that you go over the highlights with her and leave her with the rest so she can get caught up. I'll leave you to it."

It was clearly a dismissal, and that was all the introduction Talcott planned to make between me and my new partner. We both stood and exited his office, me stepping aside to let her precede me through the door. She carried herself stiffly, but even though her clothes were nondescript and a little bland, I could tell with her height and build, she'd have been at home as a model at a photo shoot. It was quite obvious the rest of the guys in the pit thought so, too, as I showed Hayes to her desk. There was utter silence and every set of male eyes in the room watched her sit primly at Trent's old desk.

"I assume administration has set you up with all your logins and passwords, but if there's anything you're not able to access, let me know and I can either pull it for you or talk to someone about getting your access bumped to the front of the line."

She stared at me as though I had something stuck in my teeth, then nodded wordlessly, pulling out drawers and assessing the state of her new space. "Where would I find office supplies?" she asked, her voice just as buttery as one would expect from such a beautiful face. She was, however, becoming more imposing as the minutes wore on and her demeanor didn't warm in the slightest. I tried to give her the benefit of the doubt, thinking perhaps she was shy or nervous about being in a new office with a bunch of hot-blooded men she didn't know. But images of Victoria's cool stature played through my head, and I gritted my teeth against them. God help me if Hayes turned out to be a carbon copy of my wife.

I gestured for her to follow me to the supply closet, and as we left the pit, I heard a few low whistles and catcalls. Beside me, Hayes stiffened. I rolled my eyes, muttering, "Neanderthals," almost loud enough for them to hear. Hayes cleared her throat, and when I opened the door to the miniscule room with a couple cabinets holding supplies, she squeezed past me into the tight space, her shoulders tense and her face unreadable.

I stepped well out of her way, pointing out everything she might need. "Make sure you grab a stapler if there is one, and lock it in your desk when you're away. They're like that Milton guy from Office Space with staplers. Otherwise, everything else you have on your desk is safe." There might have been a hint of softening in her eyes when she turned back to me and left the closet, her arms laden with pens, paper, and a valuable, if beat-up stapler.

"Thanks," she said, ignoring the stares as we reentered the main room. Dumping her supplies in a desk drawer, she turned to the file, extracting reports and photos of the scene. I held up a hand, palm out.

"Why don't we go grab a coffee and I can give you an overview of the evidence so far?" She appraised me, then nodded, slipping her suit jacket off the back of her chair. Several of the others watched as she donned it, and I rolled my eyes. I really couldn't get a read on her, but even I knew the tongues hanging out had to annoy, at least at work. It'd be better to get her away from that. Maybe she'd relax.

We headed to a nearby greasy spoon which had decent coffee where the staff would leave us alone if we spread out in one of their booths. They were used to cops and only asked that any particularly gruesome crime scene photos be well covered so their other diners weren't driven away. As we got comfortable in a booth, a waitress intent on grinding her gum into submission came to take our orders. I got a plain bagel with vanilla cream cheese and coffee, and Hayes ordered a bowl of granola and a cappuccino.

"Okay, so here's the story," I began, laying out the evidence so far, handing her reports and summarizing their contents. I didn't even bother to pull out the photos, offering to take her to the victim's house for that so she could see the room, and the pictures would fill in the gaps more thoroughly than my descriptions could. After a few minutes, she interrupted me.

"Why did you request a new partner?"

She was blunt, but somehow, despite her stiffly set jaw and steely eyes, I didn't get the impression she was judging me. I waited a beat before answering, deciding how much to explain, though I knew it was fruitless to hold anything back. The rumors had already spread like wildfire, and while the other detectives at Second were sympathetic to me, I had also noticed a few hushed conversations that died down in my presence and some surreptitious sour looks pointed my way.

"My old partner had a proclivity for the ladies and I got sick of it. I would have ignored it, but he picked one lady in particular I refused to overlook." My bagel arrived and I didn't look at Hayes as I spread the cream cheese carefully. Would she pry? Would she drop it since it was obvious I didn't relish the topic? I quickly had my answer and tried not to be annoyed.

"Sleeping his way to the top by getting in the good graces of some captain's wife?" She sipped her coffee, leaning her elbows on the table. I studied her for a moment, trying to see if she was the type to buy into gossip and was digging, or if she genuinely didn't know. If she were a gossip, she'd have found any number of ready mouths to fill her in. But she was asking me. I supposed, in a backhanded way, I should have been glad she was as direct as she appeared instead of listening to the shit around the pit.

"Not exactly. He picked my wife. Soon to be ex." That stopped her and the wicked gleam in her eyes softened. "Some of the assholes back at the station have made it clear I should have just looked the other way, but if I couldn't trust him around her, why should I trust him to have my back in a gun fight?"

"God, I hate that honor code shit. Why aren't they up in his face about betraying you?"

I shrugged. "Most of them have been understanding. It's just a few jackasses who've probably shtupped their partner's wives, too. It's not like our profession inspires solid marriages. Mine's just another casualty." I waved my hand to dismiss the subject. I was sick of talking about Victoria, and she was all anyone had asked about in recent days. "So where are you from, Hayes?" New subject, thank you very much.

Her eyes narrowed slightly, but she didn't snap at me that it wasn't my business. Tit for tat, since I'd been honest with her. "Chicago. I couldn't stand all the glad-handing and back-scratching that went on up there, and I decided a change of scenery was in order."

Interesting. Had she been caught up in some kind of scandal that hadn't worked in her favor? Was being transferred to the most dangerous city in America some kind of punishment for her? Was she running? God, I'm getting as bad as my dad.

"Husband?" I asked. "Family?"

"Nope," she answered quickly. "Like you said, this job doesn't foster stable relationships."

We turned back to the paperwork and spent the rest of the morning going over the details. I showed her around the crime scene and she took her time, walking the perimeter of the room and getting her bearings from the pictures. After a few moments, she laid the photos around George's playroom in approximation of where the evidence had been found. We spent the better part of the afternoon discussing motives, hunches, details from witness statements. She was shrewd, coming up with much the same information I'd discussed with Ben in regards to the profile he was building. She surprised me by bringing up the one detail I was having difficulty grasping about Ben's assessment.

"I don't think they're fully immersed," she said thoughtfully, crossing her arms over her chest as though she were cold.

"Why not?" I asked.

"Because it disgusts him," she answered. "Why humiliate the vic with his own implements if not to prove a point about how deviant it is?"

"Why wasn't the killer just showing he could dominate a Dom? Establishing his power?"

"Then why the marks around the tears?" she pointed out. "Why draw attention to that specific weakness?"

"Hell, you string me up on a cross, rape me brutally and whip me until my skin is in tatters, and I'd cry," I said somewhat waspishly at her judgment of how Kaiser handled his death. People faced their own demise in any number of ways. Who's to say how we'd react unless put in the exact same situation?

"I'm not saying Kaiser was weak. I'm saying the killer pointed out his tears as weak. That's the one thing that changes the game. That's the point of the murder, to show how the killer was 'better' than the vic." She made air quotes, surveying the room, her face bland. Then she clucked her tongue. "What a horrible way to go. Bastardizing something he took pleasure in and making it into a statement."

Her words softened my harsh reaction. Studying her profile, I considered her. Efficient and sharp, Hayes was more than a pretty face, and her demeanor in the office this morning shifted into place. Based on the way she'd been objectified by the good ol' boys, too many people in our male-dominated profession didn't see past her beauty to the value within, the smarts that had gotten her the detective's shield. I imagined the guys back at the station joking about how she'd slept her way into the job, or wondering if she would just smile the criminals into confessing. No wonder she was standoffish.

As we left the scene, I saw the overcast sky had grown ominous, threatening a storm, the warm May air whipping trash along the gutters in small tornadoes. I hated driving in rain. St. Louis drivers were of two varieties during a storm: they behaved as if it were icy and caused backups, or they ignored the wet roads altogether, barreling through stop signs and intersections and wreaking havoc resulting in yet more backups. I decided to try and catch Lane at his house in hopes of avoiding the worst of the traffic.

"Hey," she said, breaking the silence. "You wouldn't happen to know of a good realtor, would you? Or possibly recommend a neighborhood? There's only so much crime stats can tell you, and I don't want to live in a hotel forever."

I chuckled, noting the similarity of our situations. "I'm in the market myself, as it were. The neighborhood kind of depends on what you're looking for. If you want safe and suburban, Kirkwood or Ballwin would be a good bet, and parts of Creve Coeur. The further south you go, the older the homes get, but the higher the crime is, too. If you get close to the eastern county line, you're looking at a mix of old, abandoned houses interspersed with refurbished ones. There's a big revitalization push that's fanning outward from downtown. For a college area with an eclectic mix of artists and students, you should look around the Loop or Central West End. There are some upscale places in that area, too, but again, it's being refurbed, so there are still security concerns. The closer you get to the airport, the more industrial it is, and the housing is affordable, but it's not exactly visually appealing. The further west you go, the newer it is, but it's also kind of cookie-cutter. If you give me addresses when you come across them, I can give you a better idea."

"You're not what I expected," she blurted. I looked at her briefly before returning my attention to the road.

"Oh?"

"Not at all. Every male partner I've had has tried to get my phone number within the first five minutes. They'd spend the whole time looking at my ass when they should have been looking at evidence or talking to witnesses. I had to shove my opinion on cases down their throats for them to even hear me, and when the others at the station said shit like they did this morning, my old partners just laughed instead of calling them 'Neanderthals.' If I'd asked any of them for house hunting advice, they'd have offered to have me move in with them. You're different."

"Yeah," I agreed quietly, "I am." And the other guys would have my head if they knew why.

"Why is that?" Again, her straightforward attitude struck me. I could tell where I stood with her, and after pussyfooting around Victoria for so many years, it was refreshing.

I took a deep breath. "I try not to judge people before I get to know them. I don't like playing mind games, though I do it with witnesses or suspects when necessary. But you're not on the wrong side of an interrogation table, so I'm just seeing what you're like and how you treat people before making up my mind. I can already tell you're sharp and honest, which I appreciate. I have a feeling, if I fuck up, you won't mind putting me in my place."

She smiled, a genuine one that transformed her face from beautiful to transcendent. "I think I might end up liking you, Gavin

DeGrassi."

"Yeah, well, don't read too much into it," I joked. "I'm not as awesome as you think I am."

She snorted, relaxing back into the seat. After a brief silence, she said quietly, "Thank you."

"For what?" I asked, confused.

"For seeing me as more than a pretty face and a pair of tits."

If she hadn't sounded so relieved, so grateful, I would have made another joke. As it was, I could tell she was dead serious. "You're proving that all on your own."

"So where to now?" she asked, studying another of the photos from the file she'd stashed between her feet on the floorboards.

"Witness questioning. It's overdue, but things keep getting in the way," I answered, taking the on-ramp to I-170 and heading south.

"Who's the witness?"

"Damon Lane. Makes BDSM implements. He was one of the last people to talk to George before he left Collared."

Hayes nodded, watching the billboards sail by. Before long, we reached Lane's house. The ominous clouds had cooled the air, portending a deluge with a lightning show to accompany it. The wind picked up and whipped the tree in the front yard as we approached the door, as if railing against our presence.

Lane answered, wiping his hands on a dishtowel. I flashed my shield and we introduced ourselves in turn.

"May we come in?" Hayes asked, showing her straight, perfect teeth.

"Sure. I hope you don't mind if I continue making dinner. I don't want it to burn," Lane said, pushing open the screen and stepping aside to let us in. We followed him through the living room of a modest ranch house, the interior unremarkable but comfortable. It looked lived in, and there were pictures scattered along the walls depicting a teenager progressing into a young man, first shown with Lane and a handsome woman, and later with just Lane. School photos segued into graduation photos, then candid shots like one of the man holding a fish easily as long as his arm and wearing a triumphant smile.

"Your son?" I asked, indicating the photos.

"Yes, that's Jeff."

"Handsome kid," Hayes commented.

"I thought so, but I'm biased," Lane said, gesturing for us to follow him.

Thought? Past tense? I wondered what happened to his son, but it wasn't relevant, so I kept quiet. We sat at a table in the eat-in kitchen while he busied himself at the stove and sliced one of the biggest tomatoes I'd ever seen on the bar that separated the table from the functional part of the room.

"You were at Collared last Friday night," I began, studying his profile. There was a niggle in the back of my mind, and I knew I'd seen him before, though I couldn't place him. It had to have been at the club, because if I'd run into him elsewhere I wouldn't remember. His features only stood out insofar as they were completely ordinary. Average height and build, brown hair and eyes, straight nose and somewhat squared off jawline sporting a neat beard trimmed close to the skin.

"I was. I spend a few nights there a week. Trying to meet people, drum up business. I make equipment for the lifestyle." He deftly turned a few pieces of frying bacon over, and then laid out the makings for a couple BLT sandwiches. "Are you hungry?" he asked. "I can throw on some more bacon."

"No thank you," I answered, wanting to stick to the questions. "You see or speak to George Kaiser that night?"

Lane leaned on the counter on his elbows, brow furrowed. "Yeah, I did. Upstairs in one of the semi-privates. He was asking me about a custom flogger. Said the one he had was too wide in the lashes, that he wanted something lighter. He'd heard I was good at floggers so he asked if he could meet with me to discuss it. Brought up a couple other items of interest, too."

"Like what?"

Lane straightened, shrugged. "He wanted a custom fitted mask and a new set of restraints."

"Was that all you spoke to him about?"

"The restraints and mask were straightforward, so we mostly spoke about the flogger and its merits versus a riding crop, which is much lighter. George said he preferred the effect a flogger has on skin, but liked the sound of the crop better. Said it gives a more satisfying thwack and asked me if I could make a flogger that sounded like a crop. I remember laughing. I'd never heard it described that way, but he's right. That's exactly the sound." He seemed to catch himself. "Well, he was right."

"So you know he's dead," Hayes chimed in, her voice steady, as if she were asking Lane if he knew the time.

"Yeah, I'd say nearly everyone at the club knows by now. I heard about it when I went to Collared on Sunday. Jared, the owner, told me."

Sunday. The night I was there and left with Ben. Suddenly it clicked. He'd been sitting at the bar while I'd had my beers, watching me. He'd paid me no mind after I'd acknowledged him, so it was just a coincidence I'd even caught his eye. Well, Ben had said the community was its own small world. For a moment, I sat frozen, afraid Lane would mention my presence at the bar that night, but I'd obviously been there on my own time since I'd been drinking and had left with a known Dom. I sincerely didn't want to have that conversation with my new partner on our very first day working together.

"How did you know George?" Hayes asked, taking a couple notes as she talked, unknowingly drawing the conversation out of dangerous territory.

"I saw him come and go, either at the clubs or at munches and cons. He was well involved, so he was familiar to me, though I'd only spoken with him once or twice before." Lane flipped the bacon out of the pan and onto his sandwiches, bringing them to the table with a can of soda. He didn't begin to eat, though. Polite.

"So he wanted you to make him some equipment. Was that all you talked with him about?" I asked, getting back on track.

"We set up a time for me to swing by his house, see his dungeon and current stock of toys, find out what it was he didn't like about them, and negotiate over my making him new equipment. I was supposed to meet him Sunday evening, actually, but he never showed. I asked Jared if George had beat me there and left already and that's when he told me what happened. Shame. He seemed nice."

Lane sounded genuine, though slightly detached. It could have been because he didn't know George that well. Everyone who'd spoken of Kaiser, who'd had contact with him, had nothing but good things to say.

"What was your impression of him?" Hayes asked.

"It seemed like he knew what he was doing. I know his reputation was solid, that he treated his subs well. Even the ones who were no longer with him had a high opinion of him."

"Do you know of anyone he played with, even once, who might have had a grudge against him?"

Lane shook his head. "No, I hadn't heard anything like that. You think one of them did this?"

"We're following all possibilities," I replied vaguely.

"You should talk to Jared Nunn. I was getting ready to leave Friday night and saw him and George arguing. Frankly, I've never seen Nunn so mad."

"Do you know what they argued about?" Hayes asked carefully.

"Not really. Club music drowned them out. I did hear Lacey's name, though."

"What time was this?"

"Right before close. George had come downstairs for one last drink and Jared was leaning across the bar right in his face. Said something about George having more respect."

"Respect for what?"

"Didn't hear that part," Lane answered. "All I heard was Jared say someone should remind George what humiliation felt like. After that, I left." He was silent for a moment while Hayes wrote in her notebook. When he spoke next, it was with unmistakable curiosity. "Is it true he was killed with his own toys?"

I narrowed my eyes. "Where did you hear that?" Lane should not have known that.

"I overheard Matt Kinney talking," he answered. I didn't remembered seeing Kinney at the club Sunday, but once Ben had arrived, I'd had a different focus. It was possible Kinney had heard that tidbit of info from Mrs. Kaiser. "If it's true, that's just cold," Lane said, shaking his head ruefully, as if we'd confirmed his query. "Ultimate slap in the face."

I felt the expression fall from my features, poker face exerting itself. "How so?"

"Well, a Dom's all about control, right? They usually have an arsenal of accessories to help them maintain that control. Taking those tools and using them against the Dom, that's like using a carving knife to stab the butcher, or a cop's own gun to shoot him."

We stared at him hard for a moment, but he seemed oblivious, finally biting into his sandwich. Hayes finally spoke. "Have you heard anyone talking about such a thing? Maybe boasting about dominating the Dom?"

"No, I haven't. Whoever it is would be pretty stupid to say anything like that, at least in public, right?" Lane asked, looking back and forth between us. He seemed uncomfortable for a moment, perhaps realizing how he sounded. "Especially considering how close everyone is, how much we talk. Wouldn't take long to figure out who did it."

Hayes gave him another brilliant smile, to which Lane didn't know how to respond. She was good at unbalancing witnesses, I'd give her that.

"Where did you go after you left Collared?" she asked.

He took a swig from his soda to wash down the bite he'd just taken. "I came home." He shifted in his chair, eyes tracking both of us to gauge our reactions. "I stopped for a burger on the way, but it was late. I ate and went to bed."

"Anyone see you?" I asked, making a note. "Where'd you get the burger?"

Lane stood, leaning over the counter to a pile of papers near his phone. He extracted a checkbook from the mess and scrawled something on a sticky note, then passed Hayes a slip of paper. "This is my receipt. Does it have a time stamp?"

Hayes studied it. "Sure does," she smiled brightly, passing it to me. I looked it over. It was a drive-thru about halfway between the club and Lane's house. I'd have to check the distance to Kaiser's. It didn't rule him out since it was just before Kaiser's attack and not during, but it showed he was honest, even with the chance of looking suspicious. Hayes kept her smile and stood, sliding a business card across the table. "If you hear or think of anything else, you'll be certain to let us know?"

"Oh sure," Lane agreed quickly. "Absolutely. I'd hate for this to happen again. I'd like to keep my clients, if it's all the same. May sound selfish, but I've got a business to think about."

I stood, giving Lane a placating smile. "We have no reason to believe there will be a repeat, Mr. Lane. Your business should be safe. Thank you for your time."

He saw us to the door. "I hope you find the guy."

Hayes turned back to him on the stoop, her eyes curious. "What makes you think it's a male perp, Mr. Lane?"

He waved a hand dismissively. "Oh, I don't know for sure. Some of them women Dommes are tougher than nails. Who knows? I just hope you catch whoever did this. For Mr. Kaiser's sake. He deserves justice."

"That he does, Mr. Lane," I replied. A lightning bolt flashed brightly through the angry clouds, and the first fat drops of the threatened rain slapped the ground. Hayes and I hurried to the car as Lane retreated into the safety of his house.

"There's something about that guy," Hayes muttered, shutting her door just as the drops went from sporadic to soaking, pounding the roof of the car. "Smarmy."

I gave a noncommittal hum as I pulled out onto the road, the wipers thumping in a losing battle with the downpour.

"You don't think so?" she asked, turning slightly in her seat to face me. "A guy's dead and he's worried about his business? Not to mention he has no alibi."

"A receipt for a fast food joint at three a.m. does not a killer create. And maybe he makes a good living doing what he does, but if people are too afraid to take on new subs for fear they'll be attacked, they'll stop playing."

"Oh, come on, DeGrassi! Since when do people interrupt their lives for anything so random as a killer on the loose? Hookers don't stop tricking; women don't stop flirting; men don't stop picking up one night stands. It's in people's nature to think they're invincible, that it'll always happen to someone else."

She had a point. We also had no reason to think there were more deaths on the horizon, so people would assume it was a one-off. I conceded the argument, concentrating more on driving than the conversation, and we fell into contemplative silence. I replayed Lane's answers and body language, but my instincts weren't screaming at me. His lack of an alibi made him suspicious, as did the fact that he was one of the last people to talk to Kaiser. But the man lived alone. A drive-thru receipt was as close to an alibi as he'd have, most likely. I'd keep digging, see if anything else tied him to the scene.

Sticking to side streets to avoid the inevitable snarls on the interstates, I finally relaxed about what would have happened if Lane had said something about my leaving Collared with Ben Sunday. He'd remained quiet, so there was no point in running "could haves" through my brain. Not to mention, the more I thought about it, the more difficult it would be to keep my thoughts from my face.

"Listen, I'm heading out for the night. You have a car at the station or do you need a ride to your hotel?" I asked. I didn't have any plans, and I knew Ben was tied up for the evening with one of his patients, so I had time to drop her wherever she needed. Ben normally didn't set appointments so late, but for this one he'd made an exception. All I knew was she was a single mother who couldn't take time off work, so Ben did his best to be accessible to her. Anything else about her fell under doctor-patient confidentiality. He had, however, made it clear I was free to catch up with him afterwards.

"Oh, my car's at the station. Here," she said, thrusting a business card in my hand. It was her old Chicago PD homicide card, the numbers scratched out to reflect her current contact information. She'd written her cell number on the back. "Call me if you think of anything."

When we reached the station, I provided her with my cell phone number for the same reason. "Just don't call me in the middle of the night unless it's an emergency. I don't wake up well between the hours of midnight and five a.m."

She laughed, and I marveled at how completely different she was compared to the woman I'd met in Talcott's office just that morning. Easy going, down to earth, and smart. I felt good about the new assignment, thinking for once, I could perhaps get along with my partner in more than just a professional capacity. Maybe I had the opportunity to make a friend. At least, until I told her my dirty little secret—if I told anyone at all.

§§§

THE TRILL of my cell phone jarred me out of a deep sleep and it took me a moment to get my bearings. Cole's apartment. His guest room. Middle of the night.

"DeGrassi," I grunted into the phone, not even checking caller ID because of the blur of sleep clinging to my vision.

"Out of bed, sleepy head," a woman's voice said. I couldn't place her and frowned.

"Huh?"

"I know you said not to wake you between midnight and five, but I didn't have a choice on this one." The voice, the words, it all began to make some sort of sense.

"Hayes?"

"Yeah." Her tone took on a serious cast. "You need to meet me in thirty." She rattled off an address close to the University of Missouri-St. Louis. "It's happened again," she said, business-like with an edge to her tone.

"What has?"

"Our killer. Another BDSM murder."

That got me moving like nothing else could. "I'll be there in twenty, and I'll bring my brother."

"Huh?" she asked, but I'd already begun to hang up, her voice tinny with the earpiece so far from my face.

Padding from my room to Cole's, I knocked on his door. When I got no response, I knocked again.

"Cole?" There was an indistinct sound behind his door and I heard a stumble, then a curse. He cracked the door a smidge as though he didn't want me to see his pigsty of a room, not that I cared.

"What?" he asked softly.

"Get dressed and get your gear. We've got work to do."

He rubbed his eyes and squinted at me. "Work? What happened?"

"Another BDSM murder. Goddammit." The more alert I became, the bigger the anger swelled. I hadn't solved George's murder in the first forty-eight, and the longer it went, the less likely I was to solve it. And it had cost someone else their life. "Get a move on," I snapped.

Cole shut the door in my face and I headed to the bathroom to jump into a lukewarm shower before getting dressed. I considered brewing coffee, but didn't want to wait for it. The clock read four-fifteen am. Too early for anywhere to be open to buy any, too. When I heard words spoken in his hallway as I sat on the couch to put on my shoes, I assumed Cole was talking to me.

"What?" I hadn't caught it.

"Nothing," he said, emerging into the living room in jeans and a T-shirt.

"Who were you talking to?" I asked, realizing why he hadn't wanted to open his bedroom door. I grinned at him, poking at his ribs. He slapped my hands away and pointedly ignored my question while he grabbed his kit from the front closet, and then we were out the door. A short debate about who would drive resolved with us going separately since we would end up heading to our respective offices afterward.

Pulling up to the scene, I gathered my wits and exited my car, approaching the tape blocking off the yard and driveway of a small but quaint cottage-style house with all the lights ablaze. Cole joined me, saying nothing. Hayes stood near the front porch, holding an enormous travel mug of coffee. When we neared her, she held it out to me.

"Newbie initiation, it's my job to handle the caffeine, right?" she asked, far too perky for the time and circumstances.

"I could kiss you," I muttered, taking the cup. It was good and strong.

"Please don't, or I'll never do it again. Sorry, I didn't bring another mug," she said to Cole. "I didn't know what Gavin meant when he said he was bringing his brother." She held out her hand. "Myah Hayes, new partner."

"Cole DeGrassi, CSI supervisor and the best little brother ever."

Hayes smiled, though it didn't reach her eyes. "Looks like you'll be busy tonight. Well, this morning."

"Who's the vic?" I asked, moving toward the front door.

"Seth Adams, thirty, lived here with his boyfriend Robert Weiss."

"Another homo," Cole said.

"So what? Show some respect," I snapped, glaring at him. His head whipped in my direction, surprise in his gaze.

"I didn't mean it like that. Just unusual, that's all."

"Not really," Hayes said, looking back and forth between us. "I've worked plenty of homicides where the victim was gay. None of them were quite like this, though. These don't have the impulsivity of a hate crime, but the fact that this is the second victim interested in same sex relationships isn't something to overlook either, Gavin."

"No, it's not. It could be part of the killer's statement. Just remember the vic was human first, gay second, okay Cole?" I admonished, though my tone was far less sharp.

"I've been through the same sensitivity training you have, Gavin. I know how to conduct myself. Sheesh," he muttered, pulling on protective booties and stepping inside. Hayes and I followed suit. I bit back a retort that if he'd known how to behave, that slur wouldn't have crossed his lips.

"You see the vic already?" I asked her, looking around at a tiny but tidy living room which opened to a quaint kitchen with a small dinette set. A distraught man with red-rimmed eyes and a fistful of tissues sat on the couch, staring at a point on the floor as if his life depended on not looking up from that spot. He could only be Robert Weiss.

"No, I waited for you. Got my info from the responding officer when I arrived." She jerked her chin at the officer seated a safe distance from Robert, looking uncomfortable and trapped.

"How'd he seem?"

"The boyfriend? I haven't talked to him yet."

"No, the responding officer."

"Oh," she said, tilting her head curiously. "All right. Sickened, but holding it together. He's pretty green, but swears he didn't touch anything."

That's not what I wanted to know. If the officer wasn't conscientious of the boyfriend's grief, I was prepared to relieve him of the responsibility of sitting with the man. But I didn't know how to frame my question without looking like an equal rights vigilante after snapping at my brother. Still, I gave it a shot.

"I mean, is it a good idea for him to be sitting with Weiss, or do I need to make him scarce?"

"Oh, no, he seemed fine. Awkward, but not deliberately rude." Again, she tilted her head, studying me. I didn't elaborate on my thinking, simply turning away to head deeper into the house. Could I be any more obvious?

We followed the sounds of activity through a short hallway off the living room and down a set of wooden steps to an unfinished basement. The victim was in the center, arms stretched impossibly as his body sagged from his own weight, his chin on his chest and his hair obscuring his face. His wrists were held in place by manacles affixed to an exposed ceiling beam by heavy chains. There was no St. Andrew's Cross this time. Between his feet was a four by four chunk of wood about three feet long, to which his ankles were shackled, keeping his legs spread. Like Kaiser, Adams was naked and bloody, but the lack of a cross made the blood slick across both his chest and back and tracking down his legs more obscene. Either that, or I took it more personally.

"Oh," Hayes breathed, her eyes absorbing every detail as revulsion marred her beautiful face. It was quickly replaced by compassion, and her gaze briefly flickered to the steps as though she could see the distraught man on the couch through the walls and floor. I put a hand on her shoulder, drawing her attention.

"You can do this, right?" I asked. I had no idea of her experience. She'd spoken of working homicide cases earlier, so she was no rookie. But these were a whole different ballgame. I had to know she could handle it.

She fixed her expression into determination. "I can do this. It's just different from the photos."

I gave her shoulder a squeeze. "If you need to take a few minutes, go ahead. But I need you."

Gathering her strength, she nodded, turning back to the scene and grabbing the pair of gloves Cole extended to her. I donned a pair as well, intent on a more active role this time around. I wanted to see what similarities we could find to Kaiser's murder. The scene techs were already cataloguing the equipment, testing a flogger, a crop, and a cane for traces of blood. Only the cane came up positive. I peered at the victim's back.

"These marks are different. Wider, longer, deeper, with the skin cut only at one end of the welt." There was bruising around the edges of the reddish, raised skin, so he'd been alive when he was beaten. There were, again, the small abrasions consistent with the marks left on George Kaiser's neck, thighs, and buttocks. Speaking to Cole, I called out. "Look for a pair of leather gloves with small metal tacks on the palm and fingers. Not very big, like the business end of a thumbtack."

After a moment's thorough search, Cole spoke up. "Not seeing anything like that here. You think the killer brought them?"

"I suppose it's possible," I replied, continuing to circle Adams's body. "I do know Kaiser owned a pair we never found. Perhaps the killer found them when he did George and liked them too much to leave them behind." The thought disgusted me. "One more thing. When you're looking around the rest of the house, see if all the glasses are accounted for."

The M.E. showed shortly after, confirming evidence of rape. Once he'd had Adams released from his bonds, I was able to see the markings around his wrists and ankles—raw, chafed skin with circlets of blood smears. He'd struggled—as much as he could, anyway. Laid flat on his back on the floor, it became painfully obvious we were dealing with the same killer. Tear tracks, outlined in marker, stood out on the victim's face. His final weakness, exploited, sent as a message to whomever the killer was speaking to with these murders.

There was, however, one notable difference in Adams's scene—on the wall were the words, "Not safe," written in the victim's blood.

"Who's not safe?" I wondered aloud as Hayes came to stand beside me while the techs took photos of the wall.

"Did he mean the boyfriend? Other Doms? This one in particular?"

I glanced down at her. "Don't know. I can promise you one thing," I said, resolve crackling under my skin like a static charge. "This killer isn't safe from me."

The evidence went into bags, onto digital cards in the form of photos, and the final and most important, into a body bag to be whisked away to the morgue. We tromped up the stairs and into the living room, where Robert Weiss still sat zombie-like on the couch. The officer who'd been with him was no longer there, but posted at the door. We sent him to question neighbors as the sun crested the horizon and people rose for their work days. I hung back a little as Hayes sat in the chair next to the couch, her knee almost touching Robert's.

"How are you holding up?" she asked gently. "Can you answer some questions?"

Robert gave a nearly imperceptible nod, his eyes ever fixed in the middle distance.

"What time did you get home?" she asked, silently gesturing to me to write notes so she could concentrate on the questions.

"Around three. I'd gone out with friends to a club. My friend Kyla is moving, so a group of us went to that male strip club on the east side of the river, Boxers and Briefs, to show her one last good time. We all took Friday off work so we could be out late. I got home and Seth wasn't in bed. That's not all that weird, since he has insomnia. A lot of times, he'll get up and read or surf the web. But he wasn't on the computer or anywhere else. Last place I looked was the dungeon and-" His voice caught and a sob broke free before he tried to stifle it with a fist to his lips, his tears flowing freely.

"Do you know if Seth had plans to meet anyone tonight?" Hayes asked gently. "A friend or coworker or someone in the lifestyle?"

Robert looked at her, misery etching his face. "He said nothing to me about any plans. We always know where the other one is. If he'd had plans, I'd have known."

Something from speaking to Mrs. Kaiser struck me, about her and George having an open relationship before their divorce. Keeping my tone even, I asked, "What was the nature of your relationship with Seth?"

Robert's puffy eyes narrowed slightly, but he answered with more weariness than defensiveness. "We loved each other. We lived together. If same sex marriage were legal in Missouri, we'd have been first in line at the courthouse. He's—" his voice hitched, and he tried again. "He was my Dom."

"Was there an agreement between you to see other people?" I said, trying to take as much sting out of the words as possible.

"No!" Robert shouted before checking his tone. "No, nothing like that. We had a clause in our contract that we could bring another man to our bed, but we always talked about it first and chose the third guy together. Never once have we expanded that agreement to an open relationship. I didn't want anyone except Seth, but occasionally, he wanted to spice things up. We never picked up another sub because that's who I am—was to him. The threesomes were always a one-off, just a sheet romp and then Seth would be more into me than ever afterwards. I wasn't a fan of it, but I also understood."

"Understood what, Robert?" Hayes' voice soothed his ruffled feathers.

"That he loved me, but he found others attractive sometimes. If I'd denied him that, there was a chance he'd resent it, or would find himself trapped with me when we got older. I figured the same thing would happen to me at some point, too. No one can be together for the rest of their lives without at least fantasizing about other people. This way, it was with my participation and consent. He had no need to hide. Sort of like if you give a kid candy when they're young, they grow up thinking it's no big deal, but if you restrict it, when they get older, they become addicted to it. I tolerated the other guys because I loved Seth and it was what he needed. I even enjoyed it some of the time, when I got my jealousy in check."

"Can we get the names of some of the men you and Seth were with?" I asked, making notes in my pad.

"Honestly, I don't remember more than the first one. It wasn't like it happened often. Last one was more than a year ago," Robert said. "But I'll see what I can come up with."

"Is there anyone else you can think of who might've had something against Seth? Someone he'd previously played with who held a grudge or had some residual feelings?"

Robert shook his head. "The only one I can think of wasn't one of Seth's subs but his brother Steve. He always said Seth's lifestyle was sickening and he didn't want anything to do with us. They haven't spoken in years."

I took down Steve's name regardless, knowing that next of kin would need to be notified, and even if the chance was slim that Steve had something to do with this, his involvement or lack thereof had to be verified.

"How long were you and Seth together?" Hayes asked.

"Five years. Lived together for the last three."

"What were the places you frequented most in your off time?"

He rattled off the names of a couple restaurants, a sports bar not far from their house, and two leather clubs, including Collared. The other one, Gigi's Tool Box, I hadn't heard of before. We spent some time getting a feel for what Seth was like, the places he went, friends who might know if he'd seen someone the night he died.

As Hayes' questions began to die down, Cole slipped up from the basement and scuttled to the front door, cigarette in his mouth before he'd even exited the house. He had the courtesy to wait until he was outside to light up, but it was a near thing. I knew he'd be conscientious of his butt, but usually, he refrained from smoking while working so the temptation to just flick the butt wasn't a problem. This one must've gotten to him.

"I'll be outside, too," Hayes said, looking back and forth between me and Robert. Something passed over her features, but I didn't know her well enough to understand what it was. Perhaps she couldn't handle being in that house anymore and was as eager for fresh air as Cole had been. Maybe she was interested in my brother though I doubted this would be the time or place she'd make it known. From what I'd seen of her work, she was a consummate professional. Flirting after seeing such a heinous depiction of the evil humans visit upon each other would be callous and rude at best.

Tears silently streamed down Robert's face, and inside, my heart broke for him. He'd just lost his touchstone, the foundation of the relationship by which he identified himself. Seth had been more than a lover to him, more than a lifelong companion. The way Ben had described the power exchange, Seth had been the one to take Robert out of his own head, shake him up, and put him back together whole. Seth had provided Robert direction, purpose, and focus. In return, Robert had given Seth everything of himself and more, investing so deeply in him that I was quite sure a major part of Robert had died along with Seth.

It occurred to me that an unmoored sub such as Robert might be a danger to himself. Fumbling in my pocket, I took out one of Ben's cards. I'd grabbed a few from the holder on his desk the last time I'd been in the office, thinking that talking to Ben or his partner might be helpful to Kimberly Kaiser. I'd never dreamed there'd be another broken spouse to hand one to, and Robert was as good as Seth's husband, in my opinion. He blindly took the card, fiddling with it to keep from looking me in the eye.

"You going to be okay, Robert? Would you like me to call someone to stay with you or take you to a hotel for the night?"

He shook his head. "My sister's only a few blocks away. I already called her, and she said as soon as I was done here, she'd walk over and get me."

"How about I give you a ride and save you both a little time? If you need some of your things, I'll have to observe you packing them to make sure you're taking nothing pertinent to the investigation."

Robert nodded like a good little robot and then stood, leading me to the back room. He grabbed enough clothes for a couple days, his toothbrush, and turned to me, ready. When we emerged into the morning light, Cole had just lit another cigarette from the burning end of the first, flicking the cherry off the butt. After making sure it was fully extinguished, he tucked it into his breast pocket.

"You going in to work?" Hayes asked as I guided Robert to my car by the elbow.

"Not right away. Reports from forensics won't be in immediately and there won't be much in the way of leads until then. Uniforms are canvassing the neighbors already." I slammed the passenger door after folding Robert into the front seat and turned to her, glad he wouldn't hear me. "I don't think he's doing well at all. I want to make sure he gets to his sister's all right and then go talk to Dr. Haverson about how to approach a sub who's lost their Dom." I needed to see Ben, for more than just work-related reasons. I needed to feel his arms around me, his heart beating against my chest, the warmth of his skin. I needed confirmation that despite this horrific death, there was also glorious life and I was not responsible for it all, even if my lack of progress on Kaiser's case had resulted in another death.

"Want me to go with you to see the doctor?"

"No," I said too abruptly. She studied my face, pursing her lips like she was about to snap back, but I hurried on before she could. "I mean, I'm going to talk to him about what this is doing to my head, too. I'd really rather do that alone, if you don't mind. If you want to do the same, feel free, and I won't insist on tagging along with you. Ben's far better than any of the department shrinks, I can tell you that much."

The scowl lines in her forehead smoothed out and she let my refusal of her company drop with a sigh. "Not a bad idea, DeGrassi. I'll give him a call later." She squinted in the morning sunshine, looking around the scene as most of the CSI techs and uniformed officers began to depart in ones and twos, the M.E. having left with the body hours before. "I'm going to see if I can track down some of Seth's friends and get a read on his last few hours." She resumed her professional tone and demeanor easily. We agreed to meet up by noon and I got in my car to chauffeur Robert to his sister's house.

Robert said very little, just enough to guide me through the few turns to his destination. His sister was waiting with a fierce hug for him and a nod to me, promising to call if there was anything they needed or remembered. I quickly found myself pointed in the direction of Ben's house, calling him on my cell to warn him I was on my way. He immediately picked up something in my voice.

"What's wrong?"

"It happened again. Kaiser's killer got another Dom."

A moment of silence stretched to the point where I thought the call had been dropped. "Who?" he asked so softly I barely heard.

"Seth Adams."

"How's Robert?" Ben immediately wanted to know.

"He's a zombie, but I left him with his sister and your business card. He said he'd call your office."

"Good. That's great, Gavin. Smart thinking. Are you on your way here?"

"Yeah," I choked out, suddenly finding it hard to breathe. I was losing it, imagining my skin drying out like the baked desert and fracturing in thousands of cracks that would blow apart if I didn't reach Ben fast enough. All my years in homicide and I'd never seen something like this, never felt this weight on my shoulders. Their lives were of the same value as everyone else's, but their deaths had been such torture I had a hard time wrapping my mind around what they'd endured.

He kept me on the phone until I pulled my car up into his wrap-around driveway and got out, walking toward him in a daze, intent on nothing more than feeling him near. I didn't even remember the content of our conversation, only the tones of his voice soothing me like salve on a burn, keeping me from losing it, keeping me centered. His arms around me intensified that calm, but it wasn't enough.

"I want to try something," Ben murmured into my ear, his hands rubbing comforting patterns on my back. I simply held on tighter.

"Do you trust me?"

I nodded, my chin digging into his shoulder. When he pulled away, I swallowed a whimper, though he still held both my hands. He led me through the living room to the hallway between the kitchen and dining room and up the spiral staircase to his loft. When I first caught a glimpse of the room, it took a moment to register what I was seeing. The exposed wood beam cathedral ceiling that soared over the living room capped the loft's open space. The beams held sturdy eye hooks every few feet, though for what, I had no clue. Along the back wall, where the slope of the roof forced the ceiling angle down sharply, there was a padded bench. It looked like a weight bench without the weights and with support bars raised three feet at the corners. Heavy trunks lined the walls and there was an armoire in the corner where the angle of the ceiling allowed. Light filtered in from the enormous windows at the apex of the ceiling. It was an inviting space, except for the strange furniture. At the far end was a closed door. I assumed it led to either a bathroom or storage.

Ben pulled me to the middle of the room and wound his arms around my waist again, bringing his lips to mine with a kiss so perfect—gentle without being tentative, reassuring without being demanding—my knees went weak. I fell into it, letting him in to take what he wanted. His lips migrated down my jaw and I shivered, baring my neck to him for more.

"That's it," he murmured. "Let me have what I want."

I closed my eyes, shutting out all but his touch, his smell, his taste. I pulled my shirt tails out of my pants while he untied my tie and slid it from my collar. His hands went to work on my buttons and I hooked my thumbs in his belt loops, my eyes still closed. A flash of Seth Adams, restrained and bleeding, pounded the insides of my eyelids. I gasped and opened my eyes wide.

Ben was there, watching me, finished with the last button on my shirt and running his palms along my torso, his touch grounding me. "Gavin," he said softly. "I want to do something. You're about to fly apart. Let me put you back together again." He didn't move in, didn't nuzzle my neck or kiss me. He stared, face open and honest and concerned. "If you trust me, let me help," he whispered.

I couldn't think, fidgeting within the circle of his arms still locked around me. I could only meet his eyes for seconds at a time, and the pressure built in my chest, pulling breath into my lungs in ripping gasps. I felt so out of control, and the worst of it was I didn't know how to regain it. Ben pressed a hand to my cheek, making soothing noises while I panicked. I didn't know what he wanted, but I would do anything to get this helplessness out of my bones. I nodded, unsure if he could tell through my tremors. Somehow, I found my voice and croaked, "Do it."

"If you need to stop, you say 'thunder.' If you need to slow down, you say 'rain.' Got it?"

I didn't quite understand what he was talking about, but I nodded anyway. "Thunder to stop, rain to slow down. Okay."

"If you do say 'thunder,' I'll stop immediately, but you'll have to give me some time to get you free. Keep this in mind if you're close to panicking."

Free? What is he talking about? I nodded, standing there shivering, overwhelmed. When he spoke again, I snapped to attention. His tone allowed for nothing less.

"Take off your clothes and stand with your hands clasped behind your back." He didn't bark, didn't snarl, but he did expect obedience, and I automatically complied, eyes straight ahead while I heard him behind me. It sounded as though he was rummaging in one of the trunks. Then there was a whisper of something heavy being pushed across carpet, but I didn't turn to see. When he returned and stepped in front of me, he held up a long, red hemp rope. "I'm going to tie you," he explained. "At no time will I gag or blindfold you, and if you use your safe words, I'll immediately stop and get you free."

I gulped, eyes glued to the rope. A surge of fear clotted its way through my veins, leaving my posture rigid and my muscles vibrating with tension. After what I'd seen this morning, I didn't think being restrained in any way would help. Coupled with my naked vulnerability, I just about bolted. Ben must've seen it, because he stepped close and slid his arms around my waist, calling my attention to his warm eyes, his soft lips. He spoke low in my ear.

"Trust me," he murmured, and his hot breath sent a shiver up my spine. "You need this."

I wasn't sure, but I nodded anyway, letting his tongue into my mouth when he kissed me. He pulled away and softly commanded, "Lie down on the bench, on your back."

I turned at his urging and saw he'd moved the weight bench to the middle of the loft. On wooden legs, I moved to it, did as he directed, unsure of what to do with my hands. The bench was narrower than my shoulders, and letting my arms dangle put an uncomfortable pull on my joints. He resolved the problem for me, taking one of my hands and wrapping it around the post behind my head. I automatically grabbed the other one as well, leaving me splayed and naked, feet on the floor, thighs spread slightly to keep my balance. He was still dressed and the contrast bothered me. I shivered again, couldn't seem to stop. I needed him, needed to feel him. When he stepped close to wrap the rope around one wrist and the post, I nuzzled my face into his thigh. He let me for a moment while he secured first one arm, then the other.

The rope wasn't scratchy, like I'd expected, but it was solid. I tested its heft against my wrists. Not too tight, but I wasn't going anywhere.

"If your hands begin to go numb, tell me," he said, leaning over my torso to wrap the rope three times around my chest, affixing me to the bench. My nipples hardened as the hemp slipped against my skin. Another three passes and he'd secured my hips as well. The process, afraid of it though I was, aroused me and I felt blood rushing to my cock.

Ben knelt somewhere around my feet, and with a clanking noise, he adjusted a section of the bench. I couldn't see what he was doing very well, but I felt him lift my right foot and place it on another pad, one that hadn't been there before. Apparently, the bench had folding sections that could be adjusted and placed at various locations, widening or narrowing the surface as he saw fit. He tied my ankles to these new sections. My feet were far apart, and I had a vision of the stirrups on a gynecologist's exam table. It had the same effect, though I doubted it looked that way. I was spread open for him. On display. My dick dribbled pre-come on my abdomen despite my reservations about being restrained.

"Very nice," he said, voice low as he walked around me, assessing his work. "How does it feel?" he asked.

"Tight, but not painful. I feel exposed and unable to do anything about it."

Ben stopped beside my shoulder, bent at the waist, and rested his forehead to mine. "That's what I want. For you to realize you can't do anything. I'm in control, and all you need to do is surrender and trust me." He kissed me fiercely. The ropes rubbed my nipples again, making me moan into his mouth. I desperately kissed him back, the inability to grab and hold him fueling my ardor. I needed him closer and if that was all I could get, I'd make the most of it.

He pulled away, standing back slightly as he stripped off his clothes, neatly draping them over the loft railing. When he returned to me, his beautiful cock stood out from the trimmed thatch of hair between his legs. I licked my lips, wanting to suck him down, but he was too far away. I watched him with hungry eyes, waiting to see what he wanted. I was surprised to realize the feeling of shattering from the inside out had muted.

"I have you where I want you," Ben said, approaching me. "I can do with you what I will. You trust me not to harm you. I take that trust to heart." I tracked him with my eyes, captivated. "You may speak if you wish, but you may do nothing else without my permission, including come." I groaned as his lips found my chest, licking me where the ropes bit in. He continued to talk, his lips brushing my skin. "I'll take what I want. You'll give me what I need. In return, I'll take on your burdens, set you free."

I didn't know if it was his words, his demeanor, or the soaring vulnerability I felt, but suddenly, I wanted exactly what he described. To please him, to surrender. To my embarrassment, my chin and lips began to tremble as we stared at each other, and my eyes filled. The amount of pressure I'd been under the last week was more than I could bear. The idea of putting it in someone else's hands, just for a little while, allowed me to inhale the first real, necessary breath I'd been able to draw for days.

"Yes, Sir," I whispered, the words' significance not lost on me. I'd heard many of the subs at Collared refer to their Doms as "Sir" or "Master" and I knew what it meant that I'd said it. It meant my willingness to be a participant, rather than to merely observe others. Ben cupped my face, his thumb grazing my cheekbone. I felt a tear escape the corner of my eye and drizzle down my temple toward my hairline. Ben captured it on one finger, and then brought it to his lips, smearing the moisture over them. He dipped down and kissed me, my tear wet between us and salty on our tongues. It was that gesture more than anything else that told me he didn't think me weak, or unfocused, or a burden because of my scattered emotions. He was entrenched in them with me, and I was free to show them, to release them, and let them go. For only having known him a week, I'd have never thought it possible to feel so much for him so fast. His words rang in my head—It's also one reason D/s relationships get deep fast. There are few things hidden… I'd thought I understood at the time, but knowing something intellectually and feeling it in my bones were worlds apart.

His lips trailed down my jaw to my neck. He nipped at my collarbone, his teeth sending pleasure zinging straight to my cock. I watched his descent down my torso, helpless to move. I strained against the ropes securing my wrists, wanting so badly to touch him.

"Relax," he murmured, his lips tickling my belly button. "You're not surrendering." It was an admonishment, but a gentle one. Raising my eyes to the ceiling, I let myself feel, tried to relax and just be in the moment. For someone always in control, always relied upon to make the next move, the next decision, I found it difficult to lay that role aside. "I've got you. Let go," he said, then laid a stripe up the underside of my cock with his tongue. I groaned, my eyes rolling back in my head.

He stood and rounded the bench, standing at the foot of it and looking up my reclined body from between my feet. Running his palms up and down my shins, he watched me tenderly. He followed his hands with his lips, creeping up each of my legs and coaxing my knees apart as far as the ropes allowed. I was his to display, his to play with, and if I could accept that, I could give up what he wanted, let go of my will and give him free reign.

Adjusting the bench again so my feet were spread even farther apart, he sat on the cushion between my legs. It hurt my neck to keep raising my head to look at him, and with him sitting, I couldn't see him at all without holding my neck at an awkward angle. This, I realized, was part of the genius of his restraints. If I couldn't see, I couldn't anticipate. My only option was to let it happen. I closed my eyes and felt a shift inside, my need to control slinking away in resignation. My head thunked back on the bench as his fingers teased my inner thighs.

"That's it," he said. "You can't do anything I don't let you do." His lips grazed the skin of my thighs again, crept up until he licked the crease of my leg and balls, wrangling a shudder from me. I wanted to spread farther for him, but the ropes wouldn't allow it. I was at his mercy. I couldn't even use body language to beg for more.

"Yours, Sir," I whispered, finally, finally giving in.

"Yes," he said as he mouthed my balls, his tongue fluttering against my skin. I sighed, the heat of his mouth making my nerves sing. He rose slightly and pulled my cock upright, wrapping his hand around the base and tonguing the v-shaped groove beneath the head. My arms strained at the ropes as my body tensed in anticipation. The skilled wetness of his tongue bathed my head and then he sucked, his lips tight around the shaft, his fist pumping my length. It was heaven and hell and purgatory all rolled into one. His movements were deliberately slow, stimulating me higher and higher but not allowing me to peak.

I wanted to run my fingers through his hair, or turn my body so his cock was at my lips and I could taste him, feel his warmth, participate in some way beyond this. But it wasn't about what I wanted, I realized. He was going to take his time and that was that. Suddenly, the two hour edging session I'd witnessed at the club took on a whole new meaning. Something else within me gave way and aside from acceptance, I began to understand. This was what he'd meant by putting me back together. My responsibilities were gone. He had taken over.

My nerves were on fire as his mouth descended ever lower.

When my cock bumped the back of his throat, he swallowed. I groaned, beginning to pant, wanting to see but unable to hold the position long enough. He looked beautiful though, in the moments I dared look. His hair hung low over his forehead, and his eyes were dark and intense, watching me. His lips stretched wide over my cock and his cheeks hollowed, sucking me down. When he began massaging my taint with a finger, I could hardly stand it, needing more. I whimpered, knowing it wasn't enough to get me off, but it was too much to keep coasting.

"What?" he asked, popping off my dick. His hand continued to stroke, his finger feather-light and maddening.

"More," I whispered, not sure if I was allowed to ask, but unable to stop myself nevertheless.

"More what?"

"Pressure. Faster. Harder, Sir." My tone was just this side of begging.

"But I don't want it harder or faster," he replied conversationally. "I'm having fun just like this," and he dove back down, going even slower with his ministrations to my body. I writhed and squirmed despite the ropes, making needier sounds, trying to move toward him, get more of him, something, anything.

"Please, Sir," I whispered.

I must have pleased him, because a spit-slick finger caressed my asshole for a moment before sliding in, and I let out a cry of relief that quickly morphed into a wanton moan. He pumped it in and out. The whole time, his tongue bathed my cock in slow, sensual circles and sucking kisses, never quite engulfing me again or sucking hard enough, and his finger was never quite fast enough, deep enough, or close enough to my prostate. It was torture. Delicious, delicious torture.

The sound of a cap popping open preceded the cold drizzle of something wet on my crotch and down my balls, and I raised my head to see Ben's gleeful face as he squirted lube everywhere, like a kid given a blank canvas and free reign to paint. He tossed the tube to the floor and then used both hands to smear my pelvis and ass cheeks, getting between my legs and bathing my nuts and taint with it. His hands squelched against me, and his breathing sped up to match mine. When he spread my ass and delved at my hole, he used the tips of three fingers to massage me, and my pucker spasmed, seeking more.

"Oh yeah," I groaned. "Feels so good."

"How's this?" he asked, shoving two fingers in fast and deep with no warning. My hips flexed and I howled, the ropes digging into my hipbones and keeping me from shoving down on Ben's hand. "That good, huh?" He gave a wicked cackle and prodded my prostate.

Well, I asked for more, I thought just before all coherence left my brain and I was one big pile of sensation. His fingers played me like a maestro, and I lost all sense of anything but him and the burning need filling me.

"Please, I need to come," I begged.

"Are you close?" he asked, his composure surpassing mine easily.

"Getting there," I panted.

"Then, no. If you're not about to explode, I want to play some more." He fisted my dick with a sure hand, followed quickly by the other, alternating his hands in downward strokes that went on and on. It was endless penetration into his tight fists, and the warmth in my groin turned to fire. I whimpered, trying to fuck into his hands, but the ropes prevented it. I arched my back, feeling the hemp against my nipples bite and drag. My whole body was zapped with pleasure, and desire flowed like lava in my veins. My need was his gratification, my skin his toy, my body his to play with.

"Mine," he said quietly. "I can rub you, suck you, fuck you, and you'll let me, for as long as I want, because your only job is to give me what I desire. Your world is mine to create. I can make you focus on your dick," more heated strokes, speeding up slightly and dragging a groan from deep in my chest, "or your ass." The strokes slowed, became one-handed as I felt a blunt fingertip circle my pucker. "I can take you to the brink." His finger pushed in and mercilessly prodded my prostate. My muscles pulled taut, like piano wire at the height of its tension. I fought the climb to orgasm, though I was quickly losing the ability to remember why. "I can hold you there." For a moment, I thought I wouldn't make it, that I wouldn't be able to stop the inevitable and I would disappoint him. Something about that jolted me and from somewhere deep within, resistance to climax blossomed. If he wanted to play, he would play. I could give him that much. "And I can bring you back from the edge," he murmured, withdrawing his fingers.

The profound moment swallowed me and I began to float. I was aware of my surroundings, of Ben and his magical hands, but I was also outside it all, as though observing from afar, an interested spectator allowed to both feel and watch. When I spoke, it didn't sound like my voice, but one of calm acceptance despite the word I uttered. "Please," My chest swelled with deep, relaxed breaths, as if my body knew there was nothing more it could do, and it relented.

I surrender.

Ben reacted as though he'd heard my thought, reaching behind him and pulling the end of the rope, releasing my feet with deft hands. Next came the anchors around my pelvis and chest, and last, my arms. He pulled me to my feet and kissed me hard before spinning me around to face the bench, my back to him.

"Kneel," he instructed, and I did so, aware that he sank to the floor with me. I still had the floaty feeling and my movements were natural, though orchestrated in time with his. He pushed me forward until I rested my elbows on the bench, ass pointed toward him. He rubbed my back with his lube-slick hands, positioning himself behind me and coaxing my knees as far apart as they could comfortably go. I heard the sound of a condom wrapper and then felt the blunt head of his cock at my entrance. I arched back, giving him my body.

"Yes," I groaned low in my throat as he pushed in and I reached behind me, hand gliding up his thigh to his hip. I wanted to be closer, to feel every inch of him as he took me. He wrapped his arms around my torso and pulled me upright, his chest to my back, his body surrounding me. The need that gripped me earlier had dissipated, fueled by something greater that I bathed in completely: the sheer certainty I was safe and wanted, and no matter my flaws, Ben would care for me anyway, would want to touch me, hold and kiss me, fuck me, and guide me through.

Ben seemed to feel it, too, the measured press of his length, inch by inch, easing into me with earth-shattering deliberateness. He pumped his hips intently, his arm over my shoulder and down across my chest, his fingers tweaking my nipple. "Stroke yourself for me, baby," he spoke low and throaty in my ear.

I obeyed, keeping my strokes in time with his thrusts. The slower we went, the more intense the pleasure. Instead of gathering in the small of my back, as usual, it gathered from everywhere, my legs, shoulders, chest, all of it building in density before settling in my groin, and when it did release, it was going to rip me apart from the inside out.

"That's it," he panted, his hand resting on my forearm to ride the movements of my strokes, his cock stabbing into me with deep, leisurely thrusts. "Just like I said. You're mine."

"Yours," I answered, my slick fingers tightening on my shaft, friction sending sparks of heat shooting deep into my gut. My ass was full of Ben, my skin warmed by him, my consciousness surrounded by his control. I gritted my teeth and let my head fall back to his shoulder. He kissed my temple, licked at the sweat beading there.

"You've done beautifully, Gavin, giving yourself to me." He sped up, his cock slamming home, the change of pace driving me forward into the bench. My supporting arm gave out and my chest hit the padding. His grip changed, closing over my hand and pumping my cock fast, our fingers entwined. He drove into me, taking everything I had to give. "Close?" he asked, breathing hard.

I nodded, panicking at my inability to articulate the request to come but beside myself with determination not to disappoint him. I needn't have worried.

"Come, Gavin. Come now."

My body had been waiting for it, and with one more stroke of our tangled hands, I shot, three, four pulses that sent my spunk sailing in an arc over the carpeting. My ass clenched around Ben's cock, and he groaned, spearing me and burying himself balls deep. I released a sob that I had no chance at suppressing, my insides flayed open and his for the taking. I was grateful to give in, give him everything within me if he would only deign to take it.

I felt the thump of his orgasm reverberate through my ass, his cock twitching as he filled the condom. He collapsed onto my back, his hot breath bathing my skin between my shoulder blades. With great care, he pulled out and disposed of the condom, then returned to me and offered me his hand, pulling me to my feet.

My legs were rubbery and didn't seem capable of holding me upright as I followed Ben to the one door in the loft, dazed and drifting along in the wonderful headspace he'd put me in. He opened it to reveal an opulent bathroom that, despite the modern fixtures, had a throwback feel to it, a sleek classiness I knew was simple but expensive. Slick black tiles shone halfway up the walls and there was marble everywhere, including a giant oval tub, one of the deep ones with the jets. He ran the water, and then deposited me on the lip of the tub.

"I'll be right back. I'm going to get us something to drink. You okay?"

I merely nodded, unable to speak.

He padded back to the loft, and I watched through the open door as he bent to a small mini-fridge I hadn't noticed and returned holding two bottles of water and a Gatorade. He gave me one of the waters, which I greedily gulped in three long swallows, and I took the Gatorade when he passed that over.

"We're sharing that, so don't drink it all."

I drank deeply and then handed it back, looking longingly at the tub. Being covered in lube was becoming uncomfortable, but it was more than that. It was the realization of what had just happened, that I'd crossed a line. A long soak seemed so normal after the last hour that I craved it.

Ben stepped into the tub and situated himself, then held his arms out for me. "Come on. Sit with your back to me. I want to hold you."

I scooted in as the water lapped at my belly, chuckling when the lube proved too slick to give my ass any traction. Ben had to wrap his legs around my hips to keep me from skidding toward the drain. The water crept up, hot and relaxing, and I felt his breath at my ear.

"You're safe. You can say anything to me in this tub, and I'll listen."

It was strange how, out in the loft, the ropes had been confining, restraining, but his arms and legs, holding me just as fettered and captive, were safe and secure. Context, I guessed.

"I don't know what to say," I replied, finding my voice and letting my head rest on his shoulder. "I don't exactly know how to process what just happened."

"Okay, let's start at the beginning," he suggested. "When you got here, you were in a full panic, breathing erratically and hardly able to speak. How about now?"

"I'm good, now. Not about to shatter anymore. But I feel strange, like my body is not my own. It's hard to explain." I thought a moment, trying to come up with a good comparison. "You ever watch dancers?"

"You mean like ballet dancers?" he asked as his hands roamed my chest without intent, rubbing lazy patterns as the water finally reached an acceptable level. He raised his foot and toggled the faucet off with his toes. The silence reverberated on the tiles until Ben pushed a button on a control panel near his shoulder and the jets whirred to life. I was glad, since the sound would muffle our voices, somehow softening the import of this conversation.

"Yeah. They're so graceful, and every movement is controlled, calculated. That's how I feel right now, like my body has some kind of muscle memory moving my limbs and I'm just along for the ride."

"Subspace," Ben said gently. "It's a place inside you that brings peace. Some people meditate for it, practice yoga, run marathons. Some people find it through submission. How deep did you go?"

I lifted his hand out of the water, tangling our fingers. "Like hypnosis, you mean? It wasn't like that. I was aware of everything, just found this peace where I could let go and be only what you wanted me to be." His arms squeezed around my chest.

"And were you afraid at any time I had you tied up?"

"At first," I said truthfully. "There were a few uncomfortable moments, memories of how Kaiser and Adams were found, but then

I'd see your face, your eyes. I knew you wouldn't hurt me." Had I known, though? Maybe Kaiser and Adams had trusted their attacker as much as I trusted Ben. Maybe they'd allowed themselves to be restrained, expecting a fun night of role reversal only to be surprised and helpless when things took a turn for the worse. But I knew that wasn't true. Kaiser had been drugged, involuntarily restrained. And Adams… well, his tests were forthcoming, but based on Robert's assertion that the two of them didn't play on the side without the other present, my feeling was he'd also been tied up against his will. These thoughts intruded on an intense afterglow I didn't want to interrupt, so I shoved them aside.

"That's why I had you lie down. Normally, I would have restrained you upright and given you a good spanking, but that might have sent you over the edge."

I barked out a laugh at his frank tone in talking about whipping me so easily. I squirmed uncomfortably. "I think you're right. I'd have gone batshit."

"Plus, you haven't had any pain training, so it would have only hurt you. And made me the enemy. So it had to be ropes. I'm sorry it brought up difficult thoughts, but I had to take away your control, had to give you the chance to share your burdens. Did I succeed?"

"Yes!" I answered immediately. "You certainly showed me that not every decision made depends on me. That was…," I searched for the word, settling on, "refreshing. And a big relief." Someone was willing to take on the worst of my problems and share them with me, and it was more than being able to rely on a work partner. I could truly be myself with Ben, and he'd hold me while I fell apart. Hell, that I was even free to fall apart in front of him bowled me over, lifted a weight from my shoulders I hadn't known I carried.

Turning with some difficulty, I faced Ben, rearranging our legs so I straddled him with my butt still on the tub bottom. I took his face in my hands and looked into the warm depths of his eyes.

"Thank you," I said sincerely, leaning my forehead against his, my hands dropping beneath the water to pull him closer. He responded by pressing a gentle kiss to the corner of my mouth and pulling my head down to rest on his shoulder. I held on, eyes closed, just breathing, feeling him secure around me, keeping me safe. We stayed like that for a long time, until the water went tepid and the jets timed out. Finally, I sat back, peeling myself off him.

"I need to get back to work." The thought that I was here getting my rocks off while my new partner was doing the heavy lifting questioning Seth Adams's friends by herself made me uncomfortable. The water had finally begun to weaken the hold the lube had on my skin, and a few quick swipes with a washrag had me cleaned and ready to get out. Ben's hand on my wrist stopped me.

"Gavin," Ben said haltingly. "Is this something you'd be interested in exploring again? With me?"

His usual confidence was muted, a rarity in itself. I could see the hope plain on his face, and it melted me. I thought for a moment about taking more steps toward the life of a submissive, and it made me shiver. Could I handle it? I didn't know. Did I trust Ben to help me along? Absolutely. Was it something I wanted? I recalled how off balance I'd been when I'd arrived, how crazed I'd felt, and compared that to my current state of peace, also remembering the incredible high I'd gotten at the pinnacle moment.

"If anyone could help me embrace this side of myself, it'd be you. Let's see what happens, okay? Give me some time to think." His face barely moved, but something changed, his features softening somehow, and he nodded. I smiled. "Truthfully, pain training sounds daunting," I teased. His lips twitched at the corners. I found myself wishing I could read him better, know him better, anticipate his moods, his thoughts. Wasn't that what he was offering? More of himself, and a context in which to learn it? If we didn't continue this exploration, would he tire of me? Would he feel something was missing if I didn't allow him to dominate me?

I understood better than ever what he'd meant by the biggest gift a submissive could give was loyalty and submission.

"Pain training is a horrible name for what it actually is," he remarked, getting out of the tub, pulling two fluffy towels off a nearby shelf and tossing one at my head with a smirk. "It's more like finding out just how rough you like it."

That didn't sound so bad. I twisted my towel and whipped it at him, deliberately missing his flesh with the snap of the cloth. "We'll see. Sounds intriguing."

We dressed quickly and Ben called his receptionist to have her reschedule his morning since I had made him late. My mind shifted gears, returning to the case at hand, and something hit me that I'd been too upset to realize on the way over to Ben's.

"You knew Seth and Robert?"

"Yeah, not incredibly well, but they're acquaintances."

"You immediately asked after Robert's well-being when I told you Seth was the victim. Sounds like they're more than acquaintances to you."

Ben sighed and headed for the stairs. I followed, my tie hanging undone down my shirt front. Entering the kitchen, Ben brewed us both a cup of coffee with his single-serving Keurig coffee maker, the fancy one with the backlit display and multiple brew size options. He put mine in a travel mug.

"I knew them better a few years ago than I do now, but yes. We were once close."

My eyebrow went up and I waited for clarification.

"Robert wasn't in the lifestyle before he met Seth. They were together for about a year before they became friends of mine, and they were in trouble when I met them."

"What kind of trouble?"

"Their relationship was falling apart, and they came to me for help. I suggested they come to my office as patients for couples counseling, but they had a different idea. Well, Seth did."

"And what was that?" I parked myself on one of the barstools ringing his breakfast bar, studying him.

Ben looked at me for a long moment, as if making a decision, and then leaned forward on the counter. "Seth wanted me to train Robert. He was a fairly new Dom at the time and had only played with subs who'd had some experience. Robert had reservations about becoming a sub. It was why they were on the verge of splitting. Seth needed something more from the relationship and Robert doubted his ability to surrender, so they were at an impasse. Seth knew of my reputation as a therapist and as a Dom. He'd spoken with several of my references and he said he trusted me to recognize what Robert needed and guide him to the point where Seth could take over. Robert recognized my experience might help him let go of his reservations, and when I explained that inexperienced Doms and subs who train together often find a depth to their relationship that can't be gained any other way, he was eager to try. The idea that it was training for Seth, too, to see how to bring a sub into the fold and teach him from the ground up is what finally sold Robert. He wouldn't be the only one learning and they could grow into it together."

"Like you want to do with me," I said neutrally.

He pursed his lips, studying me. "No, not like what I want to do with you, Gavin. With them, it was instruction, finding out Seth's requirements and gearing Robert's training toward that, then releasing him into Seth's... care, for lack of a better word. I never got attached, and the longer we played, the more I turned the training over to Seth. I don't want to turn you over to anyone else. I want to keep you," he finished, gaze never wavering from mine, a slight smile playing at his lips.

"Did you fuck them?" I asked bluntly.

He blinked, his smile fading and he nodded. "Pain training

involves associating mild pain with sexual release. A handjob after a spanking, or allowing the sub to come after being tied in an uncomfortable position. Enough of that, their body starts to recognize that when the pain starts, the pleasure follows. Before long, the pain becomes the pleasure.

"When I trained Robert, Seth mostly took care of the sexual aspects of it, but a certain amount of trust has to be given to the one with the whip. I did all the aftercare if I was the one inflicting the pain. But to get Robert to understand wholehearted surrender, he had to give himself to someone. Seth wasn't competent enough to take a new sub from start to finish. So a few times, I had Robert surrender to me, to show him he would be safe, and that he was capable of trusting that deeply. Not too long after that, I backed off, let Seth take over. I couldn't have Robert becoming attached to me, or the transition to Seth would fail. There were, however, a couple of scenes where I was involved with both of them."

My gut clenched as he spoke, but I reminded myself he was a competent Dom, and to get there, he'd had to have practiced. What he'd done before we met was none of my business… as his lover. As the detective on the case, it was very much my business. I slipped into cop-mode, asking the next logical question.

"Did Robert resent you being involved with them?"

"Not to my knowledge," Ben answered. "Before beginning, I made absolutely sure he was willing, that he wasn't being coerced in any way, and if at any time he wanted to stop, he knew he could. He never safeworded."

"What about Seth? Did he have any problems after the fact? In general, or with you?"

"No. They seemed to be ironing out the wrinkles in their relationship, and every time I saw them after that, they were really happy. And grateful."

"Grateful how?" Okay, maybe that question satisfied my personal feelings on the subject, but it wasn't totally out of line.

He cleared his throat, uncomfortable, but still not looking away. "They gave me an open invitation to play with them any time. I never took them up on it. That they were happy together was enough for me."

"How long did the training take and how often did you see them after?"

"About three months, and I saw them occasionally at the club or munches. Maybe once or twice a month for a while, then less frequently for about a year. Now, I see them, well… used to see them maybe three or four times a year." He was forthcoming with his answers, not taking the time to think of the best wording—after admitting sleeping with the victim and his boyfriend—to minimize his involvement. He looked sincere, and most of all, like he wanted to help me understand, especially if understanding meant giving me a lead. I hated that the question of Ben being involved in Seth's death had even crossed my mind, but those marked-up faces haunted me and if I didn't pursue every niggle in my brain, I'd overlook something. I couldn't let Ben slide because I was fucking him.

"Where were you last night?" I asked quietly, hating myself a little bit.

"With a patient at my office," he answered just as softly. I risked a look at him, but his expression was inscrutable.

"Patient's name?" I asked, flipping open my notepad and snagging a pen from the cup on the counter beneath his house phone.

"Sorry. Doctor-patient confidentiality." His words were clipped, his jaw set. My question had crossed the line, but I saw no other way. I would do my job, no matter what.

I huffed out a breath. "Is there another way to verify your whereabouts? Was Dr. Ribaldi there?"

"No, she wasn't working last night. Building security should show me entering and leaving the office in their logs and on their security cameras. The parking garage keeps a record of every car in and out, and after hours, each visitor goes through the front desk in the lobby to be announced. I arrived around seven-thirty at the garage, was with my patient between eight and nine, and left at nine-thirty."

"Did you go anywhere afterward?"

"The club. Master Lacey can vouch that I was there until around one this morning. I'm probably on their cameras, too."

Relief flooded my veins. Even though the victim hadn't been found until shortly after three, what happened to Seth had taken time. The bruises on his body had been well risen and purplish before his death. Ben couldn't have left the club at one, inflicted the damage to Seth's body, killed him, and been gone by the time Robert got home.

"In the years since you trained them, have you heard of any other subs becoming disgruntled with Seth for any reason?" The change of subject allowed me to soften my tone and expression, and I tried to convey my regret for having had to ask the difficult questions in the first place through body language. I relaxed, leaning back in the chair and crossing an ankle over my knee, not scrutinizing him so heavily.

"Like I said," Ben's voice was chilly. "Seth was inexperienced when they approached me and Robert had never submitted before.

After the training, I never heard of them playing with another sub. Or another Dom, for that matter. I know of no one with a reason to hate Seth."

"What about before you trained them? You said Seth had played with experienced subs before he met Robert. Would his newbie status have caused him to hurt someone?"

"No. Seth had a good reputation when I met them. Are we about done, Detective? I have patients." The warmth was gone from Ben's face, and it made my stomach drop. I studied him for a moment.

"Just about," I replied, slipping from the stool and rounding the bar to stand at his side. He remained facing the counter, leaning on his hands, but he did look at me as I brushed my chest against his shoulder, our faces inches apart. "So far, I've only recognized one limit for myself, and it's a hard limit. I will do my job in any and every way I have to. Just as you refused to break doctor-patient privilege, I refuse to ignore pertinent questions. Your acquaintance with the victim tells me a lot of things, not just whether I should be concerned about your involvement. George Kaiser and Seth Adams trusted their killer. There was no forced entry to either of their homes, and one, if not both, shared drinks with him. Now that I know you have a concrete alibi, I know no one else can suspect you either. I can rely on your opinion, especially since you knew the victim quite well for a time. And now, I know I'm not looking for a disgruntled submissive because you, Mrs. Kaiser, Matt Kinney, Lance Marsh and Robert Weiss have all told me that neither victim made enemies of their previous subs." I ticked off the long list of witnesses on my fingers.

He held my gaze for a long moment, finally giving a shallow nod and breaking eye contact. I snagged his chin with my fingers and pulled his face back in my direction.

"It's nothing personal. This is just like if I get called to a scene in the middle of a dinner date. I will do my job. Hard limit."

He did smile then, remembering our conversation the night he'd explained contracts to me, the night we were first together. "All right," he murmured. "But that means we actually have to be dating for me to worry about getting stuck with the check." I went still, a tingle racing along every nerve ending and flaring across my scalp like a biological firework. "My offer to train you notwithstanding, are we dating, Detective?"

Swallowing, I leaned forward and kissed him chastely on the mouth. "I'd like to be," I answered, taking a big shaky breath and letting it out on a huff of laughter. Dating a man. I never thought I'd be strong enough to try, and it made me weak in the knees. That he was also a Dom gave it an element of danger I was drawn to, the gravitational pull of a black hole strong enough to yank planets out of alignment and into its stormy influence.

"Then if you're free tonight, would you care to come back here for dinner?"

"Sure, if I'm free." A glance at the clock on the microwave told me it was nearing ten and I needed to catch up with Hayes before she got too far with Adams's acquaintances. "I'll call you this afternoon and let you know if and when to expect me."

"Okay. And Gavin," he said, snagging my wrist to stop me from heading for the door. He pulled me back to him and straightened the knot on my tie. "I respect your position. It just didn't occur to me the questions I'd be answering in this case would get more personal than what a consultant usually fields."

"Most consultants don't end up getting so personal with the detective, either."

He smiled ruefully and let me go.

§§§

"SO WAS the doctor helpful?" Hayes asked, taking the sandwich I offered her after she climbed into the passenger seat of my car. I headed toward the station where, hopefully, forensics reports would be trickling in.

"Yeah." I cleared my throat, trying to keep any hint of humor out of my voice. It wouldn't do to break into nervous laughter while discussing such a disturbing case. "Turns out he knew the vic and his boyfriend." I dug into my pocket for my notepad and passed it over so she could read the notes I'd made after leaving Ben's house. Less uncomfortable than relaying out loud the nature of his relationship with the couple.

"How did you get him to admit all this? Most shrinks I've met are cagey as hell and incredibly good at deflecting direct questions." She sounded impressed and shook her head, food forgotten while she paged through my scribbles.

"Ben's a consultant on the case, so he was already familiar with the evidence from the Kaiser scene. He knew what things I would be asking, and I guess he figured since he was already involved, cooperating was best." I gave a shrug, hoping the fact that she didn't know me well yet would keep her from seeing how lousy a liar I was.

She cocked her head to the side. "You just called him Ben. And I don't care how wise it is, shrinks don't give up more than they have to."

"I called him Ben because he told me to. He was friends with the victim, and since he's got a solid alibi, my guess is he wants this killer caught, same as you and me. He has no reason to evade questioning. Plus, he makes no secret of the fact he's a Dom. His career doesn't depend on him staying quiet about what he does on his own time." Unlike mine.

"Wait, wait, wait," she said, holding the fingers of one hand straight up, the tips stabbing into the flattened palm of the other. "Time out. You already know he's a Dom, so all he had to say was he once played with Adams and Weiss. You got more detail than that, especially considering his interaction with them was four years ago. Why is it relevant to this case how long he played with them?"

"Establishes level of intimacy."

"That he played with them at all points to that. Why does it matter that he received an open invitation to play again?" She was relentless. Jesus.

"Because Robert said they never played with others in the lifestyle, only had threesomes with random strangers."

"No, he said they never played with other subs, because he wouldn't compete. I'm guessing Doms don't like to share their goods with other Doms, so this invitation was something special. If he doesn't tell you about the invitation, he's not required to tell you why he got into their inner relationship sanctum." I didn't correct her assumption that Doms didn't share. I assumed in certain circumstances, from the way Matt Kinney had talked about his friendship with Kaiser, and from my conversation with Ben about contracts and collaring, that Doms did share. Otherwise, why collar a sub?

"'Inner relationship sanctum?' Where'd you pick that up, Oprah?" I smiled at her and hoped she'd laugh and drop it. Turning into the lot at the station, I parked and started to exit with my lunch when the door locks clicked, locking me in. Not that I couldn't get out anyway, but that wasn't the point. I met her piercing gaze.

"Level with me, DeGrassi. Is this shrink a suspect? Looks like he's got an airtight alibi. So why'd you go after him so hard? You think he's got an accomplice or something? Like he's calling the shots and sending someone else, maybe his own sub, to do his dirty work for him? Ooh, and he's consulting to keep tabs on the investigation." She was really building up steam. I tried to interrupt her, but she barreled on. "He's a shrink. Maybe he had some dirt on the victims, something he's protected from disclosing by doctor-patient privilege, so he's safe. Maybe what he knows is so heinous he has to get revenge, but he needs a layer between himself and the victims so he won't get caught. A Dom that provides training to other Doms would be persuasi—"

"Myah," I said, holding up a hand, finally getting her to stop and breathe. "It's nothing like that." I closed my eyes and swallowed, mouth suddenly dry in a way I'd never known before. It was like I'd eaten sawdust and was chomping down on a cardboard box chaser. Did I want to do this with Hayes? Would she understand? Could I get out of it? Another lie? I couldn't pull it off, and my sinking stomach knew it.

"So what is it like?" she prompted when I'd said nothing for too long.

I looked at her, praying my poker face held. "Ben's my friend."

"Lots of killers have friends, Gavin. How do you know he's not feeding you a line of bullshit? Alibi or not, we should be checking into his background. He fits. He's in the lifestyle. He says he's a Dom but maybe he doesn't participate anymore, and maybe he uses his position as a doctor to steer people away from it."

I laughed. That was not what Ben had been doing with me.

"Why's that funny?"

"Hayes, you're barking up the wrong tree. Ben told me as much as he did to convince me not to be angry with him."

Her brows knit together. "Huh?"

I took a deep breath. "Ben's fully immersed in the lifestyle, Myah. He doesn't find it abominable, so he's not a match to the profile. I know this because... he's training me. Or wants to. Though I haven't exactly agreed yet."

Her eyes narrowed slightly. "Training you... to be a shrink?"

"Fucking hell." I looked at her then, terrified but unable to talk my way out of this. "Myah, I'm not only divorcing my wife for cheating on me. I'm also divorcing her because I'm gay, though she isn't aware of that. And after I moved out last week, Ben and I ..." I couldn't say it, not out loud. Not yet.

She stared for a long moment. "You're together. And he wants to train you? To be a sub?"

I nodded, gripping the steering wheel hard enough I imagined leaving finger marks in the plastic.

"And he told you all of this because he didn't want you to run off; he wanted you to understand how he knew Adams and Weiss and that it was old news." She gestured with my notebook in her hand.

Another nod. My heart hammered in my ears. She scrutinized me, eyes slightly narrowed and lips pursed while she puzzled out her own reaction. Would she say nothing and simply give me the cold shoulder for the rest of our working life? Would she tell everyone and alienate me so I'd have to request a transfer? Would she keep my secret and simply request her own transfer?

"Thank fucking god!" She exhaled, laughing, a big grin spreading across her face.

I whipped my head around, shocked and blinking stupidly. "What?" It came out as a croak.

"Do you know how many partners I've been through?" she asked, speaking rapidly, clearly not expecting an answer. "Seven. In three years working Homicide, I've had seven partners. Why?" I shook my head, dumbfounded. "Because every goddamned one of them hit on me. And when I refused to fall for their wily, pig-snouted ways and thank my lucky fucking stars they wanted to sleep with me, they got pissy. I was blamed for deliberately sloppy police work, had blatant lies told to my superiors to get me transferred, and one of them damn near cost me my badge. That's when I left Chicago. My complaints were ignored. Good ol' boys' club, right? So I get here, and I think, 'Shit, I have to learn all over again which assholes to avoid and who I can trust enough to do my damned job,' and then I was assigned to you. You listen when I talk; you seem to give a shit about my opinion; and not once have I caught you checking out my ass. Then I find out you're gay? Seriously, thank fucking god!" she repeated and laughed, then leaned forward and planted a huge kiss on my cheek, right in front of anyone who might be passing the car or watching through the windows of the station. At least it wasn't on the lips. That would have been bad for us both. "I'm so relieved I won't even bitch at you for getting your rocks off this morning and leaving me to do the dirty work with Adams's friends. You did get some information outta Haverson at least." My skin heated and I gave her a guilty look.

"I also made sure Ben knew Robert Weiss would be contacting him. Now that several of each of the victims' friends have stated they left no disgruntled subs in their wake, I think we can reasonably scratch that line of questioning off the list." I tried to ignore the heat in my face. "So if it's all right with you, maybe we could get out of this stifling car, eat our lunches, and see if anything's come back from forensics."

Bowing her head in acquiescence, Myah released the locks and we headed inside. I ignored several stares from the others, checking my email as I unwrapped my sandwich and took a swig of my soda. I felt a small twinge in my ass as I sat down and resisted the urge to grin like a loon. Since leaving Ben's that morning, I was calmer, centered, and more capable, the few terrifying minutes in the car with Myah notwithstanding.

"So Cole's your brother," Myah said around a mouthful of sandwich. "But you have more, right?"

I nodded, scanning my email. "I have three brothers, all of them cops. And my dad's a retired lieutenant, so I grew up with all this," I gestured grandly to the squad room.

"I kinda got that big family vibe from you. Are you close to them all? The way you are with Cole?"

I raised a brow at her. "Yeah, fairly." I'd snapped at Cole in front of her. How had she gotten we were close? I decided it didn't matter and changed the subject. "So we're not looking for submissives, and the profile says someone in the lifestyle but not fully immersed. Ben went over the scene photos for Kaiser and he could tell the technique was rough around the edges. I figure if the perp is trying to inflict damage, he won't be considerate, but Ben's the expert." Myah gave me a pointed look but said nothing. I felt my face warm again and hurried on. "So maybe it's someone who frequents the clubs, watches from afar. Someone no one thinks twice about, so he flies under the radar."

"Club owner?" she suggested, flipping through the case file for my previous notes. "Jared Nunn? He had that argument with George."

I shook my head. "We'll have to talk to him about that, but I don't think so. He seems... like he knows his way around the upstairs rooms of his own club. Makes me think he's experienced." When I'd gone to Collared after walking out on Victoria, he'd offered to set me up a scene, and I had the impression he knew from firsthand experience which patrons could have helped with my particular problem. I voiced none of this, not wanting to be overheard.

Myah took my word for it. "What about regulars at the clubs who never play? Maybe we're dealing with a stalker, that clichéd 'if I can't have you, no one can' mentality. Or maybe one of the bartenders or waitresses?"

"Stalker doesn't make sense. We have more than one victim, but it's clearly the same killer. Besides, the profile says it's likely someone with a vigilante mindset. And waitresses aren't strong enough to have secured George to the ceiling on that cross."

"Multiple perps?" she asked, finishing off her sandwich and wiping her hands on the paper before wadding it up and tossing it to the trash can three desks away. She made it, no problem. One of the other detectives gave a low whistle and leered at her behind her back. She looked at me and rolled her eyes as if to say, See what I have to put up with?

"That's a thought," I said, ignoring the others in the room. "Except Kaiser was only missing two glasses from his set. And if the killer had a second pair of hands, why would he need to drug them to get them restrained?" I shook my head. "Possible, but I don't think it's likely."

"Okay, so why not another Dom? Someone who's angry at these people for playing on his turf? Maybe Adams and Kaiser had a previous sub in common, and that person is someone else's sub now, who can't handle the thought of their guy submitting to someone else."

I toyed with a pen, considering. "Except Adams hadn't played with anyone new in five years. That's a hell of a long time to hold a grudge."

"Yeah," she conceded. "And a sub who didn't have a problem with Adams wouldn't likely have anything to tell a new Dom that would upset him enough to resort to murder. Plus, you said Dr. Haverson could tell the marks were inflicted by an amateur." She leaned forward, lowering her voice. "How could he tell, by the way?"

I shrugged. "I don't know. But he's trained other subs and Doms. Maybe he just knows what that looks like."

Myah frowned, sucking on her straw. "What if it's something these particular Doms like? Maybe they have a kink the killer disagrees with. How much do you know about this stuff? Is there something controversial in the kind of play that goes on?"

My eyebrows knitted together. I asked her for Kaiser's file and she passed it over, watching as I flipped through reports, settling on home inventory listing, particularly the different implements Kaiser had used. The account of possessions from the Adams scene wouldn't be available for another day but the one thing Adams's scene had that Kaiser's hadn't was someone familiar with the house and its contents. Robert provided a point of comparison we didn't have with Kaiser.

"I'd have to ask Ben how common some of these items are. The masks and stuff don't tell me much of anything. Oh, wait…" I paused, reading. "There was a set of ornamental knives in Kaiser's collection." I wondered why those would be included with his dungeon stuff.

"Knives? Seriously?" I couldn't help but think she was considering whether this was what I'd be signing up for if I agreed to Ben's training. Hell, I wasn't too sure myself, and made a mental note to get a better idea of his type of play.

"Yeah. I don't know. Kind of surprised the killer didn't use these, though. Don't you think they'd be a more efficient way to kill him? Strangulation isn't exactly hit or miss, but the mess he left the bodies in, you'd think a little blood wouldn't faze this guy."

"Maybe it's the strangulation that's the point," Myah mused, holding her hand out for the folder again.

"It's a very personal, in-your-face way to kill someone. I just don't know enough about it." I made a couple notes for more things to ask Ben, and then folded my hands on my desktop and changed focus. "Perhaps we aren't asking the right questions. I could ask Mrs. Kaiser what George was into. She said she tried to sub for him before their marriage failed. She probably knows his kinks to a degree beyond my questioning of her. And Robert Weiss certainly would know of all of Seth's proclivities."

Myah agreed, though I suggested we wait to question anyone else on Adams's interests until we knew more from Cole, and I wanted to find out how the knives could be used before asking Mrs. Kaiser about them. Frustration sparked in my chest again, the feeling of standing around doing nothing while our killer walked free. There was less than a week between the first and second murders. Did he kill on a schedule? Was the clock already ticking for the next victim?

Who are you? I thought, willing anything in either case to jump out at me, so the pieces of evidence could stop dancing in my head like a stubborn puzzle and fit together already. So that no one else had to die.

CHAPTER EIGHT

THE BACK door to Ben's house swung open in silent invitation, the living room beyond dark and eerily quiet. The sun had mostly set, and it was dark enough that the room was bathed in ominous shadow. A thrill of uncertainty pranced up my spine.

"Ben?" I called into the cavernous space, not touching the door to close it. My cop instincts hummed, coiled to spring. The house, always inviting and warm, was a dark cacophony of silence, the lack of sound so loud my ears rang. My hackles rose. "Ben?" I called again. I wondered if I'd misremembered his invitation, that maybe I was supposed to meet him for dinner out instead of at his house. But no, his afternoon text message had clearly said his house at eight-thirty, if I was free.

When I didn't hear an immediate answer, I began to tremble, a cold certainty I was walking into something I was unprepared for shivering over my skin like the caress of a skeletal hand. I called one more time. "Ben! Are you here?"

"Yeah, I'm here!" his voice answered, sending a wave of relief reverberating through my body. I couldn't pinpoint his location from his voice, so I shut the back door and turned on the living room lights, banishing the unsettling dark.

"Where's 'here'?" I called.

"Right here," he replied, coming through a door beside the kitchen that led down a set of steps to his basement. He held two bottles of wine in his hands, studying the labels as he walked toward me, and looked up at the last moment with a smile that dimpled his smooth cheek. "Hey," he purred, leaning in for a kiss. I didn't know he meant for it to be as lingering or heated as it quickly became, but both of us were reluctant to pull away.

My heart had resumed its normal jog, and I breathed a sigh of relief as we pulled apart. Briefly resting my forehead to his, I took a moment to soak in his proximity, his warmth and smell. His smile widened. I matched it with one of my own. Pushing away the blossom of unease that remained, I let go and followed him to the kitchen.

"Why are all the lights out?" I asked.

He shrugged. "Just got home a little bit ago. Changed clothes and ran downstairs to get the wine so I could open it and let it breathe before dinner. I hope you don't mind takeout," he said, rummaging through a drawer and fishing out a corkscrew, using it to point at the heavy paper bag I'd just noticed on the counter, which explained why his house smelled so wonderful. "I meant to cook, but had an emergency session with a patient, which pushed all my afternoon appointments back an hour. Then Laura accosted me as I was leaving and accused me of avoiding her, so I stayed to chat longer than I wanted to."

I caught a hint of steeliness in his voice, and he wouldn't meet my eyes, concentrating on sinking the point of the screw into the cork and twisting. I sauntered over to the bag and took a whiff, my mouth watering at the heavenly smell. I turned the bag around to read the restaurant's label.

"I love Rigazzi's," I said reverently. "I'd eat there every day if it didn't risk me growing out of my clothes in a month."

Ben laughed. "Yeah, it's fantastic food, but if you eat too much…" he made a face, blowing out his cheeks and bowing his arms away from his body to indicate a growing waistline.

I chuckled. "Exactly. My mother used to say to me when she caught me stealing a finger swipe of butter from the tub while she cooked, 'Gav, you want to grow up, not out,'" I adopted her falsetto as I turned to the cabinets, searching for wine glasses. I took down two and turned back to see a thoughtful expression on his face. "What?"

He shook his head. "Nothing. Just thinking."

I wanted to ask what about but decided he'd tell me if he wanted to. Reading the vintage on one of the bottles, I wondered if it was any good. Knowing Ben, he probably didn't own a bad bottle of wine, though I couldn't tell the difference between a supermarket Riesling and a five-hundred dollar bottle of Merlot. With a shrug, I poured a glass and swirled the liquid a little, taking a small sip. The tang of it hit the back of my teeth, causing my jaw to sting, so I set it down. Probably better to let it breathe, like he intended.

I felt his proximity the second before his arms slipped around my waist, his chin resting on my shoulder. "You never ask me questions about me," he intoned softly. "At least not off-duty."

Discomfort flared in my gut at the mention of my morning interrogation and I stiffened, which he had to have noticed. "I have a large family that's always trying to get into my business. I ask questions of people all the time for my job, and sometimes I hear answers that help me as a cop but I'd rather not know as a person. I try not to pry." Of course I had questions for him, and I wanted to ask all of them, but whenever I opened my mouth to ask, I found myself more interested in the other things my mouth could do with him.

Ben sighed, his lips pressed against my shoulder, his hot breath wending through my shirt and across my skin. I relaxed back into him, hands clasping his at my waist, entwining our fingers. "You can ask me anything," he said, words muffled by my shirt.

"What do you know about ornamental knives? Kaiser had a set, and I want to know why the killer chose strangulation over them." Back to the case. What was I afraid of? His answers, or getting to know him more than any other guy outside my family? That was stupid, since I clearly knew him more intimately than any other man. It just felt like rushing. I'd known him a week.

Ben let go, stepping back to lean against the counter, head cocked thoughtfully. "They're part of what we call edge play. Knives or needles, fire, erotic asphyxiation. All of them are part of something called RACK, or Risk Awareness Consensual Kink. Sadists and masochists practice RACK on a more regular basis than your average Dom or sub."

"Have you ever played like that?"

He studied me for a moment. "Not my thing. I can understand intellectually the body's response to it, how it can heighten the rush for both Dom and sub, but I'm not interested in going that far. My kink is the emotional subtlety and behavioral nuance of earning someone's submission. Pain is a means to that, but only one of many."

"Erotic asphyxiation," I wondered aloud. "Could that be what happened to Kaiser and Adams? A scene going too far?" Even as I asked the question, it felt wrong.

"Not likely," he replied, grabbing a wine glass and swirling the garnet contents. "He's inflicting injury, but he's drawing it out. It could be the strangulation is meant to mimic breath play." A thoughtful expression crossed his face. "Maybe that's the point. Maybe he wants us to see that edge play is dangerous, to see how easy it is to go too far." He took a sip of the wine and set the glass down, stepping close to me again and winding his arms around me. "But that's not the kind of question I meant when I said you don't ask me things. That's work."

I turned in his embrace and hooked my hands at the small of his back, leaning against the counter and pulling him against me. His eyes flared with heat and I smiled. "Okay, what did Dr. Ribaldi want to talk to you about this afternoon?" It was Ben's turn to stiffen in my arms. I hurried on. "If it's patient related, never mind."

Ben shook his head and disentangled from me. I watched him curiously, his body language clearly indicating discomfort as he grabbed utensils from a drawer and the food from the counter. Avoiding my eyes, he rounded the breakfast bar and set everything out. The sheer amount of food was astounding, with four entrees and three or four appetizers. His movements weren't jerky or irritated, but deliberate, as though he could bolster his answer with a confidence he obviously didn't feel. When at last he met my eyes, they were resigned but still open.

"Let's eat up here, yeah? I'll tell you what's going on. You deserve to know anyway."

A frown pulled at my lips, but I said nothing, joining him with the wine glasses. Perched on a stool, I surveyed the food, not as hungry as I had been before I'd opened my asshole mouth. But the aroma persuaded my stomach otherwise and my appetite spiked again, especially when I saw my favorite dish, the pasta tutto mare special. I groaned, pulling the mixture of pasta and assorted seafood with white sauce to me and inhaling. My mouth watered. Ben watched me, amused, momentarily forgetting his discomfort. I smiled at him, wrapped a hand around the back of his neck and pulled him in for a sloppy kiss.

"So the way to your heart really is through your stomach?" he asked mildly.

"Only with Rigazzi's," I answered, digging in with gusto. I noticed he'd also gotten toasted ravioli, breaded cheese sticks, and stuffed artichokes as appetizers. "Jesus, you spent a fortune," I said, dipping a ravioli in meat sauce and blowing to cool it.

Ben shrugged. "Wanted you to have a good dinner. I didn't realize you'd also be the entertainment." I chuckled, but didn't stop shoveling. "Okay," he turned to me, after taking a few bites of his pasta. "After work, Laura wanted to talk to me about my last sub, and to make sure I knew it was time to stop punishing myself. She's afraid I'll push you away out of fear." That got my attention, despite the delectable food. He went on. "Some people in the lifestyle would frown on me telling you this, saying it would shake your confidence in my ability to be your Dom, and that it would show weakness I wouldn't be able to overcome. Just like anybody else, sometimes Doms need to talk through their concerns and insecurities, because yes, we do have them. But talking to our subs can lead to further problems, so we often choose other confidantes. Since you haven't yet agreed to be my sub, Laura thought it would be prudent to discuss it with you. Not to mention giving you an accurate picture of what shapes my decisions as a Dom."

"Okay," I swallowed a mouthful of suddenly tasteless food.

"My last sub, Nathan, and I were only contracted for a month. He knew me from the club and his references were from some of my dearest friends. They had good things to say about him, that he was an excellent submissive and if he gave himself to me, he'd submit to anything I desired. The first few times we played, it went fine. When I presented him with a contract, he agreed to provide me with a checklist of his interests and limits. The contract was very loose, still in the early stages of our play, with lots of room for experimentation. He was frank with me and truthfully, on the extreme side for my usual tastes."

"How do you mean, extreme?"

Ben took a long drink from his wine, gathering himself. "He liked pain. A great deal of pain. He was very much into edge play. I had suspicions it stemmed from an abusive childhood, that he'd learned to associate punishment with acceptance and love, and he believed he deserved significant pain just for existing. Whenever I tried to ask him about it, he accused me of 'shrinking' him, and closed off. I told him that until I understood him better, I wouldn't pursue edge play the way he wanted. He assured me he could endure anything I put to him, and he liked it, so my concerns were unfounded.

"One of the first things I do when learning a new, but experienced sub is establish at which point they will safeword, so I can recognize when I'm approaching their limit. Nathan never safeworded, and I grew increasingly uncomfortable testing his limits. We both became frustrated, him because he wasn't being pushed hard enough, and me, because the ways in which he wanted to be tested were beyond my own limits. I'm a Dom, not a Sadist. I don't enjoy the sight of blood, nor the fact that he requested I administer pain which would incapacitate him for days. It became clear rather quickly we weren't suited to each other.

"Several of my friends suggested I try, just once, to find his limits, or I consider bringing him to a Sadist, someone who wouldn't have trouble reaching Nate's boundaries. I balked. If I was already pushing my limits and hadn't found his, I didn't have to worry about going too far. But also, if I had to find someone to play with him to ensure his happiness, I wasn't the right Dom for him. Before the contract period was up, I released him.

"Mind you, I did not dismiss him. He'd done nothing wrong, had not disrespected me or broken any rules. We simply weren't a good match. However, when I informed him I was releasing him, he didn't take it well. Told me I was an idiot for giving up someone with his ability to submit to anything and he had thought as a shrink, I would know if he wanted it, I wasn't doing him damage. I told him I thought he'd already been done damage by previous Doms, and he was a danger to himself and others until he could resolve the reasons why he required such harsh punishment.

"He stormed out, swearing to me he'd find his perfect Dom, and I was pathetic and weak and maybe I should switch to submission. I wasn't cut out for dominance, and he'd tell everyone he knew how spineless I was."

"I'm sorry," I said quietly, putting a hand on his forearm. He was lost in the past, his eyes trained on a spot in the middle distance. He looked so sad.

"I am, too," he replied, voice flat. "Within a week of his departure, he'd found another Dom to take him up to and beyond his limits, all right. He was found dead in his bed. He'd been restrained and beaten so horribly he was barely recognizable. He had shallow knife wounds all over his body, and there were blisters on the soles of his feet, the insides of his thighs, and around his nipples. Fire play. The worst was that he'd been branded. He'd found his Sadist. The cops couldn't make heads or tails of the symbol burned onto his chest. No one questioned in conjunction with his murder could figure out what the brand meant."

My appetite deserted me. I swiveled my chair to face Ben, one hand resting on his knee and the other rubbing his back. "It wasn't your fault," I murmured. "You have your own limits, and you were strong not to cross them to gain his approval. It's not your fault he found someone with less integrity, who didn't know when to stop, or he didn't want to stop."

"That's what Laura's told me for the last several months. I haven't taken a sub since and it's been more than a year. If I found another pain slut, I'm not sure I would release him, even though I wouldn't be what he needed. What if I released him to his death? The police never found the person responsible for Nate. He's still out there."

"But you didn't get Nathan killed," I argued. "You didn't beat him. You didn't arrange for him to meet his killer. You aren't the one who wouldn't stop. You aren't the one who wouldn't get help. He had every opportunity to do so, and he chose not to. You of all people should know a person has to decide when and how to get help. You can't make someone think a certain way if they're not ready."

Although, how true was that? I hadn't the first idea what a Dom could and couldn't make a sub do. Ben's skepticism told me that. I changed tactics.

"It's admirable, really," I hesitated, carefully choosing my words. "Most people with new lovers are so over the moon they'll happily ignore their own needs in the heat of the moment to please them. Frankly, that's what's been going through my head the last few days. Can I recognize my limits and stop or is the desire to please you so great I'll cross some line I'm too inexperienced to see before it's too late? For you to recognize your limits with Nathan and stick to them—amid what I'd imagine was a significant amount of cajoling—takes guts." I ran my fingers up into Ben's hair at the back of his head, tugging gently. He closed his eyes, letting me massage his scalp. "Seeing Kaiser's ornamental knives on the implement list had me thinking about you, wondering what you're capable of and if I can put myself in your hands." He looked at me sharply and my hand stilled, cupping the back of his head. "I wondered if that's something you've ever done, if you're into that. I realized I don't know how far you'd go. I have zero experience with any of this, and can't tell you my limits. Well, most of them, anyway. Then I remembered. You took me out of myself this morning without hurting me at all. You read people for a living, so you'd know if you were asking too much of me. You have been nothing but honest with me from the beginning. I have every reason to trust you." I dropped my voice to a whisper. "Especially now, knowing you won't compromise my safety for your own benefit. You'll give me the room I need to find that all-important boundary."

His eyes glittered darkly in the dim light. "I thought I was done dominating until I met you, Gavin," he murmured. "I see in you a great capacity to submit, to love, and to know the lines you won't cross, once they're shown to you. I've been afraid to take on an experienced sub again because something in Nathan's words cut me. I let my compassion get in the way of my demands, and I don't skirt the limits closely enough to achieve the high that can only come from walking the edge. This morning, you needed compassion and I still walked you on the edge. Exploring your limits with you makes me feel alive again in a way I haven't for a long time." He dropped his gaze to his hands, his voice coming so softly it was hard to make out. "Training you would give me great pleasure, true, but that's not all. It would be an exploration for both of us, Gavin. It's a big thing to ask of you, more so now since you know my confidence is shaken." He closed his eyes, looking so lost I slid off my stool and wrapped my arms around his shoulders, pressing my lips behind his ear. "I've let a piece of myself slip away, and with you, I have a chance to regain what I fought so hard to understand and master. But do I have the right to ask that of you? I don't know." He shook his head, answering himself.

My chest flooded with warmth, at how this confident man—this person who had not once judged me for my inexperience or my uncertainty, had only held my hand and unhesitatingly walked with me through the scariest revelation of my life—had wormed his way behind my closet door and given me what I'd been afraid no one else could.

Acceptance. Before I'd even found the courage to admit I was in the closet.

In that moment, I'd have done anything for him. Without hesitation, without fear, the words left my mouth on a breath of certainty.

"Train me, Ben. Let me submit to you."

His eyes found mine, dark and glittering. Lips set in a grim line softened as the creases in his forehead smoothed. He stroked a thumb across my cheek, then slipped his hand to the back of my neck and pulled me to him. His mouth was a millimeter away from mine, our eyes were locked. He smiled. With a sigh, I closed the last fraction of space and kissed him deeply, pouring my trust into him, my faith. Something in me clicked, a tight band around my chest gave way and I felt a burst of hope. It was a ray of light in the bleakness of the last week, and I recognized it for what it was. Ben had become my lighthouse after I'd been adrift for years. His steady, strong presence promised to show me the way to safe harbor, and the pounding water that kept me off balance and clinging just to stay afloat was almost through tossing me about.

He pulled back and I reluctantly loosened my grip. I wanted to crawl inside him and curl up in his warmth, his affection, his strength. Long fingers rubbed the hair bristling at the base of my neck, and then he released me.

"Let's finish dinner. Pasta doesn't reheat well." Eyes twinkling, he gently pushed me back to my stool and I resumed my seat.

After a few bites during which time I mulled over the revelations of his past, something occurred to me.

"Is this why, when I visited your office that first time, you were so unsure of where things stood between us? Because you were acting strange, whether you'll admit it or not."

Ben swallowed a sip of wine and winced, looking at me sheepishly. "I'd just told Laura I'd met someone, and as usual, she saw how hesitant I was before I recognized it myself. When you walked up, she was in the middle of a pep talk about how I needed to see where things with you could go. I was afraid you'd overheard something but had no way to ask. Then you started talking about the case, and I hid behind that, like a coward."

"But you kissed me in the elevator. That's not hiding."

"No, it was me realizing Laura was right, and I'd be stupid to let you out of my sight. So I didn't." His grin was particularly smug, drawing me into a laugh.

"I'm glad."

The rest of the meal passed pleasantly and we traded stories, him about various trips he'd taken after college and growing up an only child, and me about what it was like to grow up with three brothers, where we each went to school, and the hijinks we'd gotten up to. We laughed, and for brief moments, I could almost forget the heavy responsibility on my shoulders of finding Kaiser's and Adams's killer. Almost.

My waistband finally protested loudly enough that I listened, setting my fork down and groaning.

"I may never eat again," I intoned, glaring at my plate as if it was responsible for my overindulgence. "But that was a hell of a last meal."

"You plan on shuffling off this mortal coil then?" he asked playfully, gathering plates and carrying them to the sink. I grabbed the remaining utensils, juggled the containers of leftovers and followed him, boxing the food up and putting it in the fridge. Even if it wouldn't taste as good the second time around, I couldn't force myself to throw out Rigazzi's.

"No. But that dinner will last me the rest of the week at least."

"Carb loading. Trust me, you'll be glad you ate like that after what I have planned."

Grin tugging up the corners of my mouth, I leaned on the counter, wine glass in hand. Admiring his lean frame as he bent to load the rinsed plates into the dishwasher, I couldn't keep the curiosity out of my voice.

"What do you have planned?"

"Rule number one," he said, putting a dishwasher soap tab in the slot and starting the appliance before turning to me. "Don't ask me what I'm going to have you do. If I want you to know, I'll tell you."

"Why is that?"

"Two reasons. One, telling you would give you time to formulate how you'll respond, and that's calculated. I want genuine reactions that come from your gut, not something you think I want to see. And two, it's the unknown that gets to us the most. To tell you beforehand allows nervousness to grow to the point where you may not be able to submit wholly because it's built up in your mind as some big event. I don't want you prepared. I want you to trust I'm prepared enough for us both. The endorphin rush is greater when you feel you've walked a line, and you get closer to the edge if you're not exactly certain what's going to happen. It's not about fear, exactly, but that does play a part, and we're afraid of what we don't know more so than anything else."

To deny his words had an effect on me would be lying, but I wasn't sure how I was supposed to react. I sipped my wine, considering.

"Okay, I won't ask, then," was all I could come up with. He smiled and held out a hand. Surprise passed over my face. "Now?" Embarrassment washed up my skin like a giant wave when my voice cracked.

"Do you have somewhere else you need to be?"

I shook my head, drained my wine glass, and carefully set it on the counter before slipping my hand in his. He gave me a reassuring squeeze, and then led me from the kitchen to the spiral staircase and the loft above.

"Do you always play up here?" I asked, watching him turn on and dim the lights that ringed the low wall. The effect could have been creepy, with shadows playing on all the angles of the vaulted ceiling, but instead, it was cozy.

"Yes. When we come up here, you'll know it's to play; I'm in control, and you are to submit." He crossed the room and settled his hands on my hips. "I don't want you to think every time we're together you have to do my bidding. You're not my slave and there's something to be said for spontaneity. That's what the rest of the house is for. If I jump you in the kitchen, I don't want you thinking you have to be 'on' for me. Tonight, however, I have something specific in mind. Strip," he ordered, stepping back to allow me room to do so. "We begin your pain training."

I fumbled with the top button of my shirt and stared at him wide-eyed. I'd known this was coming, and given that I was more acquainted than ever with the types of toys Doms and subs used due to my scrutiny of the inventory of both my victims' houses for the case, this was not a surprise. Nevertheless, my hands shook, though

I tried to cover up the hesitation. Each item of clothing I removed, Ben took, folded neatly, and set aside. I couldn't deny being in the loft space, remembering that morning, our first real power exchange, made me hot and my dick was half hard before I'd even worked my briefs down.

"Now, when I have not specifically given you a pose to hold, I want you to present yourself. This is a relaxed stance, hands behind your back, right wrist clasped in your left hand, posture straight, eyes down. Some Doms consider eye contact rude. I am not one of those. I believe I can tell the difference between defiance and intensity, so if you look me in the eyes with all that fire I see in you, you won't be punished. However, if I see disobedience, I will punish you. Try it now. Present."

I widened my feet, squared my shoulders, clasped my hands behind my back, and lowered my gaze. Looking at the floor left me feeling too vulnerable, so my eyes stopped at Ben's knees. Oddly, the pose reminded me of my tenure as a waiter at a local country club when I was in college. Not a physical copy, since my feet were apart and I didn't have a hand towel draped over my forearm, but the attitude was the same. Politely attentive but silent and still so as not to make myself stand out. Although my dick, taking a keen interest in the current proceedings, certainly would have created quite the stir had it been involved in the waiter job.

"Is this right, Sir?" I asked, slipping into the submissive role more easily than I had that morning.

"Very nice, Gavin." Ben walked around me, running his hand up my arm to my shoulders, pushing between my shoulder blades just a bit to encourage me to stand even straighter. "Chin up, eyes down. I like that you're not looking at the floor, merely down. Your eyes are stunning and I can see them better that way."

Pleasure suffused my gut, the desire to please him strong and shocking in its intensity. After all, we'd only played once, and I was not used to being this passive.

It takes more courage to kneel before another than to stand beside them. Now, I knew exactly what that meant. I was afraid. Not that he'd hurt me—at least, not much. I was more afraid of giving him that much power over me, though I'd done it that morning. In the heat of the moment, desperate with desire and more than a little out of it, it hadn't felt as large as it did now. For the first time, I wholly understood the words power exchange. In giving up my power to him, he was, in turn, giving me the power to realize my value, that what I had to offer of myself was worth giving to someone, and I had to trust that particular someone to cherish it.

The realization made my whole body shake. Ben noticed, his hand on my shoulder sliding down my other arm and across my ribs as he came around to stand in front of me. His hand rested just below my ribs, firm and warm. Reassuring.

"I can already see it, Gavin," he said quietly. "You're letting go, and it thrills me." His hand trailed down to my hip, then lightened so just his fingertips grazed my skin as they wended their way toward my belly, circled my belly button, and moved lower. He plucked at my pubic hair, a sharp tug that stung, and followed that immediately with a firm stroke to my cock. Arousal flared into outright desire, and my cock pointed up instead of straight out, its length growing. Ben's hand fell away.

"Pain training," he continued, "means that when I want to see your skin glowing red from my hand, or my whip, or my flogger, you will not lose your erection. It means my preference for fucking a well warmed ass trumps your discomfort over a little stinging. It means my tying you in uncomfortable positions is acceptable if it gives me pleasure to see the beauty of ropes against your skin, to put parts of your body on display, and if it grants me access to all of you. If I want to tie you upside down, knees bent to your chest, so that your hole is showcased for my viewing and touching pleasure, you will be able to endure it. Pain training.

"At no time will I cause you true physical harm, put your safety in jeopardy, or ignore your needs as a matter of survival. Your word for me to completely stop is 'thunder,' and to slow down is 'rain.' There will never be a time when I punish you for using these words, but I must ensure you will allow me to test your boundaries. If you safeword, I need to know why. I will play mind games with you, Gavin, but only to show you the heights which you are capable of reaching. Never to do harm. Do you understand?"

I nodded immediately.

"If there's something you want to try, I expect you to discuss it with me first. If there's something I want to try, I will afford you the same courtesy. If you're amenable, these discussions can take place any time outside the playroom. I will not do something new without first discussing it with you. Earlier, I said I would never tell you what I have planned if you asked. That only applies when I am sure of your limits. If there is anything I think might give you pause, I will, of course, ask for your input. In the next few days, you will outline your expectations for becoming my sub, but I do understand being new to the lifestyle, you need context in which to formulate it. These first few sessions will be that context. Now, middle of the room."

He gestured to the spot where he'd placed the bench that

morning, though it had been moved to the side. He walked a step ahead of me, and I followed, keeping my hands behind my back.

"At some point, you'll learn to walk at my heel, but not tonight. If you have any needs at the moment, now is the time to address them. Do you need a drink or the bathroom?"

I shook my head, growing more curious and apprehensive now that the training was truly beginning.

"Good. Lift an arm for me. Either one." His voice wasn't stern, but it brooked no argument, and I raised my right arm to where my elbow was even with my shoulder and my wrist was above my head.

"Like this?"

"Mm-hmm," he replied, reaching above me to grab something. When he snapped a leather cuff with soft lining around my wrist, my heart galloped. He adjusted the strap enough that my arm was above my head and to the side slightly with only a minute bend to my elbow. "Other arm," he instructed, tapping my left shoulder. I complied and he secured that side as well. "Comfortable?" he asked. "Not too tight or too high?"

Again, I shook my head, not speaking because my voice would come out shaking and uncertain. My arms were fairly comfortable, and the cuffs, while secure, were not tight. I flexed my fingers for good measure.

"I'm not going to secure your feet," Ben said conversationally. "I want you to submit to me not because I'm forcing you to see you can trust me to take control, but because you choose to give up control. You've seen you're capable and don't need to be convinced. This time, let it go of your own accord."

He strode to the wall behind me and opened several drawers before he found what he was looking for. When he returned to me, he held up two objects. My eyes widened at the sight of them.

"This is the paddle I will use on your ass. It's a standard paddle, solid construction, and covered in leather, which will give a satisfying smack while cushioning the blow. Good for beginners. Makes your skin glow nice and rosy, too. He held up his other hand. I couldn't take my eyes from the cylindrical object, a short fat piece of rubber with two small rings at one end. I suspected its purpose, and he confirmed it for me. "This is a butt plug. You will wear this during your spanking. Because everything about this is new, including holding things in your ass, I will secure it so it will not slip out. In the future, I will expect you to be able to keep anything I insert into your anus in place without help. For the next few weeks, tell me if you need it secured, but after you get used to anal play, you won't get the luxury."

I nodded. Already trussed up, there was nothing I could do to reverse my situation, and a part of me was quite sure I didn't want to, though I recognized my terror. Chill out. You've gotten spankings before. No one's ever died from a spanking. Was it the spanking I was afraid of? The butt plug? The combination? No one but Ben would see me, and I trusted him.

Ben watched my face cycle through fear, arousal, trepidation and determination, and he stepped close, his fully-clothed body brushing my naked chest, our faces inches apart.

"Do you know how hot you look, tied up for my viewing pleasure?"

Heat coiled in my belly and I met his eyes, hoping he'd touch me, reassure me, show me the effect I had on him. But I didn't dare ask for it. He leaned forward and kissed me, quick and dirty, claiming my mouth and marking his territory with a nip to my lower lip. Despite my restraints, I gave as good as I got. When he stepped back, his pupils were blown wide.

"Sometimes I wonder if the anticipation is as much fun as the participation."

The anticipation was intense, a rising tide dumping large quantities of adrenaline into my blood stream. When he sauntered around me and I lost eye contact, it surged into anxiety and I heard him rummaging again through supplies. When he came back, he stood behind me and put a hand on my hip.

"I'm going to slick you up," he soothed, "and then put the plug in. Then we begin. Relax for me."

I did my best, especially when he rubbed his warm hands up and down my back vigorously, kneading my muscles and letting me feel his presence. I heard the rustle of fabric and felt him bare-chested, pressed to my back. He chuckled.

"Sometimes this is easier to handle when you're turned on. Are you turned on, Gavin?"

"Yes, Sir," I answered. Unbelievably so.

A hand slid around my waist and down, gripping my cock at the base and giving me one good, long stroke. I shuddered and gasped. He left off and returned his attention to my backside. His clothed crotch pressed against my ass, the buckle of his belt cold against my cheeks. The tactile sensation as well as the vulnerability of being the only one naked sparked through my nerve endings, and I leaned into him, spreading my feet further apart.

"Okay, lube now." I heard the cap flip and felt his fingers, covered in cold liquid, delve between my ass cheeks. He was as liberal with it as he'd been that morning, and it quickly warmed as he massaged my taint, his other hand still rubbing my back and cheeks. He slipped a finger inside me and I panted, the push on my opening shooting sparks through my pelvis. A second finger quickly followed and then his hand disappeared. I groaned, trying to tilt my ass toward him despite the stretch to my shoulders, seeking his fingers almost involuntarily.

A bigger press to my anus caused me to gasp, and his massaging palm was back as he slowly pushed the plug home. I moaned, unable to rein in the sound.

"That's it," he cooed. "I like to hear your voice."

Impossibly stretched, the short, fat plug pulled me wide but didn't go deep. I pushed into Ben's hand, attempting to get more, but there wasn't more to give. I felt something tickling my thighs, and realized at some point, Ben had attached straps to the rings at the base. He wound them over the tops of my thighs, stepping around to my front before gathering them around the root of my cock. He then looped them beneath my balls and drew my whole package tight, tying the straps into a bow and stepping back to survey his handiwork.

"Like a wrapped present just for me, with the added benefit of keeping you from coming," he said, eyes dancing merrily. He reached down and collected a drop of pre-come from my slit with his thumb. Holding my gaze, he brought the digit to his mouth and licked it while I watched, mesmerized. Once again, my inability to reach for him, to touch or drop to my knees and suck him off frustrated me, but quicker than last time, I accepted this as how things were.

"Now, the fun stuff," he said, disappearing behind my back again. I couldn't help it, my whole body tensed and when my asshole clenched, it pulled on the plug, which tightened the straps and caused my dick to pull away from my belly, not letting me forget that my balls had been drawn into the contraption. A twinge of not-quite-pain shot through my entire groin and into my gut. With a small gasp, I rocked forward to ease the tension. That only served to make my cock harder, which pulled tighter on the straps and wiggled the plug in my ass. I was focused on keeping still when the first blow landed.

Involuntarily, my hips skated forward. My skin stung and the blow shifted the plug, as did the movement. I hissed as my dick twitched, though the sensation was overpowered by the tingling in my ass cheek. A wave of mortification rose, but I swallowed it. This was what Ben wanted, so this was what I would give him. No, what he'll take from me.

The next blow fell across the other cheek, and the back and forth between my cock and the plug repeated. I was so hard, I ached, but I clenched my eyes to try to shut out the pleasure and focus on the pain so I wouldn't come.

"You are gorgeous," Ben said behind me, his voice calm though not cold. "On display just for me. Taking your licks like a champ." A surprising surge of gratitude mounted in my chest. He likes what he sees. I'm doing it right. I'm making him happy. With that thought, I drew a deep breath and the tight embarrassment eased.

Another smack, this time over both cheeks at the same time, driving the plug into my prostate.

"Oh!" I cried out, remembering that he wanted to hear me, though vocalizing was a touch humiliating. This is the point—to please him despite what it costs me.

Ben landed two blows in quick succession, and the pain swarmed my skin like angry bees with a vendetta against my ass. I sucked a breath between bared teeth, the air cooler as my flesh heated.

"You're beautiful, pinking up like this." He ran a hand down my flank and brushed gentle fingers up my burning thigh and over the swell of my glute, leaving stinging trails in their wake. His fingers pulled lightly at the strap over one thigh, and my erection bobbed. "Everything still secure? Breathe, baby."

"Yes," I answered, letting out a whoosh of air.

I concentrated on air in, air out as another blow to each rounded globe of burning muscle made me clench my teeth. The fabric of his pants rubbed my abused skin, spreading fire as he leaned close, his voice at my ear low and velvety.

"Yes what?" he admonished gently.

"Yes, Sir," I replied, immediately chagrined. "Sorry, Sir."

"It's okay, this time. This is a lot to take in, but next time, I expect you to remember. You're doing beautifully." Another wave of satisfaction lit me up. To punctuate his point, he ground his erection into my ass, eliciting a moan I didn't try to suppress. "Almost done," he promised, backing away. I was shocked to miss him, the need to feel him close having risen sharply despite the chafing. The urgency of my desire to please him floored me.

The displaced air from the paddle swing sounded impossibly loud, until the thwack of the leather against my skin burst across the loft. It burned, not just in my flesh but in my gut, groin, and chest. I let out a cry that was half moan, half sob, embarrassed at the non-verbal evidence of my internal struggle. Defiance—not of Ben but of myself and my lack of courage in enduring a simple spanking with grace—roared to life. I thrust my ass toward him, silently begging for more. I wanted to show him I could take it, give him the best possible performance in even this simple scene. I was his however he wanted me, whether or not I thought I could bear it. He thought I could, and that was stronger than any incentive I could come up with on my own.

"Baby," Ben murmured, his voice carrying surprise and heat. "Jesus." A final smack rang out and the paddle thumped to the floor. Ben's arms wound around my waist and his mouth was at the back of my neck, hot, sticky breath bathing my sweaty skin. The sensitive flesh of my ass stung and burned against his pants. He ground his cock into my crack, and I pushed back, crying out at the pain, the need.

"Sir," I mewled, all dignity gone.

"Gav, you—" his voice broke off, his hands scrabbling at the ribbons tied around my dick like a jaunty bow on a birthday present. His movements were jerky, urgent, and the heat from my ass spread to my groin as he fumbled with the ties, still humping me. I pumped my hips, meeting his thrusts. "Need you," he panted at my ear. I pulled at my restraints, the leather creaking with the effort, but I was going to be of no help.

Blood rushed into my cockhead as the ties finally came loose, and Ben's fingers wrapped around my iron hardness. I thrust into his hand and then back into his crotch. He surrounded me with his arms, his hands, his powerful thighs burning against my raging skin.

"Sir," I babbled. "Need you so bad, please."

His belt jingled, a condom wrapper tore, and his fingers swept gently at the base of the butt plug, pulling it from my body. My hole gaped and spasmed, looking for something to fill the void, and Ben didn't disappoint. The head of his cock trailed between my cheeks before homing in on my entrance, sliding in with decisive surety.

Thanks to the plug, there was no pain, no need to go slow, and his length reached farther into my core than the toy had, filling the naked demand within to be taken. I cried out, my body ignited in an explosion of pleasure so intense, I lost all awareness of anything but Ben, his body, and our joining.

His fist tightened on my cock, stroking brutally, and the inevitability of completion barreled full tilt at me.

"Sir! I need to… I'm gonna… Oh fuuuuuuu… May I?"

"Come, Gavin," he panted in my ear, his voice high and tight, his thrusts jack-hammering, driving my cock through his fingers.

"Nnnnngggghhh," I half groaned, half screamed as my shaft pulsed in his hand, shooting white pleasure. Ben grunted and rammed his cock deep, holding there while he came, each spasm of my ass a counterpoint to the twitches he buried inside me. We rode the pleasure until we were both spent. I let my head fall back onto his shoulder, turning my face into his neck and hiding there, overwhelmed and fighting the sting in my eyes. Strength deserted me, and I hung from the cuffs, anchored to my place by both my restraints and Ben's dick still in my ass.

"Baby," Ben murmured, his lips brushing my jaw as he nudged me with his chin to try to get me to look at him. "Gavin, babe, look at me."

The command in his voice was unmistakable—wrapped in silk and awe and tenderness, but there nonetheless. I pulled back slightly and forced my eyes to meet his. What I saw there took my breath away. Affection, sure, but also pride. I'd met his expectations, and for that, I'd been rewarded. His fingers, sticky with my come, skated the curve of my jaw, and his soft lips met mine as his arm encircled my torso and squeezed tight, holding me to him with fierce strength.

"You were stunning," he praised when we broke apart, and the tips of my ears flushed red with pleasure. "Your surrender was everything I could have asked for. Devastating, complete submission. It was an honor to receive it," he whispered against my lips.

I couldn't help it; the overwhelming cacophony of emotions—joy, fear, adoration, incredulity—refused containment. They rose and escaped on a breath suspiciously like a sob, though my eyes were dry. Ben shushed me and rubbed his hands up and down my chest, rocking me slightly. His dick shifted in my ass and I moaned, shivering at the sensitivity and giving an experimental hip tilt back. My sweaty skin caught and stuttered against his, reminding me of my reddened ass. The sensitivity burned but then subsided enough for the small bits of friction to feel good again. Intense, overwhelming, raw, but definitely good. Ben rocked gently into my rolling hips, his lips covering the skin he could reach with little nibbles. He licked at the come he'd smeared on my face, and my breathing hitched, another whimper escaping me as I felt him harden again. "Don't go, Sir," I whispered. "Stay inside me. Please." I'd learned quickly that I couldn't stand to get fucked after coming, my ass too sensitive to handle it. Not this time, though. Maybe it was the high of the scene or the overwhelming crash of emotions ricocheting through my limbs, but the shallow rocking of our hips only punctuated my desire to keep him close, to keep going.

"Let me get you down." His arms left my chest and released my wrists one by one. I looped them behind his neck, holding him to me. His pants were pooled around his ankles, and he gingerly stepped out of them, not letting himself slide out of my ass. "Bend your knees." I felt his knees behind my own push forward, unlocking my stiff legs, and I followed him to the floor. He laid me on my side, reaching for his discarded pants. "I need another condom," he said, shushing me when I clutched at him, my fingernails scraping along his thigh to keep him firmly seated in my ass. "Gav, I'm not going anywhere."

He pulled out and quickly discarded the old condom, replaced it with the new and slid home again. My head was pillowed on his arm, which he wrapped around me to grip my opposite shoulder, his forearm cradling my chin. His other hand stroked my belly and then slid along my side to lift my leg as he began to pump his cock methodically. I grasped his forearm with both hands, closing my eyes and kissing at his skin while gently rocking with his thrusts.

"Stroke yourself," he whispered, his teeth grazing my earlobe, and he licked down my neck to bite at my pulse. I reached down and gave my newly-stiff dick a long, slow pull, hissing at the spike in sensation. It was just shy of painful, a pleasure with teeth, marching in from the farthest reaches of my body. Ben never changed rhythm, never took more than the long, lazy thrusts he'd started with. He let the orgasm build slowly, with greater depth and wider breadth. It was ice and fire all at once, and I turned my face into the crook of his arm.

"Don't do that. Don't hide," he panted, his hand stroking my inner thigh as he held me open. "Look at me." I twisted my neck to do so, and our eyes locked, his warm brown gaze meeting my blue awestruck one. Our noses bumped, and we shared breath, the moment so heavy with meaning, so profound, that I wasn't surprised when a tear escaped the corner of my eye. This man, I would do anything for. Anything he asked.

A rumble swelled from somewhere deep in Ben's chest, and never blinking, he stared at me as his orgasm swept him away. I licked at his lips, wanting to taste his pleasure, feeling his strength vibrate in the slide of his chest on my back, the clutch of his hands on my shoulder and thigh. My own release came out of nowhere, throbbing from the bottom of my very soul as it coated my hand in a shocking seven pulses, all my strength and fear and need jettisoned with them. His eyes were all I could see, and in that moment, I fell into their depths and freely consented to getting lost in them. In him.

CHAPTER NINE

"OH MY god, you started your training," Myah said, primly folding herself into the passenger seat of my unmarked car, her wide greenish-gray eyes fixed on my face. I tried to keep my expression neutral, but the corners of my mouth tugged up, so I turned my attention to meticulously backing out of the parking space at her hotel. "I don't know whether to ask you about it or not," she quipped as she snapped her seatbelt into place. "On the one hand, I'm dying to know what put that look on your face. On the other, I'd be a very dirty girl to admit such curiosity about your sex life."

"What look on my face?" I asked, unable to suppress the smile. I still wouldn't look at her and concentrated on driving instead. "Coffee? I need coffee."

"The look that says you not only got laid, but you have feelings about it. If I asked you, would you tell me?"

Would I? Was I even allowed to? Maybe Ben had rules about my sharing what we did with anyone else. Maybe he would be okay with my talking about it to someone not into the scene, but not another Dom or sub. I realized I had no idea. Not only that, but the revelation that I considered his opinion before my own made me shiver. Last night had done a good job on me.

"I don't know," I answered truthfully. "Depends."

"On what?" she wanted to know.

"Well, your reaction for one. And whether or not I'm even allowed to. I have no idea."

"Whoa, you wouldn't be allowed to talk about it if you wanted to?"

"Well…" I hesitated, not wanting Ben to sound like a controlling ass. "I don't know what his rules about that are. He may have no problem with it. Or want to know who I'm talking to before I do. I seriously doubt he'd tell me I couldn't talk to someone. But I'm not going to assume."

Her saucer-wide eyes stayed fixed on me, though she pointed out the window at a passing Starbucks. "There's coffee. Now I have to ask. I can't not ask. You're not required to answer, but the detective in me will not let this go. What did he do?"

I set my lips in a line and pulled into the drive-thru before powering down the window and perusing the menu with utmost concentration. "What are you ordering?"

"It's okay to tell me," she said, ignoring the menu and my attempt to change the subject. "I can keep a secret, though it's obvious you can't. Your face, Gavin. Man. You sure you want to go to the station?"

Ugh, I forgot about that. "Well," I hedged. "We could go talk to the widow Kaiser. I have some follow up questions for her. And Robert Weiss after that. Then there's forensics to hound Cole about, and I think Dr. Jencopale is doing Adams's autopsy this afternoon. Full day."

She patted my knee, a surprising gesture considering we'd only known each other a few days. But look at the few days in question. We'd already seen a lot together, and she was the only one who knew my… preferences. I gave her a grateful smile for her concern.

"Order me a caramel macchiato and we'll go poke our noses around." She said nothing of my ignoring her questions.

Coffee procured, we pulled up to the insurance agency where Mrs. Kaiser worked and went inside. The hushed offices did nothing to hide our presence from Kim Kaiser's coworkers, and she scurried to the receptionist's desk as soon as she was notified of our arrival.

"This isn't a great time," she said, trying not to sound annoyed and mostly pulling it off. "Can I meet you for lunch somewhere else in a couple hours?"

Myah gave her a sympathetic head tilt. "It will only take a few minutes. Is there a conference room where we can go for privacy?"

"Follow me," Kim said, her near-panic morphing into a flinty expression. She led us down a hallway that ended with an employee entrance to the back parking lot, accessible by key card, which she waved in front of the access pad. Fancy, for a small office with less than twenty employees. The bright sunshine foretold a muggy afternoon, and Kim led us to a shaded area with a picnic table on the postage stamp patch of grass where a smoker's butt receptacle stood. She pulled a pack of cigarettes from her pocket and lit up before offering us each one. We both declined. She blew smoke to the side.

"Horrible habit, I know. Quit several years ago. I'm now kicking myself for starting up again after finding George. But at least we won't be bothered out here."

"Mrs. Kaiser, you told me for a short time, you tried to submit to George before you split up."

Alongside impatience, her posture took on a wary cast. "That's right. It wasn't for me."

"Why was that?" I purposefully left the question vague, fishing for anything I wouldn't have thought to ask.

The bench creaked beneath her as she shifted uncomfortably. Myah and I sat on the opposite side, not wanting to tower over or otherwise intimidate her. Myah's hands were loosely folded in front of her, her face interested, not judgmental.

"I don't like pain, Detective," Kim finally answered, taking another long puff of her smoke. "Not that George wanted to do anything abusive. But even a friendly spank or hickey would turn me completely off. George found ways to get me to submit without resorting to pain, but it wasn't enough for him. He missed the paddles and whips, and I couldn't stand those things."

I nodded, using her answer to segue naturally into my next question. "He liked inflicting increments of pain. Anything above and beyond a typical whipping?"

She shook her head. "If he liked more, I didn't know about it. When he found out how shallow my limits were, he never crossed them. When we realized I couldn't really give him what he needed, he didn't exactly tell me what he was doing with other people once we opened our marriage. I didn't ask. As long as he practiced safe sex, I wasn't interested in knowing."

I felt a flare of disappointment but ignored it. "So you wouldn't know if he actually used the ornamental knives in his collection for edge play?"

"Edge play?" she asked, paling considerably. "I don't know what that is."

"It's a more extreme form of BDSM involving knives or fire or asphyxiation."

Her eyes narrowed. "I was unaware his collection included actual weapons, Detective. They weren't part of his repertoire when we lived together."

I frowned. "You said he didn't have a dungeon when you lived together, that his play room was something he created after your divorce."

"That's right," she said quickly. "Just because he didn't have a dedicated room for it during our marriage didn't mean he didn't have his toys. And I don't recall seeing anything more than handcuffs, some rope, a few paddles and whips, and a mask. If George liked those kinds of games, I never suspected."

The mask. "Can you describe his mask?"

She nodded, stubbing out her cigarette on the smoker's corral and lighting another one. "I hated the thing. Sensory deprivation. It was one of the ways we tried my submission without pain, but it was claustrophobic and breathing was difficult. It was leather, and only had tiny nose holes and Velcro coverings for the mouth and eyes. It's supposed to make you feel closer to your partner, only able to feel their touch, but it put me off. I felt the opposite, disconnected and used, like it washed away my humanity and I was just a collection of parts to be toyed with. I couldn't see him and so his hands felt anonymous. I tried it once and made him throw it away after that." She shuddered at the memory.

"Throw it away. You sure he actually did get rid of it?"

"Yeah. He did it in front of me, to prove that even though I was supposed to give him what he wanted, he still had my limits in mind. Promised me he'd never expect me to wear one again."

"He did have another mask. It was on the same receipt from when he purchased the St. Andrew's Cross. But we found no mask anywhere in his house."

She shrugged. "Had to have gotten it after the divorce. Maybe Matt Kinney would know. He was more connected to that side of George than I was." We'd already talked to Kinney twice, and I knew a third time wouldn't get us anywhere. We seemed to be repeatedly throwing ourselves against a brick wall and it was beginning to smart.

I nodded and the three of us rose to our feet. "Thank you for taking the time, Mrs. Kaiser. I hope our presence hasn't stirred up too much trouble for you."

We trekked back toward the employee entrance and Kim held the door for us after buzzing it open. "Detectives, I appreciate all the work you're doing to find George's killer, but if I could ask you a small favor." We stopped in the short hallway, our voices automatically hushing with the quiet of the office.

"Okay," Myah said, waiting for the request.

"If you need to speak to me again, would you mind calling first, or waiting until I'm not at work? I would rather not be overheard or associated with George's lifestyle. I'm not ashamed of my relationship with him, but people here would jump to conclusions about me if they knew about him."

"I don't think that'll be a problem," Myah replied, passing one of her newly minted business cards along. "If you think of anything else, please let us know."

Climbing back into our car, I let out a heavy sigh. "That didn't get us very far."

"Not a definitive 'George used those knives for decoration, not play' so it could still be something he practiced. Though his reputation and lack of disgruntled subs would indicate if he was into edge play, he knew what he was doing." Myah's ease with accepting these relationship dynamics and a mindset she truly didn't understand astounded me. I looked at her out of the corner of my eye, thinking there were worse partners I could have been assigned. Much worse. Instead of saying anything, however, I kept to the subject at hand.

"Yeah. I doubt we'll get any more from Kinney. We need someone else who might've known George's proclivities. Someone with whom he actually played."

"Lead on, General. I will follow."

§§§

COLLARED IN the daytime was silent as a tomb. The main entrance was locked and even our reverberating knock didn't net us the response I'd hoped for.

"I guess they don't do a brisk lunch business," Myah said, knocking again. Still no answer.

"Let's go around back. There has to be a delivery area or a dock." We trooped around the building, entering a wide alley that served all the buildings on the block for trash and other business, wide enough for trucks to park and unload out of the way of general traffic on the busy streets. A beer truck was parked at the delivery entrance for the club, and Jared Nunn stood nearby, checking items off on a clipboard.

"Detective!" he exclaimed, smiling. "Give me a few minutes, and you can help me schlep all this inventory to the walk-in."

"Slave labor," Myah noted, a small smile tugging at her lips as she spoke out of the corner of her mouth. "Do you think he's a Dom?"

I looked at her sideways. "Why, you interested?"

She gave my shoulder a nudge. "Who says I was asking for myself?"

"Well, I know you're not asking for my benefit. I've got a Dom." The burn crept up my face at the idea and the freedom to say so to somebody, but I ignored it. I'll have to get used to it at some point. "Besides, I think Jared's got his hands full with this place."

"I'm thinking Dom." She assessed the man openly, watching

while he signed the bill of lading from the delivery driver and pulled a hand truck from beside the bay door, then stacked boxes of beer bottles with swift, sure movements. The muscles in his arms bulged and he grinned, pointing to another three cases that didn't fit on the dolly.

"Would you mind?" he asked. "Save me the last trip?"

"That depends, Mr. Nunn," Myah answered, face expressionless, though I thought I detected a slight upturn to her lips.

"On what?" he asked in frank appraisal, eyeing her conservative slacks and blouse.

"On just how much information you give us in the next half hour. Call it insurance."

"I call it blackmail." He grinned. He didn't strike me as someone anxious about us poking around him again. Was he that calculated or just that unconcerned?

"It's only blackmail if we threaten you. This is helping you, see? More fitting of the definition of bribery." This time, she let the smile show, which I could see disarmed Nunn like nothing I could have said.

"I'll see what I can do." Jared laughed.

I grabbed a case and motioned with my head for Myah to balance another one on top of it, then waited for her to heft the last one before following Jared through the dim interior of the club to the storage room. The wheels of the dolly squeaked as he set his burden down and moved to shuffle other inventory, keeping the rotation straight. He took the cases from us and efficiently stocked everything just so before turning to us, dusting his hands on his jeans.

"So," Jared started, looking directly at me. "What brings you back here this time, Detective? And is this your new partner?"

"This is Detective Myah Hayes. We'd like to ask you a few more questions about Kaiser. It's come to our attention that you and George had a bit of a confrontation before he left the club his last night. What was it about?"

Nunn scowled. "Which fucking busybody told you that?"

"Doesn't matter," Hayes said dismissively. "We still need to know the nature of that conversation."

He blew out a breath. "George hit on Master Lacey. Pissed me off because he knew she was in a committed relationship, and she never dates Doms anyway. She is a Domme. Occasionally, he and Lacey would discuss techniques they hadn't mastered, but if they set up a scene, they would *always* bring their own subs. That's why I was so shocked by what he said to Lacey."

"What did he say?"

Nunn shook his head, clearly uncomfortable. "Said if she knew what was good for her, she'd have let him bend her over and show her what real domination was, that she needed a little humiliation in her life. As if she doesn't know how to dominate," he scoffed. "I would have just written it off as him having had too much to drink, but he hadn't drunk enough to make him stupid. Lacey can handle herself and I know she's heard worse from a lot of assholes, so she didn't need me intervening. But that's partly what shocked me. That *George* was the one who said it. So I lost my temper and demanded he apologize. I knew the guy was getting lonely, but I didn't think it would make his judgment so poor. I didn't want him walking her out to her car, but she insisted, and when I talked to her about it first thing the next night, she said it was done, that everything was fine. I took her at her word."

"What's your opinion of Seth Adams?" Hayes flipped the subject. It was a good tactic. As Nunn focused on the argument with Kaiser, if he'd had any similar impressions of Adams, those would be the first to show on his face.

Nunn raised his eyebrows. "Seth Adams? Good guy and extremely loyal to Robert. What, is he a suspect or something?"

I shook my head, mouth grim. "Not exactly."

Staring at each of us in turn, his eyes widened, mouth forming a surprised O when he made the connection. If he were involved, his acting was stellar. "Goddamn," he muttered, leading us out of the storage room and to one of the high-backed leather booths that surrounded the sunken dance floor. "When?" His hands shook as he scrubbed them over his face, which had gone pale.

"Adams was found early yesterday morning by Robert," Myah answered. "I take it you were unaware of his death."

Nunn nodded, picking brutally at his fingernails. "I wasn't at the club the last two nights. I had Master Lacey running the place so I could deal with some personal things. How is Robert?"

"He's as well as can be expected." I flipped open my notebook and clicked my pen. "So you weren't here on the night in question?"

"No." Jaw jutting defiantly, he practically dared us to accuse him of something.

"Your whereabouts, Mr. Nunn?" Myah asked politely.

"I was helping my sister move out of her abusive husband's reach. He's terrorized her for years, but she put her foot down when he hit their son. I moved her and my nephew to a hotel across town and put their stuff in storage."

Myah clucked sympathetically. "Will she be willing to confirm that for you?"

Nunn nodded. I wasn't quite as sure, however. An argument with the first victim didn't bode well, and I wasn't convinced of his alibi for the second victim's murder. If he'd done for his sister what he said he'd done, she'd be grateful enough to cover him no matter what night it was he'd rescued her. Hotel records should show the night she checked in, however, so his story could be corroborated. I was both relieved and disappointed. Nunn was the first inkling of a lead we'd had, but at the same time, I liked the man. He had a genuine appreciation for people in the lifestyle, and protected them like they were his own. He was very much the owner of Collared in every sense of the word, from slinging drinks and schlepping inventory, to his care and responsibility for those who passed through his doors. Still, we were no closer to finding our killer.

"How well did you know Mr. Adams?"

Jared shrugged. "As well as I know any of my regulars, I guess. Who they play with, their drinks of choice."

"Do you often know what kind of play certain patrons engage in?" Myah asked.

Jared studied her, perhaps looking for any of the derisiveness my last partner had shown. I supposed he found none, because he answered her without any of the defensiveness he'd shown me the first time I'd spoken to him with Sawyer at my side.

"Some of them. Lacey tells me some things, from what she learns upstairs. Things I need to know to run a safe club as well as keep in mind if I'm trying to make a match."

"Do you do that often?" Myah queried. "Set people up with each other?"

Jared shrugged. "Sometimes new people come in and want to play. It's good business to give them a place to do so and a recommendation if I know what they like and who's free."

"Did you know what George Kaiser liked?" I asked, pen scratching against the paper of my notebook.

"George was fairly straightforward. He had pretty high standards but he was also a good-natured man, that one bout of verbal diarrhea notwithstanding. If someone wholly new to the lifestyle was looking to find a way in, George was a good bet, with the bonus of gender not being a big deal. But he wasn't always interested in initiating new subs. He had the patience, but training someone can be exhausting." I kept my face neutral, trying not to think of Ben. "George told me some time ago he was through with new initiates for a while, so I stopped recommending him. He nearly quit playing, except for two regular subs he saw, but they were there for the mechanics, not the connection. They weren't under contract with him, just casual, free-to-play type arrangements."

"Did he ever play here? Upstairs or on stage?"

"Only upstairs. George wasn't into public displays. He used the private rooms unless he knew the person well enough to take them home. He only used the semi-private rooms once, and only a couple weeks before his death. I don't know what he thought of it."

"Did George ever engage in edge play?" Myah asked.

Jared narrowed his eyes at her. "Once that I know of, but his sub had no complaints. He liked sensory deprivation, masks and such. The design of most masks makes breath play easier. Lacey never had a problem with him, and I only heard good things from his subs."

"Was he into knife play?"

"Now that, I know nothing about."

"What about Seth Adams?"

"Seth and Robert were a little more open. They used the semi-public rooms sometimes."

"How far did they go?" Myah's tone was light, as if she were asking what kind of drink Seth typically ordered.

Jared, however, squirmed uncomfortably. "Hasn't Robert told you all of this? I mean, George didn't have a regular sub, so I can understand having to answer these questions about him. But Robert would know more about this than I would."

"Robert has been very forthcoming with us," Myah assured him. "We need a knowledgeable outsider's perspective, though."

"Robert and Seth were great together. Seth was particularly skilled with a cane, and they'd often play on stage. The last several months, though, that tapered off. I don't know why, but I suspect it's because they were moving into other areas. Last time they were here, Seth asked me what my rules were about the semi-public rooms upstairs and how much display I was comfortable having. I told him I'd prefer not to have to clean up blood, but they were likely safer doing dangerous stuff here than at home. If something went wrong, Lacey would be right there if they needed her. I told him to talk to her, set up a time, and go over exactly what he had in mind before they did anything. It would give us a chance to stock the room for them and get any specific first aid supplies for the aftercare Robert would require. Last I knew, Seth had yet to talk to Lacey."

"When was this?" Myah asked.

"Three weeks ago. He told me he had a conference he was planning to attend in Colorado, and would get with Lacey when he returned. I hadn't heard from her, so I assume they never discussed it. You'd have to ask her."

"Is she coming in tonight?" I wanted to know.

"She'll be here every night from now until Saturday."

Remembering Matt Kinney had given me the names of George's most recent subs, I flipped back through my notes to find them. "Do you have contact information for Russell Price and Kristy Sutton? We'll need to speak to them."

He nodded, led us to the bar and slipped behind it, digging out a Rolodex.

"I make the regulars give me an email address and someone to contact in emergencies. I've set up a Yahoo chat group and many of the club regulars are in that group, discussing cons and munches or techniques and such. I only have phone numbers for their emergency contacts, not them." He passed over a cocktail napkin with the email addresses on them, his expression sad. "Please tell me you're gonna find this guy. I like my customers. I don't want to lose any more."

Myah piped up, surprising me with the fierceness in her tone. "I can assure you, Mr. Nunn, we are doing everything we can."

With a raised brow, he nodded at her. "Call me Jared. And if there's anything more I can do to help, just ask." He pointed to the napkin I held. "That's got my cell number on it, too. Seriously, anything you need, just call. I want this bastard stopped."

Giving him a respectful nod, we turned and left through the back door, squinting in the bright midday sun that stung after the dimness of the bar.

"So, lunch, questioning George's subs, or Adams's autopsy?" Myah sauntered down the alley, hands in her pockets like she was taking a stroll. I could tell, however, by the tense set of her shoulders, that she was faking.

"Lunch while I email these two," I held up the napkin. "Autopsy, and then hopefully, we can question George's friends. Trust me, if we don't eat now, you won't want to later."

"I've seen autopsies before, Detective," she snapped, startling me.

My steps faltered as we reached the car, but she didn't notice, merely dropping into the passenger seat with a weary sigh.

"You all right?" I didn't look at her, simply starting the car and pulling into traffic.

"Yes," came her terse response.

I let it drop. Everyone dealt with the job in their own way, and we had a long way to go before we knew each other's reactions to unpleasant circumstances. The silence stretched between us as I drove to Fitz's, a restaurant nearby that made their own root beer and had a decent lunch menu.

"Sorry, Gavin," Myah said as I pulled into the parking lot. "Most of the time, I can keep perspective, but there's always a moment in each case when I'm reminded we're dealing with real people, who had favorite foods and read books and picked popcorn out of their teeth, with loved ones who will miss them. It burns me that there are others who don't respect life enough to not take it away from someone. Nunn's response was that moment for me, and I don't like feeling like we're not getting anywhere."

"Don't worry about it. If you didn't have some kind of reaction to all of this at some point, I'd wonder at your stability. I've already fallen apart once, just not in front of you. And a lot worse than this. So I fully expect an all-out conniption by the end of the week. Understood?"

She nodded, her jaw clenched, ignoring my attempt at humor. She swung out of the car and stalked toward the restaurant, head down. Once seated, I pulled out my phone and called the precinct with a request for Lawanda, the receptionist and information guru, to track down Kaiser's two subs based off their email addresses. I decided not to go for the polite, make-an-appointment approach. Not fast enough. I wanted to meet them as soon as possible, face to face, and on my terms. It was time to get some answers.

§§§

SETH ADAMS'S autopsy proved his death was linked to George Kaiser in a few ways. One, there'd been anal penetration without evidence of lubricant or semen. Two, he'd been strangled after being brutally beaten. Three, said beating had resulted in small puncture wounds consistent with the marks on Kaiser—marks which confirmed the use of vampire gloves, tested by Cole's department using a similar set. Four, like the first victim, the ink on Seth's face outlined tear tracks. A tox screen had been sent to the lab with a full panel request, but I knew what it would say: Adams had been drugged before he was restrained.

Myah and I had been glued to our desks for days, poring over forensics, trying to find similarities between the victims, scouring for new leads. Russell Price and Kristy Sutton had provided statements about the nature of their play with Kaiser, consistent with Jared Nunn's assertion they were friends with benefits, nothing more. Russell had said there was nothing extreme about their play, but Kristy had admitted that George's interests in the weeks before his death had grown in danger and she'd elaborated on the one scene George had had in a semi-private room. She hadn't been afraid of him at any point, but she had noticed his dominance had taken on a more precarious tone.

"We talked about it before he planned any scenes with me, so everything was consensual, but I've been one of his subs for years, and he'd never been that... I don't know the word. He wasn't dangerous, but it felt dangerous. I won't lie and say I wasn't attracted to it," she said, fiddling with the coffee cup wrapped in her hands. Her slight body curled around the steam from the mug, and I suspected if we hadn't been in her tidy apartment, her willingness to talk would have been non-existent. She brushed a lock of shiny black hair behind her ear, talking without meeting our eyes. Myah hung back, sensing the girl felt more comfortable with me, somehow picking up a kindred spirit. Or perhaps my taller stature reminded her of dominance, someone to whom she wanted to defer. I didn't know and I wasn't about to take it for granted.

"What were his requests?"

Still not making eye contact, Kristy looked in the vicinity of the knot in my tie. "He wanted to asphyxiate me. I wasn't against it, but I know it's the riskiest of all the edge play. I mean, come on. You can end up a vegetable, or even *die*. Knife play, you may get a couple scars, maybe some stitches, and if you do it too often, anemic. Fire play, same thing, scars. But you're not depriving your brain of oxygen. There's no risk of brain damage with knives or matches."

"Did you agree?" I asked gently, taking a sip of coffee, doing my best to make the conversation as normal as talk of favorite books or restaurants.

"After a few conversations, yeah. I told him I didn't want a mask, that I had to be able to see his face and make sure he could see mine. I needed more intimacy from him than usual, to understand it wasn't sinister. So we agreed to manual strangulation."

It was all I could do not to look at Myah with any kind of significance.

"George was going to strangle you," I clarified.

She nodded. "With his hands, so he could feel exactly what he was doing, no gloves or scarves or ropes. He had the idea to use a bell ball in case I needed to safeword, since I would be unable to speak. All I had to do was shake it, throw it, whatever. If I passed out, dropping it would signal him to let go. I also required the scene take place in one of the semi-privates at Collared, and we have our own Dungeon Master for the entire scene. I didn't want trouble in another room to take Master Lacey away from us at a bad time. A tiny mistake, a few seconds too long, and that'd be it for me."

She took a deep breath and fell into silence, her hazel eyes unfocused with memory. I waited her out.

"It was two weeks between when we played and when I found out he was killed. The scene was everything he promised it could be, and he told me later we had quite the audience by the end. I only remember his eyes, how intense they'd been, how gentle his hands were on my neck even as he increased the pressure. He wasn't trying to hurt me, only make me fly. He said I never passed out, so I must've hit subspace really hard and fast. I don't remember much more than soaring as high as I've ever gone with any Dom. I get why people do it, now. Putting not just your safety, your trust in a Dom, but your *life* in his hands. Frankly, I was hoping George would want to talk contract with me after that scene. Obviously not right after, but a few days later. I've never come so hard or felt so much for a Dom because of a single night of play than I did that night. It gave me a new appreciation for him, someone I'd only ever looked at as a competent Dom who could scratch that all important itch for me when we were both between partners. I'm honestly sad it was the only time we got to play like that."

"I don't suppose you'd remember the faces from the audience that night," I asked, not expecting anything but a negative response.

She shook her head, smiling ruefully as well as apologetically. "Sorry, Detective. I barely remember anything but George's aftercare. It was the first and only time he stayed with me all night, and the only time we came back to my apartment instead of going to his house. Hell, even the next morning is a little blurry, like the morning you wake with a giant hangover from a drunken black-out the night before. Maybe Master Lacey remembers or the security feeds show it."

I heard Myah's pen scratching out a note as I stood to take my coffee cup to Kristy's sink and rinse it out.

"Miss Sutton, you've been very helpful. If you can think of anything else, please call or email me." I passed her a card before joining Myah by the front door. I turned at the last moment. "Oh, one more thing. Have you anyone in your past that might have learned of that scene with George who might take offense to your engaging in breath play? Someone who might think that George asking you to do such a thing was over the line and would try to protect you by harming him?"

Kristy was already shaking her head by the time I'd finished the question. "No, sir. I have a good relationship with all my past Doms, and they know me well enough to trust I can take care of myself, that I know when to use my safe words. Anyone in my past who might know about that scene would know I was completely willing."

"Thank you, Miss Sutton. Please call if you have any more information."

Overall, the conversation had yielded little, but even so, Myah and I agreed we were on the right track, however slowly we were crawling along it. Robert Weiss had much the same to say about Seth Adams, that they'd discussed taking their play to the next level and Seth had been in the midst of intense research before his death, having just been out of town for a conference where he'd met with a Dom renowned for techniques on the extreme side. This, too, matched Nunn's statement, and Adams's credit card charges confirmed a hotel room and meals for an extended weekend. Robert hadn't attended with him due to a work conflict, but they'd begun discussing what to try. Seth hadn't owned any knives as Kaiser had, so a connection to a manufacturer wasn't possible. Robert hadn't known who else had attended the conference beyond those Seth had told him about, which included half the clientele of Collared.

With a frustrated sigh, Myah threw her pen on her desk and stretched, rolling her shoulders. We'd been poring over documents for hours. The sun had finally given up and sank below the horizon, letting night press in through the station windows. The grit in my eyes reminded me that too much computer time would leave me prone to headaches, and I was dangerously close to reaching that misery.

"I can't look at this stuff anymore," she mumbled. "Do you want some coffee?"

As she stood to go to the break room, I shook my head. "Let's call it a night. I'm as burned out as you are, and if I look at these files anymore, I'll forget how to read. They're all blurring together." Despite my words, I squinted at the screen and at my pages of notes. "Another similarity is that Damon Lane had an appointment with Adams to discuss making a breath play mask for Robert. They never met, same as George Kaiser. But that's hardly a surprise, given how many people Lane makes equipment for and the fact that both men were dead by the time their appointments rolled around. The appointments didn't happen, so there's nothing there to spark opportunity."

"Yeah," Myah agreed, yawning. "All right. Let's hit it again tomorrow. I was planning on meeting up with someone for drinks in an hour anyway."

I raised a brow at her. "Oh yeah? Anyone I know?"

"Maybe," was her cryptic reply.

I barked out a laugh. "Oh, I get it. You get to ask me anything you want, but I can't ask you. Hardly fair, Detective Hayes."

"Oh, you can ask all you want," she said, her eyes twinkling. "But like you, I will simply bite my tongue and change the subject. It goes both ways, Detective DeGrassi."

"Touché. Have a good night, then."

On my way to the car, I checked my phone and found a message from Ben and a text from Cole. Dealing with the text first, I called my brother.

"Hey, I'm still at the station. Want me to pick up a late dinner if you haven't eaten?"

"Oh, I already ate, bro. I was just letting you know I'll be out, so if I don't come home you won't be worried about me."

"Got another one on the hook? What happened to the last one? Carol was her name?"

"Oh, she couldn't handle me wanting to sleep alone after sex."

"But this one, you'll be out all night for?"

"Who says we'll be sleeping?" he laughed. "Anyway, I'll tell you about mine when you decide to tell me about yours."

My smile faltered and the conversation stopped being funny. "Not yet," was all I could manage. "I'll tell you, but not yet."

"You know, it's okay that you're dating so soon after Victoria. It's not like you ever had a chance to experiment in college or play the field. Believe it or not, Gavin, I'm happy you're dating already. It means she didn't break you."

Clearing my throat, I got in my car and turned it on, cranking the a/c. "It's complicated, Cole."

There was a long beat of silence, and then he said, "You don't have to hide anything from me, Gavin. I'm your brother. I'll always be your brother. Whatever is going on, I'll back you up. Even if it's the boss's daughter."

I forced a laugh. "Well, that's good to know. Not so sure Mason or Shawn could say the same. Code of conduct and all that jazz."

"Yeah, well, you're actually happy. I don't care who it is, as long as you keep being happy."

I was absurdly touched by that, even if that was how family was supposed to be. Given the collateral damage of this particular explosion, I could see why people worried about coming out, and I was acutely aware of how keen on appearances my own family was. I'd cross that bridge another time.

"Have a good night, Cole."

"Later, Gav." He rang off.

With the night stretched before me, a resounding ache in my eyeballs, and having not had a lot of time to myself the last several days, it was no surprise that instead of going to Cole's empty apartment with a greasy takeout burger, I pointed my car to Ben's and the anticipated warmth of his arms.

CHAPTER TEN

CREEPING UP on a month since George Kaiser's murder, I was ready to crawl out of my skin with frustration. I'd spent time going back and forth between the two victims' houses, memorizing their reports, and going over witness statements for that one clue that would lead to the answers we so desperately needed to crack the case. Myah had driven herself just as mercilessly until the previous afternoon, when she'd let out an explosive groan and *thunked* her head on her desk.

"Gavin, I need a day off or I'm going to find a clock tower and start aiming."

Sergeant Talcott happened to be striding by and, overhearing her words, stopped at our desks for a moment, stoic expression firmly in place.

"DeGrassi, Hayes, go home. You can't wring blood from paper, and those reports don't say anything they didn't say yesterday or the day before. You're no good to me burned out. Take the next forty-eight hours off. If you're still here in ten minutes, I'm assigning you to the next call that comes in."

"Thank god," Myah muttered, grabbing her jacket and flicking off her monitor. "Text me if anything happens. I've got an apartment to see."

I really need to do that, too. The case had been so consuming, I'd shoved aside all else other than Ben. Two days prior, I'd gotten a call from my exasperated attorney reminding me of the mediation I was ten minutes late for. The last of the paperwork for my divorce had been finalized and all that had been left was to sign on the dotted line. Not even Victoria's cold scowl had cut through my haze of preoccupation with finding the killer, though the feeling of freedom

I'd reveled in while leaving the attorney's offices had been a nice bonus.

The only time my irritation abated was in Ben's presence, and this was no exception. The room was dark except for the flickering TV, and Ben was beneath me on the couch, on his back, with me sprawled atop him, my cheek resting on his chest. The rise and fall of his breath was comfortable, and I was content. The movie, some foreign film with subtitles, failed to hold my attention, and I let my mind wander, practically purring as Ben's fingers combed my hair.

"You couldn't care less about this film, could you?" he asked.

I raised my head, grinning sheepishly. "If it's the reason I'm plastered to you like a two-for-one perfume counter special, then I love this film."

The rumble of his laughter transferred through my arms and chest, and I rubbed my face in his shirt. When I raised my eyes again, his thumb grazed my cheekbone as his smile faded, replaced by solemn tenderness. I studied him for a few more seconds before resting my cheek once more on his pec, trying to pay attention to the words on the screen.

"Gavin?"

"Mmm?"

"I think it's time I got you under contract."

My heart began a steady gallop, but I didn't move another muscle, letting the words sink in. *A contract. His sub, for the foreseeable future.* It sounded wonderful, stable, but what if I was too new? What if I couldn't handle it? Truthfully, we'd had a couple of kinky scenes, and I was into it, but I didn't have a clue how far I wanted to go. And what about work? My strange hours meant I could go days without seeing him, and I wasn't sure that would be acceptable. Then again, he was well aware of my duties and what they did to my schedule. It had been nearly a month since we'd met, and if he didn't know now—

"Gavin, stop overthinking."

I chuckled. "I'm that obvious?"

"To me, yeah." He nudged me so we could sit up and he took my hand in his, tangling our fingers. "If you're worried about your job, don't be. I have my patients and you have your cases and there will be times they get priority over everything else. But I want more than just to date you. I want you restrained, mine to play with, to spank, to take to new heights as I see fit, and to hold as you come down. I want you kneeling at my feet, taking my paddle or the crop or cane. I want my marks under your clothes. I want to take you to Collared and let them see that you belong to me, and what a good boy you are, how well you submit."

My dick was hard at "I want you restrained"... The rest had me panting, and a thrill raced up my spine, the thought of being paraded through Collared as Ben's sub stirring something deep inside me.

"What do you think?"

"I think... I'd like a contract." My voice cracked on the last syllable and we grinned at each other.

"Stay here," he ordered. He disappeared into the hallway toward his home office and returned a minute later with a sheaf of papers in his hand and a pen. Passing them to me, he had me read it over. "This is a fairly standard contract, with spaces for negotiable bits and a page each to discuss limits."

He gave me time to read it, and while I wasn't big on legalese, there was little of that. It was more about when negotiations would happen, including weekly sessions in the "safe room," which, for us, was Ben's giant bathtub in the loft, where any concerns were discussed by either party. There were blanks for length of the contract term, a limitation that I submit only to him for the duration of the contract, and a stipulation that he adhere to safe words. If at any time I felt my safety was in danger, I was free to break the contract. If either of us felt we should discontinue the relationship, there was a clause for that as well.

"Looks like you thought of everything."

He laughed. "I've been doing this a while. Fairly standard terms. What makes it personal are the limits we set." He flipped to the back, where a page was laid out with columns describing behaviors and types of play, along with space to "rate" each on a scale varying from interested to don't even wish to discuss and whether those were linked to soft or hard limits.

"It looks so... clinical."

"It's straightforward. Best not to leave any room for confusion when it comes to limits. Speaking of which," he added, smoothing the papers onto the coffee table and writing each of our names atop identical checklists. "Edge play. I'm not into that. I can appreciate it, but I do not want to engage in it." I flashed back to our conversation about Nathan, his last sub, and understood why he wouldn't go there. I took the pen and wrote the same for edge play on my checklist. After the things I'd seen the last few weeks, I'd take a pass.

"Work," he said as he wrote the word on both our pages. "You get called in, I get called in. It happens. We stop everything and handle what needs to be handled."

"Agreed."

"Public scenes," he said, looking at me expectantly.

My insides twisted, and I hesitated. The idea thrilled me, no doubt. Hearing him talk about letting people see I belonged to him was more than a turn-on—it felt right, like I had a place and it was at his feet, proudly displayed as his and his alone. But there were other concerns. Fear of what people would think, if it would compromise my authority in front of those I might have to question. *Ginger Graham knows me.* I remembered Master Lacey's partner and sub who'd confirmed the Domme's alibi for the night George Kaiser was murdered. I didn't realize I'd spoken aloud until Ben answered me.

"She does. She also knows better than anyone the position you're in. She's in the same boat, is she not?"

"I guess so. And I didn't know about her, so I suppose people can be tactful. But Ben, I don't know where this investigation will lead. I can't compromise my position by having people I question dismiss my authority because I'm a submissive."

"Have you considered the possibility that anyone you might need to speak to would be more willing to do so if they know you understand more about the lifestyle than the average detective?"

That stunned me for a moment, and I shook my head. "No, I hadn't considered that."

"So you're automatically assuming people will think negatively of you submissive to me in public."

Panic rose in my chest, and I warred with guilt from the truth of it. It wasn't in me to lie to him, so I merely nodded.

"Soft limit," he said, writing beneath my name. "Public displays limited to lifestyle situations." He met my eyes. "Until you're more comfortable with your status." His tone was patient, his eyes soft, understanding. "It's a lot to take in, Gavin, and I don't expect you to be the perfect sub overnight." Under his own page, he wrote, speaking the words simultaneously, "Hard limit, public displays necessary."

He set the pen down and drew me into his lap, pulling my head to his shoulder. "I won't hide who I am. I will respect the situation in which I ask you to show others your true nature, but this is part of it. You're my pet and I'm proud of you. I want my friends to know you, to know what we have. I want others to see how well you behave. Other subs will envy you being mine. Other Doms will assess how thoroughly you give yourself to me and judge me based on that. It's exhilarating to earn their respect. But in the end, it's about you and me. Public scenes can heighten awareness, take you places I can't take you when we're alone, and bind you to me more fully than any other method of submission. Trust me, Gavin. You have to trust me."

I nodded into the crook of his neck, feeling the bands around my chest loosen. Still, what I had to say was easier with my face buried. "I need time. I'm not out, Ben, and especially not about this. I don't know how long it'll take me to change that. I'm afraid of my family's reaction, so I have to ask you to respect that. At Collared, okay, or other leather clubs you attend. In public, at cons or munches where anyone could be there? I can't say right now."

"We'll take it as it comes. Contract terms can change. Neither of us can see the future, Gavin. Just try for me."

I nodded and his arms tightened further. We maintained that position for a long time, discussing potential limits during actual play, my thoughts concerning certain implements, and restraints. The longer we spoke, the more I relaxed. He'd snagged the papers and despite my offer to move so he could more comfortably fill out the details, he refused, using the arm of the couch as a writing surface and holding me firmly in his lap.

The import of our discussion sank in when he scrawled his name on the last page with a flourish and passed me the pen, his eyes bright. I took the pen and willed my hand to stop shaking as I added my name beneath his. *Three months. I'm his for three months, at least.* With a finger beneath my chin to guide my face down, he kissed me, deep and tender. He was the one to pull back, and we simply stared at each other, smiling, peaceful. So when he slapped my ass, I jumped.

"Okay, time to go."

"Go?" I sat up and he dumped me onto the couch and stood.

"Yep. We're celebrating, and your first lesson in public submission begins now."

I gulped, taking his proffered hand to rise to my feet. Unconsciously, I presented, feet apart, eyes down, hands behind my back.

"See?" he asked, lips near my ear, amusement in his tone. "You're more ready than you believe. But first, a couple things before we get changed. Strip."

I wanted to ask, to know what was coming, but my knowing wouldn't change what Ben had planned, so I bit my tongue and unbuttoned my shirt, kicking off my shoes at the same time. The clothes I discarded, he took and folded neatly, resting them on a nearby chair. When I was naked before him, he circled me, inspecting.

"Stand straighter. Push your chest out. It'll feel strange but looks incredible." He could see the tension in my shoulders as I obeyed him, and he leaned close once more. "I won't parade you naked through the club. This isn't about humiliation. It's about showing me that my opinion holds more weight than anyone else's. But we have to give you the means to do so first. I'll be right back."

He squeezed one ass cheek as he sidestepped me and headed up to his loft before returning quickly with a delicate chain looped over one hand. He dangled it for me to see the ends. My eyes widened and he stepped forward, one hand moving to pinch my left nipple to stiffness. I sucked in a breath, staring at his chin.

"Gavin, look at me."

I did, and saw his dominance shining back at me, his eyes alight. My insides swirled. Trepidation fought with anticipation, and above all, the need to please wound its sinuous way up my spine. I could do this.

"I'm going to teach you to walk at heel, and while we may need more than one lesson, this will do for now." The nipple he'd peaked suddenly burst into flame as he affixed a clamp. "It hurts going on, more so when coming off, but it'll go numb in a second, and I'm not tightening these very much. I don't want to cut off your blood supply completely since you'll be wearing them awhile. Pinching, not crushing." The other nipple was given the same treatment, and he held the chain between them at equal tension. Slowly, he lowered his hand, and the chain, once so delicate, quickly became insidiously heavy as it pulled at the clamps until my nipples bore the whole weight.

Ben turned his back to me, the end of the chain resting slackly in one hand. "I'm going to walk, and you'll follow. Match your steps to mine, half a step behind me. If you fall back, the chain will let you know. If I stop and you don't, you'll bump me and your nipples will feel it. Keep pace well and you'll be fine until I remove them. Starting... now."

He took a step and I followed, but too slowly. The chain pulled and my entire chest lit on fire. I quickly widened my stride to keep with him and found the pace to match. We walked around the perimeter of the living room.

"Head and shoulders back, eyes down," he instructed, watching me over his shoulder. "It might help to find a spot to focus on, preferably on me so you'll know when I stop."

At the word, he abruptly stopped and I ran into him, hissing as the pressure flared into real pain once more.

"Again." He didn't wait for me to recover, and I didn't expect him to start so soon, so the chain tugged. I whimpered, scurrying to catch up. We paraded through the kitchen and around the breakfast bar, and I focused on his lower back. I saw most of his frame from that central point and could watch his feet. When he stopped again, I stopped with him, noting how his step altered just before he halted. His heel rose and in near perfect unison, we marched across the living room to his bedroom, the pain in my sensitive buds numbing to something I could handle. He grinned after three successive stops and starts where I didn't trip up, thanks to my observation of his body.

He stopped near an armoire in his bedroom and let the chain fall. The extra tug on my nipples made me hiss. I tried to swallow it, but he shook his head.

"I like your sounds. I want to hear them. Unless I tell you to be silent, you will let me hear you."

"Yes, Sir," I replied, presenting while he rifled through a drawer in the armoire. When he turned to me, he had boxer shorts and a pair of jeans folded neatly in his hands. He lifted the chain and walked me to his closet, where once again, he let the chain fall, more abruptly than before. I whined, my hands white knuckled and fisted fiercely so I didn't remove the clamps, didn't free myself of the small torture. Apparently, my cock liked the proceedings, though, because from the minute Ben had slapped my ass, it had been heavy and at attention. It freely leaked pre-come and I couldn't help a few small jerks of my hips. Ben, of course, saw everything.

"Ah, ah, ah." He wagged a finger in front of my face with one hand and gently slapped my dick with the other. "This is mine. I didn't say you could use it." With a groan of frustration, I went still. He tilted my chin and kissed me obscenely, keeping his body well away from me. I felt more than heard the chain fall away from the clamps, the brush of the metal caressing my heavy prick on its way to the floor. "The clamps stay on," he murmured, more to himself than me, but I answered anyway.

"Yes, Sir."

"They are your reminder to stay at my heel. If I sit, you will kneel at my feet immediately, rising only when I tell you. If you need a drink or to use the restroom, merely tell me and go, returning quickly. Any time you get yourself a drink, bring me one as well. You're free to speak to others, but I would suggest waiting to speak to any Doms until after they've spoken to you. Be respectful, but you're mine to command, not theirs. They'll know this, and shouldn't cross any lines, whether I'm beside you or not. If you're unsure and I'm not there to control the situation, simply thank them for noticing you and return to my side."

"Understood."

"Turn around." He slid a T-shirt over my head from behind and pulled it down, careful to navigate the hem over the clamps. The material rubbed my chest in an exquisite way, and no matter where the cotton touched, I felt it in my nipples. My cock hardened further. Ben slid another shirt, this one a short-sleeved button-down, up my arms and over my shoulders and turned me around to face him. "Leave this one open. It'll somewhat hide the clamp bumps with the bonus of adding pressure to them, depending on how you move. To the wall, facing it, legs spread." He pointed to a span of wall beside his bedside table and I heard him rummaging in the drawer as I complied.

Slick fingers quickly slid into my asshole, and I locked down on them in shock.

"Open, Gavin," he commanded.

"Sorry, Sir. You surprised me." Almost a month with him, and my ass had become increasingly used to being penetrated, but it was still an effort to relax while he coaxed his fingers in and out. His touch was nearly clinical, not teasing or working my prostate. He was only spreading lube.

"Bend slightly at the waist," he instructed, and I did so. Immediately, I felt the blunt pressure of a plug, this one wide and cold compared to the rubber one which I'd become accustomed to. I sucked in a breath and released it on a moan, pressing my hips back. "This one is smoother, made out of medical grade stainless steel. You will keep it inside you at all costs. Your muscles need training, and it serves the dual purpose of forcing you to work those muscles and reminding you you're mine. If you behave tonight, show them you're a good sub, I'll fuck you and maybe even let you come, and you'll be nice and stretched for me."

I gritted my teeth, fighting not to come right then. This was, by far, the most demanding he'd been of me since we'd started playing. Before, he'd held plugs in place with straps, restrained me in helpful ways, and encouraged or gently corrected me when he could see I was slipping. I understood this to be my real initiation into his world, where he would gauge what I'd learned and how well.

Gratitude swept through me like a cool wind on a hot day, and my pending orgasm, radiating from my core through my limbs, subsided. My body vibrated with pleasure, and even my nipples tingled with warmth. It was like the aftermath of a climax, without the loss of my erection or the release of semen.

"I can do this, Sir," I said as he turned me around and pointed to the bed, where he'd laid the jeans and underwear.

"I know you can, love," he answered, stepping back into his closet for his own clothes. The boxers were loose, so they wouldn't help keep the plug seated in my ass, while the jeans, new but looking well-worn, molded to my frame. They were very comfortable, which I appreciated. My focus would be split between too many goals—pleasing Ben, keeping my nipples from searing agony, and holding the plug within my body. Uncomfortable clothes would have been an unnecessary sensation that would have hindered rather than helped. The plug alone was proving difficult to manage.

Emerging from the closet in charcoal slacks that hugged his hips deliciously and a black shirt of some slippery material that looked tailored for him, Ben held two pair of shoes, his own dress shoes and a pair of loafers for me.

I slipped my bare feet into them, the plug shifting inside me in a way that weakened my knees. Ben grinned.

"Ready?"

Sweat dampened my underarms and lower back as I nodded, and he led me to his car. As he backed down the driveway, I spoke.

"A request, Sir."

"Yes?" he asked, his attention on the road.

"Please don't wreck."

"I didn't plan on it, but why?" his smile made me want to kiss him, to bite the smugness off his face, and to whisper my gratitude at his adept handling of my body with his cruel, exacting toys. I'd been his before, but this... This was a whole new kind of claiming.

"I'd rather not have the seatbelt shear off a nipple by way of the clamps."

His laughter rang through the car, making me smile. He gripped my hand as he drove, bringing my knuckles to his lips. "Everybody will love you this way."

"I'm glad, Sir, but I only care about you—" *loving me*. I only just managed to bite back the words. *Holy shit, did I almost say that out loud?* I clenched my jaw, shocked. *There's no way he missed that. He reads me better than I read myself.*

Ben, however, said nothing, merely tightening his grip on my hand, his posture relaxed as he navigated the streets to the club.

Already off-kilter from the torment to my body and nervous about publicly declaring myself Ben's sub, my mind reeled. I needed to find my center, and thinking about what almost tumbled out of my mouth was not helpful. Carefully wiping away all thoughts, I focused on breathing gingerly so my nipples hurt less, on sitting still so the plug would stay put, and on remembering the instructions Ben had given me about my behavior. It was almost a relief to arrive at the club, where my attention could focus wholly on Ben and *not* my nearly blurted confession.

True summer gripped the city, and the humidity made my T-shirt stick to my skin as we walked to the entrance with me half a step behind Ben, concentrating on his movements. The bouncer jumped to his feet when we entered the vestibule and moved to open the door quickly before seeing who was with Ben. He stopped in his tracks.

"Good to see you, Mr. Haverson," he said respectfully. I felt his eyes on me, though I didn't raise my own. "Detective."

"Just Mr. DeGrassi tonight, Juice," Ben corrected him.

I had to swallow a flash of irritation, and I considered saying something to Ben about this being exactly the stripping of my authority I was concerned about. How would that guy take me seriously now? I *wanted* him to think of me as only a detective. Bouncers see more than they let on, and this guy could be a valuable source of information—though we hadn't had reason to question him—but how likely was he to trust me if I looked weak to him?

Just as I opened my mouth to ask Ben if we could discuss it, the bouncer continued. "Welcome back, Mr. DeGrassi. It's good to see you here in an unofficial capacity. Let me know if there's anything you need."

Huh. His tone was a lot more solicitous than the first time I'd been here and spoken to him. I remembered Ben had given me permission to converse with anyone, and I was standing there gaping like a moron. I snapped my jaw shut and nodded.

"Thank you... I didn't get your name last time we spoke."

"Ronald, but my friends call me Juice. I don't do that stuff, but the nickname stuck."

"That stuff?"

"Steroids, Mr. DeGrassi." To prove his point, he flexed his massive biceps, and his T-shirt nearly whined in protest.

I nodded in understanding, feeling like a fool. "Thanks, uh, Juice. I appreciate the, uh, offer." My god, I was nervous. I resumed my downcast gaze behind Ben and waited.

"Oh!" Juice jumped to open the door, realizing we were still waiting to be let in. "Sorry, sir. Just caught by surprise."

"No problem, Juice," Ben said with a hearty clap to the beefy man's shoulder.

The club was busy, but the music wasn't overpowering as it had been on previous visits during the height of a weekend night. It was still early, however, and the crowd would swell in an hour or so. Ben made his way across the bar area to the tables surrounding the dance floor, pausing briefly to scan the faces for familiarity. I paused with him, concentrating on his feet and my focal point. When he sat with another man, I immediately sank to my knees and presented. The stroke of Ben's fingers through my hair let me know I'd done it right, and I practically purred.

"Quite the entrance, my friend," Ben's companion said. "It's been awhile since you've come in here occupied." The man was large, even sitting down, with dark hair and a neatly trimmed goatee. He was dressed casually, a leather vest over a T-shirt and jeans with heavy boots. Despite his formidable size, he had a friendly smile and an inherent casual authority that would have served him well as a cop.

"I'm not a bathroom, Steven," Ben replied, signaling a passing waitress. He ordered a merlot and a bottle of water.

Steven laughed heartily, clapping Ben's shoulder. "So you're not. But it's been a long time, yeah? Laura's told me how happy she is you're playing again, and how nice your boy was when she met him."

Laura?

At that moment, Dr. Ribaldi returned from the bar and served Steven a tall glass of beer before kneeling at his feet. With me on Ben's right, and the doctor on Steven's left, she and I were side by side. I jerked slightly at the recognition, and Ben's hand patted my shoulder. Reassurance or a reminder to be still? I didn't know. Laura couldn't have looked more different out of her professional attire, dressed in a leather bustier and short skirt that stretched with her movements. I could hardly believe she was the same woman, but the difference in her was less in her appearance than in her demeanor; with downcast eyes, she was the picture of submission, and she radiated calm.

"Thank you, pet," Steven said, his hand resting on her nape beneath the classy twist of her hair. She briefly pressed her cheek to his thigh and resumed her position. She must have been allowed to kneel resting on her heels, which made her diminutive stature more obvious beside me. I opened my mouth to say something to her, but realized that while I'd been given permission to speak, I wasn't sure she had.

"How are you, Gavin?" she said softly, answering the question I wasn't sure how to ask.

"Nervous," I answered just as low.

"You're doing fine. Congratulations on your contract." Her eyes twinkled as she looked at me sideways, still respectful and aware of her Master.

"How did you—"

"Ben doesn't bring subs to the club unless they're his. And he might have mentioned this week revising his usual first time contract period from six weeks to three months."

My skin heated and a pleased smile escaped me. "Thank you," I said politely.

The murmur of voices above us sharpened, bringing us both to attention before I could say anything else.

"Stand up, Gavin," Ben ordered. "Present."

I rose as fluidly as I was able with the plug shifting in my ass, a flush of a different kind of pleasure layering over the rush of learning my contract period was beyond Ben's norm. Ben's hand rode my shoulder down to my hip as I stood beside him, proprietary and encouraging at once.

Steven also stood, and for a moment I thought he would offer me his hand. *That's ridiculous. Doms don't shake subs' hands.* Instead, he circled me. Ben gave me a nudge to step back from the table and give Steven room for his inspection. *Duh, I should have figured that out.*

"Do you work out... Gavin, is it?" Steven asked. He ran a hand up my arm and squeezed my bicep, then let it wander across my chest as he circled around my front. One of his fingers nudged a clamp and I bit back the hiss that threatened to escape. The finger paused, returned for a lighter caress, then resumed its path and squeezed my other arm.

"When I can, Sir," I answered. *Am I supposed to call him that? Or is that only for Ben?* I had so many questions, and didn't want to make a fool of myself asking in front of Ben's friend.

"Don't get regular free time?" Steven inquired, letting his hand drop.

"Not always, Sir." Ben hadn't corrected me, so I went with it. "My schedule is sometimes erratic."

"What do you do, boy?"

"I'm a detective, Sir. St. Louis County."

Steven raised a brow and resumed his seat, whistling low as he eyed Ben with new appreciation. "Nice, Ben. Very nice. Now you don't have to worry about unpaid parking tickets."

Ben smiled. "The trick is not to get those tickets, Steven."

I remained standing for a moment longer, and then felt Ben's hand on my hip, pulling at my pocket to urge me down. *Shit.* I hastily dropped to my knees and groaned low in my throat as the plug nearly slipped out. I grimaced, struggling to stop its exit, knowing I'd just given the sloppiest present position ever. Disappointment in myself kicked into gear.

"You all right, Gav?" Ben asked.

"Fine, Sir. Just the plug," I gritted out.

"Take your time, babe. Breathe." His hand petting my hair was soothing and arousing at once, and my jeans tightened, which actually helped me regain control of the plug as the fabric constricted. The plug resettled when I found the proper muscle tension again.

"Thank you, Sir," I said after a moment.

Steven gave a chuckle and pointed to Ben's nearly empty wine glass. "Another? Or do you plan to play?"

"Not playing tonight, Steven. Gavin's got about all he can handle right now. How about you? Plan to stun the crowd with your caning technique?"

Steven shook his head. "I'm feeling voyeuristic. Figured I'd take Laura upstairs and see what's happening in the semi-private rooms."

"We'll join you," Ben said, rising to his feet. I followed suit as gracefully as I could, ready to heel.

"You say he's new?" Steven asked. "Have you been working with him long?"

"A few weeks."

"That's all? He moves like a much more experienced sub," Steven said, openly appraising me. I noticed a smile skate across Laura's lips as she also waited for the signal to follow. While Steven's eyes were on me, she winked and gave an encouraging nod. I relaxed, pleased at the validation.

"He's irresistible," Ben purred, sliding an arm around my waist to pull me close, his other hand ghosting over my crotch. My erection throbbed at the touch as well as the praise. "And he's all mine."

Steven laughed. "It's been far too long, old friend, since I've seen you this smitten."

"Smitten?" Ben snorted. "Who talks like that?"

His friend turned toward the stairs and Laura fell into perfect step with him. I studied her posture and did my best to copy as I followed Ben.

A steady pulse of music, low and sensual, pervaded the upper hallway, punctuated by sharp cracks of a riding crop from the first semi-private room we passed. Steven paused, taking in the scene before moving along to the next. Ben, content to keep up with his friend, didn't slow down. I wanted to look, but I knew if I took my eyes from my focal point, I'd mess up. I wasn't about to make Ben look bad by my lack of attention. Tension built within me, the persistent low hum of arousal ticking along as we moved on. My breath sped up and my nipples throbbed, as if the music were wired through them.

We reached another alcove and Steven stopped, the scene before him capturing his attention.

"What do you think, Ben?"

Ben took in the scene—a young man strapped to a St. Andrew's Cross, facing out. He was tied in place with red silk scarves, and their contrast to his skin was startling and erotic, even without his nakedness. Despite my downcast eyes, I could feel the arousal of those who watched—a handful of people seated in comfortable chairs just inside the arched entrance. One of the spectators held a video camera. Upon closer inspection, I recognized the pair. It was the couple from the first night I was at Collared, the Dom who'd edged his sub into the most spectacular orgasm I'd ever seen.

"I always enjoy watching Zach and Nick," Ben answered. He moved beneath the arch and settled into a leather chair that would have been at home in a library or bookstore. Steven took the one beside it and Laura and I moved to our positions at their feet.

"Gavin, keep an eye on Nick," Ben instructed. "It looks like they just started and you'll see his transformation as Zach guides him into subspace."

"Detective DeGrassi." A voice to my right spoke in surprise and I jumped slightly, my head whipping around.

Damon Lane sat in the chair to my other side, startled as he took in my position, his eyes flickering to Ben and back to me.

"This is quite unexpected," he said. The arousal I'd felt for the last couple hours dissipated as unease bubbled up like flood waters through a storm grate. I remembered Ben's words about whether I cared more about others' opinions of me than his and bit back the resulting disquiet as best I could.

"Mr. Lane. Nice to see you," I intoned politely, if disinterestedly. The last thing I wanted was for him to draw me into a conversation, and I hoped he'd take the hint when I returned my attention to the pair on display.

"So are you giving the lifestyle a try to better understand your investigation, or is this a little foray into the dark side before you don your shield and gun and forget we exist when the case goes cold?"

I bristled, mouth tightening into a line to keep from snapping at the insinuation that I was using Ben or the case would be unresolved. I kept my mouth shut, my eyes glued to Nick on the cross until I could speak reasonably. Ben, wrapped in conversation with Steven, hadn't heard, and with the spacing between the chairs, Laura had taken up her post on Steven's opposite side, out of earshot. Handling this was on me.

"I am here because Ben wanted to be here, and what he wants, I want." The answer left me unsatisfied and feeling helpless, unable to reconcile my role as a sub with my role as a police officer. The disparity in authority was too wide a gap to bridge. The cop in me would have dispelled any doubt as to my intent and dedication to finding Kaiser and Adams's killer. The sub inside was unsure if defending myself was allowed. Lane wasn't a Dom, but he was well respected in the community. I was quite certain Ben wouldn't appreciate me getting mouthy when my attention was supposed to be on Nick as instructed.

Lane appraised me briefly. "So your interest is genuine?"

"Yes," I answered. And then it hit me. I didn't need to defend myself. I would get justice for Kaiser and Adams regardless of Lane's opinion. Doubts about my motivation towards Ben could be alleviated simply by giving him my full effort. I gave Lane a brief nod and turned back to the scene.

Ben's hand on my shoulder squeezed briefly and he leaned forward. "Everything all right?" he spoke in my ear, his voice a caress to which I clung to regain my center.

"Yes, Sir. Mr. Lane was just saying hello."

Ben looked over at Damon, whose face was unreadable. Nothing about my Dom's expression changed, but the softness in his eyes was gone. Still, he was polite when he spoke.

"Mr. Lane. Haven't seen you much. What brings you here tonight?"

"Oh, Zach asked me to stick around for a while. Wants to talk about a commission, and I figured it would be smart to see him in action. Might help me anticipate what he'll request." Lane reached out a hand, and Ben shook it, returning his palm quickly to my neck, his thumb stroking my spine soothingly, if possessively. That touch did more for me than anything and I focused on it, though I continued to watch Zach, who was tormenting Nick with a feather. Nick squirmed beautifully.

"I've heard you get into your work, Mr. Lane."

"Please, Dr. Haverson. Call me Damon."

Though the words were polite, I couldn't help but feel like the prey between two circling predators, one defending territory, and one challenging.

What is my problem?

It's not like Lane had really done anything more than doubt if my interest was genuine, which could have crossed anyone's mind. Kimberly Kaiser had said more than once how well this community took care of its own. Perhaps Lane was merely looking out for Ben, not that he needed it.

"Then call me Ben."

"I do take my work seriously," Lane continued. "Especially these days, with the economy so depressed. People need each other now more than ever, and if what I do can provide the tools to enhance relationships, then it's a noble cause in my book. Despite what outsiders might think."

"That's great, Damon. Really. In fact, if you have a card, perhaps I'll give you a call to discuss some relationship enhancement."

My head snapped up, but Ben didn't acknowledge me and his thumb on my neck didn't miss a beat, except when he pocketed Lane's card. With their conversation over, Ben met my eyes, and I didn't bother to hide my curiosity. A sly grin touched his lips and he leaned down to capture my mouth in a sultry kiss.

I forgot about Lane and my discomfort, which I was sure was what Ben intended.

"That wasn't so bad, was it?" He spoke low in my ear. "Reputation still intact or do we need to leave so you can write your letter of resignation?" His teasing worked, and I huffed out a chuckle. "Now, do what I say and watch Nick."

"Yes, Sir."

Zach had moved on to a cat o' nine tails, wielding it expertly so the tips licked Nick's skin. The lights focused on them made the pink skin shine. Nick moaned deliciously, and I found myself mesmerized. Zach murmured encouragement, low enough that only a word or two was audible to those watching. When Nick, cock bobbing with every caress of the whip, began to beg, I felt a damp spot spread on my boxers. He really was beautiful.

Ben's fingers trailed through my hair, massaging my scalp, gently tugging the strands. Normally, such a massage would make me sleepy. In that moment, it heightened my awareness of the man beside me, and I marveled at how much my life had changed in a few short weeks. Openly submissive in public with my, dare I say, boyfriend and Dom claiming me both inside and out—I never thought I'd be in that position and so happy. I wondered how submitting to Ben could feel so right when I was used to control, authority, and seeing those who were responsible for crimes paid for them. Maybe it was the super hero dichotomy—saving the world when I could and reverting to mild-mannered normality the rest of the time. The difference between what Ben asked of me and what Victoria had wanted became clear. He didn't expect me to set aside my job for him. He simply offered respite from the responsibility of it. He recognized how important my work was, how I couldn't turn off the part of me that needed to see order in the world, or the desire to contribute to achieving it. In fact, he gave me order in a new way, a way in which I didn't have to think, where my only responsibility was to follow the rules, do what he expected to make him happy. He found room to take me away from the burden of heroism, from the heaviness I chose to shoulder, allowing me a sanctioned moment to set aside my responsibilities and just *feel*.

Ben tugged more insistently on my hair, and I looked up at him. He gestured to his lap, and I eagerly climbed up and settled on him, back to his chest, legs to the outside of his thighs. His hand slipped inside my T-shirt, idly rubbing my stomach. Every now and then, his hips would press up, his erection prodding the plug deeper. I moaned softly, wanting to turn my face into his neck, to nibble at him, but I'd been told to watch.

When his fingers traveled higher and grazed one of my clamped nipples, I hissed and arched my back, my shirt pulling tight across my chest, igniting the fire in my pinched flesh once more. I glanced at Steven and Laura and noted his finger coasting over the rim of her bustier, her skin flushed a pretty red. She bit her lip as his finger dipped inside to flick at her nipple. Nick and Zach were affecting everybody.

"Ready, Nicky?" Zach asked, his voice carrying over the hush that had fallen in the room.

"Please, Sir. Yes," Nick replied instantly, his hands clenching and unclenching. Zach held a bell ball in front of his sub's face, rattled it, and placed it in Nick's palm.

"Show me."

Nick rang the bell, the scarf securing his wrist not enough to impede the movement.

"Good boy," Zach praised, then reached up and released Nick's other hand.

"Touch yourself," he commanded.

Immediately, Nick fisted his cock and pumped, breath rasping. "Please, Sir."

Zach's hands caressed his chest, his shoulders, and finally settled about Nick's neck. He cradled Nick's head, thumbs beneath his jaw and fingers fanned on Nick's ears as Zach possessed his mouth in an obscene kiss. Nick masturbated faster as Zach released his mouth and they looked deep into each other's eyes.

"I love you, Sir," Nick breathed, and he closed his eyes in ecstasy as Zach's hands tightened around his throat, his thumbs digging into Nick's windpipe.

The slight undulating I'd been semi-consciously doing against Ben's pelvis stopped and I froze. Zach carried on, oblivious to the audience as he cut off his sub's breath. Nick's face turned an alarming shade of red and his hand sped up, his ass muscles clenching and releasing as he did his best to fuck into his fingers despite the restraints. My eyes passed between his hand, his face, and the bell ball clenched tightly in his restrained fist. *Should I stop this? What if Zach kills him?*

I must have tensed, because Ben's arms tightened around my waist and his voice rasped in my ear.

"Breath play. Zach won't hurt him."

"How can you be sure?" Attention riveted on the pair in front of us, I didn't realize I'd forgotten my place until Ben flicked a nipple clamp, and I grimaced.

"Sir. 'How can you be sure, Sir?' And I know them. Zach would never attempt such a thing without ample safety measures."

"Sorry, Sir," I said, chagrined at my slip. But I also knew I needed to be clear. "The job's a hard limit. If I think it's too much, I'm stopping them, Sir."

"Let Master Lacey do her job, Gavin," Ben said firmly. "This isn't the first time she's supervised edge play."

"Hard limit, Sir," I repeated, sweat breaking out on my forehead.

"Understood. Safeword if you have to."

It wasn't exactly a challenge, but I knew if I safeworded for this, Ben would be disappointed. *I thought he didn't like this stuff.*

"Nick consented to this, Gavin," Ben reminded me. His hands resumed their quiet attention to my torso. Up and down, then fanning over my hips and down my thighs. My flagging erection roared to life again, and my eyes were glued to Nick's hand frantically stroking himself. He made choking noises, which reassured rather than alarmed me. If he could breathe enough to make noise, he wasn't in danger of losing consciousness. Yet.

I didn't want to like it. I wanted to stand up and shout how wrong it was, but Ben's hands kept me anchored, soothing up and down my thighs, across my cock, and over my stomach. The result was unwelcome arousal I tried to ignore, but it was unmistakable. There was no denying the erotic tension coiled in my gut.

The choking noises stopped. Nick's mouth opened and closed with no sound. His hand flew. His hips jerked. And just as his head tilted to one side and his eyes rolled back, he spilled over his hand, semen pulsing as his orgasm shot from him. Zach's hands immediately dropped away and the sub's body sagged, the restraints keeping him anchored. The ringing of the bell ball as it fell from Nick's limp fingers detonated in the pristine silence of the room.

I heard a growl and thought it came from behind me, from Ben, but I couldn't look away from Nick long enough to check. Zach pressed two fingers to Nick's neck, searching for a pulse, as his other hand caressed the dazed man's hair.

"Nick, baby. Come back to me." Zach sounded calm, authoritative, and absolutely sure of himself. Master Lacey moved off the wall, poised to step in. Seconds ticked by.

Another growl sounded, and I realized it originated beside me. I glanced over quickly and saw Damon Lane, face twisted in what looked like pain, gripping the arms of his chair with white-knuckled strength. He was rigid, and like the rest of the spectators, glued to the scene.

"Are you all right?" I whispered. It would be incredibly poor timing if Lane had his own medical emergency at that moment.

As though slapped, Lane's head whipped in my direction and his painful scowl disappeared.

"Fine." His voice was clipped, barely controlled. "Just wasn't... prepared for this."

Join the club, I thought, turning back to watch Nick. Ben's hands had slowed, one arm keeping me leaned back into his chest, the other gripping and releasing my thigh. I could feel his arousal against my jeans-clad ass had waned as had my own, the realization of which brought me relief. He wasn't into this. His focus was on keeping me calm.

Nick moaned.

The room breathed a collective sigh of relief as the bound man came around, his head lolling from one side to the other.

"Ice," Zach demanded, holding out a hand like a surgeon demanding a scalpel.

Master Lacey passed him a blue contoured ice pack that Zach immediately wrapped around Nick's neck, quickly followed by a bottle of water with a straw. Zach held the straw to Nick's lips and he drank, coughed hoarsely, and drank again. When he opened his eyes, they were full of adoration for Zach.

"I love you too, boy," Zach said, as though the sentiment was incentive for Nick to regain consciousness. He leaned forward, kissing the man's forehead. With Master Lacey's help, Zach brought Nick off the cross and wrapped him in a blanket. Everyone stayed in their chairs to allow the pair a quick exit so Nick could be tended to. He was supported by Zach, but mostly moving under his own power.

"That wasn't quite what I expected," Steven said from Ben's other side. He'd gathered Laura into his lap, and her legs draped sideways over the arm of his chair while his hand rested on her thigh. She was as composed as before, but her eyes seemed distant. "What did you think, pet?" he asked her, his voice steady but his eyes empty of his previous friendliness.

"I was afraid," she admitted. "Edge play makes me queasy. If it pleases you, I'd like to go home, Sir."

Steven nodded and stood, cradling her to his chest a moment before setting her on her feet, as though she wasn't the only one who needed the contact.

"Ben, it was good to see you again," he said, holding out his hand. Ben shook it but made no move to stand, gave no indication that I was to resume my position kneeling at his feet. "Congratulations on your contract."

"Thank you, Steven. Call me for a drink sometime this week, if you're available. Laura, I'll see you at the office."

She nodded, and followed at heel as Steven moved to the stairs.

"Turn around," Ben ordered.

I stood, turned, and reseated myself across his legs, a mirror of Laura's position with my feet dangling over the chair's arm, pointed at Lane, who hadn't moved.

"What did you think?" he asked quietly. Murmurs from those around us had gradually increased to normal crowd decibel, and I resented it. I needed a quiet moment with Ben, and wanted everything else to go away.

"I don't understand it, Sir," I admitted. "But that's the cop talking. I've never experimented with erotic asphyxiation, so I don't know how good Nick felt."

"Is it something you'd ever think of trying?"

I looked at him, startled.

"I don't know, Sir. I thought you weren't interested."

"I'm not interested in inflicting pain, which the rest of edge play centers around," Ben said. "And we're just talking now, not deciding."

Beside us, Lane stood, leaving the room wearing a dazed scowl. I thought I saw him shoot me a barely concealed look of rage, but decided I was just being sensitive, both to what we'd all just witnessed as well as to my first public submission.

"I'm not interested in trying, Sir," I decided. "Too many risks, and I know from my first aid training that oxygen deprivation is as dangerous as a drug. It only takes once to cause permanent damage."

"Agreed," Ben said, his voice soothingly close to my ear. "Even if it's not painful, it's too dangerous for me to consider. But for a moment, I thought it was turning you on."

Heat roared up my cheeks. "No, Sir. That was your hands on me."

"Was it now?" he asked coyly.

"Yes. You were rubbing me and holding me against you, and I

felt restrained and safe, despite what I was watching. Your voice in my ear commanding me to let Master Lacey handle any intervention reminded me I'm to surrender to you, to trust you." I looked at my hands, curled limply in my lap. "I almost safeworded, Sir." The admission embarrassed me. "This was far too close to my limit for comfort."

"I know, Gavin. And I'm proud of you for knowing you were approaching your boundary. Believe me when I say I would have understood. But also believe me that Master Lacey has things well in hand for these scenes. Nick probably never truly lost consciousness. Zach wouldn't knowingly go that far."

"You seem to know a lot about them, Sir," I said, trying to keep my voice neutral, but I couldn't help wonder if Zach and Nick were another pair Ben had "helped" in the same manner he'd assisted Adams and Weiss.

"Zach and I once developed a Dom's training workshop together. He owns a bed and breakfast at the Lake of the Ozarks. Unlike most B&Bs, this one has a dungeon in the basement. He provided room and board for weekend workshops and Doms were invited to bring their subs for extensive instruction in a secluded setting. I taught techniques in sensory deprivation. Zach and I, and by extension Nick, got to know each other over the three months the workshops were scheduled. He's a good man, a good Dom."

I wanted to ask just how well he knew the Dom, but no matter how I framed the question, I'd look jealous and possessive. Ben had his past, I had mine. He'd accepted my past so I tried to push my insecurity out of my mind.

"Stand up, Gavin," Ben ordered.

I did so, presenting for him with such focus as to drown out everything else: the others milling about the room, a few of whom were locked in passion in the chairs still occupied, and my insecurities. One thing I had learned after witnessing that scene was I was certain edge play did not interest me in the slightest. Ben and I were on the same page there, and it was a relief. But something else he'd said to me rose to the surface.

"Sir?" I asked, moving out of his way as he stood.

"Yes?"

"What sensory deprivation techniques did you teach?"

"Ah, now there's a good question. Most people think of water tanks when it comes up but those are not necessary." He turned toward the stairs, leading me down to the main floor and outside. I was glad. We hadn't been there long, but the intensity of Zach and Nick's performance had left me feeling oddly disjointed and drained.

Once in the car, he continued his explanation.

"The senses can be muted in many ways, and touch is the most difficult. I taught ways for a sub to feel very little the Dom didn't want them to feel. Whole body suits can be used for this, but even that amount of effort isn't necessary, with the right circumstances. A lot of it comes down to psychology. A good mask, earplugs, and the right headspace can make a sub float as well as a water tank can, if done right. I taught the headspace bit."

"Is it dangerous?" I gingerly buckled my seatbelt and squirmed in my seat, trying to get comfortable, though my awareness of the plug increased again.

"Not any more so than anything else we do."

I was silent for the remainder of the ride, letting my mind wander.

"Gavin? We're here," Ben said, grasping my knee and squeezing. I jumped, and then smiled sheepishly. The entire evening had me off balance, and I didn't like it, but I didn't know how to regain my equilibrium. As we exited the car and walked to his house through the back courtyard, I concentrated on staying at his heel, the practice calming me. In this, I was able to let go, to keep from thinking too much.

Once inside, Ben went through his usual routine of locking up for the night and setting his security system. Unsure of what to do, I waited in the living room, fidgeting, putting my hands in my pockets, taking them out, fiddling with my watch or the buttons on my open shirt. That reminded me of the nipple clamps, and once I became aware of them again, the discomfort reared anew. Ben returned and caught me frowning down at my chest, wondering if my nubs would ever be the same.

"Time for those to come off," he murmured, gathering the button-down shirt to push it from my shoulders and then lifting the T-shirt beneath carefully. Stretching my arms above my head pulled at my nipples, and I hissed, looking at the reddened flesh once my torso was bare.

"Painful?"

"Some, Sir. Not as much as I would have thought."

"They're designed to have adjustable tension, and I went easy on you. Normally, they'd be tighter, but I also wouldn't have you wear them as long as I did tonight. You know what? Follow me."

He turned and led me by the hand to his bedroom, flipped on the bedside lamp, and gestured for me to sit on the bed. I complied.

"Relax," he intoned. "They'll hurt like hell coming off, but it's short-lived." In one smooth motion, he removed the left clamp and icy fire flared in my chest. I groaned in pain and then pleasure as he very gently licked my abused nipple. The heat abated quickly as he swirled his tongue over it, and a pleasant ache followed. My sensitivity went off the charts, and I was rock hard in seconds. The other nipple received the same treatment, and I sighed in relief after a moment of watching his tongue play over the swollen flesh.

"Now, on your back."

I obeyed, finding comfort in his commanding tone. The discombobulated feeling lingering from the club scene dissipated. Ben's deft fingers undid my jeans and pulled them down and off, along with my boxers. The plug in my ass shifted, making me whimper. He climbed up the bed and lay on top of me fully clothed, staring down at me for a moment.

"You're a little freaked." Of course he would see it on my face, and he had that superhuman gift for reading people, but truthfully? I was glad he'd broached the subject.

"A little, Sir."

Ben's shirt rubbed against my chest, and my chafed skin sang at even the slight movement.

"Which part of the night unsettled you?"

I took a moment to think, wanting to be as honest as possible. "Being in public wasn't as difficult as I'd expected, Sir, so it wasn't that, though I think it'll take some getting used to. It was more the scene we watched. And the helplessness."

"I've had you helpless before," he said, his hips beginning a slow rock into my own. I spread my legs and sighed as he settled firmly against me, the undulations more pleasurably comforting than arousing, though the plug made me very aware of my body.

"This was Nick's helplessness, Sir, not mine. I can handle my own because I trust you to see me through it. My upbringing centered around helping people. Having a cop for a father and being groomed for a career in law enforcement beat that into my head. You see someone in distress, you fix their problem, whether it's medical attention for an accident victim or catching the burglar so their victim can sleep at night. But I've never been told how to help someone who invited danger. We train for all sorts of situations, from suicidal people to hostage negotiations. All that psychology is geared toward making people safe. Nick doesn't need mental help, and yet he still consented to the danger. I just... I don't know how to handle what I saw, Sir."

Ben's eyes were warm, his voice a liquid balm on my frayed nerves. "You don't handle it. You let Zach take care of his boy. You let Master Lacey do her job. You let Nick negotiate his own terms.

It's not up to you. That's why I held you back tonight. Not every decision, or every person, is your responsibility, Gavin."

I closed my eyes and let my hands trace up and down his back, gently meeting the pressure and release of his hips. It was erotic and soothing and pleasure built in my lower back, but I didn't chase it. I wasn't after a climax, and the simple act of rubbing against Ben was so good, so achingly sweet, that I didn't want to ruin the moment by speeding up or begging for more.

"You're not even your own responsibility," he murmured huskily in my ear. "When you're surrendering, you're *my* responsibility, just as Nick is Zach's. Ultimately, you trust me to take over, or you don't. Nick gave Zach the ultimate trust tonight. As dangerous as breath play is, it's also quite intoxicating for both sub and Dom. I'd love to find out if you can surrender to me that much." He nipped my earlobe, sending a shiver rippling over my skin.

"I'm confused, Sir. You don't like edge play."

"I don't. But I think I can get you to that level of surrender with sensory deprivation, take you so far out of your body your very existence is mine."

My dick, already heavy and full, became steely, weeping pre-come at the very thought. "Please, Sir," I whispered, arching my back so my sensitive nipples stretched and my aching cock rubbed into his crotch, his pants a tactile scratch on me.

"Please what?" Ben's lips migrated down my neck and I bared it for him, shuddering at the wetness of his tongue.

I didn't know what I wanted, just that I needed more of him, needed more friction, more pressure, more surrender.

"Please take me. Use me. Make me yours."

Ben purred against my throat, then leaned back to rip off his shirt and pants. He settled on me, skin to skin, and we rocked together. One of Ben's hands slithered between us to press at my taint, jostling the plug. I gave an open-mouthed groan and tilted my hips to his hand, seeking more.

He gave it, lifting up on his knees to stroke my cock and massage the plug through my perineum, sending shockwaves reverberating through my entire pelvis. I didn't know what to do with my hands, but I had to touch him. I ran my palms up and down his arms, feeling the muscles flex, and when he stopped touching me to lean over for supplies from his nightstand, I grabbed at him, not wanting to lose the contact for even those few seconds.

"Greedy boy," he smiled, leaning down to kiss me heavy and hard, his tongue dancing with mine. His knees at the back of my thighs were the only other contact between us. I heard the crinkle of a condom wrapper and the snap of a lube bottle, and then he leaned up, staring down at me while he ran his dry hand up and down my leg. When slick fingers delved between my cheeks and gripped the base of the plug, my eyes rolled back in my head, and I hooked my hands behind my knees to hold myself open.

The pressure inside me moved, pulled, and suddenly I was empty of the hard, knobby metal, leaving me both relieved and bereft. But not for long. Ben dropped the plug to the floor and pressed my knees to my chest, lined up, and shoved in.

"The beauty," he said in time with his thrusts, "of plugs… is that… you're open… when I want you. Waiting… for me." His breath was steady, his eyes focused on me as he spoke. I writhed. So many things about the night confused me, but this I knew: I needed to give myself to him, needed him to take over for a little while.

"Yours, Sir," I mumbled. The stretch of my hamstrings brought the pain I'd come to appreciate with his taking of me, and I went boneless as he filled me, overtook me, owned me. He pinned my hands above my head and kissed me breathless, relentlessly, deliberately fucking me. Because he never increased the pace, the build of ecstasy was slower, but ultimately more devastating when I tipped over the edge, howling in pleasure so strong, my vision faded at the edges.

He fucked me through it, his control never slipping until the last thrust when he buried himself to the hilt and grunted from deep in his core. The weight of his body descended, and I felt safe and cared for, cherished, in the crush. A swell of emotion on the heels of my orgasm laid me to waste. Here was a man who had, in only a month, held me through the worst of my terrifying sexual preference admission, took the time to guide me into the core of my submissiveness, and made me feel worthy and adored. Ben knew my deepest secret, and still, he wanted me, saw my value, and appreciated that I'd put that value in his hands for safe-keeping. I never wanted to let him go.

He raised his head and smiled down at me, brushing my hair back from my forehead. The tenderness of the gesture walloped my already wide-open heart.

"No matter what happens, what scares you, what thrills you, I've got you. Do you believe me?"

I nodded, looking away. It was too much. A month! Feeling so strongly for him after such a short time overwhelmed me. I clamped my lips shut and breathed as evenly as I could through my nose, afraid if I opened my mouth, I'd say something I wasn't ready to examine. I'd fallen for him. I knew it. He probably knew it. But in all my years of pretending, of going through the motions and having societal and familial expectations define me, I'd never faced such life-changing feelings, let alone voiced them aloud. I'd never dealt with overpowering adoration or the desperation to be near someone as much as I needed to be near him. Victoria had been, while atypical of the definition, a trophy wife. My family, I'd tried to please by following their standards, not by being myself. I played the good son, the good brother. But on these occasions, with Ben, I didn't have to pretend, to grandstand and puff up my feathers to prove myself. He could see me on my knees, begging to be whipped, red ass waggling in his direction and pleading for more, and still know I was a good man, not in spite of my desires to please him, but because of them.

Ben, to his credit, didn't force me to do more than ride the wave of emotions. He simply held me, kissed the bridge of my nose, smoothed my eyebrows with gentle fingers, nuzzling my jaw. In unspoken ways, he let me know he was there for me. In that moment, I would have done anything for him.

CHAPTER ELEVEN

"I HAD this idea," Myah said, setting coffee in front of me as I perched carefully in my desk chair, more on one hip than my ass. Ben and I had had a thorough, if slightly rough, shower before leaving for our respective offices. If Myah noticed, she didn't mention it.

"I hope you didn't spend your whole two days off thinking about the case," I admonished playfully as I sipped my coffee and grimaced. It was the break room stuff, and I had trouble believing stress was the reason for most cops' ulcers rather than the acid we were expected to drink. I set it aside, not that desperate for caffeine.

"No, I got myself good and laid, same as you, Gavin," she muttered, heaving a brown file box onto her desk with a loud thump that kept others from overhearing her. I tried to sit straighter and winced. She merely grinned at me, then handed me a sheet of paper with a long list of cases. "I was thinking our killer really knew what he was doing with George Kaiser. There wasn't a fiber on the body. There wasn't a footprint in the mud outside. No tire tracks from a vehicle. No prints. No fluids. Nada. No one is that thorough without being one of us." At that, she gave me a pointed look and let her eyes wander around the room skeptically. "Or having had some practice. I'm thinking Kaiser wasn't our guy's first dance."

I looked at the list of cases, nodding. "You're probably right. So this is...?" I held up the pages.

"All the unsolved cases in the last three years that had cause of death listed as asphyxiation due to strangulation. Domestic violence, mostly, but a few were violent attacks, mostly rapes against women. Not all of them are murders. But maybe, just maybe, there's a needle in that list of needles that will shine brighter, poke harder."

"Good thinking," I said, albeit with a grumble at the thought of yet more paperwork on which to go blind. "Give me a handful of files."

We read for hours, our chairs creaking as we shifted position. Twice, Myah stepped out, once for real coffee, and once for lunch at St. Louis Bread Company. As she set my bag on my desk, mindful of the cup of soup within, I couldn't help noticing the smile on her face.

"Something I should be aware of, Detective?" I asked, eyebrow raised. She surreptitiously slipped her phone into her pocket and shook her head before sitting down and digging into her salad with gusto.

"Just a nice phone call. Carry on, nothing to see here."

I smiled but said nothing. The difference between her demeanor now and the waspish, defensive woman I'd met only weeks earlier was substantial, and I was pleased she had let her guard down with someone, whether I knew who it was or not. She'd said I knew them, but I was content to wait until she felt comfortable enough to tell me. By far, she'd become the best partner I'd ever had, due in no small part to the fact that I'd been open with her about Ben. Yeah, I hadn't exactly wanted to spill those particular beans, but it was reassuring to know another person besides Ben freely accepted my choices. It gave me hope that when the time was right to open up to those closest to me, maybe it wouldn't be the disaster I feared.

"Hey, did you find an apartment yet?" I wondered, breaking off a hunk of baguette and dipping it in my french onion soup.

Talking around a mouthful of lettuce, Myah said, "A couple possibilities. There's one in Webster Groves and one in Kirkwood. One has in-unit washers and dryers, and the other one's in a nicer neighborhood. Both about the same price, and I just have to pick."

"Hey, I can ask my brother. He lives in Webster Groves. He can let you know more about the neighborhoods, if you're interested."

A hint of a smile touched her lips and she shoveled more food into her mouth, merely nodding. When she swallowed, she cleared her throat. "That would be good, thanks."

I pounced. "If you want, I can talk to him about taking you around the area. He's a fun guide."

Her eyes darted quickly to my face, then away. *Uh-huh. Not imagining it.* It all suddenly clicked—the night she had said she was having drinks was the same night Cole had planned to be out and I shouldn't worry about him. I'd noticed on the nights I was at his apartment and not with Ben, he hadn't brought anyone home. Myah kept getting phone calls here and there throughout her workday that brightened her mood. When I'd stopped over the weekend to pack a bag, Cole had actually been whistling while he did dishes, a chore he abhorred.

"I'm sure he is. I'll talk to him," Myah mumbled. Suddenly immersed in another file, she wouldn't look at me. When a piece of lettuce with vinaigrette dressing dropped from her fork onto the file, she cursed a little too loud, drawing attention from the detectives in the desks nearest ours.

"There are no rules about it, you know," I said nonchalantly, dusting the crumbs from my hands into my empty soup cup and throwing it in the trash before grabbing and unwrapping my sandwich. I didn't look at her as I spoke, my tone soft and conspiratorial.

"Rules about what?" she asked, voice equally low.

"Cross-departmental dating. Fraternization rules only apply to people in the same departments, or between supervisors and their subordinates."

"Different rules everywhere," she mumbled. I risked a glance at her. To anyone else, she'd have looked fascinated by her reading material. I knew better by the quirk of her mouth before she took the last bite of salad. With her eyes still averted, she tossed her trash. "But thanks for telling me."

"No problem." She did look at me then, and I winked. She smiled. And like that, it was done. She was dating my brother and I'd let her know I was okay with it. During the next couple hours, she relaxed a lot more.

Until she sat up abruptly and exclaimed, "Holy shit!"

I startled, gaze snapping up from my file on a rape victim attacked on a Forest Park jogging trail at night.

"What?"

She read, "'Victim is twenty-eight year old Jeffrey Demarco Lane, found by his father, Damon, after the victim failed to answer his phone for two days. Cause of death, asphyxia, probable strangulation, as evidenced by petechial hemorrhages around the eyes and cheeks. Signs of anal intercourse, presence and quantity of lubricant suggest consensual. Victim was restrained at the wrists and ankles, and posterior abrasions indicate a lash or whipping implement was used.'" She slowly tore her eyes from the file to stare at me. "Case open, unsolved."

"How long ago?" I demanded.

"Five years."

"He didn't say a word about it," I sniped.

"Why would he? We weren't there to talk about his son, and we have no reason to think they're connected."

I pointed at her. "Yet. We have no reason to believe they're connected *yet*. But I want to look into it. It's too coincidental and there's no way I'm leaving any questions unanswered on these." I ticked off on my fingers. "Victim was restrained and whipped. Strangled. Perhaps this is one of the practice killings. If his son's case was never solved, it had to have crossed his mind that whoever was responsible for Jeff's death could be responsible for Kaiser and Adams."

"Agreed," she said, picking up the phone on her desk and punched in a number from memory with the eraser end of her pencil. "Cole DeGrassi, please."

She stuck her tongue out at me when I raised a brow at her.

"Real mature," I mouthed silently.

"Hey, it's me," she said into the phone with a familiarity that made me grin. "Can you look up evidence we might have on file for an old case?" She rattled off the case number and waited for him to see where it was stored. Because multiple police departments used Cole's lab, the lab itself handled all evidence collected and analyzed in the basement. The cavernous evidence room was meticulously kept, and while it was irritating to be unable to immediately access something from our precinct, the county-staffed security personnel acted as messengers, so the wait was not prohibitive. The storage locker was a well-oiled machine, and because of the security protocols involved in removing, transporting, and returning evidence, there was very little lost or corrupted. Myah put in a formal request for Jeff Lane's case evidence to be sent over and hung up. She opened her mouth to speak, but was interrupted.

"DeGrassi, call that shrink of yours."

My heart skipped a beat at Talcott's no-nonsense voice calling to me from behind the front desk several feet away. *Why do I need to call Ben? What's wrong?*

"What?"

"Just got a call. Your killer's done it again. I want Dr. Haverson on hand, if he's free. Maybe he can tell from the scene if something's triggered the killer into escalating."

"Escalating?" I gulped and came abruptly to my feet, drawing my cell out of my pocket with one hand and grabbing my suit jacket with the other.

Talcott strode over, handing me the address the dispatcher had scribbled as she took the call. A hush fell over the room and Talcott lowered his voice.

"Multiple victims. A couple was found by their cleaning lady. Fits your killer's MO."

"Sonofabitch," I cursed softly, looking at the address. Ladue, the most well-to-do suburb in the county. My stomach did a slow somersault.

"Three kills means Feds, Gavin, and four cements it," Talcott continued. "Definitely a serial. I'll do what I can to keep you on the case, but you know how the Feds are. Buncha badasses who think because we're county police, we're backwoods country boys, no matter what city we serve. We'll officially cooperate in every way. You're lead liaison for any task force they set up. Get out there now, before I make this call, and do what you can to preserve our momentum. If they see what a good job you're doing, there's a chance they'll defer to you. Make it happen, Gavin." He slapped my shoulder and I nodded, determined to do this right before the rug got yanked from under my feet. *If I've been doing such a great job, two more people wouldn't be dead.*

As we marched out the front doors, I unlocked my phone and navigated to Ben's number. "Myah, call Cole. Have him meet us at this address." I handed her the slip of paper and got behind the wheel just as Ben's assistant came on the line.

§§§

I DIDN'T use the siren or lights on the way to the scene, but people got out of my way when I barreled up in their rearview mirrors and made cursory use of the brakes before sliding around them. The neighborhood to which we were headed wasn't one of the most affluent of Ladue, but the lots were still massive, the houses expansive. It made me nervous because if this set of victims was high profile enough, keeping the media off our backs would be harder than ever.

We pulled up to a sprawling ranch-style house and were met by the responding patrol officers, one of whom comforted a young woman hunched against their squad car, weeping. She wore the smock of a local cleaning service, and I made a note in my pad to check the accounts of the other two victims to see if they used the same service. Gesturing to the patrol officer not speaking to the woman, we moved a few paces away.

"What do we know?" I asked him.

He read from his notes. "Victims' names are Zachary Campbell and Nicholas Parker, the residents of the house. Saturdays are their regular cleaning day, and when they didn't come to the door, the cleaning lady used her key. She went about her usual duties until she reached the room with the bodies. Called emergency services immediately. But half the house has been cleaned."

I grimaced, wondering what evidence we'd already lost until my brain stuttered to a stop and my insides went cold.

"Can you repeat the victims' names?"

"Zachary Campbell and Nicholas Parker."

Oh god. Zach and Nick.

Fighting a wave of dizziness, I put a hand on the trunk of a nearby tree to steady myself.

"Detective, are you all right?" the officer asked.

I nodded, clearing my throat. "Yeah, I'm good."

Just then, tires squealed at the curb and the sound of a car door slamming caught my attention. Ben strode straight to me just as Myah stepped over from her short conversation with the cleaning woman.

"Gavin?" Ben asked, his voice alarmed.

With him, I couldn't hide the pained expression, but I refused to avert my gaze.

"It's bad, Ben," I said, voice low with misery.

He nodded and put a hand on my arm. "Okay. Have you been inside yet?"

I shook my head. "Waiting for CSI and the M.E. Some of the evidence was lost when the cleaning lady started her job before finding the bodies."

"Bodies?" He paled.

I gulped, still holding his eye. "Two victims. Zachary Campbell and Nicholas Parker." I knew he'd know, knew it would hit him worse than it had me. They'd been his friends. He sucked in a breath and looked away, lips tightening on whatever words wanted to escape. Myah looked back and forth between us, confusion plain on her features. As Ben moved away for a moment to himself, she stepped close to me.

"What's going on?" she murmured.

"He knew them. They hadn't been close recently, but..." I cleared my throat again, trying to swallow the acid that had risen sharply. "We just saw them last night."

Immediately, she opened her notebook. "Where?"

"At Collared. We got there about nine and they were already there, in one of the semi-private rooms upstairs."

"What were they doing?" Her voice had switched to interrogation mode, and while I understood it, I didn't like being on the receiving end of it. I hesitated, not sure exactly how much I wanted her to know about what Ben and I had been doing there.

"They were already doing a scene when we came into the room. Nick was tied to a St. Andrew's Cross with scarves and they…" my voice trailed off and I swallowed thickly. She waited patiently, her face a mask of blankness. "They were engaging in erotic asphyxiation."

She nodded, her pen scratching on the paper. "Notice anyone in the room paying undue attention?"

"Everyone in the room was glued to what they were doing," I answered.

"What were you doing?"

"Myah…"

She looked at me hard. "Gavin," she said, her lips tight. Her hand landed vise-like on my elbow and she dragged me further away from listening ears before wheeling on me. "I don't care what you were doing, but like it or not, you're part of this one. What you saw, who you saw doing it, those things are more than we've had on either of the other two cases. If it's irrelevant, I won't write it up."

She was right. I knew she was, but making myself say the words, knowing they could end up in an official report… I wasn't sure I could. However, this was an investigation. What she didn't find out from me, she'd get somewhere else. I blew out a breath.

"Ben and I went to celebrate my signing a contract with him. He wanted people to know I belonged to him. We met up with his business partner, Dr. Ribaldi, and her Dom, Steven. You'll have to get his last name from Ben. After a couple drinks, we went upstairs to see what was going on, and Zach and Nick were already set up. Zach was teasing him with a feather when Ben and I arrived, and then he moved on to a cat o' nine tails. After that, he gave Nick a bell ball, untied one of his hands, told him to pleasure himself, and while Nick complied, Zach choked him."

"Did he pass out?"

"Hard to say. When he… finished, he sagged against the cross with his head bowed. Zach checked his pulse and coaxed him back, and when they were done, Nick walked out of the room under his own power."

"What time was this?"

"I don't exactly know. Maybe ten-thirty, and I don't know where they went."

"Did you see who else was in the room?"

"The only people I knew by name besides the victims were Master Lacey and Damon Lane."

"What were they doing?"

"Master Lacey was overseeing the scene and Lane was there to observe, like everyone else."

"Did he seem particularly interested?"

"Everybody in the room was interested, Myah. It was intense. But..." Something prodded my memory, and I recalled the look on Lane's face. "I thought he was going to have a heart attack or something. He looked like he was in pain himself." Realizing he might have been, given how close the scene was to his son's death five years prior, I saw his reaction in a new light. "I asked him if he was okay and he said he was fine, just unprepared for what Zach and Nick had done."

"What was he doing there? He's not a Dom or a sub from what he told us."

"Said he had an appointment with Zach and Nick, and he figured he'd watch them in action to see if he could anticipate what kind of equipment they'd order."

Her eyes widened. "Lane had an appointment with them?"

"Yeah," I replied absently, watching as Cole and Dr. Jencopale arrived simultaneously. The already busy street became crowded with more vehicles. Ben stood off to the side, hands shoved deep in his pockets with his head down while other patrol officers began stringing crime scene tape across the driveway and around the perimeter of the yard.

"Gavin." Myah's voice snapped me back to attention. "Lane had appointments with all the victims."

"But he never made it to any of them. They were all dead before he could."

"Doesn't mean they weren't well enough acquainted not to talk to him outside the appointments."

I gave her a skeptical look. "It's flimsy, Myah."

"It's coincidence and you don't believe in coincidences."

I nodded grimly. "Make a note of it. We'll talk to him again."

"We have to stop meeting like this," Cole said, joining us as we walked back to the crowd of officers waiting for orders. A few more of Cole's crew had arrived and were checking their kits.

"From what I understand, you *have* stopped meeting like this," I gave him a pointed look, my eyes flickering to Myah and back. Perhaps the relief at his interruption showed on my face, because his startled look morphed into a grin, then quickly resumed its somber cast. Myah found her shoes suddenly very interesting. I dropped it. This wasn't the time or place.

I turned, hollering for the gathered officers milling about to pay attention, and handed out the assignments to canvas the neighbors, walk the perimeter, and check the exterior of the house for signs of break in, although I knew we would find none. I left the responding officers with the cleaning lady and the rest dispersed to perform their duties. Dr. Jencopale and Cole's team donned their protective gear and entered the house, leaving Myah, Ben and me a moment to ourselves. I motioned for her to go ahead of me as I turned to my lover.

"Ben, if it's too much, you don't have to do this."

His face grim, he nodded. "Yeah, I do. For them. I want this bastard caught for all of them." I noted the lines around his mouth, the determined set of his jaw, but none of that compared to the haunted look in his eyes. I wanted to wrap my arms around him, offer what comfort I could, but there were officers everywhere. I settled for placing a hand on his shoulder and brushing my thumb against his neck.

"Okay. Anything you can tell us will help."

He took a deep, shuddering breath and turned his focus to the front door. Together, we went inside.

§§§

THE CLACK of the keys was clinical beneath my fingers as I typed up my notes of the scene, starting with my observations about the body positions and visible trauma they'd suffered. They'd been tied to another St. Andrew's Cross, this one suspended in the middle of their play room, which allowed room for them to be restrained back to back, the cross between them. The walls had been covered in mirrors, so the horrors within had doubled and tripled when we'd first entered. Jencopale had worked quickly and as a result, the time spent with the victims' dead gazes watching us had been minimal. Still, seeing Ben attempt a clinical perspective as he described his impressions of the killer's behavior had been pure torture. He'd hunched in on himself, repeatedly pausing to regain his composure as he'd noted more trauma to the bodies than had been present in the previous two cases. The marker on both victims' faces had been a mocking purple instead of the macabre black, insulting in its jauntiness. It was as if the killer was saying, *Look how pretty my work is. Admire it. Respect it.*

Cole's team had worked efficiently, and shortly after the bodies were transported to the county morgue, they'd had everything in the room catalogued, tagged, and removed for further testing. As soon as they'd announced the room was clear, Ben had made a beeline for the front door. I'd followed, catching him at his car and placing a hand on his back. He stopped and turned but didn't look me in the eye.

"I need to see you tonight," I murmured.

"Gavin, I don't think I can—"

"Not for that," I interrupted. "I don't think you should be alone. I know I sure as hell don't want to be." Lowering my voice, I willed him to look at me. After a moment, he did. "I need you."

His lips tightened, but he exhaled a pent up breath and nodded, averting his gaze again. "Don't expect much. I'm not in the mood."

Given the circumstances, his reaction was understandable. "Ben." He didn't answer, just stared into the distance, pain evident in every line of his face. "Sir," I tried again, softly. He closed his eyes and swallowed.

"Gavin, I have to go. I can't be here anymore."

There was so much I wanted to say, but it would have to wait for a more private location, so I stepped back and watched him drive away.

Hours later, I was finishing up my personal observations as quickly as I could. Myah sat across from me, glaring at the file on her desk on one of the many strangulation victims she'd dug up.

"Detective DeGrassi? Detective Hayes?"

We both looked up, me turning in my chair to look at the pair of stone-faced men standing in the pit. They wore nondescript suits that screamed Feds. Both of them were tall, one solidly built, the other lanky.

"Yes?" I asked, coming to my feet.

"Special Agents Price and McGraw. We're here about the BDSM murders."

It was the lanky one that spoke, though whether he was Price or McGraw, I didn't know. I shook the proffered hands and Myah rounded her desk to do the same.

"Yeah, good to meet you." The response was rote, polite despite my having no interest in their help. On the other hand, federal resources might help us find the killer, so I bit back my distaste about sharing or relinquishing responsibility. It didn't look like I'd be seeing Ben anytime soon, and for once, I resented the pull of a case interfering with my personal life.

"Is there somewhere we can set up to go over the case files?" Lanky asked, surveying the room for an empty desk.

"Sure, follow me." I led the men down the hall to one of the smaller briefing rooms with a long conference table inside. "You can spread out in here. There are ethernet cables and a power strip if you've got computers to hook up and need Wi-Fi." I pointed to the spiderweb of wires sticking out of a hole in the middle of the table.

"The files for the first two murders—crime scene reports, autopsy reports, and photos of the scene—are available electronically. If you're using your own laptops, I can email them to you. Probably faster than waiting for the county to issue a temp laptop with network access. The file on Campbell and Parker has only just been started and hasn't been scanned in. None of the reports are in either, but I will email you my notes. Lawanda can set you up with the Wi-Fi password."

Suddenly, the last place I wanted to be was at work. Either these men would boot us off the case and take over, or they'd let us continue, acting as consultants on our investigation. Whether I stuck around or not would not sway their decision. I had a report to finish, and then I was going home. There was no way I was going to sit around babysitting Feds while they got caught up. I reached into my pocket, extracted a business card, and handed it to Lanky.

"Cell number's there, if you need to reach me."

Abruptly, I turned on my heel and almost plowed into Myah in my haste to exit the room. I slammed down in my seat and glared at my screen, trying to pick up where I'd left off. Dull anger throbbed in my chest and I ignored my partner as she resumed her seat a few minutes later.

"I helped them set up their computers. They're good to go."

I said nothing, clenching my jaw to keep from snapping something rude.

"Are you all right, Gavin?" she asked quietly, leaning forward.

"No," I replied tersely.

"Talk to me."

"We don't need the Feds' help, but there'll be no convincing anyone of that. I just want to solve this fucker, forget I ever saw anything to do with whips and restraints, and move on to the next case."

"Does that include forgetting Ben?" Her eyebrows rose when I looked at her, but her expression wasn't unkind. I blew out a shaky breath and sneaked a look around to see who might overhear. At nearly 9 pm, there were few to eavesdrop in our corner of the pit.

"I don't know." I shook my head, more confused than ever. The night before, I'd been so sure of myself, so sure I'd found where I belonged, kneeling at Ben's feet or wrapped in his arms. But in the harsh reality of daylight, with the threat of additional murders hanging over my head, I didn't know if it was worth it. I hadn't missed the derision on the faces of some of the patrol officers when they'd reported back to me their findings at the scene or their questioning of Zach and Nick's neighbors. My family wouldn't approve, and my parents would be horrified, not only that I'd been intimate with a man, but in such a deviant way. I wasn't sure I was strong enough to defend my choices, and I certainly didn't want to face the vulgar ridicule my fellow detectives would heap on me should they ever find out.

What would my brothers say? Cole would probably high five me, but Mason would definitely have a problem. He was the closest clone our father had, and reputation was important to him. Shawn... I had no idea how Shawn would respond. His girlfriend Chrissy would likely be a big part of how well he accepted that his gay brother liked to be spanked, and I was fairly certain Chrissy would be supportive, no matter how shocked. She'd make sure Shawn either accepted it or never made me uncomfortable over it.

My mother was a whole different story. She wanted more grandbabies, not that I could give her any since leaving Victoria. Mason and Sandra had made it clear they wanted no more than the two girls they had. Shawn and Chrissy weren't married yet, and Cole... well, he wasn't even close to walking down the aisle with anyone, even if Myah was incredible, and if Cole settled down any time soon, I hoped it would be with my partner.

My partner. Who was looking at me with concern in her eyes, waiting for me to speak. I opened my mouth but didn't know what to say. She had her own problems: getting used to a new city, earning respect and building a good reputation that didn't center on her looks, proving herself by solving her first case, which had turned into quite the doozy. This was rapidly becoming my most difficult one, and I was frustrated that after four murders, we were no closer to an answer than we'd been when I'd first stepped into George Kaiser's house. She had to be feeling the pressure.

I ran a shaky hand through my hair, turning back to my screen and staring blankly. That's when it hit me what my problem was.

I'm afraid. Of everything. People finding out about me. Not solving the case. My reputation, my family's response. In finally taking a chance on something *I* wanted, I'd put everything and everybody I knew in a difficult position.

Except Ben. He accepts who you are and wants you anyway. Finally, I looked Myah in the eye.

"No, I don't want to forget about Ben," I said softly. "He's the only one who's asked what I want, and not once has he worried what people will think of him being with me." He was the only one with whom I could be myself. And hell, the night before, he'd been showing me off as his. "Besides, I just signed a contract."

"You said that earlier," she smiled, her voice so low I barely heard her. "Congratulations."

I got a flash of warm excitement and my confusion dissipated. Whatever my life was with Ben, we were building it on my terms. Even when I gave him all the control, he still respected my needs and desires. He still respected *me*. That was more than I could say for my ex-wife. More than I could say for my family, Cole exempted.

I needed to see Ben. Right then. It didn't matter there was still work to be done. Didn't matter a killer was still out there. Ben was my anchor. And at that moment, I knew he was hurting.

I shut down my computer and stood, throwing my suit jacket over my arm. "I'm heading out. I'll see you tomorrow. Say hi to my brother for me." Myah smiled in reply and I left.

§§§

"BEN?" I called, sticking my head through the gap in the door. He hadn't answered my knock and my heart thudded at my crazy thoughts concerning his whereabouts. I'd tried the knob to the back door and sighed with relief when it turned easily.

The living room was dark, the under-cabinet lights in the kitchen barely penetrating the gloom. Every other light was off. I saw enough to recognize the outline of the man on the couch. Letting the door shut behind me with a quiet click, I removed my shoes and tie, draping the latter over the back of the couch as I rounded it. I couldn't see his face, but his utter stillness sent a chill prancing up my spine and I shivered.

"Ben," I said softly, sinking to my knees at his feet. I put a hand on his knee, felt the muscle of his thigh jump against my fingertips. This wasn't the present position of a submissive, it was that of a friend, a lover, wanting to offer comfort when words failed. I laid my cheek against his other leg and the smell of his laundry soap surrounded me as his hand reached to grasp mine. His grip was tight, but I could still feel the shake in it. "I'm so sorry," I whispered.

His fingers carded through my hair, and though he said nothing, I felt him seeking the contact, taking what he needed. Impulsively, I rose and sat beside him, lacing our fingers together.

"Anything new?" he asked, his voice raw, as if he'd just woken. Or been weeping.

"No. Preliminary comparisons show the same pattern, but we knew that." Both men had been raped, Zach so much so that he'd bled significantly. It sickened me to think that Nick might have seen that in the mirrors. I had no way of knowing if Nick had already been dead at that moment, but something in my gut told me the killer wouldn't have spared either of them the torture. They'd been forced to endure every pain possible before the finality of oblivion. "The cleaning lady confirmed three glasses were missing, so I'm pretty sure they were drugged. They knew him, same as the others. Let him into their home, served him a drink, and he drugged and killed them."

After a long moment of silence, Ben spoke. "It's hard not to take this personally." I rubbed his thumb, trying to soothe him. I understood him not being in the mood for a scene, but he wasn't pushing away my affection. For that, I was grateful, because I needed to be near him, to hold him. It was still a surprise when he laid his head on my shoulder. Ben was the strong one, the one in whose arms I could fall apart. It felt strange, this small role reversal, but not uncomfortable. I let his hand go and put my arm around his shoulders, pulling him closer.

"I didn't know Kaiser well, but I'd talked to him. And Seth was a friend, albeit one mostly in my past. But Nick and Zach... It's like this guy is taunting me. I have no reason to believe he even knows who I am, but it feels like he does. Who's next? Steven and Laura?"

"I doubt that." I squeezed his shoulder, my other hand squeezing his thigh. I pressed a kiss to the top of his head. "It seems like this guy's focus is on same-sex couples. Steven and Laura are probably safe."

Ben raised his head, and the little available light made his eyes glint. I put a hand to his cheek, caressing his cheekbone with the backs of my fingers.

"It's not about you," I murmured, my lips a fraction of an inch from his. "Just like I can't shoulder all the world's problems, neither can you. It's not your responsibility. You can let go, Ben. You're not weak if you do."

Every tense line of his body relaxed and he sagged into me. I leaned back, drawing him with me and lying down. For a moment, we shuffled to bring our legs onto the cushions and get comfortable, but we eventually settled, Ben's head on my arm and me with my back to the room. My top leg was draped over his hip, and I pulled his leg between mine with my ankle. We lay in silence for so long, I thought he'd fallen asleep, until his voice vibrated against my throat.

"I'm afraid of this guy getting to you."

"What makes you think he will?"

"It's no secret you're working the case. And now, because of my ego, everybody knows you're in the lifestyle. Maybe he'd see it as a bonus to take out the detective on his tail as well as another sub."

I couldn't help the small smile that tugged at my lips. "That's not going to happen," I reassured him.

When he spoke again, his lips brushed against my neck. I tried to ignore the rush from it. This wasn't the time.

"How can you be so sure?"

I really couldn't. "Because I'm careful. My partner's with me for most, if not all, the questioning, and the only other person I'm ever alone with that knows about me is you. Obviously, I've got nothing to worry about there."

He chuckled, the puff of breath on my skin wafting heat across my neck. I tilted my chin, inviting more if he were so inclined. His hand trailed from my leg up my hip and across my back, then down again.

"I'm not so sure you shouldn't worry about me," he murmured. "Every time I see you, I want to... do things to you."

"What things?" I shivered.

"I want to blindfold you, plug your ears, gag you, tie you up. Make it so the only thing you know is my touch. No sight, sound, or taste to distract you. I want you hyper-aware of my fingers on your skin, of my lips and tongue exploring every inch of you. And I want you unable to move, so when I have you that helpless, you can only do one thing—surrender to me."

There was no mistaking my arousal at his words, and he spoke them against my throat, pausing only for his tongue to flit out and taste me. "I want that, too," I croaked, sliding my hand beneath his shirt and trailing my fingertips along his waistband.

"But right now," he continued, raising his head from my neck so I could feel his breath on my lips, "I want to fuck you. Feel your heartbeat through your cock while I suck you. I want you to pant my name on every breath. Make you sweat and cry out. I want to feel you alive under me, around me."

I captured his lips in a deep kiss that, while tinged with desperation for the very things he promised, was sensual and unhurried because he made it so. He controlled the sweep of our tongues against each other. He held me with a reverence I'd never experienced. He made me feel accepted and wanted and desirable, so perfectly myself I couldn't believe I'd had doubts earlier. It was inevitable, my falling for him. Like one more wall coming down, I surrendered to it.

"I love you."

He pulled back to look at me, searching my face in the dim glow from the kitchen, but for what, I wasn't sure. Uncertainty? Deception? Doubt? He found none, only my devotion, my absolute certainty that no matter what happened with the rest of the people in my life, I belonged to him. I belonged *with* him.

His kiss was fierce, claiming, and open. He moaned into my mouth, and I swallowed it, returning his attention fervently. He shifted me to my back and settled on top, slotting his hips between my thighs and pumping. The sounds he made, growls and grunts, told me how much he needed me.

"Bedroom," I hissed as he pinched a nipple. He quickly climbed off, held out a hand to me, and led me to his room, his bed. He did everything he promised and more, giving as much pleasure as he took. There were no commands, no toys, nothing but the two of us, and though he hadn't returned the words I'd spoken, I could feel it in every look, every kiss, every stroke of his body against mine. I wasn't the only one who had fallen.

CHAPTER TWELVE

THE SMELL of bacon roused me from sleep at an hour that should have been illegal. I pulled on my discarded boxer briefs, visited the bathroom, and shuffled into the kitchen in search of coffee, food, and a kiss from Ben, not in that order. He smiled when he saw me, giving my ass a slap as I passed him on my way to the coffee maker and picked out a flavor of his ridiculous single serving brews. The first sip burned my tongue and I grimaced but otherwise ignored it.

"What's with the early morning, Benjamin? I think even the sun would call you crazy for rising at this hour."

"What are your plans for the day?" he asked with a grin. I realized it was Sunday, Jencopale wouldn't schedule an autopsy for yesterday's murders until the following morning at the earliest, and Cole's department would be a ghost town. I wasn't about to go to the station and babysit Feds. There was little I could do until preliminary reports came through. I did want to catch Damon Lane and ask him about his son. And there was something else I'd been dreading.

"I need to check with Hayes to chase down a lead and I don't want to sit on this just because it's Sunday, but there also won't be much else to do. Jencopale estimated time of death between three and four am, and I don't need to question people about when they were last seen." The killer had taken a few hours for his ritual, and doubling the body count meant that when the couple left Collared after their scene, they'd likely walked straight into their killer's waiting jaws. "But before all that, I'm supposed to have brunch at my parents' house at eleven." My eyeroll was evidence enough of how much I looked forward to the third degree for missing family time the last few weekends, but if I waited much longer, my dad would send out a search party, then a lynch mob. "So don't make a lot of food for me."

"Poor baby," he teased, his voice tinged with fake sympathy. "Once more into the breach, correct?"

"You got that right," I grumbled. "A couple hours of how pitiful my life is since I left my wife and how I should let them crowd me because they're just trying to help. I think I'd rather scrub the toilets at Busch Stadium with a toothbrush after a World Series game."

Ben gave me an appalled grimace, then turned back to the food and cleared his throat. "There's something I want to talk to you about."

He turned bacon on a griddle beside the stove, then cracked a couple of eggs into a bowl and began to whisk them. His whole body shook, and I couldn't help appreciating the smooth planes of his back, the flex of his shoulders. Instead of concentrating on the frisson of unease his words brought, I let myself ignore it for a moment.

"This is a good look for you," I gestured to his sweat pants, no shirt, and an apron draped over his neck and tied loosely behind him.

"Have you ever splattered bacon grease on your stomach? Hurts like crazy," he drawled as he removed bacon from the griddle and carefully poured the eggs into the leftover grease, using a spatula to chase the runaway dribbles threatening to drip into the grease trap.

"No, but I've ruined more than one shirt with grease stains that way. Still, you should wear that in bed." I sipped my coffee, then took a breath. "What did you want to talk about?"

"Yesterday, before you called, I made an appointment with that guy, Damon Lane, to talk about a special order for you. But I want to make sure it's something you really want."

My voice clogged in my throat and I gulped coffee to dislodge it. Myah's suspicions from the previous day floated up. Hadn't I told her it was flimsy? There wasn't much of a connection between Lane and the victims. My discomfort didn't listen to my logic.

Ben seemed to take in my face, my lack of response as a negative. "I can cancel."

Willing myself to speak, I drew circles with my finger on the countertop beside my cup. "What kind of special order?"

He seemed to weigh whether or not to tell me, and I remembered him saying when I asked what he intended for future scenes, I wasn't always going to be told. This wasn't the beginning of a specific scene, though. He was negotiating. How much did I trust him?

I told him I love him. That's gotta mean something.

"It's a special suit. I saw one at a con several years ago and always meant to see how well it worked. Sensory deprivation suit. It has a mask that covers the eyes, nose, mouth, and has special plugs inside for the ears. The rest of the suit is lycra lined with silk, which picks up the wearer's body heat, and the stretch fits like a glove. The original was made for a woman, and the owner swore it was as good as a water tank. There were hooks for suspension in mid-air, so I could have a custom rig put in the loft that would allow you to be horizontal without lying on anything. You'd be totally floating, unable to speak, see, or hear."

I relaxed marginally. It didn't sound anything like edge play, but for one feature. "The nose is covered?"

"There are breathing holes and the mask has to be custom fitted so the holes are lined up. I don't have access to a tank, and while I did teach that workshop at..." he paused, taking a shaky breath. "Zach's B&B about achieving deprivation-like conditions without the use of water, I'm not equipped to do it in my house. I've not had anyone I was interested in playing with to make the necessary renovations worthwhile. Until now."

How paranoid was I about an appointment with Lane being dangerous? We had nothing to connect him to the murders. He was less acquainted with the victims than Ben. His alibis weren't complete, but a man living alone didn't have much corroboration. That didn't make him a criminal, either. I couldn't help wondering if Myah's original impression of him had colored her opinion of his involvement. Hell, Jared Nunn would have been a prime candidate but for his alibis. It could literally be anyone in the community.

I want you unable to move, so that when I have you that helpless, you can only do one thing—surrender to me.

I wanted that, too.

"Keep the appointment. When is it?"

"Tomorrow morning, nine." He turned and spooned the eggs onto plates, then set them on the counter and perched on the stool beside me. He ignored the food, facing me, his knee pressing into my thigh. "I'll understand if you need time. You only just signed a contract, and after yesterday… It's okay if you need distance from this right now."

Did I? Last night had been heaven with just the two of us, no rules or expectations other than to be close to each other. I took a moment to gather my thoughts before speaking, but when I did so, I looked him in the eye.

"Let's order the suit. We don't have to use it right away. When the time's right, we'll know. And yeah, I'm really unsettled, but I also know I haven't felt this comfortable in my own skin since I was a kid. It's not just being tied up and letting someone else decide what happens to me. It's you, Ben. Your calm, your command of my body, of *me*... it feels right. You'll take care of me, and I'll take care of you. When I'm with you, I can do anything. I like who I am with you."

His palm rested against my cheek, its warmth radiating into my skin. I closed my eyes and leaned into him. There was nothing sexual about it, just proximity. A quiet joy unlike anything I'd ever felt built in my chest, such a simple thing but so profound, it refused containment. We ate our early morning breakfast in companionable silence.

Heading to my parents' house just after ten, I tried to reach Myah on her cell while I drove, but the call went straight to voicemail and I briefly wondered if Cole would make an appearance at brunch or if I'd be the lone soldier sneaking into enemy territory. I didn't want to dread seeing my family, but I knew what was in store, and avoidance had seemed the easiest way of handling it. I couldn't do so forever, though, and I figured the excuse of my divorce had run out of grace period. Unable to reach my partner, I dialed my brother.

"You'd better be at Ma and Dad's to back me up, fucker, or I'm disowning you," I growled when he answered sleepily.

He laughed, and I heard a muffled whisper. "I'll be there. Maybe a few minutes late," he conceded. I grinned. Cole sounded happy, and while he was generally an upbeat guy, his voice was more content than I'd ever heard it.

"While I've got you on the phone, roll your slutty ass over and rouse my partner. I need to talk to her."

"What makes you think Myah's here?"

"I'm not stupid," I replied conversationally. "I promise I won't keep her."

"And what if I told you her mouth's busy right now?" There was an indignant yelp in the background, and Cole laughed around the word, "Ow."

"I'd say bullshit, because I just heard her and I know from recent accidental eavesdropping what you sound like in the throes of passion. I really need to find my own place."

"That you do, brother," Cole agreed amiably. "Hang on."

Myah came on the phone, her voice a dichotomy of growl and smile. "What's up, Gav?"

"I'm making no assumptions on how to answer that question, Hayes. I don't wanna know." She growled again, this time at me.

"Are you busy later? I think we should try to talk to Lane this afternoon."

"Can't today. I've got appointments to see four apartments and I'm going to be rushing as it is. I've already rescheduled an obscene number of times."

"I suppose we could do it in the morning. Lane should be available after—" I hesitated, then cleared my throat. "I'm supposed to meet with him about something tomorrow morning. We can meet you for coffee afterwards."

The joking tone left her voice. "What are you meeting him about?"

"Uh, just some personal stuff. Shouldn't take too long." I pulled onto my parents' street and parked in front of their house, shifting into park and closing my eyes. I wanted to kick myself for bringing it up with her lying next to Cole. *Stupid!*

"Please tell me you're not meeting him for Ben," she said through what sounded like clenched teeth. Irritation at her made my face flush.

"Please tell me you didn't just say that in front of my brother, Myah." My voice took on a low, dangerous tinge, one I hoped Cole wouldn't hear beside her. "You want to tell him Ben and I are fucking while you're at it? Maybe you could join him for brunch at our parents' house and let them all know how much I enjoy taking it up the tan track."

"Don't be an ass," she snapped. "I'm allowed to be concerned."

"If you breathe one word—"

"Gavin," she interrupted. "Cancel it. We'll meet with Lane together tomorrow and find out what the story is with his son, then go from there."

"Ben will be with me, so I don't know why you're worried, but when we're finished, I'll call you and you can meet all of us at the Coffee Cartel."

"Yeah, because Zach and Nick were safe as a pair," she bristled.

"Myah, I swear, if you say one more word in front of Cole, I will never tell you another personal thing again." *What the fuck is her problem?*

"All right, Gavin," she said quietly. "But I want you to call me as soon as you're finished."

"Of course." Swallowing my anger took effort. I knew she wasn't being indiscreet on purpose and it was my fault for bringing it up right then. "I'll talk to you later." Without waiting for her reply or for her to give the phone back to Cole, I ended the call.

A knock on my passenger window startled me, but it was just my niece, Marcie. She was barely tall enough to see into the car, even standing on the curb, but she tried to shield her eyes from the glare on the window, pressing her nose flat on the glass. I chuckled, getting out and rounding the car to pull her into my arms.

"Where have you been, Uncle Gavin?" She projected every ferocious ounce of bossy indignation she could, her face a perfect scowling replica of my brother Mason's.

"Didn't your father tell you your face will freeze like that if you leave it too long?"

"That's not true," she huffed, putting her arms around my neck and squeezing me tight. I returned the hug, her slight build light in my arms. "I just missed you."

"I missed you, too, sweetheart."

"Nana says Aunt Victoria won't be around anymore. That true?"

Oh god. How do I explain divorce to a six year old? Or worse, her four year old sister?

"Yeah, that's true. Aunt Victoria and I aren't married anymore."

Marcie wrinkled her nose as I carried her up the porch steps to the house. "She was real pretty, Uncle Gavin, but she never smiled."

Out of the mouths of babes.

"No, sweetie, she didn't. Maybe now that she's on her own, she'll smile more."

"Will you smile more?"

I gave her a peck on her cheek and set her down beside her sister on the living room floor. "I already do." Tweaking her nose made her giggle, and I stood and surveyed the room. Just the girls in the middle of a game of Memory and voices from the kitchen. I followed the noise, taking a deep breath before stepping over the threshold into view.

"Gavin!" Ma exclaimed, hastily wiping her hands on her apron and hurrying over to throw her arms around me. I bent down to return the embrace, letting her decide when to let go. She cradled my cheeks in her hands and scrutinized me. "You okay, hon? You look good, but how are you really?"

I laughed. "I'm okay, Ma. It's for the best."

"Well," she huffed, returning to the cinnamon rolls she'd been icing. "I don't know about for the best, what she did to you. If you need anything…"

My dad came down the back stairs from the second floor with a newspaper tucked under his arm, stopped briefly when he saw me, and then strode across the floor to shake my hand.

"Son, it's good to see you. Your Ma's been worried."

"I just wish he would have called, that's all," she crowed, not looking up from her cooking. Sandra, Mason's wife, winked at me over Ma's shoulder as she got butter from the fridge.

"Gavin's staying with Cole, isn't that right?" Sandra looked to me for confirmation. When I nodded, she continued. "He's had family taking care of him, even if it wasn't his Ma. I'm sure Cole's made sure everything is okay."

"Speaking of Cole, where is the golden child?" Mason asked, stealing a carrot from a veggie plate Ma had set out for munching until the main event was ready.

"I just talked to him. Said he was running a little late, but he'll be here," I answered, standing off to the side and out of the way of the two bustling women. "What about Shawn and Chrissy?"

"They're down at the Lake of the Ozarks for the week. Vacation." Ma's eyes lit up. "I think they might come back with some news," she sing-songed the last word, doing a mini-jig. I rolled my eyes. The pressure never let up. Either it was on me for a promotion or a kid, or on Shawn to propose to his girlfriend, or on Cole to find a girlfriend. That last thought made me smile.

"If Shawn's ready for that, good for them," I said, swiping a cracker with cheese and heading back to the living room. "I'm going to check on the girls. They've been quiet for too many minutes in a row." Sandra chuckled, tossing a thank you over her shoulder. Mason followed me, settling into Dad's recliner and eyeing me over his daughters' heads as I sat on the couch.

"You really okay, bro?" he asked. His face said he was concerned, but his tone said he didn't want to pry. I appreciated the sentiment, even if I was already tired of talking about it.

"I'm really okay, Mason. Can we change the subject?"

"I'm a much more interesting subject, anyway," Cole breezed through the front door, his hair still damp from what had to have been the quickest shower on record. He dashed into the kitchen to tell Ma he'd arrived, then darted back into the living room, giving me a meaningful look and a head tilt to follow him. Just like that, he was back out the front door.

Reluctantly, I went after him, my earlier anger at my partner returning. Arms crossed reticently over my chest, I leaned on the porch railing.

"Okay, what the fuck, dude?" he asked, careful to keep his voice down as he lit a smoke. "After you hung up, Myah practically snarled at me when I asked why you meeting with someone had her so upset. She marched me into the shower, yelled at me to, and I quote, 'Talk to your goddamned brother for a fucking change,' and when I got out, she was gone. Start explaining. Why am I in the doghouse and I didn't even do anything wrong?"

Ice wrapped its insidious fingers around my spine and I couldn't look at him, could only stare at my feet. Of my whole family, Cole was the one I trusted the most, was the one with whom I could be the most honest. But telling him meant I had the most to lose.

"She thinks I'm putting myself in danger by meeting with a guy who's on the periphery of the BDSM investigation, and she was concerned. That's all it was."

"That's all. That's a pretty big 'all.' *Are* you putting yourself in danger?"

I raised my head to look at him. "No, I'm not."

"Because whatever this meeting is about, you're going with Ben? And Ben's the psychologist consulting on the case? The guy at the last scene who looked a little green around the edges?"

"Yeah." *I might get out of this one yet.*

"But you told her to meet up with you and the periphery guy after you and Ben meet with him, right? I'm confused. Why can't she go with you to the first thing? I know it would make her feel better."

Maybe not. My shoulders slumped and I let out a breath, shoving my shaking hands in my pockets. A quick glance at the front door showed no one nearby, and I couldn't even hear the girls in the front room anymore. *Now or never.*

"Cole, what I'm about to tell you, you cannot repeat under pain of death. I mean it like I've never meant anything before. Swear to me."

His whole body went rigid, and he stepped forward, putting a hand on my shoulder, kneading the muscle. "You can tell me anything, Gav. Haven't I always said that?"

I nodded. "This little appointment I have set up with Ben and this other guy is personal, not work. Well, it sort of is indirectly, but only because I know about the guy from working the case."

Cole shook his head. "I don't understand. What's the appointment for?"

I winced. I couldn't tell him about the toys, or the contract with Ben, or being a sub. I just couldn't. My eyes pleaded with him to let me off the hook. He waited patiently, hand still massaging my shoulder, comforting.

"Okay, fuck." I pulled away from him and whirled, abruptly sitting on the porch swing, my head in my hands, elbows on knees. I felt his weight fall beside me seconds later, the swing creaking and swaying. Without raising my eyes, I spoke.

"Ben's consulting on the case, but he and I have been spending time together outside of the case, as well. Socially."

"That's good, right? Hanging out with him is probably better than moping around my apartment pissed at your ex-wife. Talking to a psychologist, too. Smart, Gav."

I finally looked at him. "Socially as in… seeing each other."

"Yeah, it's a little hard to hang out with someone without seeing them." He finished his smoke and flicked the butt into the bushes.

"Cole, I'm dating him."

My brother squinted at the street, his lips in a grim line as the import of my words hit home. He sniffed, fidgeted with his hands, tapped a foot, and all the while, I waited to see if I would lose him over it. It was the most agonizing minute of my life, waiting for him to process the revelation.

"Can't get in trouble, since technically he doesn't work for the department," he murmured. "Seemed like a nice enough guy from what I saw yesterday, especially in less than ideal circumstances. You happy? He treat you all right?" His blue eyes pierced me, looking straight through all my bullshit, and I felt a thousand tons lift from my shoulders; his expression held no judgment. His words sank in and my racing heart slowed to a brisk trot.

I couldn't suppress the smile, so I looked at my hands. "Yeah, Cole. I'm happy. Finally happy."

"So you're gay," he added, not really a question.

"Yeah, I'm gay." For saying the words to family for the first time, they weren't all that difficult. Or maybe that was because it was Cole to whom I said them.

He clapped me on the back. "Okay then. But why's my girlfriend pissed you and your boyfriend are meeting some dude?"

I stared at him open-mouthed. "Girlfriend? I don't think anyone's ever reached girlfriend status with you."

"Don't deflect," he snapped.

"She thinks this guy has something to do with the murders."

"Does he?"

"I can't see how. Just because he's…" I trailed off. I'd nearly said *in the lifestyle*, which would have led to more questions I sincerely didn't think I could answer.

"Wait," Cole said. "If Myah thinks he could be related to the case and dangerous, then he could be the killer, which means he's into the BDSM stuff." His eyes widened. "But you're meeting him for personal reasons. Are you and Ben into that stuff?"

My throat closed, blocking any words I might have tried, not that my brain could form words. I gaped at him, my mouth opening and closing. I couldn't quite understand the look on Cole's face. Disbelief? Disgust? Wonder? Worry about cooties since he'd just touched me?

"You kinky son of a bitch!" he exclaimed, then flinched and lowered his voice, looking sheepishly at the house. Leaning closer, he whispered conspiratorially, a sly smile on his lips, "Don't worry, I won't say anything." He winked at me, and then grew serious. "You sure you know what you're doing?"

It was a moment before I found my voice. "For the first time in my life, yeah. I know what I'm doing. And Ben's great about what I don't understand or am uncomfortable with."

Cole nodded, stood, and held his hand out to pull me up. He yanked harder than necessary and when I stumbled into him, his arms wrapped around my shoulders to steady as well as hug me.

"You're my brother, Gavin. If you're happy, that's good enough for me. But if Myah thinks you need to be careful tomorrow, then you be goddamned careful." He pulled out of the hug to stare at me fiercely. "I fucking mean it. Watch your back."

"I will," I promised. "Or your girlfriend will kick my ass. Since when do you do girlfriends?" I teased, poking him in the ribs as we headed back inside the house. I only hoped the rest of brunch would go as smoothly as coming out to my brother had.

§§§

IN THE car on my way to Ben's the next morning, my thoughts were anywhere but on the appointment and the reasons for it. Instead, I replayed the conversation from the day before, one of the most honest I'd ever had with Cole. Ben had understood when I'd called to let him know I was staying at my brother's and why. Long into the night, Cole and I had talked. I told him about my best friend in college, Pete, and how he'd been the one person I'd ever let know about my orientation. In retrospect, the way I'd told him—planting a drunken kiss on him after a frat party when Pete helped me back to my dorm—left a lot to be desired. It was Pete's reaction more than the predestined future laid out by my family that had convinced me to stay firmly in the closet all those years.

"He punched you?" Cole asked incredulously.

I smiled, a reaction very different due to time and distance than the one I'd had immediately following the punch. "Yeah. Damn near broke my nose." I pointed to the minute scar across the bridge. "His class ring."

Cole squinted at it, then shook his head, getting up from the kitchen table to get both of us another beer. "I liked Pete. Never did figure out what happened, but I assumed your classes changed and you just drifted apart."

"Our classes changed because he dropped the ones we shared so we wouldn't have to see each other. He vanished." I grabbed a chip from the bag he'd set on the table between us and gathered up a large dollop of salsa from the adjacent bowl.

"I'm sorry," Cole said, eyes sad. "It bugs me that people are so narrow-minded. What difference does it make who you love, as long as you get to?"

"Yeah, well, I don't see Dad having the same opinion."

Cole waved me off. "Dad will come around, when you decide to actually tell the rest of them."

I stared at him, wide eyed. "Mr. Your Lives Are Mine To Plan being okay with this? Doubtful. He's going to hit the roof." I gathered a deep, cleansing breath. "But I don't care anymore." I paused, thinking, and then chuckled. "I just lied to you. I do care. I just don't want to. What I don't want even more is living on their terms. About time I grew up and said so. Just... maybe not quite yet."

Cole's expression couldn't be anything but proud, which startled me. "Look at you, putting on your big boy britches." He sat back, shaking his head. "I just can't quite believe the britches are leather with D-rings to tie you up."

I threw a chip at him. "I don't ask you about your bedroom Olympics, so don't ask me about mine. Speaking of, what's the story with you and my partner?"

The sheepish grin was unlike any I'd seen on his face when it came to talking about his dates. "I like her. We were discussing some of the evidence from the Adams scene and it was clear how much it bothered her. So I asked her to get a drink with me, to get her mind off it. I had no intention of anything more happening than a couple drinks, some conversation, and maybe a sandwich. I guess she could tell I wasn't after her, not that I normally wouldn't have been. She's fucking gorgeous. That evening, I walked her to her car and when I asked if she was okay, she kissed me and said, 'I am now.' Blew me away."

I chuckled. "That's probably why she did it. If you'd been trying to hit on her, she'd have blown you off with the coldest shoulder you've ever felt."

He smiled wryly. "So I've been told."

The chirp of my cell jarred me back to the present, sitting in my car at a stoplight. I settled the earpiece and hit the button. "DeGrassi."

"What time is your appointment?" Myah's resignation transmitted loud and clear.

"Nine. I'm on my way to Ben's now."

"You're meeting at Ben's house?"

"Yes. Lane wants to look at the loft and see how it's fitted out so he can tailor the…" I trailed off, not wanting to go into more detail. "He needs to see Ben's setup so he can customize the order."

My answer was met with silence.

"It shouldn't take more than an hour, but I honestly don't know, Myah. I'll call you when we're headed to Coffee Cartel."

"Okay. Just… do me a favor. Be careful, Gavin. I don't want to find a new partner."

I didn't answer her right away, lost in thought at the stoplight. Staring. At the traffic camera designed to catch red light violations.

"Cameras…" I mumbled.

"What? Gavin, are you paying attention?"

Something gnawed on my brain, barely out of reach, and the more I strained for it, the more it danced away. A car behind me honked, and I waved them around, earning myself a finger from the irritated driver. Turning right, I pulled to the side of the road and stared blankly out the windshield.

"Myah, has forensics submitted the inventory listing of Zach and Nick's house?"

"Cole said he'd have it to us this morning. Why?"

Cameras. Holy shit!

"Every time I saw Zach and Nick in a scene, someone was filming them. Check the list for camera equipment in their play room. It's a long shot, but what if, Myah?" My voice took on the breathlessness of excitement. "What if they had a setup at home to record them all the time?"

"It would have to be motion activated or a security camera to be of any use," she said, and I could hear her typing furiously in the background. "Nothing yet. Let me call and find out the ETA on that report. If I get a hit, I'll let you know."

"Do that." She hung up and I returned to the road, pondering the shift in our luck if my hope was true.

When I arrived at Ben's, another car sat in the courtyard drive, and I pulled alongside it. I sat a moment, my thoughts a jumbled mess. With a breath to calm my nerves I entered the house through the patio door, and found Ben leaning forward on the countertop, talking with Lane who sat at one of the breakfast barstools.

"Good, you're here," Ben said, rounding the counter and giving my lips a peck. "We can get started. Damon, would you care for anything to drink?"

"Coffee would be good," Lane answered, picking up a bag at his side. "And an electrical outlet." He removed a laptop from the bag and set it on the counter, then unwound a cord and plugged in to the nearby outlet. "You mentioned masks and I want to show you what I've done before. What, specifically, are you trying to accomplish?"

It all seemed so businesslike, though it shouldn't have surprised me. This was Lane's line of work, so talking about elaborate getups for sex scenes wasn't embarrassing to him in the least. Ben was even less nervous or shy, but I felt the color rise on my cheeks as Ben described his intent with the mask.

"I want to control all five of his senses. I don't want him to hear, see, taste, smell, or feel what I don't allow. Total sensory deprivation, and the mask combined with this suit," he said, sliding over a paper on which I assumed was a description or some other depiction of what he'd found at the con, "will give me control over everything. It all needs to fit him like a glove and be lightweight enough that he can forget he's wearing it. I'd like it to include built-in D-rings and, of course, access to his cock and ass, as well as provide stability through his center of gravity so I can suspend him from my ceiling."

I carefully set Lane's coffee in front of him, then Ben's, while mine finished brewing. I couldn't meet either of their eyes, not that I expected them to be looking at me. It was just so... *clinical*, Ben's wishes laid out in such a manner. It took all the intent out of it, the whole *reason* I submitted to him in the first place. Yeah, it was to give him control, but more, to *share* myself with him. The way he'd just spoken, it was like I was a side of beef to be strung by a hook from the ceiling.

Which, of course, called to mind another picture of restrained men, no longer breathing or living, just so much fresh meat discarded by a callous and sadistic killer who had no respect for what had made those men human.

"Ben, can I talk to you for a moment?" I asked, pouring my coffee into a mug before heading to the kitchen door leading to the hallway.

"Sure, babe." He excused himself and followed me to where I stopped just past the bend in the hall. "What's up?"

I swallowed tightly, unsure how to express what I needed to without sounding like a virgin at a sacrificial altar.

"That's not all this is to you, is it?" I didn't quite stutter, but it was damn close. "Not just about the control, but also the connection between us?"

His warm palm cupped my face as he stepped closer and his thumb stroked my cheek. "Of course, Gav. I don't want a robot who can submit to me and then walk away like it was nothing. I put too much of myself into being a Dom for it to just be about the kink."

"But you've... taught others, people you didn't have much of a connection with."

He looked to the side, choosing his words carefully. "Yes, but that was different. I gave them my knowledge knowing they'd take something with them, that even if they weren't getting a specific piece of me, they would use what they'd learned to enhance their own relationships." He took my face in both hands, forcing me to look at him. "Babe, I don't play casually. You know that. You also know you're the first person in years I've wanted to do anything like this with. This is as much about giving you an experience you'll never forget, as it is about Domination and submission. But if you're not ready, it's fine. We go tell Damon that we're still thinking about it and will be in touch. No harm done. Or, like you said, we order the suit and wait for the right time to use it. Okay?" He pressed a feather-light kiss to my forehead and wrapped his arms around me. I buried my face in his neck and held on tight. This was right, with him. No matter what happened, if I was with him, I'd be okay.

"Let's order it. I don't know how long it'll be before I'm ready to use it, but at least when that happens, it'll be finished and waiting."

"You sure?" He pulled away to look into my eyes.

I nodded and we turned to go back to the kitchen just as Lane peeked through the doorway. "Everything all right? Your coffee's getting cold."

"It's fine," I smiled, exhaling a marginally shaky breath I hoped he didn't hear. "Just double checking something."

"Good, good," Lane replied, resuming his seat and taking a sip from his cup. "Mmm, this is excellent coffee. I've never seen it brewed that way outside a coffee shop. Are the individual filter cups expensive?"

I grabbed the basket of coffee servings Ben kept beside the machine and took them, along with my mug, over to the counter where Lane perched. Ben explained how it worked and how much less mess he dealt with while Lane pawed through the flavors. I took a generous gulp of my own hazelnut blend and sighed in contentment. Ben's kitchen was becoming as familiar as my own when I'd lived with Victoria, though much less difficult to relax in. I watched the two men talk and tried not to get too lusty when my eyes were drawn to Ben's throat as he drank deeply.

Looking into my cup, I frowned into the contents. It was two-thirds empty, but it felt so heavy all of a sudden.

"Shall we get back to your requirements?" Lane asked, pushing the basket to the side and turning his laptop screen to face Ben, who blinked at it in confusion. A high pitched whine infiltrated my ears as the world muffled, and I gripped the counter when the room spun.

"Ben," I croaked, and barely heard myself. He leaned over the barstool beside Lane, shaking his head as if to clear his vision. In horror, I watched as his grip slackened on the stool and he slid to the floor. "Ben!" I shouted from miles away, trying to make my leaden feet go to him. My knees betrayed me and I reached an arm out to steady myself, knocking my mug to the floor. The last thing I heard was the crack of ceramic as the cup's pieces skittered across the tile. Then, oblivion.

CHAPTER THIRTEEN

THE PAIN in my hands battled for dominance over the pain in my head when awareness crept in. The first attempt to open my eyes failed, and my head lolled, thoughts fuzzy and slow while I tried to make sense of my body. I heard a moan and took time to decipher it wasn't my own, but came from several feet in front of me. When my eyelids finally cooperated, the weight of my predicament slammed home. *The loft.*

"Ben?" I whispered, vision focusing one increment at a time. He was five feet in front of me, naked, his hands high above his head and held in place by rope tied so tight, his fingers were an angry red. His shoulders strained as he fought the position, but his balance was made precarious by the hobbling block between his ankles. He struggled to find his feet, and I felt similar sensations from my own wobbly legs as I sought balance. Looking down past my own nudity, I saw a similar block between my feet, chains clinking from the cuffs around my ankles which affixed them to the hooks on the block. There was no give, and the wide open stance made it difficult to hold myself up. My hands screamed from the weight of my body, and my fingers were purple and swollen, like fat sausages straining their casings.

Ben moaned again, head coming up, brow furrowed as he managed to open his eyes. He stared at me, took in my position and realized he mirrored me.

"Gavin," he murmured, his voice scratchy and dry.

I whimpered, and with every flex and pull of my muscles as I struggled to support my weight and relieve the tension to my arms and hands, I awoke further. Realization dawned.

Lane.

"Oh, goody! The two lovebirds are awake. Time to get started." The incongruously cheerful voice reached the loft before the man it belonged to emerged from the stairwell. "Sorry to leave you alone. Had to run out to my car for supplies."

With detached familiarity, Lane pulled on a pair of vampire gloves, and I closed my eyes against the rest. *Fuck, Myah. I'm so sorry I didn't listen to you.*

"Lane," Ben croaked, his head straining to look behind him where the man—no the heinous, sadistic killer that had haunted both of us for more than a month—donned a leather pony mask, the equine shape of it giving his whole demeanor a sinister cast. The discovery in Ben's voice of who was responsible for the murders solidified in my soul just how very, very fucked we were.

"Yes, love?" Lane asked, scratching his needle-pocked palm across Ben's back. Ben flinched, though from the touch or pain, I wasn't sure. "Not so dominant now, are you?" he taunted. "Not so sure of the pain you'll inflict, the danger you'll put others in, huh? Good."

He smacked Ben's back and the sound reverberated through the rafters. I winced, and the realization I would watch Ben die forced a gasp from my throat. I began to shake, the chains linked to my ankles rattling with each tremor. I lowered my head, desperate for breath, for some kind of understanding. But I would never understand what made men like Lane do what they did. I could never fathom the taking of another life.

When I saw boots on the floor before me, I squeezed my eyes shut, refusing to acknowledge him. He would coax great pain from both of us before ending our suffering. I made myself no promises to remain strong, that I wouldn't give him the satisfaction of seeing me break. I knew better. I'd seen the damage Damon Lane had done. *The pain those men had endured.* Little shards of awareness pierced my heart as I understood, not only would I have to witness Ben's torture, he'd witness mine. I did raise my head then, looking past our captor, our reaper, and into Ben's eyes.

And I saw love. Pain, fury, incomprehensible fear, but also reflected back at me was my own desperation to *do something* to save my lover, to spare him the agony not only of enduring Lane's perversions, but of watching them inflicted on me. My eyes filled with tears, and I knew if I had no chance of being strong for myself, I'd be strong for Ben.

"Don't watch, Gavin," Ben ordered, every bit in command of me as he'd been the night he'd shown me off as his at Collared. "Don't look."

"Yes, Sir," I replied, memorizing his face, the light in his eyes, that adorable gap in his front teeth. "I love you," I mouthed, smiling when he said it back.

Resolutely, I shifted my gaze to Lane, who stood watching with hands on his hips, fingers curled into his palms so as not to snag the gloves' spines on his clothes.

"That's all very touching," he intoned. "But you will watch if I have to cut off your eyelids. You will see his humiliation and he will see yours. You will witness what your disgusting ways have led you to."

From where the courage came, I didn't know, but I glared at Lane, took a heaving breath, and spat on him. It landed on his neck and shirt, and then made its slippery way beneath his collar. With a force that didn't surprise me, he slapped me so hard my head rocked back. My cheek was engulfed in the flames of pain inflicted by the glove. Inside, I found the place in which I could endure the beating. I was not weak. I was not disgusting. And I was not an animal to be slaughtered. Whatever he took from me of my dignity, my courage, he would not take my humanity. He could not touch my soul.

With as much leverage as I could muster, I leaned toward him, tasting blood from a split in my lip, and whispered with as much hatred as I could, "Bring it, you bastard."

Lane's eyes widened in the eyeholes of the mask, he blinked a few times, and then shook himself as if to rouse from a daydream.

"All right then. Since the good doctor is the one so hell bent on seeing you on the brink of death by suffocation, I think we should give him his ultimate fantasy, don't you think? Dr. Haverson?" Lane turned to Ben, but I kept my eyes averted. I was not to look. Ben grunted. "You want to see him give up control of everything, submit so beautifully that he forgets he has a body? Now's your chance. Your only chance."

Striding across the room, Lane perused Ben's inventory of toys, rummaging for some time before coming back to me with a cane slapping scratchily in his spiked palm. I couldn't help myself.

I started laughing.

In an instant, Lane had a fist in my hair, yanking my head back so I was forced to look at him. The violence did nothing to stop my laughter, which rang out through the loft.

"What. Is so. Fucking. Funny?" Lane gritted through clenched teeth.

"You," I wheezed, trying to form the words through the gales that swelled in my chest. I took my first deep breaths since waking in restraints. "You're trying to go for intimidating and you just look stupid," I managed. "Big man. Bully. No better than the high school jock beating on the nerd. Take me down and show me you can beat me fair and square, asshole." Suddenly the humor was gone.

"Oh, but that's not what you like," Lane sing-songed. "You want to submit. You want to be told what to do, how to look, what to say, what to feel."

"Not by you," I snapped.

"Too bad." He slipped the cane into his armpit to free both hands and shoved a spiny finger in my mouth, forcing my jaw apart. The taste of leather burst over my tongue. I bit down as hard as possible, ignoring the needles sinking into my gums. Lane grunted, dropped the cane for better leverage, and punched me in the temple two times in quick succession. I reeled and when his finger invaded my mouth again, I was too stunned to bite. The cold press of metal would have been soothing if not for the stretch to my mouth and the force smashing my lips to my teeth. One of Ben's anal plugs. The stainless steel was dry, the knob too wide to be anything but agonizing as he forced it into my mouth. There was a *chink!* sound within my head as one of my teeth chipped. As wide as the plug was, there was no spitting it out. An effective, strap-free ball-gag if there ever was one.

"Now maybe you'll shut up," he murmured. Turning back to Ben, he cheered up. "Doesn't he look so pretty with a plug in his mouth, Doctor?" His words were met with silence. "Look at him." Nothing. "Look at him!"

With my eyes anywhere but on Ben, I had no idea what Lane did to him when he charged across the room, but there was a grunt, a groan of pain, and heavy breathing. Yet still Ben did not answer. Steps thundered down the stairs, and I heard a door slam in the far corner of the house. I had no idea what to make of that. Every nerve-ending screamed at me to look at Ben, to get one last glimpse, but I couldn't. He'd told me not to, and I knew how I must've looked, blood trickling down my chin, mouth stretched wide around the plug, hands beyond numb to the point where circulation was a distant memory. I couldn't let myself see him, meet his eyes, get one more chance to show him my love, to see his for me. It was too much to hope for him to look at me, and he'd ordered me not to. I would obey. In my final moments, my submission was for Ben and Ben alone.

The unmistakable sound of a swatch of duct tape being torn from a roll ripped through the air as Lane returned, silver strips in his hands which he tore into small pieces. I heard Ben grunt, his chains clinking as he struggled. The sound of long strips being wound around something had me utterly confused, but I would not look. Would not give in.

"There. Can't avoid it now even if you had to."

Returning to me, Lane retrieved the cane from the floor and held the roll of tape in front of my face. "Do I have to tape your eyes open, too?" he snarled. I met his gaze with every ounce of defiance I had, then deliberately nodded.

Grunting, he pried my eyes open, slapped tape on my eyelids, and then wound several strips around my arms with my head in the middle, securing my face forward, eyes wide open. Using a trick I'd learned as a kid to avoid harassment from my brothers during scary parts of movies that I couldn't hide my face from, I gently crossed my eyes, deliberately blurring my vision. Ben was a blob indistinguishable from the furniture and the doorway to the bathroom behind him. It took effort to hold, and when the caning started, I used it as a distraction.

The pain was excruciating, but I didn't scream, didn't whimper. All Lane got out of me were grunts now and then, and a sob I couldn't hold back when I felt blood trickle down my spine. When a dildo was unceremoniously shoved up my ass dry, it was the closest I came to shouting. The burn was like nothing I'd ever experienced, a lick of fire from the very pit of Hell, and all the more torturous for the devilish laugh that erupted from Lane. I heard nothing from Ben's side of the room, and for that I was grateful. Lane's preoccupation with me allowed Ben to look away. He didn't have to see my violation, my step by step deconstruction. In that moment, I wished for the sensory deprivation mask, wished for darkness and the internal pounding of my blood being the only sound I'd hear. Tears welled and spilled over, scalding my cheeks. It would be over soon.

Lane had apparently gotten bored with me, because he moved across the room, back to the array of whips, and there was a swish of what sounded like a cat o' nine tails. I heard Ben's intake of breath when they struck his flesh. I heard the sharp whistle of the tails through the air. I heard grunts of exertion from Lane. There was movement in my deliberate blurriness, but I didn't analyze it. When Ben shouted, it was muffled, and I wondered if he'd gotten a plug, too. I would not satisfy my curiosity. I felt as though I would vomit when Lane murmured, "What, no hard-on for this? Don't you get off on it?"

The shouting continued, and I wanted to close my eyes. The tape pulled at my eyelashes and forehead.

Oh my god, let it be over. Please, let it be over quickly.

CHAPTER FOURTEEN

IT WAS a wish made in vain. Lane had just started.

But something about the tone of the shouts changed, got my attention. It wasn't just Ben. And it wasn't only in the loft.

"Police! On your knees, keep your hands where I can see them!"

"Iyaaaah!" I screamed behind the plug, all hope for dignity gone, my courage a puddle at my throbbing feet. Myah's voice, so authoritative, so incensed, was the most gorgeous thing I'd ever heard. I focused on the thrum of feet flooding the space and soon saw uniforms swarm the masked Lane, who stood dumbfounded long enough for the officers nearest to bully him to the floor. His arms were twisted behind him and his wrists zip tied, the sight of him subdued sending bolts of relief through my abused limbs. I sagged against the restraints. As Lane's mask was ripped from his head, he glared at the officers in front of him, who read him his Miranda rights as they led him from sight.

"Get them down," Myah barked, holstering her weapon and coming to my side. Tears of relief washed down my face; my breathing was harsh through my nose as her gentle fingers gripped the base of the plug in my mouth and slowly pulled. I wrenched my jaw wider to get the wretched thing out, conscious of the drool on my chin. As my arms were released, two officers positioned themselves at my sides to guide me to the floor.

"Get the paramedics and Cole DeGrassi up here now!" she snapped. "Don't touch anything."

Over her shoulder, I watched two more officers lower Ben to the floor, his body quivering and his mouth covered in tape. With my arms and head still taped together, I had little room to move, and as much as I wanted to be freed, I knew I had to wait. Evidence.

Cole charged up the stairs and stopped dead when he spotted us. "Oh my god," he breathed.

"Cole," Myah ordered, her voice both commanding and understanding. "Get two of your most trusted techs up here to help."

He snapped into motion, striding to the loft rail and hollering to his men below. After pulling a camera from its case, he moved first to Ben, ordering the officers already helping him to stand back while he murmured an apology and rapidly snapped off a handful of pictures. As soon as the photos were done, he spoke quietly to the other officers and the paramedics who had just arrived.

"Get him loose, and everything goes in here." He left them with evidence bags and hurried to me to repeat the process. Camera slung to the side, he cut through the tape securing my head and arms together, and carefully peeled my eyelids free. Humiliation washed over me as the medics checking me over discovered the toy I'd been trying not to lie on protruding from my ass.

"I've got you," Cole whispered as he extracted it himself, quickly deposited it in a paper bag, sealed it, and made a notation on the label. I shook uncontrollably.

"He's going into shock," one of the paramedics said, covering me with a blanket. I turned my head to look across the room, seeking, finally giving myself permission to look for Ben. He was similarly covered and on his back while his blood pressure was measured. His eyes were unfocused, staring at the ceiling for a moment before he turned his head. His nose was bleeding and puffy, and I could hear his breath whistling from across the room. Our eyes locked, his so glazed I wasn't sure he recognized me. He blinked a few times, and I held my breath.

Then he smiled.

Relief flooded my veins, a palpable force that made my whole body jerk. I tried to return the smile, but a mask was shoved over my face and sweet air forced into my nose and mouth. I was rolled to my side, and fingers gently skimmed the cuts on my back, the latex from their gloves making me wince as it dragged at the skin.

"Several lacerations and contusions, but nothing still bleeding heavily. He's going to need a lot of stitches. His hands will need attention," one of the medics said, easing me onto a backboard they used to lift me onto a stretcher. Cole held my hand, twined his fingers with mine and worked my wrist in a circle, shaking gently to ease circulation back into it. I only saw the gesture; I didn't feel it.

"You should have listened to me," Myah said gently, brushing hair back from my forehead. I met her gaze and saw so many emotions there I couldn't identify them all. Fear, relief, fury, and comfort were chief among them. All I could do was nod.

"We'll be right behind you and Ben," Cole promised. He must have seen the question in my eyes, because he answered what I couldn't ask. "He's okay. About as banged up as you, but okay."

I nodded again and closed my eyes, the adhesive that remained on my lids pulling the delicate skin. Shame slammed home as I grasped the reality of what I'd just been through, how we had to have looked to the responding officers and my partner. *My brother saw me like that.* My eyes filled. Cole brushed the tears away as they fell.

"None of that. We got him, bro. *You* got him. You didn't do anything wrong."

The paramedics maneuvered my stretcher down the stairs after securing me with straps. I had a moment of panic when the restraints were tightened, but Cole immediately whispered in my ear, "Just to keep you from rolling off the stretcher and down the steps. For your safety. Nothing more." As soon as we were downstairs, Cole unhooked the chest strap to free my arms over the protests of the EMTs. He turned and did the same for Ben, a gesture that brought fresh tears to my eyes.

They put Ben and me in the same ambulance, two medics sitting along the wall closest to the cab monitoring us, two up front for the drive to the Barnes-Jewish hospital. The ride took only minutes. Words were beyond me but I couldn't stop looking at Ben, devouring his pale face, sweaty brow and haunted brown eyes as he stared back at me. When he reached across the gap between our stretchers, I fumbled for him, clumsily grasping with the claw of my hand, which was still numb from lack of circulation. Nothing worked right—my brain was sluggish and my throat was clogged. When we arrived at the emergency room doors, they pulled us apart, whisked us inside, and we were swallowed up in the crowd of people waiting—nurses scrambling to bring us in, and doctors taking over for the medics.

After the obligatory "squeeze my hand" instructions, I let myself drift.

§§§

HOURS LATER, I was deposited in a semi-private room, my hands wrapped in massaging gloves that restored my nerves to excruciating pins and needles, and a body pillow strategically placed behind me to keep me from rolling onto my freshly-stitched back. I didn't think they had much to worry about, since I wasn't positive I'd ever lie on my back again. I was high as a kite on painkillers, and the doctor said several of the lacerations could have potentially damaged nerves that would manifest as numb spots. He didn't think I would have lasting damage that would impede movement.

Cole and Myah were in the room, my partner standing at the window with her arms crossed as if holding herself together and Cole slumped in the visitor's chair. The nurse parked my bed and locked the wheels, telling me the doctor would be by shortly before exiting. Cole sat straighter and scooted the chair closer. Apprehension speared me at the recollection of him seeing me in such a horrible position, but he quelled it by reaching for my hand. The massaging gloves got in his way, so he squeezed my forearm instead, his face showing nothing but concern and relief.

"I'm so glad you're okay," Myah said from the foot of the bed, her hand finding and squeezing my ankle through the blankets.

"How'd you know? Lane?" My lips barely cooperated through the haze of Vicodin and fatigue.

Cole quirked a one-sided smile. "Cameras."

Events marched blurrily through my brain and I knew I was supposed to understand what he meant, but I couldn't focus. I looked to Myah for an explanation.

"I beat down Cole's office door right after you told me to look for the cameras. They hadn't finished cataloguing Zach and Nick's possessions, but photos of the scene showed cameras in the corners of the ceiling. Motion activated. You were right. Zach and Nick liked to film themselves, and everything that happened in that room was saved on a server in Zach's office. We dragged a computer expert in to crack the files and found the entire murder, including Damon Lane tying the victims to the cross before he put the mask on. His face reflected in the mirrors as clear as if he'd been posing. Because of you, I knew where to find him. I called in the cavalry."

"Thank you." My throat constricted on the words, but they squeezed out in a croak.

Just then, the rest of my family filed in. Embarrassment flooded my face as I realized they had to have heard something about the state in which my partner had found us. I wanted to feign sleep, but they had already seen me awake. *My kingdom for these awesome drugs.*

"Oh, thank god!" Ma exclaimed, coming to the head of the bed so she was face-to-face with me, her gentle hands pushing my hair soothingly off my forehead. Despite wanting time before facing them and their questions, her touch was comforting. "Thank god you're okay," she murmured, kissing my forehead.

"Let him breathe, Ma," Shawn said, putting a hand on her shoulder. They gave me some room and my dad placed a reassuring hand on one of my feet. Mason stayed by the door, and Cole vacated the chair for my mother, retreating to the window with Myah at his side.

It was Cole who broke the silence, explaining the doctor's assessment and wanting to keep me overnight for observation. The blows to my temple had me loopy and apparently passing out during the initial examination hadn't offered the medical staff much reassurance.

My dad cleared his throat. "Anything on why this sicko did this to my son?"

Myah spoke from behind me. "The investigation is ongoing, Mr. DeGrassi. I'm sure you understand." I wanted to kiss her.

"Of course, of course," he said quickly. If I hadn't been so stoned, it would have bothered me that he couldn't look me in the eye.

Commotion at the door drew everyone's attention as Ben was wheeled into the room. He was propped on his side as I was, facing me as they locked the wheels of his bed into place. He appeared to be asleep. Deep bruises had formed around his eyes behind the bandages that bridged his nose. The nurse was followed by Laura, who wore a worried though composed look.

"Oh," she said, seeing everyone crowded around me. She began to turn away, but I clumsily waved her in before letting my unwieldy gloved hand thump to the bed.

"C'mon," I slurred. "You're okay."

There was an awkward silence as she perched her tiny frame on the chair between the beds. Not looking at me, she asked, "How are you, Gavin?" Her speaking my name garnered curious looks from my family since they didn't know her or how she knew me.

"Stoned. 'M good."

Shawn snickered and earned himself a smack on the shoulder from Chrissy, and all the tension bled from the room.

"What 'bout Ben?" I had to know, and I didn't care if my family knew. Not that I could keep a lid on the secret anymore.

"He's got bruised kidneys and a broken nose, but otherwise, just some stitches in his back," Laura answered, her eyes trained on Ben. "They're keeping him overnight because of the kidneys to make sure he doesn't develop clots."

"Me, too. Head." I said, gesturing both gloved hands awkwardly toward my face before settling again. It wasn't quite the night together I would have wished for with him, but we were alive. I'd take what I could get.

Ma straightened in the chair, patting my leg. "When you're released, we want you to stay with us for a while." The offer surprised me, and I stared at them until my dad finally looked at me, giving a tiny nod. Cole's hours were erratic and I had no idea if Ben would want to see me again. I suddenly wanted very much for my family to leave so I could ask Laura if she'd talked to him.

I swallowed thickly, and then mumbled gibberish meant to acquiesce. My eyelids began to droop, my surroundings to fade. I felt another squeeze to my foot, and they all moved to the door with barely-heard promises to return the following day. One more bleary look around the room showed me Cole and Myah had stayed, settling themselves in with an extra chair from somewhere. The combined weight of their hands resting on my leg was the last thing I knew before sleep swallowed me whole.

EPILOGUE

"IN A St. Louis County courthouse today, Damon Lane, the Breath Play Killer, as he's been called since his arrest thirteen months ago, was found guilty of four counts of first degree murder, two counts of aggravated criminal sexual assault, and two counts of assault in the first degree. Details of what police are calling the most heinous series of homicides the county has ever seen have kept this case in the spotlight since an astonishing press conference held by Lieutenant Jacob Mitchell of the Second Precinct shortly after Lane's arrest. Lane's son, Jeffrey, died by bondage-related strangulation six years ago. The prosecution asserted that Lane's motivation stemmed from a desire to exact vigilante justice against participants of the lifestyle in which his son died. Testimony from the two survivors, saved in what can only be described as a dramatic, made-for-Hollywood rescue, Detective Gavin DeGrassi and Dr. Benjamin Haverson, depicted Lane as a merciless killer who perpetrated his attack with cold calculation, determined to show BDSM sexual practices to be degrading and immoral. Prosecutors submitted as evidence Lane's journal, which has become known as Lane's manifesto, in which he promises to avenge his son's death by eradicating the leather culture one Dominant/submissive pair at a time, particularly those interested in erotic asphyxiation.

"Detective DeGrassi and Dr. Haverson were present for the verdict, hugging each other upon hearing the jury's decision. DeGrassi comes from a family of respected police officers, including retired Lieutenant Herman DeGrassi, his father. Lieutenant DeGrassi has supported the detective with his continued presence, but refuses to answer questions about his son's role as both investigator and victim. The attorneys for the case, however, gave statements from the steps of the courthouse at the conclusion of the proceedings." The news broadcast switched from the anchor desk to the courthouse, where attorneys for each side expressed their opinions on the jury's decision.

Ginger Graham, the prosecutor on the case, gave the camera a subdued smile, looking nothing like the submissive I knew her to be. "Today, justice worked as it should, with twelve everyday people able to look past the sexual orientation and lifestyle of the victims, and consider their lives as valuable as anyone else's. Damon Lane's mental faculties certainly played a part in his commission of these murders, but not to the extent he has claimed, and the jury honored the victims' memories by putting the man responsible for their deaths in prison. This case is a tragedy all around, and Jeff Lane's memory is as important as those of George Kaiser, Seth Adams, Zachary Campbell, and Nicholas Parker. He should be remembered for who he was, not who his father became."

Lane's defense attorney blustered about Lane's failed insanity defense, calling him a victim of a deviant lifestyle and of the verdict, which prohibited access to quality healthcare for him. Lane's lawyer promised to appeal the jury's recommendation for four consecutive life sentences.

I threw the book, ignored in my lap since the beginning of the broadcast, at the screen. Ben clasped my hand with a chuckle. The news anchor returned to wrap the story.

"The country's changing political climate with regards to equal rights for same-sex relationships has made this case a hotbed of controversy. Equal rights activists are demanding tougher hate crime laws in Missouri, and are outraged that only crimes to property, not person, carry the stricter penalties a hate crime designation allows. Religious and right wing political advocates have made Damon Lane the face of their fight, claiming had his son, Jeffrey, not been homosexual and engaged in the BDSM lifestyle, he would not subsequently have been murdered, and Lane would not have suffered the psychological trauma that put six homosexual men in danger."

The picture cut to a pastor who had preached fire and brimstone from his pulpit for months, claiming Lane as a martyr for the cause and all but demanding we deviants burn in hell, as if it were up to him. He'd even come close to offering to help us pack. Ben scoffed, killing the broadcast and placing the remote on his bedside table. He rolled to face me, his hand finding mine beneath the covers.

"You okay?"

I squeezed his hand, not looking at him. "As okay as I'll ever be.

You?" My eyes cut to him sharply, but darted away again.

"Same as you. I just want to go back to my life without wondering if my trip to a baseball game or restaurant with you will become front page news."

I nodded. Many had expected our burgeoning relationship to fizzle quickly after the arrest, thinking the strain would be too much for us to handle, but the opposite had happened. While so much of our beginning had been wrapped up in the case, the aftermath had been about us, about healing. During that time, we'd grown as close as two people could.

Once released from the hospital, I'd stayed with my parents for a few days and explained the entire situation. I'd left out only the most graphic of details, and I even told them about my contract with Ben. My dad hadn't understood at all, but he'd tried to. He'd sincerely tried, though I could see the pain on his face when he looked at me. I had diminished in his eyes, though he swore I hadn't. He betrayed his lie when he asked me if he'd done something wrong raising me. Ma made her opinion more than clear when those words left his mouth. She threw him out of the house, telling him I was their son and I deserved respect, and if he couldn't see I was still a good man regardless of who shared my bed and how, then he could leave. I deserved the chance to love whom I chose and live life my way, because their way had landed me with Victoria, and look where that had gotten me. By the time she was done shouting, both Dad and I were staring at her in shock. Chagrined, Dad left, staying at a hotel for two nights before begging to come home. Ma cried, both when he left and when he returned, but she wouldn't tolerate anyone thinking less of me, including my dad.

Shawn and Chrissy were fine with my big gay revelation, but Mason kept his distance. I'd assumed he was embarrassed or disapproving. His wife came to visit with the girls, who wanted to make sure their Uncle Gav was okay, a few days after my release, but Mason wasn't with them. Sandra leaned her head on my shoulder, a surprisingly tender gesture from her considering we were friendly but not close. Speaking softly in my ear, she said Mason was having a harder time dealing with how I'd almost been killed than my sexual preference, so she didn't want me thinking he was homophobic.

"It really hit him how dangerous a line of work his entire family is in. He'll come around, if you can give him time." I kissed the top of her head and thanked her for easing my mind.

After two weeks with my parents, I was climbing the walls. My mother treated me like I would break and my father tried to "man" me up, shoving more sports down my throat than I could stomach.

Finally, I'd told them I needed Ben and left.

Ben had no family to speak of, so his sole support had come from his business partner, Dr. Ribaldi. When I'd shown up on his doorstep, he'd wordlessly let me in and offered me the guest room, but physically, he'd kept his distance. What both of us were too afraid to discuss had him assuming I felt obligated to finish out my contract but would break it as soon as the three months were up. I assumed he didn't want to be reminded of our ordeal and tried to give him space while desperately seeking to regain our equilibrium. After three days of tiptoeing around each other, Dr. Ribaldi had stopped by to see him, taken one look at us, and told us she wasn't leaving until we opened up. We had, and so began our first unofficial counseling session with Dr. Ribaldi that continued even now, and we had long since submitted her as our therapist of record with both my supervisors and the State Board of Psychiatric Services, who were working with Ben to get him back to practicing. I felt more comfortable talking to a submissive who not only wouldn't tell me I was better off not engaging in kink, but was helping me come to grips with how afraid I was of still having the desire to submit.

Ben, hearing my fears, began to voice his own thoughts. He wasn't concerned for himself or that he couldn't control his dominant tendencies—what Lane had done to him hadn't challenge his nature the way it had challenged mine—but concerned for me. He feared my limits had drastically changed and he'd inadvertently push me too far before I recognized the need to safeword. The more we talked, the clearer it became how much we needed each other. Ben finally began to believe I was there because I loved him, and not out of obligation.

When the contract expired, we'd let it, acknowledging the terms weren't conducive to either of us healing. We'd torn up the paperwork together, and Ben had immediately taken me in his arms and asked me to stay with him. I'd agreed and moved into his bedroom. With Laura's guidance, we had a pretty good handle on our combined headspace.

Until we tried a scene.

I'd safeworded every time. Frustration didn't begin to cover it. Laura had helped by suggesting I submit in ways that had nothing to do with sex but gave me a sense of safety, things like Ben feeding me by hand while I knelt at his feet. I took care of him in little ways, like drawing his bath or doing laundry, and he set rules for keeping the house going for which I was responsible—inanities that meant little if I failed because they could easily be redone, but had become important because I was following his orders and needed the structure.

Myah was my rock. Despite being with a new partner until I returned from my extended leave of absence, she kept in touch almost every day. When I was overwhelmed, tired of being analyzed, or just plain needed the shoulder of someone who wouldn't try to fix me, I turned to her. We lounged on her couch watching ridiculously bad gay and lesbian indie movies, stuffing ourselves stupid on junk, and being lazy slobs whenever I needed to. Sometimes, Cole joined us. I understood she couldn't put work on hold for me, but for the most part, she made time where she could.

She and my brother were still going strong, much to my parents' delight. They loved her down-to-earth nature, her beauty, and her ability to put a ridiculous smile on Cole's face. What they didn't love was that she and Cole were in no hurry to move their relationship to the next level. Myah had outlasted any previous girlfriend of Cole's, but she wouldn't cave to the pressure my parents exerted for them to move along, get married, start a family. I think my dad gave her more respect than he did me in those early weeks after the entire story came out. She stood her ground in a way any cop could respect, and any father could admire in the woman who'd civilized his wildest son.

And Myah was the only one besides Ben and Dr. Ribaldi who encouraged me to embrace my submissive side. She knew how torn up I was that Ben and I had only succeeded at vanilla sex. Fantastic and frequent vanilla sex, but we hadn't completely recaptured the soul deep connection we found in a scene.

"You're awful lost in thought," Ben said gently, kissing my shoulder.

I gave him a nervous half-smile. "There's something I want to try." It had actually been Myah's idea, much to my surprise. She'd just shrugged and said I wasn't the only one who could claim some depravity.

"What's that?"

"A scene. But one I set up." Most Doms would likely refuse that request. They were the ones in control. Most Doms weren't Ben, and most subs weren't me. He knew part of my sense of security came from knowing what would happen. It was no longer his desire to surprise me. At least, not until I was well on my way to reclaiming my submission.

"Okay. How so?"

I climbed off the bed and knelt beside it to retrieve a long wooden dowel about two inches thick and several feet long from under bed frame. Lightweight, sized for a good grip, and versatile, it was possible to use anywhere in the house, since we no longer had a play room; Ben had dismantled his loft, turning the space into a home gym with a hot tub and sauna. I never went up there, except for the hot tub, and even that was rare.

I returned to the bed and shoved my pillows onto the floor, then wedged the bar into the brackets designed for restraints we would no longer use. Bondage was off the table permanently. The brackets were a good fit for the pole, which had a couple inches of gap between it and the headboard. The most important feature of this was the choice.

"I will hold onto this pole while you do what you will with me. Toys, plugs, flogger, crop, whatever you want." Except a cane. He no longer had one of those either. "You order me not to let go, and I won't. Yours to command, Sir, but not forced. This way, my grip will be my choice to obey you. Like it's my choice to kneel for you."

"I like it," he smiled, cupping my cheek. "With one adjustment."

I raised a brow and waited. He was exerting his dominance in this small way, taking my plan and changing it to suit him as well as me. Instead of speaking, he lifted the bar and lowered it to the brackets closest to the mattress. I didn't understand until he moved to sit sideways, scooting to the edge of the bed.

"Lie across my lap so I can spank that gorgeous ass. Grab the bar and don't let go," he ordered, voice commanding and soothing at once. I scrambled to obey, draping myself over his thighs with enough room to reach up and hold on to the bar.

"Thunder for stop, rain for slow," he repeated my safe words as he'd taken to doing every time we'd tried a scene since the incident. As if I could forget them when I'd used them so often. I nodded, feeling his cock rise and press just below my hip bone. His big hands lovingly caressed my skin from shoulders to thighs. "So beautiful," he murmured. I arched into his touch, both wanting and fearing it. It wasn't unlike the first time I'd submitted to him, how his touch made the out-of-control tightness in my chest ease while I was filled with wonder and the unknown.

The first smack was barely more than a love pat. The second and third were each a little harder than the last. My breathing sped up, and my dick filled in the space between Ben's thighs. With each successive blow, I became more aware of Ben's body than my own—the tense flex of his thighs before each blow, the heat from his torso against my side, the gentle caress of his fingers playing with my skin between spanks.

I need this. For so long, I've needed this. Needed him.

The next blow wrenched a cry from me and a wriggle of my hips

I couldn't suppress.

"That's it, pet. Let me hear you. Let me see how much you want this," Ben encouraged, and I complied. I felt my heated skin, the welts his fingers caused. With each caress between blows, Ben mapped the evidence of my submission as though inking our mutual desires into my flesh.

It went on for a long time, until every strike made me cry out. Pre-come dribbled from my glans, and I whimpered when Ben's fingers slipped between my thighs and slicked it up and down my shaft with three thorough strokes. Using two fingers, he played in it, smearing it along the ridge of my head and coating his fingers, which he then trailed from tailbone to taint, glazing my crease. The warmth of his fingers as they slipped into me spread as though my insides were frozen and his skin was the blanket of heat I needed.

"Roll over, Gavin." His voice was rough as he leaned back to give me room to move. "Middle of the bed on your back."

I climbed off and crawled into position, immediately taking up my hold on the wooden bar again. Ben's composure betrayed itself in the shake of his breathing and his blown pupils. He settled over me, trapping our cocks between us, his weight pressing my scorching ass into the roughness of the covers. It was delicious and painful and beautiful. Maybe I hadn't reached subspace, but that didn't mean I wasn't flying high on every sensation he wrested from me. The thrust of his tongue matched that of his hips as he pumped our swollen flesh together, and I opened wide to him with my legs, mouth, heart and soul. The slide of his tongue made me ache for the slide of his cock.

"Please, Sir. Please fuck me. Take me, all of me," I begged.

His body weight disappeared as he rummaged for a condom and lube before returning quickly to blanket me in his need and heat. Suddenly, I couldn't breathe, couldn't open my eyes, could only lie there as a slow panic stole over me that this would be the last time we were together. It was irrational, and we were through the hard part, but still. I couldn't stop it even if I tried.

"Rain," I said through gritted teeth. Ben's gaze turned soft as he hovered over me, lube in hand, about ready to stretch me. "Rain, rain, rain," I chanted.

He threw the supplies aside and crawled up until he hovered over me on his hands and knees. I didn't let go of the bar, though I wanted to, wanted to flee to the bathroom and see the proof of my hauntings on my face. Ben laid his head on my chest, his ear right over my heart, listening to it pound.

"Talk to me, Gav," he said, kissing my nipple and nuzzling his stubble into my chest.

"I'm sorry, Sir,"

He raised his head and crossed his arms over my chest, resting his chin on the back of his hand. "Don't apologize for slowing me down, or even stopping. Don't apologize for getting the time you need. But what's going on?"

I swallowed, staring at the ceiling. I felt a tear slip out of the corner of my eye and trickle into my hair, already damp with exertion. "I'm afraid of losing you, Sir."

"Why?"

"Right this moment why or whenever I feel like this why?"

"We'll start with this moment."

"I need you so badly, Ben." Under normal circumstances, his name would have been a slip, changing the dynamic from Dom and sub to lovers on the same playing field. He didn't nitpick. "I've started to wonder if you're still here with me because I'm your fixer-upper, and once that's done you'll tire and dismiss me." It was the one fear I had from before the attack, but had never voiced. Fix the closeted gay man and show him the beauty of the lifestyle, and then move on to the next project.

"Why would I do that, Gavin?" He punctuated the question with kisses to my sweaty skin.

"I don't know, Sir," I whispered, shivering not from cold, but fear.

Ben's hips slowly began to writhe against mine, keeping me focused on him, reminding me I had slowed, not stopped him.

"I think you do. What would prompt me to leave you?"

I swallowed, the words coming in a whisper. "You'll get bored with me. I won't have anything left to learn, and I'm already more trouble than anyone you've ever trained."

His lips trailed to my collarbone, and I twisted my head to bare my neck to him, exposing my vulnerability. When he reached my ear, his sexy voice held more than want and desire; it held love.

"When you were working, did you ever think you'd stop learning?"

I shook my head, leaking tears freely and not trying to hide them.

"And with your family, did you ever think they'd grow too tiresome to be around?"

"No," I whispered.

"Would you ever stop learning about me? About how I mumble in my sleep, or like my eggs, or someday want to buy a cabin in the Rockies and retire?"

I finally looked him in the eyes. "You do?"

The gap in his teeth peeked past a reassuring smile. I smiled back. "Yeah, I do," he said. "And the whole time you're loving your family and your job, you don't stop learning. Gavin, we're going to grow old together, and whether you pick up a gardening hobby, or learn to make your own sushi, or even decide to learn an instrument, I will be right there with you, growing with you. We'll share our whole lives, our quirks and bad habits. It's not just learning your past and who you are today; it's getting to see who you'll become tomorrow. I want to be there for that." Emotion swelled in my chest, and when he caressed my face, I leaned into his palm like a cat seeking human touch. "We're more than a Dom and sub, baby." He kissed the tip of my nose. "We're doctor and detective. Ben and Gavin. The bed hogger and cover stealer. The one who cooks and the one who reads."

"The one who pitches and the one who catches," I grinned through my tears, lifting my hips into his flagging erection.

"That one, we may switch up now and then," he murmured, ignoring my shocked expression to kiss me breathless as his hands skimmed my sides and up my arms, then back down. "But not right now. Hold on, Gavin, because I'm about to blow your mind."

He slithered down my torso and knelt between my spread thighs, lubing his fingers and gently massaging my hole before sliding inside. With his other hand, he oriented my erection to his lips and kissed the head, then pushed me into his mouth through the pillow of his pursed lips. Tight suction enveloped me even as his wiggling fingers drew gasps from my lungs with their clever massage. He bathed my shaft with his tongue and swallowed me whole, bringing me right to the edge.

"Rain, rain, rain," I chanted for a different reason. He pulled off my dick and his fingers slowed but stayed inside me. Reading my face, he gave me a devastating smile as I breathed through an impending orgasm and banished it, my breathing ragged. "Too close. Need you in me, now, Ben."

"Sir," he chided gently, tearing open the condom and suiting up. The pressure of his cock at my anus swelled as he breached. He leaned over and looked directly into my eyes. "I love it when you call me 'sir,' Gavin. It does something to me."

"Please, fuck me, Sir."

"Oh yeah," he nearly growled, rearing back to his knees, hiking my legs higher and pounding me into the mattress. He gave me everything he had, didn't hold back in touch, strength, or desire, and held my gaze as he shifted angles and nailed my prostate, the hair of his thighs scratching my over-sensitized ass. I howled, never letting go of the bar, giving myself to him so completely that when my orgasm broke over me, it shattered and demolished me. Ben's pleasure soared as I coasted through my climax, my ass clenching and milking his dick.

"Coming, oh fuck," he groaned, snapping his hips and only closing his eyes at the last moment when he couldn't control it anymore.

We lay breathless, Ben collapsed on me, lazily planting kisses along my sweaty, aching shoulders. "I love you," he murmured. "So much. Never get tired of you. You're mine in every way, Gavin."

I grinned and kissed his head as he finally went still.

"Sir, may I let go now?" I asked. He raked his eyes up my face to my hands and back again, lips quirking at my slightly smartass tone. When his expression sobered, I knew with his next words he meant more than just my hands.

"Only if you let me catch you."

I nodded and let go.

ABOUT THE AUTHOR

It began with a Halloween themed short story assignment from a second grade teacher, and from then on, AJ Rose fell head over heels in love with writing. Even an active social life through school, learning to play the piano in a passable imitation of proficient, and a daring cross country move couldn't stop the tall tales about imaginary people that refused to be ignored. With college experiences came a change in perspective to romance and passion. A propensity to slash favorite TV characters brought AJ to where he is today, writing mostly M/M for publication. But don't be surprised if the occasional ghost still pops up.

Printed in Great Britain
by Amazon